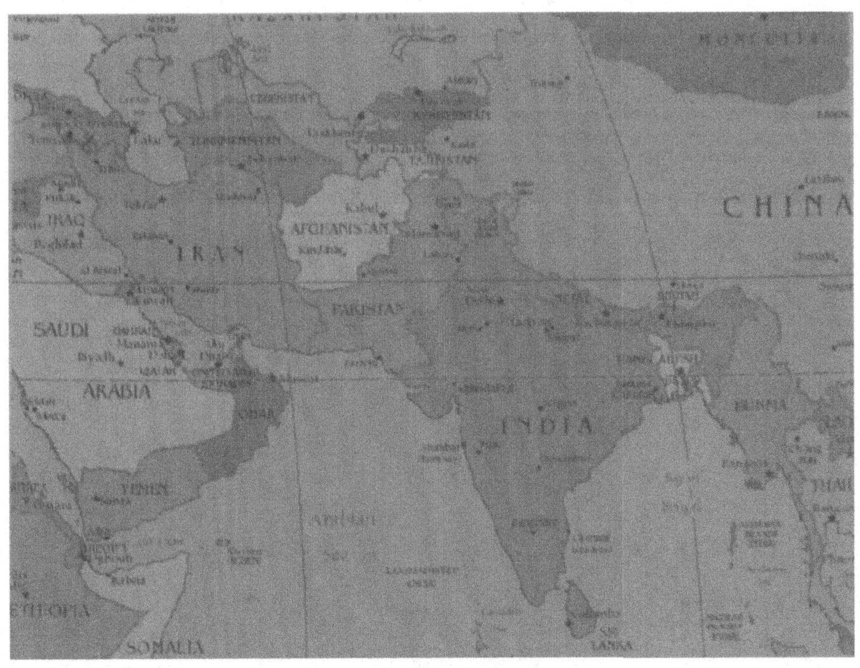

Southwest Asia

THE ASSASSIN'S MACE

Brigadier General (Ret.) Bob Butalia

iUniverse, Inc.
Bloomington

The Assassin's Mace

iUniverse books may be ordered through booksellers or by contacting:

iUniverse
1663 Liberty Drive
Bloomington, IN 47403
www.iuniverse.com
1-800-Authors (1-800-288-4677)

ISBN: 978-1-4620-1658-7 (sc)
ISBN: 978-1-4620-1660-0 (e)
ISBN: 978-1-4620-1659-4 (dj)

Library of Congress Control Number: 2011907620

Printed in the United States of America

iUniverse rev. date: 8/1/2011

Dedication

I dedicate this book to the gallant Officers, Junior Commissioned Officers, and Men of Hodson's Horse, past, present, and future, and to my comrades-in-arms in the Indian Army, with whom it has been my honor and privilege to serve. *Tyar-Bar-Tyar*

Author's Preface

The Assassin's Mace is a story of armed conflict and terror, and the human motivations and political miscalculations that trigger cataclysmic events. The setting is globally current with a resurgent China and the People's Liberation Army increasingly setting the strategic agenda, and an economically enfeebled US at geo-political odds with China over Iran, Afghanistan, Russia, Pakistan and India. This work should enable any reader who even casually glances through a daily newspaper or catches just the news headlines on TV periodically, to immerse himself/herself in a fast paced plot with a lurking sense of déjà vu. The reader will possibly get a chance to get a good, hard look at what can happen in the real world behind the headlines of the day. It is also the story of a courageous woman who is catapulted into a position of authority as Prime Minister, following a massive terror strike on her country, to deal with a situation involving millions of lives.

There were two real-life disparate incidents that triggered a stream of fictional events in my mind and resulted in this work. I actually started research on March 21, 2009, the day after the first incident described below.

On March 20, 2009 a nuclear-powered US submarine the, Hartford, collided with a US Navy amphibious assault ship, the New Orleans, with a thousand on board, in the Straits of Hormuz, the narrow passage through which much of the world's oil must pass on its way to markets. Both ships were damaged in the crash, and fifteen sailors on board the submarine, the Hartford, were slightly injured. The other vessel, the New Orleans, ruptured its fuel tanks and spilled twenty-five thousand gallons of fuel into the sea. The vessels were involved in what the US Navy euphemistically calls "maritime security operations." The Fifth Fleet covers an area of 7.5 million square miles, running through the

Persian Gulf, the Red Sea, the Gulf of Oman, and parts of the Indian Ocean, touching twenty-nine countries.

The second event actually preceded the first chronologically in order of occurrence, but on its own was not a trigger for initiating a work of fiction. More than ten coordinated shooting and bombing attacks by a group of terrorists across India's largest city, Mumbai, killed 164 people and wounded more than 308 on November 26, 2008. Ajmal Kasab, who was captured alive, disclosed that the attacks were planned and directed by Lashkar-e-Taiba militants in Pakistan. The brutal attack was carried out by ten young highly motivated armed jihadists trained and sent to Mumbai by sea, and directed from inside Pakistan via mobile phones and VoIP. Under international pressure Pakistan arrested a few members of Jamaat-ud-Dawa, the front organization for the Lashkar-e-Taiba and briefly put its founder under house arrest. Till today, Pakistani authorities continue to stonewall the investigation with serial excuses.

US investigators believed that Pakistan's Inter-Services Intelligence (ISI) officers provided support to Lashkar-e-Taiba militants who carried out the attacks. The attackers had planned and rehearsed their mission over several months. In October 2009, two Chicago men were arrested and charged by the FBI for involvement in terrorism abroad, David Coleman Headley and Tahawwur Hussein Rana. Headley, a Pakistani-American, was charged in November 2009 with scouting locations for the 2008 Mumbai attacks. On 18, March 2010, Headley pled guilty to a dozen charges against him, thereby avoiding going to trial. In December 2009, the FBI also charged Abdur Rehman Hashim Syed, a retired major in the Pakistani army, for planning the terror attacks in association with Headley. In November 2010, families of American victims of the attacks filed a lawsuit in Brooklyn, New York, naming Lt. Gen. Ahmed Shuja Pasha, the Chief of Pakistan's Inter-Services Intelligence, as being complicit in the Mumbai attacks.

After the attacks, Indians severely criticized the ineptness of their political leaders. Political reactions in Mumbai and India included a spate of forced resignations to appease the public, including the Home Minister responsible for internal security. The attacks also triggered a chain of citizens' movements across India. There were vigils held across all of India with candles and placards commemorating the victims of the attacks. It was, however, business as usual after a few weeks during which politicians piously declared at multiple funerals that their thoughts and prayers were with the victims, their families, and the people of India. Proactive actions to preclude similar occurrences were barely discussed.

No nation can survive an indefinite status quo as this fictional work strives to show. The reader needs to look no further than the recent revolts against dictatorships in the Arab world in Egypt, Tunisia, Libya, and Bahrain and the stirrings caused by the Jasmine Revolution in China. The US had earlier invaded Afghanistan after the Taliban-run government refused to turn over Osama Bin Laden and his Al-Qaeda Terrorist network responsible for the 9/11 attacks against the US, whom they were sheltering.

In India, however, there is a near obsession with the comfort of a status quo amongst politicians. This permits India's neighbors to constantly cause "death by a thousand cuts" as so expressively put across by Pakistan's former military dictator General Zia ul Haq. The Indian military, where I served in the tank corps, took the military dictator seriously, as also his development of extremely close strategic, including nuclear, ties with China, but failed to get the message through to an obdurate political class.

One reason I resolved to write, even while I was working full time as an advisor to a US multinational in India, was to challenge the status-quo political mindset, something that is almost impossible for a serving soldier. A mindset that is petrified of using military force to safeguard national interests, primary amongst which is the security and well being of its people; a mindset that thrives on cover ups and half truths. Kicking the can down the road has disastrous consequences, as I have sought to underline in this book. The first draft took a full year from June 2009 when I actually started work. The Indian political management, for it would be futile to call it leadership, refrained from taking any meaningful steps after the terror strikes to prevent a recurrence of a similar tragedy later. The other reason was that it was sheer unadulterated fun; it provided a constant adrenaline kick to write fiction that posed a credibility test of merging what one hammered out on a keyboard with factual real world developments almost on an hourly basis!

I cannot give adequate thanks to the many former comrades who maintained the faith to completion. Infantry veteran Raghu Raman, a weekly defense columnist for "Mint" the exclusive partner of the *Wall Street Journal* in India, pointed to the need to fill a gaping hole in the genre of contemporary politico military fiction with an Asian bias. Tej Pathak, a former three-star general and paratrooper, constantly urged sticking to a tight timeline before the national memory faded. He also volunteered to fill in crucial research gaps using information publicly available all over the world. Pushpinder, former tank corps colonel and a dear friend, found and cajoled iUniverse to publish an unknown author. Over many months, he shepherded the flow of communication with many false starts through trying times. Prakash Katoch, again a three-star general and paratrooper, and Arjun Katoch, a combat veteran and colonel with long experience of United Nations disaster management, were incisive in their comments to plug loopholes in the plot. Former naval commanders Ashok and Samir enabled the Russian aircraft carrier Gorshkov to set sail in the story and did much to orientate a landlubber like me to matters nautical! I have been remiss in still not being able to meet former Air Marshal Parnaik whose knowledge of the aeronautical world is profound and who responded instantaneously to requests to partake of it. Former Wing Commander Prasad with decades of commercial flying experience was ever gracious in responding to calls for clarifications of current aviation practice in and around airports. The cover design by Colonel Harkirat of Hodson's Horse is the work of a gifted amateur artist and serving tank corps professional soldier who shuns the limelight.

Last, but not least, to my immediate family. To my wife, Rekha, for injecting repeated doses of healthy cynicism to keep me on track; my soldier son Sahil and journalist daughter Nivriti, who appear fleetingly in the plot as themselves, for their irreverent unstinted support, and my mother, Jasbir, for her unshakeable belief in my ability to stay the course!

Finally, this is a story woven with large strands of the factual bounced off virtual mirrors but still only a tale for which I am solely responsible.

Contents

FOREWORD

I TAKE GREAT PLEASURE IN WRITING THE Foreword to Brig. General (Ret.) Bob Butalia's *The Assassin's Mace*. I have known Bob since 1970 when I assumed command of Hodson's Horse, an Indian Army Tank Regiment, where he was already serving. It was the 1971 Indo-Pak war which brought us closer when he, as my Intelligence Officer & Executive Assistant, was a member of my tank crew.

I congratulate Bob for writing a book on a subject that is not only topical, but which concerns the entire world community at large. He has very deftly woven realty into fiction, yet retaining the essence and flavor of the main topic—the curse of terrorism, which is a worldwide phenomenon.

The story unfolds with a touch of contemporary historical characters, later merging seamlessly with those created by the author to portray a vivid and chilling picture of terrorism, intertwined with all the major and many smaller nations of the world reacting in different ways, keeping their individual intrinsic national interests in the forefront.

The United States of America, The Peoples Republic of China, India, Pakistan and the major players in the Middle East, with their oil resources and intrinsic strategic interests, are all players on the sweeping canvas of *The Assassins Mace*, which spans the entire global political landscape in its conception, and has emerged through the author's deep understanding of current global political events, and meticulous research, which enables him to portray the main characters in a manner that reflects the innate anxiety of various national governments, if terrorism is allowed to succeed, with India placed in the epicenter of this terrible fire-storm.

A page turner, *The Assassin's Mace* has short but crisp chapters which make for easy and enjoyable reading. I am certain the book will be well received and will carve a place for itself in the present day literary world.

I wish Bob and *The Assassin's Mace* all the very best, and every success!

Lt. Gen. (Ret.) R. M. Vohra, PVSM, MVC
Formerly Eastern Army Commander, Indian Army
GURGAON—122002 (Haryana), India
May 30, 2011

PROLOGUE: SONAR SIREN

As Janet Chang finished jogging her second lap around the outer periphery of Leavenworth Park in Syracuse, New York, a man in a navy blue tracksuit and woolen cap, a man who went virtually unnoticed, caught up with her. He kept pace with her for a while and said in a low voice, "Go to work early tomorrow. Stop dragging your feet. You need to move faster on the project."

"I am doing as much as possible, and you know it! What good will going early for one day do?" she asked the man she knew only as Nick.

"Get to spend some time with David Dean when there is no one around. You could do it over a cup of coffee. He is always in by seven. Try to make it look accidental in case anyone else is around. His wife is out of town visiting her mother."

"How do you know?" she blurted out.

"Don't ask stupid questions!" Nick snarled. "Just do what you have been told and get him to your apartment for dinner and fuck his brains out!" Nick increased his pace, and then he was gone.

Deeply perturbed by the unexpected meeting, Janet halfheartedly did a few stretching exercises and headed home. It was unusual for Nick to lose his cool; he had rarely done so in all the years that she had known him.

Nick had guided her conversion with an unerring focus. He had created a beautiful woman from a shy, flat-chested, awkward creature with acne scars, protruding ears, and crooked teeth, albeit one with a doctorate in mathematics and a master's in computing both from

Stanford. As a teenager, she had secretly yearned to look like the buxom women she had seen in magazines and not just perform brilliantly in her class. That was all too easy to achieve with her solid work ethic like almost all migrant kids from Taiwan. Nick had opened the world of her dreams and paid for all the doctors.

"In America, even scientists have to look good to command above-normal salaries and promotions," Nick had said. "You have the brains and the education to succeed in the technology race. For the rest, we have cosmetic surgeons of Chinese origin. These racist bastards all want to dip their wicks into classy Chinese pussy. Let them have their delusions so long as China gets the technology it needs for its submarine program to match the American Navy."

"If you say so, Nick," she added hesitantly, her face coloring at the choice of words. "But won't they select white American candidates for such work?"

"They would if they could—except for the fact that there is little chance of most born-and-bred Americans taking up science-related work. There is too much hard work for young, pampered Americans to pursue careers in hard science. They also feel there is not enough money to compensate for the effort. Whereas with your training, once you are in, you will quickly become indispensable. After a few years, you will also be affluent and beyond suspicion, especially if you marry a white American."

Two years of visiting an orthodontist, chemical peels, otoplasty to pin back her ears, and some discreet breast augmentation later, coupled with a rigorous physical training routine that Nick had insisted on, had transformed Janet. She had become a beautiful, confident scientist who would slow down traffic downtown when she sometimes took a walk, showing off her stunning figure and flowing hair. The transformation and her vigorous academic credentials had also ensured a job in cutting-edge sonar research with Lockheed Martin Naval Electronic and Surveillance Systems.

At 7:00 a.m., as David Dean walked briskly to the coffee machine for his caffeine kick before work, Janet turned around with a cappuccino topped up to the brim of the disposable cup, pretending not to see him. As she completed her turn, she banged smack into David, spilling a few drops of coffee on his sleeve. Apparently flustered and apologetic, Janet looked all set to burst into tears.

"I'm sorry, David," she said, putting her cup down on top of the machine and grabbing for a clutch of tissues to wipe at his sleeve. "It's incredibly clumsy of me spilling coffee on you! I didn't realize you were here!"

"That's okay, Janet. It's only a bit of coffee. I won't melt." David looked fleetingly into the limpid pool of her dark eyes and perhaps imagined a hint of tears while she dabbed at his sleeve to soak up the stain. "What are you doing here so early in the day? Normally, I'm here all by myself for at least an hour."

"I had this crazy idea last night when I was about to go to sleep. I thought of improving the Los Angeles sub-sonar array capability using the latest commercial, off-the-shelf components. I saw them at the trade fair in Seattle last week."

"And—" he prompted.

"We should be able to save at least two million in integration costs if it works! I couldn't sleep, so I thought I'd come to work early and do some preliminary calculations to see if it works … and I was grabbing some coffee, but my mind was way out there," she ended lamely.

"You'd better come into my office and tell me about it," David said, gently steering her toward his corner office. Normally, there would have been no one else there for another half an hour, which was how he liked it. His most productive thinking had always been accomplished early in the day. David Dean, Lockheed Martin's corporate vice president and guiding hand behind all complex projects of the company with unremitting deadlines, was unaware of the consequences of his kindly action. Father of four facing an ongoing battle with skin cancer—currently dormant—David Dean wasn't used to the type of feminine attention he was getting. He was primed to allow his disciplined self to be led by the stunning and young math wizard in directions that he had not dreamed of for years.

"David, I've never had the chance to tell you how much your support and suggestions have meant to me while working for Lockheed. Would you like to attend a small dinner I'm having for some friends along with your wife, Liz, tomorrow at 8:00 p.m.? The notice is a bit short, but I didn't have the courage to ask you, fearing you may feel offended by a junior employee taking such liberties!"

He had been surprised by her invitation to dinner but had accepted with grace. "I'm sorry that Liz is out of town for a bit, but I will certainly be there."

Later that night, she opened the door seconds after he rang and carried a huge bouquet of roses and a bottle of champagne inside. Wearing a low-cut designer black sheath of a dress that provided a vivid contrast to her glowing skin, she held his hand a little longer than was strictly necessary while she welcomed him into her home.

"Am I too early?" he asked. "Where are the others?"

"There are only two of us now—you and me," she said with pure mischief in her eyes, holding out a drink for him.

After he rode her smooth, almost virginal body two hours later and only occasionally thereafter in furtive meetings in small hotel rooms as decreed by Nick, David Dean would agree to the small, eminently sensible changes she suggested for successfully installing the new sonar systems in the Los Angeles class of submarines due for major refits.

Not so coincidentally, a similar scene was being played out at Digital System Resources. The systems-integration expert at DSR working on the same project, Liu Shao Chi, thirty-three years of age and a slow, dreamy talker, was lovingly removing the bra and freeing the pendulous aroused breasts of his project manager, Caroline Crane, ten years older and supposedly wiser. Getting her to agree to minor changes was always an intellectually stimulating challenge. Her mind was always firmly in control of her emotions … or so she believed.

"Some day, I would like to take you with me to my parents' home in China near Shanghai and perhaps visit parts of the Great Wall!" Liu Shao Chi said afterward.

"Do you think we could go to Lhasa as well?" Caroline asked, squirming with pleasure as Liu gently nibbled at her breasts.

"Sure, in a couple of weeks after we finish with the submarine upgrade. As a matter of fact, I have a small suggestion that can really speed up the project and in the process enhance your reputation as well in managing complex projects" Liu answered momentarily raising his head.

Nick had given Liu Shao Chi and Janet Chang a mission that they were told was crucial to the functioning of the PLA Navy. He had explained the issue separately to both Liu and Janet.

"The PLA Navy is unable to track United States submarines at critical junctions. Submarines that take advantage of hiding under ships to sneak through the straits of Hormuz and Malacca and to close into shallow waters bordering PLA Navy submarine bases in the South China Sea are almost impossible to detect. With tensions rising between China and America, a solution to this problem is immediately required."

The answer to discouraging such tactics, Janet told Nick, was to try to discreetly sabotage the Los Angeles–class submarine sonar. If distance to the target readings in certain water conditions could be falsified, submarines would tend not to get in too close as a matter of routine.

Janet explained to Nick, "The Los Angeles–class submarine array is far smaller than conventionally passive towed arrays, and the frequencies used for detection are lower than low-frequency active sonar (LFAS). This results in reduced bearing resolution and accuracy until enhanced. This enhancement is achieved by a synthetic aperture technique called an "extended towed array measurement" (ETIM) algorithm and another algorithm known as the "minimum variance distortionless response" beam former (MVDR). If these algorithms, which are basically a sequence of instructions, are altered in minor ways that appear innocent and logical if discovered, interesting operating results will ensue in shallow waters. Trouble-free operations in the deep oceans would, how ever, continue as usual.

Janet Chang had found the answer to downgrading the sonar by pure persistence and her extraordinary grasp of the math involved. She tweaked a minute change in the range-only motion analysis algorithm under the guise of working on integrating the sonar with other vital instrumentation. This minor change created acute problems of range estimation for the Los Angeles class submarines. This was, however, only in water depths up to ninety meters and for the normal, run-of-the-mill sonar operator. The really good ones, who were few, could cope to an extent.

The system integration was executed by Caroline Cray, the project director at DSR. She was persuaded to do so by Liu Shao Chi stoking her carnal desire at every opportunity. The sonar tweaks on submarines coming in for upgrades turned out to be relatively simple and attracted little attention, with swarms of workers doing different jobs at the same time creating the perfect opportunities.

CHAPTER 1 STRAITS OF HORMUZ, MARCH 20, 2009

"Sir, we have just received information that the Israel or American strike against our nuclear reactors at Bushehr and Natanz you were discussing is possible within the next few hours!" The admiral's flag officer walked into the small room and interrupted the discussion that had been going on for the last two hours between his boss, Admiral Habib Sayyani, and Commander Ali Reza Tangsir of the Senior Revolutionary Guards.

"Thank you. Keep me updated, but please leave us now!"

"I don't believe that they can be so stupid and take the chance of provoking the Russians," said Ali Reza Tangsir. "There are almost 1700 Russians working to get the reactor going!"

"Nonetheless, let us be prepared to retaliate!"

The staff officer was back in ten minutes. "Sorry to disturb you again, sir. There is more news from the Chinese that an American submarine is trying to sneak through the straits and may meet with an accident!"

"What rubbish! The message must have been distorted by a translator. How can they say the sub will meet with an accident? Put the boats on ten-minute notice to lay mines in the shipping channels! Keep me posted if any American aircrafts are picked up by radar." Admiral Habib Sayyani spoke in a cool, controlled voice.

Twenty-one to thirty-two miles wide, the Strait of Hormuz (SOH) presents a formidable, twisted, waist-like entrance to ships passing between the Persian Gulf and the Gulf of Oman, carrying 40 percent of the world's oil traffic. Thus, the SOH was easily the most vital choke point in the world. Shipping channels were restricted to marginally over two miles, one each for incoming and outgoing traffic with an intervening two-mile gap. No international waters existed in the SOH, as the straits are shared by Iran and Oman, and passing through by all ships was under the right of innocent passage recognized by the United Nations. Use of ship weapons in the passage was therefore not permissible.

In March of 2009, the Iranian Navy had just three Kilo-class diesel-electric submarines procured from the Russians, who were more than happy to make money for their wilting arms industry. More importantly, the Russians were delighted to create a permanent headache for the United States Fifth Fleet based at Bahrain in the Persian Gulf. The fact that the US Navy had sunk two Iranian warships and three armed speedboats during the Iraq-Iran conflict in 1988, blown up two Iranian oil producing platforms, and shot down a civilian airliner by means of the USS Vincennes while illegally in Iranian waters was difficult to forget.

It was very much on the minds of Iran's Navy Admiral Habib Sayyani and Senior Revolutionary Guards Commander Ali Reza Tangsir as they grappled with the opportunity that had opened up in the early hours of March 20th. They were both acutely conscious of the fact that the opportunity could easily turn into the biggest threat that their country had ever faced. While the fading economic strength of the United States would probably ensure that there would be no full-blown conflict like the invasion of Iraq, any punitive military action against Iran that did not generate an immediate response would surely lead to one of them being made a scapegoat and publicly executed to satisfy political ends.

With a great deal of Chinese assistance, Iran's Islamic Revolutionary Guard Corps had deployed more than a thousand fast patrol boats in and around the straits. The vessels, armed with cruise missiles, mines, torpedoes, and rocket-propelled grenades were up to twenty-three meters in length. Some of them could reach a hundred kilometers per hour with throttles open.

The concept of "the swarm doctrine" encouraged by the PLA Navy was simple and low tech; it envisaged a group of more than a hundred speedboats attacking a target, which could have been a Western naval vessel or a commercial oil tanker from four or five different directions, making effective defense extremely difficult. All that was needed was for one boat to get through to sink or cripple a US aircraft carrier slowed down by shallow waters.

The doctrine was a response to an Iranian assessment that the United States was considering an air strike on Iran's nuclear facilities. It seemed like a no-brainer for the Iranians to send an unambiguous signal to the United States. Any such move would invite retaliation. While Iran would undoubtedly suffer grievous damages, it would definitely still be able to disrupt oil supplies from the gulf immediately. This would automatically send oil prices spiraling skyward and disrupt the US and world economies dependent on the flow of oil in a matter of weeks.

On March 20th at 1:00 a.m., the USS Hartford (SSN-768), an improved Los Angeles–class submarine, was tasked with sanitizing the USS New Orleans (LPD-18) against hypothetical Iranian Kilo-class subs. The USS New Orleans was blissfully unaware of these instructions for what may have been an oversight in spite of standard operating procedures laid down. This task of sanitizing was to be done while the sub was entering the Straits of Hormuz en route to Bahrain after an extended deployment exercise.

The USS Hartford was trying to hide under USS New Orleans to disguise its entry into the Persian Gulf, using only its passive sonar to keep track of the position of the New Orleans. The maneuver was not coordinated in advance, and the New Orleans crew was not even aware of the Hartford's presence. When subs didn't want to be found, they went quiet and depended on their sensors to pick up noises from other vessels. Of course, if there was a Kilo-class sub with upgraded Russian stealth technology better than Hartford's sensors, a situation could exist in which two subs could not see each other, even if they were literally within kissing distance.

The acoustics in the Straits of Hormuz caused by shoal water, heavy traffic, and the presence of a large number of sea mammals gave even seasoned sonar operators nightmares. Tankers in particular were hard to hear as the oil/ballast acted as a sound masker for propellers at certain angles. As far as Hartford's sonar was concerned, the performance of passive broadband on the spherical array was not spectacular to start with. This was reckoned by the technical specialists who had installed it. Expectedly, it was degraded by the high background decibels, and it was mobbed by biologics. However, as far as the institution of the US Navy was concerned, Hartford's passive sonar was as good if not better than any sub in the world. What thc US Navy was blissfully unaware of was the fact that the passive sonar capability on the forty-seven Los Angeles–class submarines operating worldwide had been severely compromised by Janet Chang's efforts over two years earlier during an upgrade program.

When Hartford's radar mast and sail of HY-80 steel rammed into the New Orleans in the wee hours of March 20, 2009, and tore a fifteen-foot hole in a fuel tank, 95,000 liters of diesel spilled into the Persian Gulf, worsening the already high existing pollution level. Fifteen of the submarine's crew also suffered severe injuries. The $150 million worth of upgrades that the sub had undergone at the Portsmouth Naval Shipyard two years earlier also became history.

Hartford's crew was fortunate that the Revolutionary Guards swarm of the first hundred boats with their engines idling was told to stand down after they had been at action stations for most of the night. The swarm crews were informed that they had successfully passed the test of operational readiness ordered by the supreme commander in case of war with the United States. In actual fact, no US air attacks had materialized against any nuclear or nonnuclear facility.

The US Navy would do what all navies did to whitewash themselves in times of trouble: Sack the commander, also known as the sub driver, hold a court of inquiry to apportion blame to as low a level as possible, and get back to the business of running down the US Marines, the US Army, and the US Air Force, not necessarily in that order.

It was Saturday night, March 21, 2009, when Janet Chang idly watched a news report on TV showing the US Hartford's smashed radar mast and sail while she sipped cask-conditioned ale at Clark's Ale House at 122 W. Jefferson St., Syracuse, New York, in a sheer, body-hugging red cocktail dress, apparently enjoying the crowd.

A man brushed past her at the bar. Nick said, "Excuse me," and then in a low tone, he murmured, "Admiring your handiwork? Should take a few years to remove the dents? David Dean is dead. The big C caught up finally. He recommended to the Lockheed Board a few weeks ago to promote you to do his work. The Board has just accepted this recommendation. Congratulations!"

CHAPTER 2
PROPHET OF DOOM

"THANK YOU FOR HUMORING AN OLD man, Durga," the PM had said without preamble in the brief evening meeting the previous day. "I know how devoted you are to your constituency, but I need you to sensitize the national security advisory board (NSAB) for a couple of hours. The NSAB can then issue a wake-up call to the National Security Council (NSC). Since I head the NSC, I will ensure it wakes up. That's how coalitions are managed!"

It was payback time. The old man had extracted his pound of flesh with consummate ease. Until her recent death, Durga's grandmother had virtually terrorized the congress party to respond to her every whim. Getting a noted former economist like the PM, who owed his elevation to the top job in the country to her grandmother, to write a foreword for her book required just a thirty-second phone call. It also ensured that Durga's book was a runway success.

Durga Vadera smiled as she finished the last bit of her address to the audience of dour, grim-faced men. "Just too bad for this bunch of male chauvinist pigs," she told herself. "They had little choice but to put up with her today."

"Gentlemen, thank you for the singular honor of having given me an opportunity to address the national security advisory board. I believe that this is the first time these hallowed portals have been opened to a woman? When I authored *The Perils of Fiscal Stimulus*, the PM was kind enough to write a foreword for the book. However, I never even dreamt that it would be read by more than a handful of academics or it would result in this address to you. May I respectfully suggest that instead of business as usual, we should be treating the economic situation in the world and the general weakness in the United States as a wake-up call for our national security interests?

"This is definitely becoming an Asian century again after a five-hundred-year pause. The power shift away from Western Europe and North America is, however, unlikely to play out without considerable violence—or so the history of the world indicates.

"With the United States continuing to lick its wounds from what is already coming to be known as the greatest depression of the modern era, the pretender to the US throne, China, will stake its claim to greatness. It will do so, but with the secrecy and stealth a democracy cannot provide. The Chinese have a golden opportunity with the United States in disarray to see what they can do to cut India to a size that suits them.

"The United States cannot help us, although it is in their geo-political interest to do so, at least openly. They owe the Chinese a trillion dollars and change and need to kowtow suitably to the dragon. In the next decade, China will have no potential competitor in Asia if we are also rolled over. History suggests that China will do what it takes to avail this opportunity. The only successful colonizer of the twentieth century that has managed to retain its colonies has been China. Think Tibet and Xinjiang!

"The national security council needs you to prod it and suggest what surprises China can spring on us … and what we can do, if anything, to protect and safeguard our interests! Rest assured, gentlemen, that we stand alone, and to quote our prime minister, who asked me to give you this brief, "We stand ill-prepared to face the music in store for us!"

The advisors to the Indian National Security Council were known collectively as the national security advisory board (NSAB). They were a collection of trusted and retired civil servants, armed forces, and police officers, along with a smattering of the nation's technocrats, including ISRO, the national space agency, and the atomic energy commission. They looked uniformly grim, but they were also noticeably impressed as Durga Vadera wound up her talk.

Ten days later the head of the NSAB, Ashok Chand, a former police officer not known for springing major surprises or rocking the boat, asked for an off-the-record meeting with the prime minister.

Ashok Chand came straight to the point of his visit. "Sir, the national security threat from China, Pakistan, Indian insurgents, and non-state terror groups in the next few years is going to go beyond business as usual. It is going to be of a level and dynamic that requires extraordinary, 24-7, dedicated, out-of-the-box countermeasures to cope with."

Durga has indeed delivered, the PM thought to himself. "Are you telling me that our institutions are incapable of dealing with this threat?" he asked the NSA.

"That is exactly the case. Across the board in a spectrum including defense, foreign policy, internal security, science and technology, and finance, they require help. Many radical measures are needed that would be more effective if carried out by stealth without forewarning our enemies, by quick decisions and within a tight band of secrecy."

The PM then asked, "Is the NSAB in agreement, or is this your individual view?"

"Sir, the entire NSAB is on board with this. It has never in its brief history unanimously agreed on any issue before this one. The prevailing structure of government and practices, including those of the part-time National Security Council will be unable to cope with the unfolding security challenges."

The PM said, "Let me think about it."

He had, in fact, been thinking about it for some months. He thought to himself, *A small select group of nationalists of proven credentials from various fields with a proven capacity to work miracles and deliver on promised timelines could be an answer to critical problems screaming for attention. This could work provided whoever was the PM had the will to give them the space to perform. Needless to say, unquestioned and adequate financing was a prerequisite. The group will also need to be out of the media limelight, working without being obviously visible!*

CHAPTER 3
MAVERICK

"LET'S MEET ON THE LAWNS OF the Gymkhana Club on Safdarjung Road at 5:00 p.m., and we can have a talk?" Durga Vadera had suggested. "It'll give me a chance to play a couple of sets of tennis before that." Nivriti Butalia, a columnist from the national Indian daily *Hindustan Times* who wrote the weekly column "Know Your MP," had readily agreed.

After he arrived early, Nivriti Butalia watched her from the sidelines as Durga clipped the sideline with an elegant overhead smash on match point and yelled in delight.

"I don't get a chance to play in Chandauli, so I try to get a game here whenever I am in Delhi." As she put on a navy blue tracksuit jacket to ward of the chill, Durga continued, "Let's get some tea and chat in that corner of the lawn, where we won't be disturbed."

"You could have had a great career as an economist and author after the success of *The Perils* warning the world of the economic depression to come by 2007. Why the sudden plunge into politics as an independent candidate for parliamentary elections?" Nivriti Butalia asked.

"In a sense, I was born a default politician but never realized it," Durga Vadera responded with a smile. "After both my parents were assassinated by Maoists in Chattisgarh, my grandmother brought me back to her constituency in Uttar Pradesh. You may be aware that Varanasi almost made it into the Guinness Book, as it elected her a record twelve consecutive times, till she died. I learnt the nitty-gritty of ground-level politics at her knee. I still recall the names of many of the poor that unfailingly voted for her."

Some weeks earlier, Nivriti had made the journey by passenger train to Chandauli, the hellhole in UP where Durga Vadera had chosen to make her home. The train had spent more time waiting at small wayside stations in the darkness than actually moving. No electricity, bad water, marginal roads, and no sanitation characterized the constituency. Detailed background knowledge before setting up an interview was always useful.

"Durga lives here, and she cares for us," a bunch of women transplanting paddy had told Nivriti. "The other politicians just come before elections to make empty promises and buy our votes with money and liquor. And they accused her of doing the same when she won. We heard that she resigned and there was an enquiry of some kind. But she is back. She spoke to us about sending our girls to the new school last week in spite of what our men say. Three of us have already gotten admission for our daughters."

To Durga, the miserable state of Chandauli was, however, a supreme opportunity to become indispensable to the dirt-poor constituency by doing the obvious, something that had never been attempted, namely improving rice productivity with better seed, having narrow tarmac roads constructed to facilitate market access to small farmers, refurbishing two small rural hospitals along with half a dozen rundown school buildings, and dredging the vital canal that brought timely water for sowing. More than anything else, she was a familiar sight early in the mornings on her cycle, traditionally dressed with her head covered, listening to people and doing whatever it took and what no politician in the state had dreamt to do.

"Why did you then not stand for elections from your grandmother's constituency when you took the plunge into politics?" Nivriti probed.

"I would be lying if I said that I was not tempted, and it was offered to me on a plate. However, when I looked across South Asia, women have traditionally used free rides associated with families to achieve political power. Benazir Bhutto in Pakistan, Indira Gandhi in our country, Khaleda Zia and Shaikh Hasina in Bangladesh, Sirimavo Bandaranaike and her daughter, Chandrika Kumaratunga, in Sri Lanka—all moved into power under dramatic circumstances involving assassinations and coups primarily. I want to be regarded differently and be viewed as a part of a normal, long-drawn-out process that most politicians have to undertake from the grass roots to reach the pinnacle of political power!"

"So you have your eyes set on being PM one day?" Nivriti inquired.

"Certainly, I have that ambition like any normal politician. It may take time—say twenty years or so—if it is to happen. By then, I would look the part of the traditional Indian politician as well, with gray hair, a more weather-beaten look, and perhaps a cardiac condition and arthritis!"

"Is that the reason you joined the congress after being reelected for the second time?"

"Independents can only play a limited role in government. I don't want to be confined to that. The congress has also been a family affiliation for almost a century. Besides, the prime minister, who had been a close colleague of my grandmother, strongly advocated my following in her footsteps."

"How do you reckon an exception being made in your case for the top job as PM some day, given the sexist thinking about a woman's role in India in spite of the Indira Gandhi exception?" Nivriti prodded further.

"For a start, I got elected to Parliament initially on my own as an independent. I used my training at the Indian Institute of Management, Ahmedabad to see if I could actually make a difference at the grass roots level. I have also—and it is still a work in progress—built 'Durga Vadera' as a sort of brand for good governance. In that sense I am following the Chinese example of professionally trained people getting into politics. Even in India competence certainly should count."

"What do you regard as your core strengths, where you are different from other politicians?"

"I can only answer the first part of your question. I am an extremely good listener. I picked it up from grandmother. She managed conflict so wonderfully between various factions of the congress, primarily because she was always prepared to hear everyone out for any length of time, along with the unsaid nuances that she absorbed from body language.

She would always ask me to repeat what people had said at the end of each day of being with her."

"What other strengths do you have besides the ability to listen and register the others point of view?" Nivriti asked.

"I think that my other core strength is that I can make decisions quickly even in the absence of clear-cut inputs—IIM, Ahmedabad has refined that process in my thinking. I think I am also open to admitting when I have it wrong for midcourse corrections to be made."

"What do you visualizc as thc single biggest threat to the idea of India?"

Durga Vadera replied forcefully, raising the pitch of her voice a bit for the first time in the interview, "I have no doubt in my mind that China is by far our major threat. China has been emboldened by past and continuing success against a comatose Indian polity to continue to raise the ante. We are a country without any allies, practicing hide-bound, flat-footed diplomacy and without the backbone to match force with force and guile with guile!"

"Hasn't all this transpired on the watch of congress governments controlling the reins of political power much of the time?" Nivriti queried.

Because he was expecting a politically correct response, Nivriti Butalia was surprised when Durga Vadera said, "I cannot deny the past and any blunders my party may have made. However, we need to draw our strategic lessons from it and change course for the future. I will play my part, given a chance, if and when the time comes!"

"My last question is on a personal note before I finish. You are acquiring the reputation of being almost a nun. Do you have any intention of getting married in the near future? Your name has been linked to a few men who were also acquiring management degrees along with you at Ahmedabad." Nivriti asked the last question that had been sent as an SMS by her editor two hours earlier.

"It didn't work out perhaps because of what could perhaps be called ideology gaps. The men I liked needed to prove their success in the commercial world. Both are hugely successful venture capitalists in the United States and have survived the depression brilliantly. I think I am married to the idea of India as it could be. I have no intention of being another Margaret Thatcher with her husband and children causing more problems than the opposition!"

"But you have adopted children yourself, so it could well happen to you as well?" Nivriti could not resist asking the loaded question.

Durga laughed and said "Amir, Dilip and Tony are less than ten years of age so it will take time for them to reach that stage. Hopefully, they will have a different value system when they grow up! I would appreciate it if they are kept out of the media glare and you don't give the kids more than a passing reference in your piece? However, as a mother I'm always happy to talk about them off the record. I cannot imagine life without them."

Nivriti said "I won't mention them if that's what you want. I'm, however, curious about your decision to adopt three boys and no girls?"

"I did not really have time to think about my decision. I was staying in a small cottage in the Himalayas in Mussoorie where I spend time when I need to be by myself. One evening a van bringing these children back from a vacation to St. George's a century old boarding school near my cottage rammed into a bus coming down a hair pin bend at speed. The parents of the kids, who were escorting the kids, were all great friends. They had planned on a week-long break in the hills after dropping the kids off at school but were all killed in the collision" Durga said her eyes moist with held back tears.

"What happened then?" Nivriti prompted.

"I was sitting inside reading a book when I heard this awful crash and ran out of the gate. The van driver and the parents of the kids were quite obviously dead from the impact. The door of the van had been flung open by the impact and I heard this moaning sound from the back of the van. Miraculously the three boys who were sitting in the rear of the van playing survived with severe concussions. With the help of the bus passengers, including one who was a doctor, I got the nearly unconscious children out and into my house."

"Where were the police and the highway ambulance?"

"The road was narrow and had been completely blocked by the accident. On top of that it was getting dark and heavy rain had started. The police and ambulance took two hours to arrive."

"And then what happened?" Nivriti asked.

"The children had nowhere to go when they recovered. All of them came from nuclear families with distant relatives they had rarely come across. A strong bond has been forged amongst them by the traumatic experience they went through. They sort of adopted me. So here I am an unwed mother with sons almost the same age from three different faiths-Muslim, Hindu and Christian and I love it! They are still studying at St. George's, the same school."

Nivriti Butalia yawned as she punched in the last paragraph, struggling to meet the deadline for the weekend edition.

"In India, Durga, the mythical consort of Lord Shiva, is the embodiment of feminine and creative energy symbolizing female power or 'Shakti' in different ways. Alternately fierce and creative on one hand and calm-faced and smiling on the other as the symbol of cosmic harmony, Durga is depicted as a warrior woman riding a lion or a tiger. Her multiple hands carry weapons and assume a series of mudras (symbolic hand gestures) widely incorporated in some of the rich classical dance traditions of the country. Durga Vadera will have to transform herself virtually overnight to become all or most of these things to a country crying in the wilderness for a savior. The biggest threat to a developing brand 'Durga' is the continuing distaste of the congress for maverick politicians in the party ranks!"

CHAPTER 4
BEIJING-REVIEW

THE NINE MEN OF THE STANDING committee of the Chinese politburo who were present at Zhongnanhai, the "Central and Southern Seas" because of two lakes located west of the Forbidden City, had listened in pin-drop silence. They were not amused as Premier Wen Jiabao finished his presentation.

"The US economy is in the deepest recession in a century, and Obama is continuing the gross mismanagement of the economy and reckless spendthrift habits of Bush. We need to be worried about more than the seventy thousand shutdown factories and twenty million jobs lost in the last one year ... but compounding the problem is that close to 1.4 trillion dollars of our foreign exchange reserves invested in dollar-denominated assets are losing value."

"Dump them and buy commodity assets like oil, iron ore, and fertilizers that we desperately need!" Wen Bangguo, chairman of the National People's Congress Standing Committee, interrupted.

Wen Jiabao patiently explained, "Obama knows that we are in a bind and cannot afford to dump large amounts of his treasury bonds. We cannot afford to let the bond markets slide by offloading our holdings except marginally, or we will shoot ourselves in the foot by letting the market panic. For years, it suited us to supply the United States with an unending line of credit to buy the stuff that our factories produce. Our own consumers are not stupid to buy the millions of Barbie dolls that we have dumped on the United States. We were essentially blind to follow the example of the Japanese and Koreans to be obsessed with exports, thinking like fools that the good times would never end."

"We will be bigger fools going forward. You have forgotten to mention that with all the warning signs in place of a plunging US economy, we persisted in buying US treasury bonds and virtually doubled our holdings since!" Wu Bangguo snapped. "We seem to forget that the reserves belong to the Chinese people and should have been used to boost our domestic economy by now. The Weng'an County rape case recently involving a fifteen-year-old girl would have been like any individual crime problem quickly forgotten by the public if we had taken some steps to boost the economy. Instead, the locals are burning down the police station out of anger at job losses and workers coming permanently back from our coastal special economic zones. Cui Yadong, the Provincial Public Security chief, is still trying to keep things under control without using too much force. With the world's media watching, we can't afford to do otherwise for the time being."

"At the moment, the US government bond market remains more or less the only asset class that is large enough and liquid enough to accommodate our foreign exchange reserves. There was nothing much that we could do," said Wen, maintaining his cool. "We had to buy United States Treasury debt. We have, of course, done other things like topping up our strategic petroleum tanks with thirty-five million barrels of oil and secretly buying up large amounts of copper, aluminum, zinc, titanium, and indium cheaply through the Strategic Reserves Bureau to build up our stockpiles."

Hu Jintao, the president intervened, "We don't have the luxury to repatriate foreign exchange dollars earned via our massive trade surpluses. This would only drive up the Yuan, making our exports much more expensive and uncompetitive. We can't do this in the midst of the biggest global slump that the world has possibly seen! We are, however, continuing to scout for opportunities for some of this money to be channelized into picking up energy and base metal assets in Africa and Central Asia now that valuations are beginning to look affordable."

Wen continued, "The United States, too, is dependent upon us. This dependence was fully exposed when Hilary Clinton was dispatched to Beijing immediately after Obama became president. She virtually begged us to continue to buy US Treasury bills. Quantitative easing that sounds so harmless but only entails printing huge quantities of dollars is essentially the tool of choice of the United States. While making soothing noises about protecting the value of our dollar investments, the United States has to pay more attention to reassuring the markets. It will do so by creating enough inflation to get the economy moving. Obviously, this will fail. Bonds will sink, and gold and commodities sitting in our warehouses will rise.

"However, that is part of the reason we are here today. With the world economic turmoil likely to continue for years, we need to take a strategic view as to how we can use it to our long-term advantage. We need to emasculate the United States by the time the economic turmoil is all over and gain enough freedom and clout in the emerging world order for the Chinese people to take their rightful place in the sun. This recession is clearly swinging power back in our favor after five centuries, and we should grab this opportunity with all our resources. We'll have a short break now before the President tells you what he has in mind for the future."

CHAPTER 5
ASSASSIN'S MACE

PRESIDENT HU JINTAO SPOKE SLOWLY IN careful precise terms, indicating the way forward to the Politburo. "We cannot afford to be distracted by temporary difficulties and personality clashes. It's not the purpose of this meeting, and history will not forgive us for losing out on this opportunity. Our rise in the past three decades has lacked one essential feature, an accompanying decline in the West. Now in the space of a few short months, Europe and Japan, embroiled in the worst depression in living memory, are not worth considering as rivals anymore. America, the superpower, has passed its peak.

"In the next two decades, we need to use this threat to the wealth of our people as an opportunity to finish off the United States as the foremost power in the world. Our intelligence estimates, based on thousands of inputs worldwide, show that it has never been easier to destroy the position of preeminence that the United States has enjoyed since World War II. To achieve this destruction, all of us must maintain a great deal of strategic perspective. I will therefore now ask General Xu to touch on the historical perspective that we have in formulating our national strategy. This should serve as a reminder to all of us when steering a course in the turbulent times ahead."

General Xu Caihou stood up and raised a hand for attention before he spoke. "Shashou Jiang, in our ancient Chinese strategic thinking, conveys the idea of 'the assassin's mace.' It is a concept that stresses that whenever possible, avoid a fight. If you do need to fight, then fighting by whatever rules of war are accepted as norms in the world need to be cast aside. You need to think out of the confining box of conventional wisdom and so-called civilization-driven behavior. Overwhelming an enemy should be with 'Shashou Jiang,' figuratively, the club with which the assassin ruthlessly destroys the enemy."

"Would you like to share a more modern perspective of the concept of using 'Shashou Jiang,' General Xu?" Wen Jiabao asked.

"Certainly, I shall endeavor to do so. The first use of a nuclear weapon by the United States in immediate response to the attack on Pearl Harbor would have nicely fitted the conceptual framework of 'Shashou Jiang' in case nuclear weapons had existed. That the United States did use nukes at a time when Japan was already on its knees does not detract from the concept. Our invasion of an unwary India in 1962 could fall into this classical ancient category. We hid intent behind the smoke and mirrors of negotiations while preparing to overwhelm India with 'Shashou Jiang.' Refinement of this concept over the last several decades now stresses that the political objective should be achieved by economy of force as well. Economy of your resources includes their substitution by proxies. Like we use Iran and North Korea to confront the United States on an ongoing basis in different parts of Asia and bleed it bit by bit."

"And we use a willing Pakistan to bleed India even more. It is a delicious irony that the United States also helps us by generously supplying arms free to Pakistan and saving us the trouble," Wen added.

Xu continued, "The great Mongol warrior Changez Khan was probably our role model in evolving this concept initially. His battle hardened, ultra-mobile, golden hordes backed by superb cartographers created a sort of primitive global-positioning system to position, overwhelm, and destroy much larger forces. Changez Khan did this as a matter of near routine. Fortunately for us, much of his attention was taken up destroying the Persian Empire. He achieved this by sudden multidirectional attacks carried out by stealth and speed, where overwhelming superiority and shock action was achieved at the point of decision. Panic setting in the enemy ranks thereafter ensured the disintegration of numerically superior forces. In the twenty-first century, however, the People's Liberation Army is just one component, albeit still the most important one, of multidirectional attacks aimed at the political, economic, and social cohesion of the chosen enemy."

Hu Jintao took over again, "The United States will still seek to eke out its preeminence with a new set of allies. These will be added to NATO, Japan and South Korea, the former Soviet Republics, and the Gulf Royal families around the world. It still has the wherewithal to react viciously by air and maritime forces to any overt attempt to thwart its perceived power and influence. In our region, however, where do all of you think the danger lies?"

Wu Bangguo replied, "In Asia Pacific under the fig leaf of shared democratic ideals the US pawn in the making is undoubtedly India … a country that is coming out in relatively good shape from the recession. Given adequate support from the United States, India would seek to undermine our Asian supremacy for its own security. George Bush, for all his perceived failings, was actually the first American politician to have instinctively realized this. He prodded a strategic rethink to boost Indian capabilities to counter our destined rise. However, we should be quite clear that in the Asian sky, there cannot be two suns!"

There was a loud murmur of agreement. Hu Jintao then said, "You are absolutely right! India is the US pawn in the making. Still, from our experience of the last sixty years, India can be compared to a frog. When dropped in boiling water, a frog will immediately try to jump out. However, if you put the frog in a large vessel of water at room temperature and gradually heat it, it will go to sleep. It will be lulled by the warmth and not react at all. It may actually appear to be enjoying itself, oblivious of the impending danger.

"The Communist parties in India, with their presence in parliament, will ensure that we get what we want without more than a few bleating sounds of protest. India, with its bunch of squabbling, petty-minded politicians, has the least political will in our region to assert itself. We know that the Indians are still conditioned from their 1962 defeat by the PLA and our redrawing our borders with it. We have left more than four thousand kilometers not demarcated and called it the Line of Actual Control (LAC). India will not oppose us in any meaningful way. Our unopposed occupation of Tibet before that and making the Dalai Lama irrelevant met with no resistance. Our military assistance to Pakistan, Bangladesh, Myanmar, and Sri Lanka go unchallenged. Nepal will fall firmly in our lap if we ensure that the Maoists are firmly placed in power. India is unable to lead the South Asian nations by example."

General Xu Caihou said, "I will give all of you a quick update on the current security situation in India. The internal security situation in a third of India's six-hundred-plus districts is precarious. The Naxal or Maoist movement that we are now supporting secretly has at least fifty districts where their writ is absolute and virtually unchallenged by the Indian government. This area is also the core of India's resource base. This is where they mine uranium and coal and iron ore. We made a strategic mistake of not giving this movement adequate support ten years ago at least. We are encouraging the Naxalite communists in India to increase recruitment of their cadres. They already have more than ten thousand trained men and women. If they can double this strength in the next three years, they will force India to divert large parts of the army as well, aside from paramilitary forces. These formations can only come from infantry divisions against Tibet to start with. Indian paramilitary forces are poorly led and untrained. To give you some perspective, in Pakistan, less than twenty thousand Taliban-controlled tribes have tied up half a million men, including much of the Pakistan Army.

"That kind of force level committed to internal security for the last twenty years in turn has made the job of the PLA to keep the border issue with India fully alive even easier. We have pushed PLA patrols into India on at least seventy occasions in the past year without any effective response from India beyond halfhearted protests. Geopolitically, we need to ensure that India remains as irrelevant as at the time when Bush decided he could change the rules of the game and put some spine into the Indians. Pakistan is creating strategic space for us as well by encouraging local insurgencies and inducting terrorist groups in India. Breaking up India into smaller bits over time has never been easier.

"We also have a lot of scope to tie up large numbers of Indian troops in Assam and Arunachal Pradesh by giving better support to various insurgent groups to tie up the additional army divisions that the Indians are raising in their northeast region. We are also hopeful of getting one of the politicians we have been regularly paying off elected as a chief minister in one of the tribal areas in Eastern India. This will further disrupt the anti-insurgency efforts of the Indian central government."

President Hu Jintao continued thereafter, "We need to be focused and ruthless like Mao when he liberated China. We have taken a small but important step in safeguarding our maritime interests. We initiated action a few years ago to erode the enormous advantage that the Americans have in projecting power through their submarine fleet. Yesterday, we were finally rewarded with some success. We arranged the collision of the USN Hartford, a Los Angeles class submarine with one of the new American warships, USN New Orleans, it was trying to escort through the Straits of Hormuz. Extensive damage has resulted that should keep both vessels in dry dock for the next few years. We also gave the Iranians a few hours notice to watch the fireworks and left no doubt in their thinking that the collision was our doing. Information was fed to the Iranians that the Americans were all set to bomb their nuclear facilities. The Iranians had their swarm patrol boats supplied by us equipped and ready to retaliate by sinking the USN Hartford.

"President Mahmoud Ahmadinejad should now be happy to let us expand our presence in the Iranian oil program. Also let us set up a naval station on one of their islands in the Straits of Hormuz. I have committed to help Iran keep an eye on the US Fifth Fleet operations out of Bahrain if they cooperate by making a base available. This will also be another important step in squeezing the Indians further out of the Iranian oil and gas sector."

There was a palpable air of excitement in the room as the meeting broke up. The time had finally come to claim China's place in the sun! They would be the lucky ones to try to shape China's destiny and cast aside centuries of shame and subjugation by the West.

Hu Jintao closed the discussion when he said, "I am setting a seven-year target for ourselves to dismember India. We have estimated that the United States will have to live through a sustained period of economic turmoil and will not be able to interfere with what we are going to do. By that time, we would have let the frog boil itself to death! The United States will have little choice but to live with the new balance-of-power equation that we create."

CHAPTER 6
MENWITH HILL, HARROWGATE, ENGLAND

MENWITH HILL IN ENGLAND IS THE largest electronic monitoring station in the world. It is run by the US National Security Agency (NSA), which monitors the world's communication for US intelligence. Menwith Hill employs more than 1,200 US civilians and servicemen working around the clock inside "hardened" buildings, intercepting and analyzing communications mainly from Europe, Russia, and the Middle East

Dr. Asha "Ash" Conway with an IQ of 160 held a doctorate in political science from the Harvard-Kennedy School along with an online-acquired master's degree in computation and game theory. She also had outstanding vernacular skills in Farsi and Chinese. With striking good looks, shoulder-length, lustrous black hair, and glowing with obvious good health enhanced by an hour-long yoga workout six days a week, she was still occasionally offered modeling assignments at age thirty-six. Ash scanned the latest downloaded intelligence from SIGINT satellites covering Iran amongst other countries, making brief notes on a scratch pad as she worked. She was a very important but temporary desk warrior on a two-year contract at Menwith Hill. The base, though controlled by the NSA, was classified as a Royal Air Force facility.

In spite of her obvious aptitude for intelligence-related analysis Ash had opted out of a permanent assignment at the NSA. She hoped to revert to developing game-theory models impacting national security and international trade negotiations. Normally, the NSA would never have employed her with her marked reluctance to a long term commitment. The times, however, were far from normal, with Iran trying to acquire nuclear weapons, China giving silent support to the mullahs running Iran, and a near absence of people who were proficient in intelligence analysis involving both languages.

Ash had become highly skilled in a few months at utilizing the highly automated system called Echelon. The system used computers known as Dictionary to select messages that included combinations of specific names, dates, places, and subjects. Dictionary automatically searched through intercepted messages, looking for particular subjects and people from target lists. Those matching particular criteria were sent for further processing by analysts. Key words for message interception were numerically coded and included diplomatic messages and regional communications.

Ash's computer skills were directly attributable to a strong homegrown foundation with long hours sitting and learning from her father, Mike Conway. His work as an independent oil drilling consultant had driven him to operate in some of the remotest areas of first Iran and then China for two decades in the oil exploration business as a data analyst. He was also a self-taught software programmer. This was out of frustration with the limitations of what was available in the market for locating oil and gas reserves. Ash's language skills and stubbornness in analyzing problems could be attributed to her mother, Lata, who was from the small Himalayan town of Dharamsala in Northern India.

Along with their only child, Lata had accompanied Mike everywhere he had worked. She had insisted on Ash going to local schools and learning fluent Farsi and Chinese by the time she was fourteen years old. Lata was herself proficient in English, Hindi, and Tibetan. Tibetan happened to be the language of a number of her playmates, playmates whose parents had been uprooted from their native land, Tibet. They had accompanied the Dalai Lama into Indian exile in 1958, fleeing the wrath of the invading Chinese People's Liberation Army. Over time, a thriving Tibetan community had come up in Dharamsala, the seat of exile of the Dalai Lama.

Ash soon discovered that since the incorporation of a movable satellite-signal-suppression shield in some of the newer satellites, the quality of information being picked up had noticeably improved. The technology suppressed the laser, radar, and infrared signals of a satellite, which made spotting it a tough proposition. The space-communication shield was deployed in the form of a rigid, inflatable balloon that deflected incoming laser and ultraviolet energy beams into outer space rather than back to the ground detectors, creating a cloak of invisibility for itself.

The brief and enigmatic telephone conversation that the SIGINT satellite had picked up, which Ash was trying to make sense of, involved Admiral Habib Sayyani and Ali Reza Tangsir, the Senior Revolutionary Guards commander. It had taken many days without much sleep to work that one out. Asha played back the recorded conversation, looking for something she may have missed.

"I don't trust the Chinese. The bastards are a pack of liars!"Ash was eventually able to figure that Admiral Habib Sayyani was talking to Ali Reza Tangsir.

"I agree with you. Definitely, they were lying to us, hinting that the Americans were going to attack. However, the Chinese did tell us two hours in advance that the Americans were sneaking a submarine into the strait!" A voice match showed the speaker to be Ali Reza Tangsir.

"Rubbish! They just hinted that something would happen. One of their satellites must have picked up a transmission from the Hartford or a rescue boat. I see no reason why the Chinese should be given any base facilities for essentially worthless information!" it was Admiral Habib Sayyani again responding to the Senior Revolutionary Guards commander.

Ash figured that she had done her bit by figuring out the personalities involved. The newspapers had all picked up the story of the American submarine that could not sail straight. *Let someone in the National Security Agency work out the reason*, Ash decided. *Or toss it to someone at the CIA headquarters at Langley.* She turned to the set of intercepts in Chinese, thinking that if there was some sort of collusion between the Chinese and Iranians, someone in China might talk about it—if they got a mite careless.

After almost a hundred hours of effort, the intercept of the conversation between Navy Captain Li Zhiquan of the South Sea PLA Fleet and his mistress was retrieved. It provided the connection. "I know I promised to be there for your birthday party, but there is an emergency about to take place between the American and Iranian Navy. And my admiral wants me to remain here. I'll make up, I promise, in a day or two, when this dies down, and we can fuck the whole night!"

Ash Conway had also been following the development of strategy debate in China for two years through intercepts of conversations and Internet communications. These were roughly five thousand powerful people all over the Chinese establishment. These also included leading academics of one type or other who were an entrenched part of a system that created inputs for the Chinese politburo. Almost without exception, the ones who were given predominant hearings for their views were the ones with advanced degrees from the West.

The list included the functionaries of the China Institute for International Studies responsible for organizing an unending series of conferences bringing together academics and leaders in business, the military, and the government to drive strategies for the top rung of the communist party. Foreign affairs inputs seemed to come in a steady stream from Justin Yifu Lin, director of the China Center for Economic Research at Beijing University, and his immediate staff. Most importantly, the Chinese neo-cons, in particular Yang Yi and Yang Xuetong from the Chinese Academy of Social Sciences with fifty research centers and four thousand researchers, were mooting a return to great power status.

There was a broad consensus that there were two kinds of order. The "Wang" or "King" system, which was based on a dominant superpower, with primacy on benign government rather than coercion or territorial expansion, was a suitable model for use within China. Outside China, the "Ba" or "Overlord" system, which was classically hegemonic, urged that the most powerful nation restored order on the periphery. China was well positioned to adopt "Ba" in Asia, with Japan in geriatric decline and Russia demographically crippled. India, the only potential challenger, needed to be quickly snuffed out. A wonderful window of opportunity existed with the United States, the world's hegemony in a deep financial mess. Attempts to undermine the United States further in

Asia should have been pursued by supporting Iran firmly and squeezing India's strategic space to reduce its value as a potential US ally against China.

Ash hummed tunelessly to herself as she started to write her last quarterly intelligence summary. In a week, she would be back in New York. She ended with the following sentence: "There appears to be a likelihood of China trying to provoke a low-level conflict against India in the next three to five years. The aim would be twofold—undermine the US presence in Asia further and degrade India's ability to be a potential challenger to its hegemony in Asia. A play for a naval base in SOH will continue as it fulfills its objective."

In a few weeks, Ash's report, though unknown to her, made its way to the US President as an appendix to an assessment by the US National Security Adviser, Lieutenant General Jacob Long (retired) from the US Marine Corps.

"What are we doing about following up your assessment?" the president asked.

The general replied "The FBI is quietly investigating the chances of a leak in the submarine upgrade program. The Chinese aims seem logical enough. We would have done exactly the same in their place. It's, however, a golden opportunity for us as well, I reckon. We should quietly raise the stakes for the Chinese. It won't make them change their minds, but the idea is to make it so expensive by the time they are done that the idea of challenging us remains on the back burner. At least for another two decades."

"And how do we do that Jake?" the president asked.

"Sell lots of arms—say four or five billion dollars worth through the Foreign Military Sales Program—to Taiwan first as a warning to China. Follow up with permitting a complete basket of India's defense needs to combat the Chinese as purely commercial transactions. This will also keep Boeing, BAE, General Dynamics, Raytheon, Sikorsky, and Lockheed Martin, amongst others, happy for the next twenty years! These companies in turn will ensure that substantial contributions are made for funding your reelection. In the meanwhile, we sit back and watch the fun. A drawn-out, low-level conflict between China and India with an unsatisfactory ending may well ensue. It will slow down economic growth and clip the worldwide perception of China's growing power. It will also ensure the Indians don't get too big for their pants dealing with us!"

The president smiled for the first time in weeks. "Go for it, Jake. Best news I've had the whole damn year!"

"Okay, boss. I'll call the Indian ambassador and tell her that we will approve sales of what she is desperately angling for. I'll tell her off the record that if India asks for say the F-16 or F/A-18 fighters, the C-17 Globe Master-III giant strategic aircraft, harpoon missiles, PAC-3 antimissile systems, H-92 Super Hawk helicopters, or for that matter, M777 155 light howitzers, I will ensure quick clearances."

The president terminated the discussion. "Also tell her that we'll guarantee delivery and spare parts no matter what! The Indians have always been suspicious of our ability to just clamp down on arms deliveries because of domestic pressures. They've witnessed it happening to Pakistan and trust the Russians more than us! Besides, the Pakistan Army doesn't pay us for what doles we give them."

CHAPTER 7
MASTER OF THE GAME

Brigadier Syed Ali had learnt his trade from the best teacher in the intelligence game. Lieutenant General Hameed Gul (retired), former head of Pakistan's Inter-Services Intelligence, the equivalent of a CIA-FBI combination, had arguably been the most powerful man in Pakistan after General Zia ul Haq before he had hung up his military boots. During the war against the Soviet occupation of Afghanistan, Syed Ali had been an apt learner with a brilliant mind, a fondness for intrigue, and a gift for tactical innovation.

As a young officer, Syed Ali had soaked up the power trails that his general, who had treated his staff officer like a favored son, had generated over the years. Syed Ali had seen more live action than any three other contemporaries put together had. He had been Hameed Gul's ear to the ground, coaxing and cajoling militant groups and earning their respect by being with them in the thick of their battles against the Soviets. He had a photographic memory and an evocative gift with words that made him invaluable.

By a process of osmosis, notable segments of the old man's power and strategic thought had shifted ownership to him. Syed Ali was now powerful in his own right. Power came because of his beliefs, strong leadership traits, and track record in promoting Jihadist groups with whose leaders he had once been an intermediary. He had also developed an incredible hold on the more fanatic religious leaders in Pakistan in the process. These had looked at him as a rock-steady ally. The power he had earned had always been exercised from the shadows with great circumspection and secrecy.

He had drifted into being an "informal strategic adviser" to Pakistan's extremist religious political parties for the past decade, but he had been closest to the Taliban and Osama bin Laden. It was a pity that Osama had been slow to heed his, Syed Ali's, advice to move his hide away to Karachi from Abbotabad and got himself killed by US Navy Seals. At close quarters, Syed Ali had watched the evolution and running of a hundred-and-fifty-thousand-strong intelligence agency that had been largely responsible for driving the Russians out of Afghanistan. It had also helped that he had been a pillar, albeit only a middle-ranking one, of the only establishment in Pakistan that had always mattered, namely the army. It had also helped that the interests of the army and the men he had nurtured had roughly been aligned for the most part. Both had had an implacable hatred for India and now anything remotely connected with the United States.

Syed Ali was the one, the Taliban openly acknowledged, who had thought of the brilliant innovation of hiding explosives in cameras to kill Ahmed Shah Massood, the Northern Alliance warlord. His skill in organizing the logistics of inducting the Jordanian doctor Khalil Abu-Mulal al-Balawi as a double agent and suicide bomber into the CIA operating base at Khost to kill seven CIA officers was also loudly praised! The CIA suspected that Brigadier Syed Ali had been the master mind behind the incident, and that had been the main reason why they had forced the Pakistan Army chief to retire him prematurely.

After the Russians were kicked out of Afghanistan, Brigadier Syed Ali was at least largely responsible for the huge impetus given to Jihad in Kashmir and the recruitment of hundreds of Muslim Kashmiri youth. Literally under the noses of the Indian security establishment, Syed Ali also knew a great deal about promoting the use of illegal nuclear materials as biological and chemical weapons in Pakistan. He was a solid bridge between the more radical elements of the Pakistan Army and the Taliban, trusted implicitly by both and distrusted completely by the United States.

Brigadier Syed Ali arrived at the little stone farmhouse thirty kilometers northwest of Quetta a little before sunset. His much younger companion, a bodyguard clutching an AK-74 rifle, eyes roving from side to side for any threat, waited outside the little farmhouse under a tree when the brigadier strode in. They had walked the last ten kilometers along mountain paths with a GPS and watched the building through binoculars from early in the morning to ensure there were no unpleasant surprises. Amir Mullah Omar Amir-ul-Mumineen—the commander of the faithful and spiritual leader of the Taliban—was accompanied by a little-known aide, Hakimullah Agha, and Abdullah Sa'id, Al Qaeda's Paramilitary Force commander. After the formal salutations were done, the one-eyed Mullah Omar spoke his mind.

"Things are not going as well in Afghanistan as we would wish for. Although we have widened our attacks in the North and the West, where we had very little influence, we are taking too many casualties from superior American firepower. Funds are also a problem, as too many couriers carrying opium have been intercepted by NATO patrols. We are also seeing for the first time signs of a slight drop in recruitment because of recruitment by the Afghan Army and regular pay. I am concerned that by the time the Americans actually leave, we may be so weak that there will be fewer chances to take over the Afghan government. The Tajiks controlling the government have become far too powerful. They have earned enough from American-sponsored contacts to sustain themselves against us Pashtuns once the Americans leave. The old Northern Alliance may be recreated with enough money and guns."

Mullah Omar continued, "Within Pakistan as well, the fight with the army, which is secretly permitting American predator UAVs to target Taliban leaders, is not doing us any good. Baitullah Mehsud getting himself killed fucking his new wife was of course a pity. I had warned him to be more careful, but the suicide-bombing successes had gone to his head. Of course, it was one of his own people who gave him away for American gold. It will take us years to replace him—if that is possible. I can see no one with the prestige or talent as a fighter to get thirteen tribes to act as one."

Hakimullah Agha added, "To carry out really catastrophic acts of violence like our attack on the World Trade Center years ago, we require sanctuaries, sanctuaries that provide time, space, and improve our ability to perform competent planning and staff work. Sanctuaries are needed that provide opportunities and space to recruit, train, and select operatives with the needed skills and dedication. We had gained these in Pakistan under your advice, and this led to an influx of our operatives and money into the tribal regions."

Abdullah Sa'id added "We now have about three hundred trained recruits ready to do our bidding, but our funds are starting to dry up because of several financial restrictions that the Americans have managed to create. The drug network in Helmand, too, is temporarily dysfunctional, as everyone is busy fighting the Americans. They have also accidentally captured some drug shipments to Iran as well."

"In short, you are worried that even after withdrawing some army brigades from Afghanistan, the Americans will continue to have the upper hand as it appears today?" Brigadier Syed Ali asked.

Mullah Omar responded "True, although we have more than one tool at our disposal to postpone this for a long time—rapid deterioration inside northern Afghanistan that will surely divert the Americans in the south, striking at NATO allies, disrupting NATO supply lines originating in Pakistan, assassinations, and even possible strikes on American facilities and citizens."

Brigadier Syed Ali continued "I have a suggestion. One other tool may also be considered even if spoken of earlier—lure Washington into negotiations. Already, the propaganda machine of your brethren from different corners of the world, including some journalists inside the Western media, has been pushing the idea that discussions with what they call the 'good Taliban' is a viable and pragmatic option."

Seeing he had Mullah Omar's interest, Brigadier Syed Ali spun out his suggestion further. "Recently, a particular push for considering so-called radical Islamism as a 'fact of life' to be recognized has materialized in a publicized *TIME magazine* article. Painting jihadists as credible partners in a peacemaking equation is, in fact, part of our maneuver to gain time and delay US-led efforts to defeat the network in Afghanistan. Similar moves are being undertaken within Pakistan as well. All you need to do is to give these a little push. Let your emissaries say that you will distance yourself from Al Qaeda and not grant it sanctuary in Afghanistan."

Mullah Omar interjected, "In order to delay Islamabad's government in its preparedness to confront the Taliban once and for all, our suicide bombers target officials and civilians alike, while offers for ceasefires from local allies are made daily to the authorities and guarantee a truce for a while. With time, the agreement will be used to our advantage to indoctrinate the youth, recruit fighters and suicide bombers, and eradicate government presence. All this, of course, we have done before. What do you think of trying to do more of the same? Or do we now need to change track to create strategic surprise?"

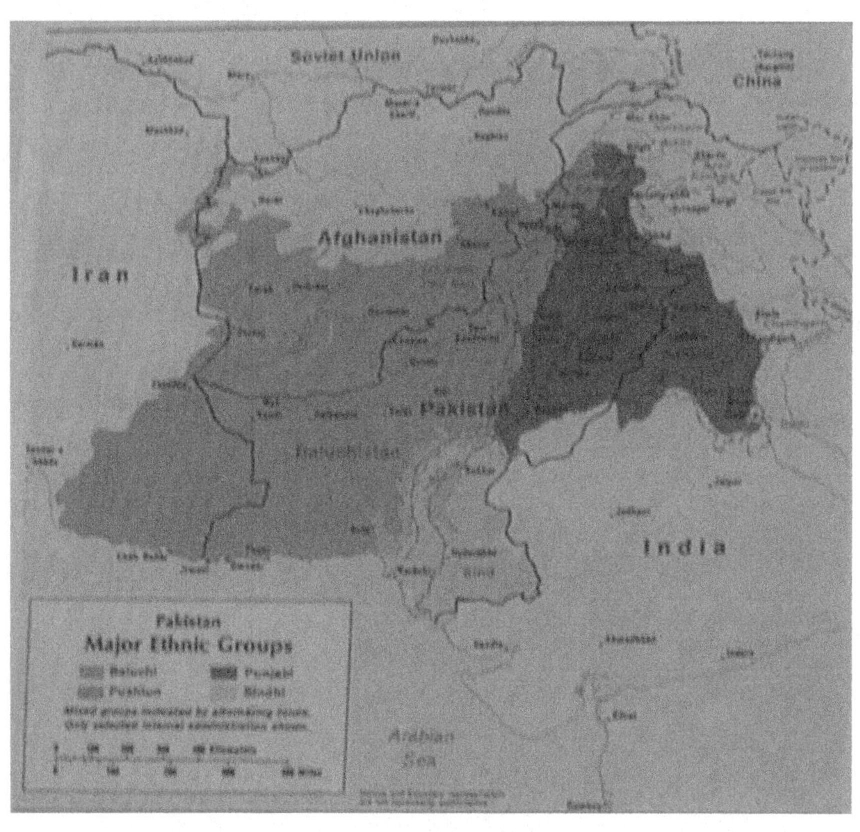

Afghanistan-Pakistan (AFPAK)

CHAPTER 8
THE CHOSEN ONE

BRIGADIER SYED ALI LOOKED FLEETINGLY AT the circling eagle riding the air currents of a chilled blue sky, weighing his words carefully before looking squarely into the one good eye of Mullah Omar Syed, Ali still remembered the time Mullah Omar was a small time commander in the fighting with the Russians in Afghanistan when he, Syed Ali, as a young captain was an important intermediary for the ISI chief. Mullah Omar's rise had thereafter been meteoric after he had earned the respect of his people while leading the uprising against former Mujahidin warlords in 1994 around Kandahar.

Syed Ali had been thinking about what he needed to put forth for weeks, biding his time for this meeting but not wishing to bring up the subject himself. It was important that the three men continued to defer to him. It was a reflex action that went back many years to a time when they had less power to shape events. Now it was his moment as a man of acknowledged wisdom to say things that would be mulled over, dissected, analyzed, and debated but never rejected out of hand, even if not immediately acted upon.

"The biggest advantage that you have right now, irrespective of how badly things may actually be going in the long run, is that American people and politicians do not believe that they can win in Afghanistan. In addition, the Pakistan government has completely lost credibility by their mismanagement of the Indus floods and millions of homeless people for years to come. With the worldwide economy showing little signs of improving, the Americans cannot afford to continue in the same way that they are doing currently."

Abdullah Sa'id nodded vigorously and said, "So we should increase the intensity of fighting and kill more Americans and NATO soldiers quickly to force them out?"

Brigadier Syed Ali smiled grimly and continued, "Just the opposite. We should decrease the intensity of fighting. This will give the Americans an excuse to show we are losing the war and our support base. This, in turn, will start the 'good Taliban, bad Taliban' debate again amongst America's allies. We do all we can to give them an excuse to leave quickly and save your base of operations to quickly finish off the Afghan Army after the Americans leave. The pressure to disengage and leave will greatly mount as the US presidential election campaign picks up steam, especially if fighting in both Afghanistan and Pakistan is greatly reduced. The Pakistan Army in any case is not cooperating fully ostensibly, because a lot of army formations are committed in the flood relief of twenty million Pakistanis."

"What you are saying is that our interest and the American interest in Afghanistan are in complete alignment?" Mullah Omar asked disbelievingly.

Brigadier Syed Ali smiled for the first time. "You want the Americans to leave right now; they want to do the same but with some saving of face. This face you can provide them by calling off all major operations. Creating an illusion of peace is yours to do whenever you like. You just need to ensure that the moment the Americans leave, you simultaneously target the Tajik heads of the intelligence services and their families with sustained attacks in Kabul. Taking over Kabul will then be easy."

"And what do we do about the Pakistan Army?" Mullah Omar still looked skeptical.

Syed Ali patiently amplified, "There is a need to keep the dialogue with the Pakistan Army going as well. The army is overstretched, and bringing the fighting in Pakistan to a halt will suit them. That will tempt the Americans to leave even quicker while claiming that American objectives have been achieved. All that is required, the Americans will presume, is to provide financial support to the Afghan government over the long term."

"If what you suggest is done and it succeeds, what can we do next?" Abdullah Sa'id asked.

"You have often spoken of expanding the Jihad into neighboring countries. The time has come to do so now but indirectly through your brethren in the other Jihad groups in Pakistan, especially the Lashkar e Taiba and Hizb ul Mujahidin, who have become comparatively powerful enough to be made better use of."

"I don't trust them!" Abdullah Sa'id was vehement.

"Nevertheless, you must use them!" Syed Ali emphasized looking him full in the face.

Syed Ali continued his pitch "You don't have to like them to use them. The Lashkar and the Hizb must be encouraged further to build up operations in Kashmir and other parts of India. You have much to teach them. Offer them your people to facilitate their training."

"And who will carry this message to the Lashkar and Hizb? We don't have a continuous running relationship. Will they really trust our messenger and not carry on seeking clarifications and changes for months?" Abdullah asked, unconvinced.

"I will carry the message if you wish. They know me well enough to trust my word!" Brigadier Syed Ali offered, looking at Mullah Omar. "Remember, instigating operations against India will invariably distract the Pakistan Army to meet the Indian retaliatory response. Once the Pakistan Army's focus turns toward India, the American and NATO operations in Afghanistan will automatically falter. In turn, this will ensure that you have the time to reorganize, train, and recruit. It will also give you time to turn your attention toward our Uyghur brothers and Xinjiang.

"You have lost Mullah Abdul Ghani Baradar, who was widely respected by everyone fighting the Americans, sold out for ten million rupees, I'm told, and you need some one senior to maintain links with the field commanders. The loss of Khalid Habib, Abu Jihad al Masri, Usama Al Kini, and Najmiddin the Uzbek, amongst others, have also been major blows to you. Your operational planning needs to be strengthened, with so many of the Shura having been killed in recent years. Leadership is everything in this battle. It does not matter how many of our young recruits get killed. More will come. It takes more than ten years to create good leaders. These then can get recruits to follow them because of their personal qualities."

"Go on" Mullah Omar said seeing Syed Ali hesitate.

Syed Ali continued "If you like, I can get four or five outstanding majors and colonels who are being forcibly retired from the army along with me under US pressure because of their close links to you to help. They have all organized covert operations in India and also exercise good control over the so-called Indian Mujahidin (IM) in more than a dozen Indian cities. I have personally organized thc training of some of the IM leaders in Karachi, so I know what I am talking about. One of them is also familiar with the key Pakistan nuclear sites in Wah, Fatehjang, Golra, Sharif, and Kahuta in case a site has to be targeted at some stage."

"Will you personally vouch for each of them?"

"All of them have been trained under my supervision for years and are simply the best available anywhere in the world. Let them help you with planning operations. They will do their work quietly and efficiently. Most importantly, keep them updated on a daily basis and listen to their suggestions. The Taliban is indeed fortunate that they will no longer be used against you."

Mullah Omar nodded in agreement, keeping his eyes glued on Brigadier Syed Ali, and said, "We will require a lot of time to organize all this. There are many who will not understand the logic of easing operations against the Americans, especially with their predators firing hellfire missiles, continuing to pick off the leaders every few weeks. Is there anything else we can do in the meanwhile that will bring us long-term benefits?"

Brigadier Syed Ali was waiting for just this moment. "We need to plan an attack against India as well. This needs to happen soon, before it gets its act together and their National Counterterrorism Center becomes fully functional. At the moment, fortunately, the Indian state as usual is pulling in disparate directions with its political, administrative, intelligence, and enforcement elements still continuing to work at cross purposes."

"We have been hearing that the Indian home minister has gotten their act together after the ISI directed attack on Mumbai through the Lashkar? Hakimullah Agha asked.

Syed Ali acknowledged the observation of Hakimullah Agha with a nod and said "Unfortunately the Americans gave the Indians access to Daood Sayeed who had earlier worked as a CIA informer under the name David Headley. This was before the ISI recruited him to do the reconnaissance for the Mumbai terror strike at the Taj Hotel. The ISI has, however, still managed to weaken the Indian home minister by organizing a recent attack against a Hindu cremation site in Varanasi frequented by lots of foreigners. The Indian establishment is also distracted by the recent Maoist success in wiping out a full company of their central reserve police force in eastern India. I have very good information that the Chinese have a hand in this by providing the Maoists with satellite-based intelligence of police reserve movement. You can take it from me that if we do something big enough, the Chinese will find a way to bleed India further."

Brigadier Syed Ali continued, "On the negative side, the Indians have been able to network twenty-one databases that contain vital information and intelligence under what they call NATGRID. I have been keeping a close watch on what they are doing. I have also established a presence in India that will not show up on any of their databases until it is too late. By the time the Americans finally leave, we should be in a position to strike India. That will give the Pakistan Army an excuse to pull out from the tribal areas to face India. You can thereafter focus your efforts fully on reestablishing control over Afghanistan."

Mullah Omar nodded his agreement and turned toward Abdullah Sa'id. "You'd better get some rest before you start travelling. As our brother has suggested, you need to talk to at least twenty leaders one-on-one in the next few weeks. Do not give those you visit more warning than is strictly necessary, or you too, may fall to a predator attack. We will discuss the exact message that you will need to convey and, of course, the exact warning to those not inclined to hear you out."

As he turned back to Brigadier Syed Ali, Mullah Omar asked, "It will take an extraordinary man to lead and guide the strike against India. None of my men have the knowledge and the capability that is required. Will you do it?"

CHAPTER 9
PRAETORIAN GUARD

General Mohammad Ali Jafari, commander of the Army of the Guardians of the Islamic Revolution of Iran, also known as the Islamic Revolutionary Guards Corps (IRGC) had ordered the meeting in the secure lead-lined room where there was no chance of being bugged or overheard. "We are the true keepers of the Ayatollah Ruhollah Khomeini's Iranian Revolution, since our sacrifices and service in the Iran-Iraq War. Qassem, we have no option but to retaliate against Jundallah in Pakistan who the CIA is funding and equipping. We cannot wait for the clerics to give the orders."

"What do you wish to do, General?" Brigadier General Qassem Suleiman asked. He was the head of the Quds Force, mentor of Hezbollah in Lebanon, and master of clandestine operations in other countries.

The deaths of Brigadier General Noor-Ali Shoustari and Rajab-Ali Mohammadzeh have to be avenged suitably. The CIA having fifteen of our best men killed in Sistan-Baluchistan, including our colleagues, is something we cannot tolerate. The Americans cannot be permitted to instigate trouble across the Pakistan-Iran border at will to keep us unbalanced. I want Abdolmalik Rigi's head. Obviously, he has learned nothing from his brother Abdulhamid's hanging. However, we need to do so in a manner to issue a plausible denial. Get the Indians into it as we discussed last week!"

"Leave it to me. Killing two birds with one stone will be truly just," Brigadier General Qassem Suleiman stated confidently.

Alirezah Khalilzad, long-term friend of Sohrab Mehrotra since the time they did an MBA fifteen years ago in Harvard, greeted his friend warmly as Sohrab came into his study in his biking gear for their weekly chat. A shared passion for biking to keep fit and save money on transportation had brought them together initially, not to mention a focus on excelling at their studies. Ever since Sohrab had moved to Tehran to take over the family oil services business and other varied interests they met regularly to shoot the breeze, challenge each other's ideas and have fun. They also lived within an easy bike commute of each other in the Aryashahr locality.

"The IRGC is the new 2.0 version of the erstwhile Imperial Bodyguard of the Shah of Iran. It exerts the type of awe, power, and sheer reach into every facet of society the Shah's Praetorian Guard could never ever have dreamt of" Alirezah commented.

Lounging in his friend's study, Sohrab Mehrotra observed, "That the president is a former Praetorian is not incidental. Like an overindulgent father, the president bestows continuing largesse to fuel the Revolutionary Guard's voracious appetite. It uses the clergy as a façade to hide its tentacles in every niche of Iranian society including business and industry. Khatam al-Anbia, one of the Guards companies I work with, is arguably the largest contractor in industrial development, spanning dams, electric power, and locomotion. There are also other IRGC companies that control a thriving fifteen-billion-dollar black-market smuggling activity for products banned by sanctions."

Alirezah laughed "Don't be sanctimonious since helping these sanctions busters and implicitly trusted by the corps is an Indian friend of mine—namely you Sohrab Mehrotra!"

The phone rang and Alirezah picked it up on the third ring. Sohrab saw the amusement in his friend's eyes rapidly vanish as he listened for the most part for the next ten minutes.

"Brigadier General Qassem Suleimani wants to meet you at your convenience? He knows you cycled to my place half an hour ago" said Alirezah Khalilzad.

Sohrab wondered what the secretive and powerful head of Niru-ye

Qods, better known as Qods Force in the Western media, had in mind. "Any idea what he wants Alirezah?" Sohrab asked.

"None at all, but it must be important for him to take the trouble to personally contact me. He met me a few days ago at a friend's place during a party to perhaps make it look like an accidental meeting. Obviously, he has done his homework, for he seemed to know more about your family in India than I did, including the fact that you had measles at eleven! One of his minions could have just called you up or picked you up from the street. Obviously, it is something more than smuggling in another diamond necklace for his wife!"

"Okay, see if you can set up the meeting for tomorrow around midday."

"Consider it done! He said to confirm any time suitable to you. He will send a car to fetch you from your hotel at eleven. By the way, he also requested that you make no mention of this to anyone else."

The ancient black Mercedes with tinted windows took him to the Quds Force headquarters in Tehran in what was previously a US Embassy until the Iranian Revolution. Sohrab suppressed a shudder. *Fifty-three Americans had been held hostage there for 1,444 days from November 4, 1979, to January 20, 1981, a period that included an abortive rescue attempt code named "Eagle Claw," which had eventually resulted in the death of eight Americans and the loss of two aircraft.*

"It was very kind of you to have come to see me so quickly, Mr. Mehrotra," the head of the Quds Force said as if Sohrab really had a choice in the matter. "You have been a great friend of Iran since the revolution, and we really appreciate the vast risks you have taken. Risks that, of course, have brought their own rewards; however, even two billion dollars paid to you as commissions over the years have been worth every dollar."

"Thank you, General Suleimani," Sohrab said, guessing that the screws were going to be applied. "Iran is my second home, and I went to a village school here when my father started an oil services company at the government's suggestion. If you recall, before that, he also helped setting up your first shipping company to run the oil blockade during the war with Iraq. A large portion of my heart lies in your great country."

"Besides, you have been given opportunities here that have made you a very rich man, worth hundreds of millions of dollars!" the general added.

Sohrab ignored the comment. "Is there anything that I can do that may be useful to the Iranian people? You only have to point the way, and as usual, I promise to do my best to deliver."

Suleimani said, "As you are aware, your country, India, had carried out a series of five nuclear tests in May 1998, including a forty-five-kiloton fusion device. Some of your scientists said in retrospect that the tests were a failure. We believe otherwise for reasons I am not in a position to discuss. We believe that there is considerable unrealized synergy between the Indian nuclear program and ours."

"And how do I come into the picture, general?"

"We are aware that your family and that of the former chairman of the Indian Atomic Energy Commission, Dr. Anil Kak, are friends for over fifty years apparently?"

"That is a fact," Sohrab confirmed, nodding his head.

General Suleimani continued, "Dr. Kak has publicly stated that India's nuclear tests were sufficient to build fission and thermonuclear tests up to two hundred kilotons. He has also said that India has developed state-of-the-art computer simulation capability to predict the yields of nuclear weapons."

"What you say has been widely reported by the media," Sohrab agreed.

"You more than most of my countrymen are aware that Iran has struggled to create a minimal nuclear capability to prevent the Americans from squeezing us further to do their bidding. Obviously, we cannot carry out any nuclear tests and risk retaliatory action by the United States and the West. But you can help us do away with any requirements to test. The West may be convinced that we have nuclear weapons. That gives us considerable leeway to deal with the United States and EU. The problem is that we need to be convinced as well irrespective of what our scientist tell us. A sort of private audit of our capabilities is required," the general said.

"And … you want me to arrange the private audit?" Sohrab asked.

"This is too sensitive to play out through normal diplomatic channels. I would like you to convey to Dr. Kak our request to confirm

Iranian nuclear capability through computer simulations so we don't need to test."

"And invite UN sanctions, general! I can tell you now that there is no way that he will even listen to this proposition," Sohrab said emphatically.

"Not necessarily if it is kept quiet. This does not involve the export of sensitive nuclear material and equipment that can be picked up by UN sanction inspectors. Dr. Kak will obviously have to take it up quietly with the Indian government. We believe that it is in India's interest to do so; you are being squeezed out of Iran by China, and you have a chance to reverse the process."

Sohrab said "I doubt the feasibility of your proposition, general."

Suleimani continued, "India has also lost out on trade opportunities in refined petroleum products for fear of your companies like Reliance Industries being blacklisted by the Americans. The Americans, on the other hand, looked the other way for decades, creating problems for India. All this while, Pakistan was acquiring nuclear weapons and helping the Chinese to put up the uranium centrifuge plant at Hanzhong, with technology stolen from Urenco."

Sohrab's ability to control any show of emotions was legendary in the shipping and oil business he ran. As he kept a neutral look on his face, he asked, "And what does India get out of this proposal, general?"

"Whatever your country wants from Iran can be negotiated!" Suleimani responded. "Trade access, a million barrels of oil a day from the new Yadavaran complex, natural gas from North and South Pars by sea instead of through Pakistan, guarantees on Afghanistan, perhaps increased access to Baluchistan, although it really does not suit us … you name it. Be realistic. We will acquire the nuclear tools that we need in any case. Why not ensure that it is through India and earn our goodwill and secure your energy needs as well."

Sohrab replied "Very well general, I will convey your message!"

"Good. Your country needs to read the writing on the wall. The sun is fast setting over the United States reign as a superpower like it did with the Soviet Union and the British Empire earlier. Ask its ally, Israel, and newer ones, Georgia and Poland, how much comfort they get these days? The short answer is zilch. I have taken the liberty of booking a first-class ticket for you this evening that will be delivered to your hotel. Do well by us, Mr. Mehrotra, and you will find us not ungrateful!"

"You can rest assured that I will not fail, General Suleiman! There is too much at stake for both countries."

"The last issue that I wish you to touch upon is the fate of Afghanistan. Once the Americans and NATO leave the Taliban, Pashtun factions will undoubtedly reassert themselves with the help of the Pakistan Army. The Chinese will be the major beneficiaries. The ISI will ensure that the Taliban permit China to extract the great mineral wealth of Afghanistan, especially copper, and eliminate the Indian presence in economic development. India needs to develop its links to the Persian-speaking Tajik and Hazara from the north dominating the Afghan Army's ranks currently to prevent this. This will be easiest to continue to do through us!"

"One last observation, general—your message will be taken more seriously if I can convey some kind of proof of your good intentions!"

"I will immediately provide proof of our intentions that will be acceptable to India before we sit down to negotiate. While you are in India, when you confirm that our message has been communicated to the Indian prime minister, we will announce that Iran has decided for the time being against giving China access to a base in the Straits of Hormuz. The timing of the announcement can be made in consultation with India if you wish."

"And if the Indians do not agree?" Sohrab asked.

"If India does not agree, it will only be because of concerns of US retaliation. India should worry less about what the US reaction is likely to be. Sooner or later, America will have to come to terms with Iranian power in the region and the fact that nuclear weapons are required by us to safeguard this power, like in the case of Israel and India. America is no longer the economic power it once was to go to war over an issue that basically does not affect its security. Not being able to bring Iran to heel only affects its prestige."

"That does not answer my question, general," Sohrab said bluntly.

"For a start, we can always reconsider the cancellation of the base to China."

A passionate gardener who found the process of looking after plants a favored method of destressing, Dr. Kak was trimming his roses when Sohrab arrived at his small home. The former scientist and head of the Indian Atomic Energy Commission lived by himself on the outskirts of Gurgaon, an hour's drive from Delhi. His wife had died the previous year. The two men shook hands, and the scientist hugged him briefly.

"I've not seen you for at least five years, Sohrab, but I've kept a tab on you through your family. Thank you for coming to see an old man when you have so many things to do. Let's sit out of the sun under my mango tree and have a beer!"

Sohrab had always called him "Uncle," a term of endearment going back to his childhood. Sohrab and the scientist's son, Suraj, who had since migrated to Australia, had been inseparable friends. "I've been meaning to visit you, Uncle, since Aunty passed away, but work pressure in Iran prevented me coming to India up till now."

"Doesn't matter, Sohrab, but I was touched by your call immediately after Sheila died."

"How are you keeping yourself busy after your retirement?" Sohrab asked.

"The PM asked me to head a committee to approve future plans for nuclear plants in India. The work keeps me fairly busy, and I travel a lot within the country to examine potential reactor sites."

"So you are in constant touch with the PM and the political and bureaucratic leadership?"

After a long pull at his beer, Dr. Anil Kak said, "Out with it, Sohrab. What brings you here and to me? What deal are the Iranians trying to swing? You've never asked me for a personal favor!"

"I'm really thankful that my business rivals don't know me half as well as you do, Uncle, or I'd be on the streets without a job. The IRGC has sent me as a sort of unofficial emissary to sound you out. It wants to convey an informal message to the Indian government. Iran wants a confirmation of the workability of their nuke, since they don't entirely trust what their own scientists claim. The IRGC figures that Indian scientists could provide an answer quite easily and sort out their uncertainty," Sohrab explained.

"And in return, Iran will give us more oil and gas, I suppose?" Dr Kak asked.

"Something like that I reckon, as well as cooperation in Afghanistan and Baluchistan," Sohrab agreed.

"The PM should find this pitch interesting!" the former scientist commented. "I'll try to speak to him next week. By when do you have to take back an answer?"

"A couple of weeks, I guess? But whenever I confirm that the offer has been conveyed to you and is being seriously viewed in India, the naval base facilities offered to China will be withdrawn by Iran. This will be done as a proof of friendship. In the meanwhile, I'll be staying at the Taj Hotel in Delhi, in case you want me," Sohrab replied, handing over a piece of paper with his contact details in India.

CHAPTER 10
THE SWISS CONNECTION

"You will simply have to go through the motions to keep the opposition in check in parliament, but there is no chance of the Swiss playing ball," Durga Vadera said emphatically. "Even if you send documents, they will find them insufficient. Let's face it. UBS is more important for the Swiss economy than India—at least as of now! But you knew all before sending me to Zurich."

"True, the UN conference was just an excuse, and you have impeccable credentials as an economist to have attended and met the contacts you made while working on your book," the prime minister agreed. "It's still good, though, to get a second opinion. So how do we leverage the money lying in Swiss vaults for development?"

"Long term, you need the leader of the opposition to play ball to ensure continuity of purpose. Why not sound him out?" Durga suggested.

It all started in the backdrop of the infamous Hasan Ali Khan case, where a stud farm owner by that name in Pune, India, was discovered to supposedly hold eight billion dollars in Swiss bank accounts. A back-of-the-envelope calculation would have shown that irrespective of the pedigree of racehorses reared by anyone in India. Even a million dollars would have been difficult to retain after expenses. When the Swiss Federal Tax Administration was asked for details, it refused to share bank-related information on the grounds that information regarding bank deposits of Indian residents was covered by bank secrecy laws.

For more than sixty years, Zurich had remained the summer stopover of choice for India's rich and infamous. After all, it made sense to personally oversee investments that started with the parallel or so-called "black" or the cash economy in India. The parallel economy had resulted in colossal gains for a few, and Indians had more than a trillion dollars sitting in numbered accounts in Switzerland. It generated at least 30 percent returns for conventional business, including non-invoiced sales within the country, over-invoiced imports, and under-invoiced exports that evaded taxes.

Generating tax-free income was regarded as being street savvy and attracted no social stigma in India. Money thus generated could return laundered and ready for deployment anywhere in the world if required. Criminal activities, including murder, blackmail, and kidnapping, naturally produced greater returns in spite of the general low level of investment required both in capital and in the quality of human resources deployed. Even after paying a service premium for conversion into US dollars or Swiss francs via the so-called informal *Hawala* route, it was definitely worthwhile to squirrel cash away in numbered accounts that were at least inflation-resistant if not inflation-proof. They also provided absolute secrecy from prying wives and tax authorities.

The Indian Income Tax Department had carried out raids on Khan's premises as early as January 2007. One of the documents recovered contained information that Khan had been permitted to withdraw six billion dollars by UBS AG out of his holding of eight billion dollars on deposit. Consequently, the Enforcement Directorate of Income Tax approached the Swiss government for further information on Khan's account to initiate cases against him under both the Income Tax Act and the Foreign Exchange Management Act.

However, the Swiss authority stonewalled and responded that the documents sent to them from India had been checked out with UBS AG and were confirmed to be forged. The Indian government thereafter started the cumbersome process of renegotiating Article 26 of the Organization for Economic Cooperation and Development Model Tax Convention with the Swiss government so that they could receive and share information relating to tax purposes with law enforcement agencies.

The leader of the opposition in the directly elected, generally all-powerful Lower House of Parliament in India was escorted ceremoniously into the office of the Indian prime minister. There had been many years of traditionally acrimonious relationships between the government of the day and the opposition that had plagued India. In many cases, the interests of the country had been sacrificed to score brownie points and supposedly gain votes and money from special interest groups on more than one occasion.

The recent changes in personalities on both sides of the fence of the governing alliance and the opposition had ushered in a totally unexpected change in the working environment in parliament. The prime minister pushed back his glasses, stood up, and walked around his work table to courteously shake hands with the brilliant lawyer who could have been heading a coalition government sitting in his place but for two dozen renegade abstention votes.

"Thank you for coming to see me so promptly," the prime minister said, walking his opponent around to the somewhat dimly lit corner of the room, the comfortable, upholstered, somewhat worn chairs around a low coffee table.

"To keep the prime minister to a billion-plus Indians waiting, especially one with your moral authority, would be unforgivably rude. Our differences aside, decorum must be maintained as we had agreed earlier. However, for the record, this sort of meeting has been rarer than a solar eclipse, I'm told."

"Touché, you are right, of course. Perhaps you and I can reverse the course of history in the months ahead, if we see it as our dharma or moral duty. The time has come when we really have no choice but to look at our obligations to India as distinct from our obligations to our political parties."

"I recall Pervez Musharraf saying something similar when he justified taking over Pakistan years ago and locked up the duly elected Prime Minister Nawaz Sharif before exiling him!"

The prime minister smiled for the first time. "It was also the same Musharraf who decided in a few hours to support the war against the perpetrators of 9/11 terror attacks in New York and got Pakistan off the hook of American retaliation. Sometimes there is a requirement of democracies to act quickly and decisively as well. We are unfortunately not structured to do so."

"Yes, perhaps it does help to take out-of-the-box decisions to resolve a crisis. Does this have anything to do with the Khan case and the refusal of the Swiss government to cooperate in freezing his accounts?" the leader of the opposition queried.

"In an indirect way, it has everything to do with it," the prime minister replied. " Why waste a good crisis! We have a country to run. Admittedly, none of us have done a particularly brilliant job of doing so in a long while.

"Did you know that between 1783 and 1843, as a distant precursor to our Ministry of External Affairs, we or rather the British colonial power had what was called 'The Secret and Political Department' to deal with the proliferation of princely states within the Indian subcontinent? It had a remarkable track record in winning undue influence and trade privileges for the British. Asian neighbors were also constantly outwitted by this small coterie of dedicated people.

The cutting edge to this dedicated team was provided by agents in the field with wide-ranging powers. There was also an understanding that for more than occasional coercion, an expeditionary force of some cavalry and one or two battalions of foot soldiers would always serve as a backup at short notice. We seem to have lost or rather frittered away this diplomatic and military edge!"

"And you want to regain this by putting in place a modern version of the same thing bankrolled by what you can extract from the Khan billions for protection against prosecution and confiscation?" the leader of the opposition posed the question. No one had ever accused him of being slow on the uptake.

The prime minister said "There are lots of people in the same category other than Khan. We will provide the Swiss with the necessary documentation in the case of some medium-sized fish that will take the heat of the treasury benches in parliament accused of protecting tax evaders."

"And I presume that we will do our best to ensure that the Swiss can easily get away with denying information in the case of the large fish by not providing the detailed information and documentation required to freeze an account. Or worse … substitute bogus documents for the originals like in the Khan case?" the leader of the opposition completed the prime minister's statement.

When he saw the affirmative nod by the prime minister, he continued, "Aside from the fact that in our country, it is virtually impossible to keep a secret for more than two hours, do you really think that I can make the Bhartiya Janata Party (BJP) a party to this outlandish notion of reclaiming a doubtful diplomatic legacy? There are too many problems with this concept even without a robust analysis of what you propose."

"And these are?" the prime minister prompted.

"It is completely illegal, not to say immoral, for a prime minister to even suggest such a thing and make the leader of the opposition an unwitting accessory! You cannot fabricate or destroy evidence and blackmail your own citizens to part with their wealth without recourse to the courts. The constitution does not permit it! You have a dozen instruments of state like the Ministries of Defense, External Affairs, and Home, the Cabinet Committee on Security, Research and Analysis Wing, the Intelligence Bureau to safeguard national interests—"

The prime minister interjected firmly, "And we operate in a world of constraints that can only be overcome in the long run by the leader of the opposition agreeing to what is being done. Kautilya wrote the *Arthashastra* treatise that helped overthrow Macedonian rule in North India and establish the Mauryan Empire in the fourth century BC. Nothing much has changed since then. Our country is in grave danger, and our territorial integrity is up for grabs in Arunachal Pradesh, Assam, West Bengal, and in Jammu and Kashmir, besides the Red Corridor within India from Bihar to Karnataka, where the writ of India is questionable and being questioned.

The United States is fully in retreat. For the next decade at least, it is basically going to focus on maintaining economic ties with China, its main creditor. The United States will avoid all political complications other than their ongoing headaches, especially in Asia. Our fundamental strategic interests are threatened primarily by China, with Pakistan as a distraction we can well do without. The Bangladesh opposition and fringe fundamentalist groups want to follow, following an unofficial Nazi-like state policy of Lebensraum or expanding living space in India to solve its population problem at our expense. At least 150 legislature seats in Assam and west Bengal are controlled by illegal immigrants. Myanmar, Nepal, and Sri Lanka are all ceding strategic space to China that we took for granted a few years ago.

Our existing intelligence institutions are tied up in knots by the stranglehold of bureaucracy. Worse, they have been penetrated and compromised. We don't have the luxury of time to redo all this, even if the political will in the national interest could be aroused. The left parties, even in their enfeebled state, would fight this along with half a dozen regional stakeholders!"

The leader of the opposition put up his hand and said, "All very plausible and undeniable … but what has changed? This has been the case for years. Every hack in half a dozen government-funded think tanks has pointed out the same things. Perhaps this is just an attempt to get people like Khan off the hook so that we don't make much noise in parliament to bring illegally expatriated money back from the Swiss and your party continues to receive funding for the next elections! This is just one big charade to become prime minister again with my connivance!"

The prime minister half smiled and said "That at least is not possible! At most, I can continue for a year till my party can agree upon a replacement for me. I have been diagnosed with Crohn's disease, which has affected my large intestine. There is no pharmaceutical or surgical cure, and treatment options are restricted to controlling symptoms. I am trying to use the interim period when I am reasonably fit to try to resolve or at least start the process of resolution to some of our more intractable problems. There is every chance that after the next parliamentary elections, you will inherit many of these legacy issues. The choice is yours—to let someone else do the spade work and perhaps reap the benefits or start at a time when the stakes have gone through the roof."

"I am sorry to hear about your illness—it is tragic for the country in these difficult times. I hope and will pray that you remain in remission and have a long, useful life ahead of you. I would perhaps have agreed in any case to your suggestion, after a few weeks to mull over it, to satisfy myself that it was for a greater cause."

The leader of the opposition continued "All I will insist upon now is that if you have little choice but to try this route, you need to rope in the best available talent to tackle intractable national security issues. We need people irrespective of their politics with a long track record of putting India before self to execute this. Give them a limited mandate like evolving a coherent strategic riposte to China and recommend expenses outside the budgetary process that can create credible responses. An implicit authorization for deterrent covert operations that do not fall under the ambit or capability of your other agencies will probably have to be included. If you wish, this compact can be reduced to writing and put away safely somewhere. Later history can judge whether in breaking our national laws we acted in the nation's interests or acted just as any other greedy, self-seeking, petty politicians as believed by most of our countrymen."

Both men rose, conscious of having committed to an undertaking fraught with uncertainty, high risk, and danger but also one that someone should have taken a long time ago.

"I promise you one thing," the prime minister said, walking the leader of the opposition to his car in the driveway. "Whichever way this plays out, this meeting of ours will open a new chapter in the way that India will take strategic decisions in the future. I will personally keep you fully informed of how the execution of this agreement progresses. If ever you have strong reservations against something being done that is repugnant to your way of thinking and there is a better way, we will alter course. This will ensure that a change in the government will not affect continuity of policy."

As the leader of the opposition entered his car, he said, "Get Mathew on your team. He's a lone wolf but an out-and-out nationalist! You need his vision. The use and denial of energy may be the key in creating strategic space. It may also be best to keep this effort under wraps for the time being!"

CHAPTER 11
CHINA—MIND GAMES

Asha "Ash" Conway was surprised to see that the old, unpolished brass plate at the office entrance had been replaced. It now read, "Carlos Rodriguez Ash International (CRAI), Computer Simulation Specialists." As she stepped into the office, she saw Carlos, her boss and former professor at the Harvard-Kennedy School, and his secretary, Venus Cray, grinning from ear to ear, awaiting her arrival. Carlos quickly escorted her by the arm to a tiny office that had a brand new sign that said, "Asha Kumari, Partner." Venus had procured a small chocolate cake with icing that read, "Welcome Home Ash," along with a cake knife with a ribbon wrapped around the handle and placed it on the computer worktable.

Totally at sea, Ash said, "I don't understand. What's this all about?"

"You brought us an investment of $750,000 for developing the national security game model further! Admiral McNeil was so pleased with your work at Menwith Hall that he arranged the funding. It has come with the proviso that the national security adviser's office would get priority for future projects. In other words, we have some guaranteed work."

Carlos was making it sound simple. He had been assisting the NSA as a consultant for over three decades. It was true that the NSA had been desperately scouting around for someone with a high level of expertise in both Farsi and Chinese. It would make it easier to keep track of the growing collusion between Iran and China. However, the assignment at Menwith Hill had come her way to broaden her exposure only at Carlos's intercession with the NSA. The two-year contract also provided the NSA time to look around for a replacement for Ash.

Later that day, she received an e-mail from her Indian cousin, Nivriti Butalia. The two women were in regular touch and had spent a few days in London together a few months earlier.

> Dear Ash,
>
> I am in Geneva with an Indian delegation covering a UN session on disarmament. The Indian Foreign Secretary was having a chat with me off the record. He mentioned that it would have been great if India had some think tank with a robust, reliable national security simulation computer model. I told him of your impressive work and experience (adequately spiced up by how good you look). This related to game-theory models and their efficacy with respect to national security and trade issues if adequate inputs could be provided.
>
> You are invited on the 15th of March on his behalf and jointly by the Ministry of External Affairs and Commerce Ministry co-sponsors of the seminar to give an hour-long presentation. This will be at a seminar in Delhi next month attended by senior government bureaucrats. The subject is "India's neighborhood security threats in the next quarter century." The formal invite will follow in a couple of days if you are agreeable.
>
> Love,
> Nivriti
>
> PS: Don't forget that I can read your mind. No, Carlos is not the right guy! You have equal gravitas if you don't smile like a jackass all the time.

A week later, Carlos strolled into her office and asked, "How are the preparations for Delhi going, Ash?"

"I'll run through my final presentation with you in a few days, but I've got most of it together already," Ash replied.

Carlos said, "I played golf with the admiral over the weekend. He wanted to borrow your services again to look at, interpret, and analyze some intercepts."

"Why? He's got enough of his own people now." Ash asked.

"They are still wet behind their ears, the admiral claimed. When I mentioned your trip to India, however, he requested that you keep on the lookout for any interesting tidbits on Iran, since you already have a great insight on what is happening there from your previous job. Lots of influential Iranians are present in India for one reason or another. We will need to talk to the Iranians outside official channels sooner rather than later, and you never know what information can come in handy."

Although her presentation in India had been the final one at six in the evening, no one attending the seminar had wandered away. Thin attendance seemed otherwise the norm in government-sponsored events. These were normally regarded as a waste of time and resources. Everyone wanted to attend to more pressing matters like picking up the kids on the way back home or having a haircut. That thin attendance had characterized the previous day of the seminar, when the national security adviser was making a pitch to the half-empty auditorium, which was now an indicator of the novelty value attached to Asha Kumari Conway. It was also indisputable that her trim figure in a crisp, white cotton sari with a gold border rather than a western dress that she otherwise favored was definitely easier on the eyes than the weather-beaten myopic look of the NSA.

This may also have had something to do with the fact that she had made a definitive observation about a Chinese Naval base likely being permitted soon by Iran near Bandar Abbas in the opening discussion of the seminar. This had already come true as reported by *CNN* that morning, creating a favorable ripple of opinion to hear her out on other issues.

She ended her presentation by saying, "To give you an example of how the status of decision-makers matter in arriving at out-of-the-box solutions, we need to look no further than Libya. Gadhafi lobbied for Abdel Basset Ali al-Meghrahi's release. He was the Lockerbie bomber, who had been held guilty of the Pan Am aircraft bombing in 1988 by a neutral court. This he did even while taking steps to end Libya's status as an international pariah.

"To ensure his own survival unlike Saddam Hussein, arguably even more powerful than him, Gadhafi first renounced terrorism and his nuclear ambitions in 2003 and signed off on a written Libyan mea culpa to the United Nations. By 2008, he completed a compensation agreement for the families of the dead in the United States. Still, he continued making statements in public that Libya and al-Maghrahi were innocent. The resultant ambiguity and confusion in the public mind expanded his power instead of diminishing it till the Jasmine Revolution recently ended it. You are all aware, on the other hand, of what a host of bad decisions did to Saddam Hussein!"

She was now answering the last question raised by an assistant secretary in the Commerce Ministry, Anand Sharma, on understanding the Chinese mindset.

"Is there really a difference between the decision-making process of China and India, or is it more hype than reality?" he asked.

"The democratic processes along with Naipaul's much heralded million mutinies have forced your hand and permanently altered the status quo. It has ensured that all of you as representative of the governing class have given or been forced to give up a measure of control over the destiny of the poorest of India's people. The ones most affected by your decisions can now have some sort of a voice in the decisions affecting them more often than not. This is not so in China. Chinese institutions have evolved in a manner to deny any such control and use force, both physical and psychological, to do so."

"From the Chinese media, it appears that their minorities now have a significant voice in improving their living conditions," Anand Sharma more of a statement than a question.

Ash responded, "The minorities have little say. Hans take all the decisions affecting the lives and culture and politics of their minorities, whether Tibetan, Uyghur, Mongolian, or Korean, and keep them on a tight leash. And logically, from their viewpoint, why should it be any different? The policy of cultural assimilation forced on to the minorities has the unstinted backing of the Han Chinese population. Although Tibet and Xinjiang occupy a third of the landmass of the country, their combined population of ethnic people is far less than 2 percent. They don't matter one bit to the majority Han.

"The Han find the minorities genuinely ungrateful. In the Han opinion, all the heaven-like development that has been brought to Tibet and Xinjiang at such great cost is wasted. Bloody-minded repression is favored by the majority! So it is a no-brainer to continue with it as state policy … then apply the same yardstick and logic of ungrateful minorities to dealing with India. India consists of dozens of troublesome ethnic groups … so why not eliminate the power of one country that can be a serious competitor to China in future and create a dozen Indias by encouraging break-away tendencies amongst the better organized groups … closer to borders that can be easily financed and influenced? In a decade or two, the problem of an unreasonable neighbor disappears!"

There was polite but genuine applause when she finished. She still had to deal with the minister of state for external affairs the next afternoon.

CHAPTER 12
TOSS OF A COIN

The amiable and very dapper Hari Narayan, minister for external affairs, had asked to meet Ash the next day at his office in North Block. Last she heard, he belonged to a political family with a fortune from illegal coal mining to humor his regional party. This was an essential sop, because his party was an important part of the ruling coalition's struggle to maintain a parliamentary majority. The external affairs minister who gave little leeway to his junior minister was in hospital for a few days. This was the result of overexerting himself on behalf of candidates from the ruling party during the recently concluded state-level elections.

"Am I to understand that your computer model will predict the outcome of any situation where countries are trying to persuade or coerce each other? And your model will do that with a hundred percent accuracy?" Hari Narayan queried, reveling in his newfound but temporary importance.

Ash answered patiently, "Not states trying to persuade or coerce each other. It is the handful of human beings and their teams of people that control states. We call the groups that run a country 'selectorates.' I'm sorry if I am treading on any of your deep-seated beliefs, but we work on the premise that there is no such thing as national interest. There are only leaders trying to stay in power by building coalitions within a 'selectorate.' I'm sure your own experience would bear this out as well. I am not claiming infallibility for the computer model we use, but certainly more than 90 percent of the time, we do get it right."

"And to do this modeling, you want access to the meteorology department super computer?" the minister asked.

"Not necessary. I can jury-rig a cloud computing effort, but you may well have security issues tied up with my doing so. Any secure super computer will do. I will probably only require access for sixty minutes a day. The backup stuff can be handled through high-end PCs and laptop modeling. Small interactions with players can get complicated. To give you an example, with five players, there are 120 possible connections, but with just twice that number and ten players, it becomes 3.6 million possible interactions. For most complex problems, there may well be seventy to eighty personalities involved, so the computing effort is considerable."

"And what are the types of inputs that we will need to give you for the model to play out?"

Ash replied "Well, for the democracies of the Western world, we can probably do a lot of the stuff ourselves, as lots of information is freely available and interviews with opinion-shapers are easy to get. For some countries where expertise and open-source data is hard to come by like for China, at least in certain crucial areas, you will need to give inputs. Some of these will already exist and be filed away somewhere as institutional memory. Some will exist in the minds of people without being reduced to writing. While we do have sources and offices in China and Hong Kong, the primary inputs I need are in respect of some of the following issues: Who are the players involved in the problem or crisis? What do they say they want? How focused are they on achieving their goal? Last but not least, how much power do they command?"

"Could you be more specific about the power-commanding aspect?" Hari Narayan asked.

"Sure; look at the network relation and analyze it, although it may be a subjective call. The extent to which certain designations reflect power, such as 'foreign secretary' or 'defense minister' or 'secretary of state' in the United States is well understood, but back-office influences often predominate and are not so easily pinpointed. Sonia Gandhi in India was widely understood to influence all matters of state policy in India ... and Bill Clinton in the United States could change the nuances of dealing with North Korea and a number of countries by an off-the-cuff observation to a TV channel.

Ash continued "Bit regional players in India with swing votes have made a mockery of economic reform, and so, they obviously have power. We need to pay attention to not only the obvious head honchos but also the smaller ones, the faceless wheelers and dealers that influence them. Take, for instance, the cases of personal assistants of long standing many with no obvious qualifications. They arrange or deny access to their bosses, thus exercising power."

"This is how democracies work, Ms. Conway!" Hari Narayan said shrugging his shoulders.

Ash said "Apparently this happens even more frequently in India. One chief minister takes no major decisions without consulting boyhood chums. These friends wield clout in different ways. Add to that spouses often exert disproportionate influences to slot their kids, friends, friends of friends, and so on! Once the linkages are laid out, it becomes relatively easy to predict outcomes."

Out of the corner of her eye, Ash could see Hari Narayan gritting his teeth. Without realizing it, she had insulted him by her comments on his type of political affiliations. He was just not interested in her pitch and more so, she suspected, because of deep-rooted prejudices about women stereotypes.

Hari Narayan dismissed her abruptly. "Thank you for coming to see me. I will consider all that you have put across. Someone from my office will get in touch with you to see how we can take this forward if required."

Ash retorted, "It has been a pleasure talking to you and getting a renewed insight into how little has changed in India as far as political mindsets are concerned!"

If she hurried, she would be able to catch the train to Pathankot and take a cab to Dharamsala up in the mountains. Already, she had put aside her disappointment at her apparent lack of success and opened up another highly personalized space in her mind, which was looking forward to seeing her parents. Both had made a ritual of making annual visits to India for at least a few weeks.

Two days of relaxation and family bonding followed. Later on the third day as she checked her e-mail, as was her wont early in the morning, there was a short and enigmatic note from her cousin:

> Ash,
>
> Well done! I am proud of your efforts. I'm told you floored them with your presentation! Never mind about the Ministry of External Affairs not following up and giving you some exploratory work. All related to internal turf battles!
>
> I want you meet Dr. Santanam (mobile number +919818299195) on your way back. He heads the prime minister's business advisory council and has booked you at the Taj Hotel for the 14th and 15th of this month with my prior approval. I'm out for two days for an interview in the boondocks, but see you Friday before you go.
>
> Lots of love,
> Guardian Angel,
> Nivriti

CHAPTER 13
THE CATALYST

AFTER AN UNEVENTFUL FLIGHT, SHE HAD barely checked into her suite in the Taj Hotel when the telephone rang.

"Good morning, Ash. I'm Raja Santanam. I trust you are comfortable in your room."

"Thank you, Dr. Santanam. It's a delightful suite. I'm looking forward to our meeting."

"Good. Please call me Raja. Everyone does, including my son! Whenever you are ready, we can have a chat. There is an executive lounge on the ground floor where you will find me. We can have breakfast there as well."

As she walked toward the reception desk to check out the location of the lounge, a cheerful young executive greeted her and introduced himself as Dr. Santhanam's personal assistant, Anthony D'Souza. He escorted her into the large, well-lit lounge, where Raja Santanam was waiting. Of medium height, dressed in a superbly tailored business suit, sparkling eyes full of laughter and fun, Dr. Raja Santhanam exuded energy even in a state of repose.

An extraordinary and talented scientist and self-made business tycoon, he had set up an off-patent generics pharmaceutical empire in under two decades and had supplied medicines to combat AIDS in particular at ridiculously cheap prices to a hundred countries. This had earned the wrath of all the global majors, Pfizer in particular, who was one of the first to accuse him of unethical market practices. The fact that this was upheld by US courts in cases that had nothing to do with Santanam years later only enhanced his reputation. Barely a few years over forty, he had put all his business holdings into a charitable trust and had taken an unpaid assignment as head of the prime minister's Business Advisory Group. Widely admired for his chutzpah in taking the fight to global corporate majors for Indian market share, he also had his detractors, who credited his success mainly to luck and benign market conditions.

"Your presentation on your last visit was very impressive. I've seen it, including an update on the Q&A session. The call on Iran agreeing to give naval facilities to China near the Straits of Hormuz should have been an eye-opener to our external affairs minister, who unfortunately insists that we have known about it for the last year! He, however, had no answer when a reporter asked him if he had been able to do something to counter the Chinese.

"Nivriti, your cousin, has interviewed me on and off the record in the past on the political economy of India. She gave me a paper that you had written about the main opposition political party here—the BJP and the internal struggle for power. This, you claimed, was under the guise of establishing accountability for the mauling the party received during the last parliamentary election. You had predicted in the paper that Jaswant Singh, who was a key minister in the last government the BJP ran, would be expelled. For someone living in the United States, even an Indian, to make that call is extraordinary!"

Ash was pleased by the comment but still puzzled by the purpose of this meeting. "Thank you, Raja, but if you had been working with the CRAI model for some time, this call would have been a no-brainer. It was just a question of putting together the known affinities and track record of about twenty people connected to the BJP and maybe another half a dozen outsiders."

Raja opened the slim folder lying on the table and took out an unsealed envelope. "Here is a check for $300,000 drawn on UBS New York as a retainer for this year. I would like your company to work for me on some projects. However, I also need a confidentiality agreement signed so that none of the results of this work can be publicized for ten years—and then with my permission."

"I can sign that right now," Ash replied, taking a letter out of her bag and extending it to Raja. "I am a partner in the company, and I am carrying a board resolution to be able to do so."

"Good. We can start straight away then."

"Raja, I'm a little puzzled. It's a great honor for me to get to meet you, but it leaves me curious. Why select us and to what purpose?

"Ash, let me give it to you straight. You probably know that I head the prime minister's Business Advisory Group. It's not public yet, but I have also set up the Santhanam Trade Foundation, which has offices in Mumbai and Delhi and seeks to suggest ways and means to make India more trade competitive.

"This includes seeking new markets in Asia, South America, and Africa, besides further developing our traditional ones in North America and the EU. Our current government institutions and industry-sponsored inputs have too many hidden agendas and make for poor continuity in policy. I need your help to set this right … or at the very least more right than it is. I want you to assess country risks for India in particular!"

"Raja, in spite of the fact that I have just accepted a retainer without any questions asked, surely there are lots of people who can do this far better than us? Our expertise is adapted more toward the foreign policy sphere." Ash explained.

Raja smiled. "Trust me—there is a great deal of overlap. If I'm wrong, it won't take too long for it to become obvious. Even then, I figure the investment in trying to leverage your model will have been worth it."

"Okay, Raja, where would you like to start? Do you have a proposition for us to examine, or would you like to e-mail it to us later?"

"Bear with me in one thing. I'm paranoid about security. I have witnessed too much being lost out of carelessness! No e-mails are to be exchanged with me as a general rule except with 128-bit encryption in case of emergencies."

"It will be impossible to function without ongoing contact at least initially."

"I would prefer that you work out of India as far as possible after the first two months or so to get yourself organized, but you can discuss this with Carlos. In the interim period, I have planned to make trips to the United States every fortnight for two days for some meetings. We can catch up while I'm there."

"I'm not sure that we can set this up in India so quickly."

"I have already set aside enough secure space in the Santhanam Foundation office here in Delhi for you to work. Adequate access to a stand-alone supercomputer of Indian design will be available whenever you want."

Obviously, Santhanam seems to have thought this through in his mind, Ash reasoned to herself. Arranging open access to a supercomputer was not something arranged on the fly. Also, expensive office space in the heart of Delhi was not something you arranged without a purpose. And his willingness to visit New York for ostensible meetings every fortnight for a couple of months must have taken days of scheduling.

"And what is the first proposition that you want us to vet for the Santhanam Foundation, Raja?"

"Simply this … there is negligible expertise in India about China. We need to plug this gap until institutional capability can be built up within the country to do this. This may take a decade. Maybe much more. In the meantime, we need an estimate of China's strategic intentions. What does China want from India? A time frame in which China will seriously try to change the status quo and what triggers will it look for to affect changes? What proactive steps can the Indians take to dissuade any serious military escalation in tensions?"

Anthony D'Souza materialized again without any perceptible signal from Raja and stood quietly by their side.

"Since you are here just another day, Tony will take you around and show you the space that you can utilize in the Santhanam Foundation offices. Let him know anything that you need to become functional—people, communications, interiors redone, or anything else."

As Tony left with Ash, Raja poured himself a cup of tea from the flask at his side and pondered his next move. So far so good!

Of course, it was a bit of a gamble, but with the extremely limited choices that were available, it could be the thin edge of the wedge to a better understanding of what faced India.

As Tony and Ash were leaving the impressive Santhanam Foundation office, a slim, athletic-looking man called out to Tony from a corner of the reception where he was sitting and leafing through a newspaper. "Hello, Tony! I thought I would take a chance and see if Raja was available? I'm back in India after more than two years."

"Good to see you, Mr. Mehrotra. He is currently at the Taj in a business meeting. You can meet him there if you wish?"

"What a coincidence! I'm staying at the Taj myself."

"Ms. Conway is also staying at the Taj. Perhaps you can travel back together?" Tony said and introduced Ash to Sohrab. "Ms. Conway, this is Mr. Sohrab Mehrotra. He runs an oil and gas exploration business in Iran. Ms. Asha Conway is a political scientist from New York."

"There was a girl who went to the same village school as me in Khuzestan in Iran a quarter of a century ago whose nose turned up at the tip just like yours," Sohrab said in Farsi, pure mischief in his eyes when they were both seated in his BMW.

"And I recall a snot-nosed brat by the same name as yours tripping over his own shoelaces!" Ash retorted fiercely but equally fluently in the same language. They gazed at each other for a moment, and simultaneously, both burst into laughter.

"I wasn't aware that you knew each other," Raja said as he met them at the reception.

"Believe it or not, we went to the same school in Iran for a bit as children," Ash clarified. "And thanks to Tony, we met again a little while ago."

Raja escorted them to the Emperor's Lounge, where they ordered tea. Sohrab brought Raja up to speed with the business prospects in the energy sector in Iran. "Raja, Iran is desperately in need of refining capability and investment in oil and gas exploration. The Western sanctions really bite but have also eliminated competition from the likes of British Petroleum, Exxon Mobil, and Chevron. Bring a delegation of Indian businessmen to Iran. I'll take care of the logistics and the invitations from the National Iranian Oil Company (NIOC), Arandan, Pars Oil and Gas, and more if needed. The Chinese are having a free run at present!"

"Sounds like a great idea. I'll see what I can do, Sohrab, to get the PM behind this," Raja said before he left.

As they ordered some more tea, they all seemed reluctant to break the magic that seemed to pervade the air around them. Ash then said, "It's strange, but I feel as if I've known you forever, Sohrab. And we've barely met."

"I feel exactly the same. This is our *kismet,* our destiny perhaps to meet again after so many years," Sohrab said seriously. "Recognizing each other almost spontaneously after such a large time gap is surely an indication of fate. By the way, since we are both here for a few days, let me show you the Mughal Emperor Humayun's Tomb and the lovely thirty-acre garden surrounding it early tomorrow?"

"Sure, I look forward to it, although many years ago, I visited it. Jeans and sneakers, I guess, if we need to walk?" Ash accepted the offer.

"You won't recognize it. The Aga Khan Trust along with UNESCO has done such a fabulous restoration. Did you know it also served as a model for the Taj Mahal?"

Ash and Sohrab were amongst the first visitors at 6:00 a.m., when the Mughal Emperor Humayun's Heritage Complex opened. Barefooted, they leisurely walked around the ancient mausoleums, and after some time, as if it was the most natural thing to do, hand in hand, they made their way through the highly geometrical and enclosed Paradise Garden. It was divided into four squares by paved walkways and two bisecting central water channels, reflecting the four rivers that flowed in *Jannat,* the Islamic concept of paradise.

"Let's walk through the garden," Ash suggested taking Sohrab by his arm.

"Look there," Sohrab said and pointed. "The central water channels seem to be disappearing beneath Humayun's tomb and reappear on the other side in one straight line. The design concept is from the Quran, which talks of rivers flowing beneath the 'Garden of Paradise.'

"I'm fascinated with the thought that Hamid Begum, Humayun's wife, conceived this tribute to her husband. This, especially after she saw so many women being taken into Humayun's harem after he married her?"

"You will have no complaint from me," Sohrab said, turning toward

Ash and kissing her gently and then with increased passion as the first rays of the sun broke through to light up the tomb in front of them.

Later that afternoon, both slowly and leisurely undressed each other in Ash's suite and made unhurried love on the huge king-sized bed and drifted off into sleep entwined together. After some time, Ash felt him become hard again and turned him flat on his back, easing herself onto his maleness while sitting astride him. As she rocked back and forth, her pendulous breasts rubbing against the hair of his chest, she felt the first of a wave of orgasms engulf her.

"This may not keep me going until I'm back from New York!" she said, happily nuzzling into Sohrab's armpit. The phone rang softly, and Ash lazily stretched across Sohrab's naked body to pick it up.

"So you couldn't keep out of mischief since I left you to your own devices?" Nivriti asked Ash, barely restraining a chuckle.

"Who told you, cousin?" Ash asked, squirming with delight at Sohrab, who had his mouth enclosed firmly on her nearest nipple.

"We journalists all have our trade secrets. In your case, it was a friend of my brother, Sahil, who provides security to the Taj Hotel. I had asked him to keep an eye on you just in case you got into trouble while I was away!"

Back in New York two days later, Ash briefed Carlos about her experiences in India, and they discussed the new project with the Santhanam Foundation.

Carlos said, "Ash, this whole thing sounds a bit out of kilter. Santhanam sounds logical, but I can't imagine anyone going so overboard on security for commercial reasons?"

"You are dead right. Since Raja advises the prime minister, it's possible there is a government angle to it. There is no reason for it to worry us as long as we're getting paid."

Later, Carlos asked her, "Anything I can convey to the admiral in Iran?"

"Not yet, but we need to set up a secure process to communicate with each other while in India. Believe it or not, I have a new boyfriend working in Iran who is apparently commercially connected with the IRGC in Iran. We were in school together as kids.

"Sounds interesting; don't lose him!" Carlos said.

CHAPTER 14
THE RAZOR'S EDGE

He had been more than surprised when the prime minister had sent for him a month ago.

"India needs to do what the United States has been always doing to get the government moving and improve things in the country" had been the prime minister's preamble.

As he, too, played the game, Raja expectedly replied to the icebreaking gambit, "The US government seems to be moving in reverse gear as far as their economy is concerned. The mess is just getting larger."

"Perhaps so, but by and large, without creating ripples, each president gets in fresh talent from public life in accordance with his own agenda. The anointed people finish the job, and after that, they go back to teaching or running businesses or whatever else they please. Unfortunately, we try to make do with whatever existing talent there is in the system."

"What do you have in mind, sir?" Raja queried, almost floored by the subsequent answer.

"India stands today on a razor's edge, and we are blissfully unaware of it. The Chinese are gnawing away at our vitals. Indian security is being severely jeopardized, and coordination between our foreign and security policies, to put it mildly, is suboptimal. Coalition politics compounds the problem. Our regional parties in the coalition have no time for national security issues unless their vote banks are immediately affected. I'm stuck with a dilemma that leaves me between the devil and the deep blue sea. Morally, the choice is clear, but *realpolitik* demands something else. We desperately need to play catch-up for decades of benign neglect in the process of streamlining national security voids.

"We need a stopgap measure or a buffer to gain time while we undertake institutional reform of the government to create and seize opportunities in consonance with India's interests. I want you to be part of a very small group of maybe seven to not more than ten people who can act as a catalyst or a firefighting team to safeguard India's security and geopolitical interests and buy time.

"I need a team that can plug national security strategy voids. It must encompass top of the line political, economic, and military expertise to create synergy with what is already being done and deliver quick results. Suggest names of suitable candidates. I have some in mind and have individually spoken to them but will not share these with you at this stage. This is to try and avoid a groupthink situation in picking candidates.

"We need a small, entrepreneurial, quick-acting team, because bureaucracies cannot move as quickly as non-state actors like the ISI, Al Qaeda, and the Taliban. Moreover, we have a national security adviser hamstrung by lack of a staff to give an ongoing strategic perspective. The political coalition is still shy of using the armed forces headquarters as the underpinning for strategic inputs. They refuse to see that the house is on fire!

"Figure out where the greatest dangers from our enemies, primarily China, Pakistan, and sundry terrorist groups, lie in the immediate future. Also, look at how we can manage these dangers more effectively and faster. Manage either with out-of-the-box solutions or known solutions that can be sped up by various means.

"We need independent, reliable estimates of what our enemies are specifically going to be doing going forward both in the short and medium term. Thereafter, find ways and means of disrupting these threats or preempting them in addition to using our conventional capabilities. All I get about threat assessments are vague generalizations at present from within the establishment couched with words like 'plausible,' 'likely,' 'in the long term,' etc. Everyone is clearly bent on covering their asses!

"Already, Pakistan's piling up of nukes with diverted US-supplied funds, and Chinese incursions into Ladakh and Arunachal are mounting. We've kept a lid on it for some time; however, the media has now got hold of the issue, and the pressure is mounting on me to do something—or at least show that we are doing something!

"I want you to also consider, being a part of something patently illegal as well, to get this show on the road. It is against the laws of the land, as I will come to in a minute, but it needs to be done immediately! It is also something I believe that India desperately needs to do for some years ahead.

"Nothing of what you say is illegal or against the laws of the land as far as I can see," Raja said. "I'm truly honored that you consider me worthy to be a member of a group like this—and on top of that to suggest names for others to join the group. With all humility, I accept this onerous trust that you are placing in me."

The prime minister grimly said, "You have not asked how this group is going to be financed? To do things in a hurry, you will need vast amounts of money. That is the illegal bit that needs to be organized very quickly by you while the opportunity exists.

"I am proposing that we squeeze say three to four billion dollars for starters from two dozen of our more solvent but far from worthy citizens. These people have stashed more than an estimated trillion dollars in tax havens abroad especially Switzerland; along with thousands of other somewhat smaller fry who have done the same. This money should get you started as a sort of venture capitalist for India's strategic interests on a strong footing."

"And where do I find these gentlemen, sir? And what do I do to persuade these worthies that they need to be good boys and dole out their loose change for the future of India?"

The prime minister clarified "We have a list of them to start with after many years of backbreaking investigation. We also have some gentlemen from our income tax department who have played ball with them under the scanner. I'm sure they will cooperate to bring their informal clients in line when the only other option is disgrace and perhaps fifteen years in jail. We do have the ability to legislate a minimum sentence still. As a sop to their egos, you can promise suitable national awards on Republic Day and a meeting with the president!"

"And how do you propose we handle the money that we may get?"

"Raja, you handle the money like you would handle a family trust. Put it in off-shore locations where you need to pay minimum taxes. Much of it is already in such places. Invest it so you get a decent return that can be spent on projects that all of you agree upon which are vital to India's security. Include projects that are not being done by anyone else like the RAW and DIA or are not being funded properly. Invest in technology wherever necessary. In short, use your best judgment. Set up a foundation that can ostensibly examine national security issues. That should provide an appropriate cover for this crisis management team."

"Sir, there is a real danger that with all the good intentions in the world, the money will inevitably be used badly sooner or later! It may become like budgetary allocations to your ministries that are spent with such callousness without regard to outcomes. We will have too much power without clear-cut responsibilities."

"We'll cross that bridge when and if we come to it. Selecting the right people to whom India comes first and every time is part of my insurance. Your responsibility can't be more clear-cut than this—protect your country in ways that are not being currently achieved.

"I want all of you to set a benchmark for what you hope to deliver. You may like to set the bar with what was achieved by Pakistan's Dr. A. Q. Khan to start with. Single-handedly, he managed Pakistan's nuclear proliferation network, involving the United States, China, Germany, Iran, and perhaps half a dozen others for at least two decades and has still kept them ticking over. Think big. If we are going to be crucified for illegalities, we may as well do it for world-class, game-changing projects."

"I can only promise you that I will do my best and drop every other project and process that I am involved in until you want me out!" Raja concluded.

CHAPTER 15
THE GAME CHANGERS

Raja's brief presentation on the commissioning of the Asha Kumari led CRAI simulation model to gauge China's intention met with surprising open-mindedness with a general wait-and-watch attitude. This may have been due to the implicit backing of the prime minister to the initiative. The first results were not likely to be available for another few months because of the massive groundwork required to carry out a large number of one-on-one interactions to facilitate the modeling required.

It was only the second meeting of the select group on national security crises at the Santhanam Foundation. They were clearly worried. There was no precedent for what they were doing—at least not in any democratic, open society. The enormity of what the prime minister sought from them weighed on them, not to mention his carte blanche charter to decide and execute. They had decided in the first meeting that terrorism, internal security, China, and Pakistan, not necessarily in that order, should be their starting points, along with removing common technology irritants. They needed to focus on nimble, game-changing agendas that could deliver in the short and medium terms.

Lieutenant General Randhir Singh was the first to offer a suggestion. "Our government seems to be leaking information like a sieve, most of which seems to be through infected communication equipment and computers. We need to find some quick answers to find out who is doing the damage while the long-term fixes are being put in place. Otherwise, whatever we try to do will be compromised sooner rather than later."

Randhir had spent most of his service career combating insurgencies in Assam, Nagaland, Manipur, Jammu, and Kashmir in ranks ranging from captain to lieutenant general till he sought premature retirement when he was slotted as an army commander so that he could look after his wife of thirty years, who had terminal cancer. His request for premature retirement had closed with an observation that invoked the oath that he had taken on commissioning as an officer almost four decades ago.

"In the final analysis, I cannot take the chance that in case of an emergency, my mind is even 1 percent distracted by the condition of my wife to the detriment of my nation!"

She had been barely dead a week when the call had come from the prime minister's office commiserating the death of his wife and wondering whether or not he could spare a little time to meet the prime minister when he was free. That was how it had all begun. There had been no time to grieve.

He continued then, "What we need to investigate terrorist or spy networks is a user-friendly search tool that can investigate terrorist networks by scanning multiple data sources at once. This is something that was just not possible with existing search tools. However, an information technologies start-up company run by a former tech-savvy army major who worked under me for some years may have an answer. He was wounded and partially disabled for life in an encounter with terrorists. After leaving the army, he founded a company 'Abyss Neural Limited,' which is looking at funding for a tool like what we need.

"The company was initially working on a project with seed money from the United Nations for the visually handicapped where audio inputs from multiple data sources were required to coordinate with visual images to train near-blind people. The owner could see the potential in an adaption for intelligence gathering and offered a six-month trial to the army. The results have been amazing in the initial tests that were done with fairly current data in the Kashmir Valley."

"Amazing in what way, general?" interjected Sridhar, the former maverick boss of the research and development wing who had turned the focus of India's external intelligence collection to Tibet and Xinjiang in China.

"During a brief spell of president's rule while I was commanding a corps in the state, we persuaded the governor of Jammu and Kashmir to knock some heads together. This was done to put one year of intelligence data regarding terror attacks in the state onto a common grid. The army, SIB, IB, CRPF, RAW, border security forces, and the state police CID were roped in, and all very reluctantly permitted access to their records. This permitted the use of a tagging technique similar to that used by the search functions of most websites.

"Every bit of data made available from each agency was tagged separately, such as first names, last names, phone numbers used, next of kin, locations of spotted and known associates. The army was able soon after to create new links and track patterns in attacks on their logistic convoys, and the state police was soon thereafter able to foil an attack on the chief minister's house. The icing on the cake came following a routine enquiry from the Delhi Police. This followed from their interrogating a bombing suspect. The suspect's name also showed up from other tags that enabled the Jammu and Kashmir police to arrest two IED-making accomplices in Anantnag.

"All this could be done within just a few weeks. Unfortunately, before we could make more headway governor's rule was terminated, and the new political dispensation had no interest in taking this further. One of their own elected ministers was hand in glove with the insurgents, although it was difficult to prove it."

Sridhar commented, "General, why don't you get hold of the company again and guarantee long-term backing for the product? A tool like that will be like a disruptive technology and potentially enable our small pool of analysts specializing in this field to deliver better. They can quickly track connections among a group of suspects, money transfers, phone calls, and modus operandi of attacks all over the world for the last three decades if required. The beta version Data Integrator Software already creates import routines to suck data into Quickbooks from other agencies' save formats.

"Currently, analysts have to query different databases, and some of the ones needed may not be accessible to them because they do not have the requisite security clearances. This can also be because of turf battles.

Often, they have to make laborious written notes to create relationships that can be analyzed. There is a crying need to be able to draw inferences when confronted by an enormous amount of data. This may just be part of the answer!"

Santhanam offered a suggestion, "Let's give them an equivalent of ten to fifteen million dollars from our Mauritius account to start with. We already have a nonprofit venture capital firm 'Quest India' for channeling the money. Abyss already seems to have enough software engineers working. We can take out a lease of one of the software outfits that has collapsed recently and retrofit it with whatever additional equipment they require so they can be operational in a larger space by the end of the month. They can simultaneously hire additional people they are sure to need sometime down the line."

Ashok Sobti, the former cabinet secretary with a mind hardwired like a chess grand master always looking two steps ahead, was generally a man of few words. Universally admired by juniors and colleagues for his straightforward, no-nonsense approach, he was the informal head of the group. He added, "Abyss Neural needs to be kept under tight control for security reasons by acquiring a majority stake. Perhaps we can look at expanding the Santhanam Foundation to include the company? Abyss has a head start on NATGRID, with the added advantage that it can be selectively inducted at the state level and used even by field agents on the move."

Sridhar added, "We also need a process to keep an independent track of web chatter on undiscovered terrorist websites and a record of those who visit these websites, which often have doctored videos of persecution, atrocities, and terrorist rants to attract potential recruits. This time, we cannot afford to be caught napping. With the Americans largely gone in the foreseeable future from Afghanistan, it's only a matter of time before Al Qaeda and gangs that include the Lashkar e Taiba turn attention toward India once again.

"We need to use other directly intelligence-related assets to pick up the signals as well—maybe tourists- and trade- and commerce-related options. We also need to create similar sites ourselves for targeting Chinese and Pakistani minorities for future operations. It could also give us an inside track to sharing information with Western intelligence agencies. We will only get as good as we give!"

M. J. Mathews, fluent in Russian and an academic and energy consultant, was an oddball in the group. He had an eclectic energy background starting with an electrical engineering master's degree from the prestigious Bauman Moscow State Technical University followed by a doctorate in mining geology from Michigan Technological University. He was still a respected visiting professor there as well as at the Lomonosov Moscow State University with more than two thousand international students. Many of his students were ensconced in the higher reaches of decision-making in Russia, Africa, and the Central Asian republics. At various times in his checkered career, Mathews had also worked on projects for Exxon Mobil in the United States and Gazprom in Russia, and he was on a first-name basis with half a dozen former KGB senior people who were now businessmen but retained their old connections in the intelligence community.

He was actively disliked by the Indian nuclear energy establishment for advocating the use of fast neutron reactors from Russia and mining investments in South Africa, Mongolia, and Kazakhstan as a solution to the uranium fuel problem. That he was on this team at all was thanks to the word dropped in by the leader of the opposition. Mathews had spent many hours deposing in front of a parliamentary subcommittee on energy independence that the leader of the opposition had headed.

"India will always be held to ransom until it can achieve energy independence. Conventional reactors can only use 5kg from a ton of uranium, whereas fast neutron reactors can use 700kg. Thorium fast breeders to make use of India's considerable thorium reserves are a fantasy technology for at least thirty years. In the interim, develop shale oil technologies for the billions of barrels of oil equivalent reserves in the northeast."

Years earlier, he would turn down an offer from the oil minister to become an energy adviser, saying, "I love my country, but no one will listen to what I suggest. I also do not have the political skills to work the system! Working from outside the government, the media and the opposition will occasionally make you pay more attention to what I suggest."

"We should also look for other foreign companies that we can finance or take over for solving other technology-related issues—or for that matter, hire scientists for in country projects," Mathews now said.

"Like which companies from where?" Sobti asked.

"Like Israeli defense research–oriented outfits working on next generation remotely piloted vehicles. I would like to see, for instance, three or four solar-powered RPVs that do not need to be refueled for perhaps a year or more, keeping vigil over the LAC, for instance. Raja would be the right guy to handle this. He already has a pharmaceutical company in Israel, has an abiding interest in aviation as well, and is in and out a couple of times a year anyway, I reckon."

As Raja nodded acceptance, Sobti prodded further, "And what else?"

"And tap some of the forty-five closed cities in Russia dedicated during the Cold War years to research and development. Znamensk, for instance, located southeast of Moscow out in the barren steppe for developing rockets or Arazamas-16, the home of nuclear engineering. They are all short of money for supporting their infrastructure and lab facilities. Fifteen to twenty million dollars a year will get us plenty of options! I particularly like the work they are doing on quantum computing."

"Can we use any of it in the near future?" asked Ashok Sobti.

"We need to hire a couple of hundred skilled software developers and a dozen Chinese language experts from around the world through the Santhanam Foundation. They can work with the Russian team doing the hardware development on quantum computing to do a lot of developmental work quickly. I think we could put together a working model of an automatic system for translating text on computers within a few months, just focusing on Chinese in the first instance by scanning millions of multilingual websites. To ensure security, we will need to adopt a suitable segregation model so no one is aware of what the others are doing."

Raja Santhanam interjected, "Side by side, they could easily build on the work done on voice recognition systems to conduct web searches by speech commands. To make up for our dearth of Chinese language specialists, we could develop a software capable of understanding a caller's voice say from intercepted phone calls or radio intercepts from PLA troops in Tibet. It could nearly simultaneously translate it into a synthetic equivalent of Hindi and English. We could also get valuable inputs on selectorates in target countries for the CRAI simulation models in a dozen languages over a period of time!"

"Let's get a move on and do it! We already have a rider by the PM on utilizing 25 percent of funding for cyber war-related development," Ashok Sobti directed.

Randhir then added, "It would be absolutely brilliant if we could also develop a nonnuclear electromagnetic pulse generator through such assets. The DRDO has done some work, but it needs to be taken to a usable model. If push comes to shove, especially with the Chinese, we need something out of the box at the tactical level, short of a nuke, to level the playing field somewhat. It will take at least five years before we can get half-decent roads up to the LAC. If major incursions by the Chinese take place, we will need to react very quickly to prevent a complete rout. Taking out all the communications, radars and communications of leading Chinese divisions will set up the stage nicely for disrupting operational time frames, if not for our counterattacks."

"Will you organize this EMP bit in Russia, Mathews? It won't be easy but I suspect the Russians will go for it, as it will help them modernize their nonnuclear EMP systems to integrate nanotechnology options and reduce maintenance and storage problems that are widely reported. We can pull some strings through the PM when he meets Medvedev next month here in Delhi."

"Give me a month, Ashok, and leave the PM out of this. I need a good reason to be in Moscow. I've been invited to participate in a seminar by Gazprom next week. That should create a good opening to speak to scientists who fear retirement and are willing to work in India."

Mathews added, "We will also need deep-sea reconnaissance assets. I am aware that the Experimental Design Bureau of Oceanic Engineering at the Russian Academy of Sciences has helped India to create a multifunctional, unmanned underwater vehicle with the required immersion depth and capacity to process manganese, nickel, cobalt, and copper nodules from the Indian Ocean floor. Adapting this for our navy in three or four years may not be difficult since we can push the funding envelope. It could be an interesting way of keeping tabs on Chinese subs in the Indian Ocean area, not to mention US Navy assets.

Joint ventures with South Korea, Taiwan, and perhaps Japan, ostensibly for seabed exploration, could be a way forward."

Vice-Admiral Shankar Menon, a former naval aviator who was the latest addition to the group, added, "I agree. Nonconventional undersea-operable assets may also be useful in the South China Sea to keep tabs on the undersea Hainan Island Chinese submarine base. I think the one really effective step to reduce force imbalance with the navy is to get another aircraft carrier inducted into the navy soon—also perhaps another nuclear submarine."

Sobti intervened, "Admiral, you know better than anyone that these assets take decades to create. We have been struggling to get the aircraft carrier Gorshkov by the Russians for years!"

"Exactly," said Shankar, "and we are still quibbling over money. Aircraft carriers are just not available at any price. The US Ford-class costs ten billion dollars and change, but it's more than twice as large. What I suggest is that we ask Mathews to speak to the Russian Defense Minister and quietly give them an extra hundred million dollars off the record that will sort out all the Russian objections to overprice negotiations. Give it provided they complete the sea trials by the end of next year! It may be a great opportunity to also put in a bid for another Nerpa Akula II-class nuclear submarine on a ten-to-fifteen-year lease to India."

Nasruddin Babbar had been the director general of police in Chhattisgarh following a long tenure in the Kashmir Valley on deputation as an inspector general in the Central Reserve Police. He was introduced to the prime minister during a visit by the latter to the state capital, Raipur. He had been mildly surprised when the prime minister had sent for him late in the evening at the state guesthouse.

"I have something extremely important for you to consider, Nasruddin. Your country needs you in a different setting for a difficult mission."

"Why pick me, Mr. Prime Minister? You have a whole lot of brilliant police officers to choose from. Besides, I have my hands full with the Maoists currently," he had responded.

"Of course, I have considered many others. I need you because of your experience of dealing with the Maoists in the Red Corridor, including our major problem area in Jharkhand, where the chief minister is giving the Maoists a very long rope by curtailing operations. Your personal awareness of the functioning of Kashmiri terror and insurgent groups is critical as well. I don't want anyone who has to climb a learning curve. I need someone who understands the big picture to hit the ground running. You also have two sons in the police in West Bengal and Jharkhand, so your commitment is unquestioned as far as I am concerned."

"And perhaps most importantly, Mr. Prime Minister, because I am a Muslim!" He had blurted, and from the pain in the prime minister's eyes, he knew he had struck a raw nerve.

He knew then he had no choice but to accede to the command disguised as a request.

His impact on the small group had been electric from the first session he had attended.

"Our counterterrorism and counterinsurgency strategy does not exist. Our top leadership refuses to learn. We need to keep it simple. Eliminate the leaders any which way! Unfortunately we have been targeting the *piyadas*, the pawns if you will, because it is simpler and no coordination is required across state boundaries. The pawns are on sale at a few thousand rupees a dozen."

"Policing is a state responsibility, and we have never been able to coordinate effectively across even two states," Sobti countered. "So how do we do this?"

"Terrorist leadership is unique to a large extent. It requires vision, foresight, the ruthlessness to survive and eliminate opposition, even if it is a brother, high energy, and the charisma to perpetuate a myth. How many have all these qualities and the luck to avoid a bullet in the head? Very few. Maybe one out of a few hundred recruits to start will have the warrior instinct to so completely dominate others. Conceptually, if we prioritize and target a dozen terror leaders both in India and elsewhere in our neighborhood and succeed, the game changes!"

Randhir agreed, "Nasru is absolutely right. We've killed and captured hundreds of dumb recruits with no ideology. They were brainwashed in a few weeks of training to believe that they would become important by killing as many Indians as possible and achieve martyrdom. However, the leaders have remained safe and keep sending more and more of these greenhorns, knowing that many will die but some will get through."

"As far as coordination across the states is concerned, the place to start the process is through the old-boy network of Indian Police Service Associations over a drink. My sons will help through their own contemporaries. I will initiate this dialogue," Nasruddin said. "However, we need to give them enough dope through national technical means to show that we mean business."

Sobti closed the discussion, "Conceptually, we need to follow the Pakistan ISI model, even if it is late in the day. Always, in every group, there is ingress of the ISI. And that is the efficiency, the effectiveness of the ISI. You must have ingress so that you can influence all insurgent groups at critical stages. Buy the access, Nasru. Pump in money, even if a lot goes to waste, as long as we can get the leaders eliminated!"

CHAPTER 16
THE ORACLE

DR. S. RANGANATHAN WAS POPULARLY KNOWN as "Speed" to his students for his ability to quickly explain complex economic theories. The name had been acquired when he was still a young economist with the World Bank for the manner in which he could strategize and get large consultancy projects in developing countries completed always under budget in weeks instead of the norm of years. After two decades of teaching at the London School of Economics and European School of Economics, he had started a hedge fund that had correctly timed the recession and shorted the Dow Jones Industrial Average, S&P 500, and the Nasdaq Composite in late 2008.

Unmarried and bored with a hundred million dollars in assets, he had returned to India after accepting a challenging invitation from the prime minister over a phone call.

"Speed, you are wasting your talent, and you have nothing further to prove to anyone. Your father and I were childhood friends, and he went to jail as part of India's freedom struggle when he had barely joined college. He worked sixteen-hour days doing two jobs simultaneously to give you an education. That hard-won freedom is now under threat again. Come back home. I need you to do things for India. Things that are strategic in nature cannot wait and desperately need doing!"

He had not asked any of the obvious questions.

"Give me two weeks, Mr. Prime Minister."

"Good, come and see me as soon as you arrive."

It had taken him less than a week to arrive in Delhi. *Money helped in some ways*, he thought to himself. An aide of the prime minister had hand-delivered the tamper-proof envelope with the CRAI simulation report enclosed.

"Dr. Ranganathan, the prime minister has requested you to have dinner with him tomorrow at 8:00 p.m. There will be just the two of you present," the aide had said. "I have also been asked to convey to you that Ms Asha Kumari Conway will be here to meet you at 5:00 p.m."

Speed broke open the tamper-proof seal and read with interest: *Extracts from CRAI preliminary computer simulation report on Chinese intentions versus India prepared for the Santhanam Foundation by Asha Kumari Conway, CRAI.*

To put the China-India issue into historical context, the 1962 Cuban Missile Crisis between the Soviet Union and the United States and the threat of nuclear war had effectively removed the focus of attention of the superpowers from meddling with the renaissance of the Chinese military. This opportunity had been quickly seized to defeat the Indian Army in detail in a two-front conflict.

The long-drawn-out worldwide economic depression has again created adequate strategic space for China with respect to India that was now viewed as the only serious contending actor with China in Asia. The mood in Beijing was adequately reflected in the tight orchestration of anti-Indian hysteria through the controlled media, opaquely funded websites, and the blogosphere.

The strategic space was invitingly wide for China, with the only national superpower embroiled in a no-win Vietnam-like situation in the Afpak region and China's own rising economic capacity. There appeared to be near unanimity in the Politburo, fed by the perception of the PLA that there was a bare three-year window to dismantle India.

The Chinese geopolitical view was that this should be done before the US economy restructured and efforts to groom India as another junior partner like Japan and Australia kicked in. This would happen in any case with sizeable infusion of superior technology, maritime- and air-based weapon systems, and covert intelligence inputs. There was also a growing fear that the Russians might have been far from averse to counterbalancing Chinese power, given the poor state of the Russian economy.

There is a 95 percent chance with an upward bias that Beijing will reinforce its attempts to prod India into providing a casus belli to instigate a conflict. Border incursions will increase exponentially, particularly in winter. Appreciating that a currently supine West is desperate not to antagonize China, the Chinese diplomatic offensive will ratchet up several notches to further undercut Indian sovereignty over Arunachal Pradesh.

Pakistan will be encouraged to believe its strong ties to China will extend to Chinese military intervention against India, along with any Pakistan offensive into Kashmir, to accommodate Pakistan interests. The caveat for this support, of course, will be the continued development of Gwadar Port on the Makran coast as the main Chinese naval logistic and replenishment facility in the Indian Ocean region. The development of the oil pipeline linking Gwadar to Urumqi in Xinjiang will also be linked. Feeding this oil pipeline will also make it imperative that commercial and political ties with Iran are constantly improved by investments in oil and gas, not to mention China playing the spoiler in Iran-Indian ties.

Similarly, the final push against India would be preceded by other parallel developments in South Asia. This would aim to leverage economic and political ties in Nepal, Myanmar, Bangladesh, and Sri Lanka, granting military bases or at least enabling facilities. Iran would then become an important part of this calculus to create energy supply imbalances.

India's present default strategy of improvising responses and bending backward to accommodate Chinese moves appears to be distinctly unviable. Statements by defense ministry officials that there is no significant increase in Chinese incursions embolden China to step up the pressure further.

Therefore, there is a question mark on the continued viability of Sino-Indian trade beyond the next two years. It is, however, possible that the strategic opening that the Chinese envisage with respect to India may be constrained by internal pressures arising out of natural calamities like earthquakes, floods, and droughts of a sufficient magnitude.

The internal security situation in China and the preservation of harmony may be affected by the stimulus injected into the economy running its course without a distinct improvement in job prospects. Twenty million educated aspirants that need to be employed every year can be a powerful and disruptive force if not accommodated. It may also be constrained by restive minorities creating large-scale disturbances in Tibet, Xinjiang, and Inner Mongolia. The probability of this happening is less than 10 percent in the next two years.

The economic impact of any conflict between two major hot spots of economic activity in the world will be considerable. This will, however, need to be a part of a separate project that will take at least six months to complete. As of now, there is near unanimity of opinion worldwide that if pushed, India's geostrategic interests will have to be sacrificed to its economic interests. India will have to make considerable territorial concessions to avoid conflict.

He had just finished reading the report when Ash arrived at his hotel. After he ordered coffee for both of them, Speed said to Ash, "I'm very impressed with the report that you have prepared and more so with the near certainty of your convictions."

"Dr. Ranganathan, the conclusions stem from the data. This is the message that has emerged from simulation exercises that include the views of hundreds of people in China-shaping policy. I have personally checked the translation efforts in a statistically significant number of cases for inaccuracies. The message is loud and clear. There is no ambiguity that I can fathom. Provoking a conflict with India is in the Chinese's national interest!"

"What can deter a conflict taking place, Ms. Conway?" Speed asked.

"The only way China can be deterred from annexing so-called disputed territory is for India to have sufficient nuclear and missile capability. The nuclear capability will have to be demonstrated, as unsavory bickering in the nuclear establishment has convinced China that India's deterrence claims are a huge fraud."

"Does China envisage any effective competition from India in any sphere?" Speed asked.

Ash replied without hesitation "Yes, in energy matters there are a lot of concerns that India is ideally placed to provide much of what Iran needs. This is primarily related to developing its untapped energy potential. India also has the market to absorb Iran's exports. It also has the refining ability to provide Iran's needs for finished petroleum products with negligible shipping costs. Moreover the Indian private sector has the ability, along with the Indian government, to bring in large amounts of capital from all over the world into Iran."

"So what do you make of it, Speed?" the prime minister asked after the simple vegetarian meal was over. He had already explained his initiative of setting up the small group of overachievers to plug strategic short comings in the country.

"Do you remember the Noah Principle, sir? The best time to build the ark is when it's not raining! The report, as far as it goes, clearly implies that China has you over a barrel. There is no way that you can improve your nuclear and missile capability in the medium term to deter China."

"So we become like sitting ducks for Beijing's dinner?"

"Perhaps in the end, it may well happen. But what you have done is important. From a strategy of reactive improvisation followed by our country for many decades, we seem to have shifted gears to proactive improvisation! It, however, needs a focus, since there is little time to experiment. Undoubtedly, the initiatives taken by your unofficial crisis management stalwarts are needed, but are they enough?"

"What are you getting at, Speed?"

"I need some time to think this through. Conceptually, our country can't increase its nuclear and missile potential to create the necessary deterrence before the Chinese act. Maybe we should be looking at something else or some other things? Something or things that China fears enough to prevent it from carving out further geopolitical space at our expense for long enough to level the playing field."

"Think it over and war game it with Sobti's group when you join them next week! I need a clear set of options presented to me. I have been getting the feeling for the last few weeks that time has run out!"

CHAPTER 17
CONTINGENCY PLANS

IT WAS A SUNDAY AND SUPPOSEDLY a day of minimal engagements at the prime minister's house. The small, enclosed, lead-lined meeting room had been electronically swept for listening devices minutes before the unofficial crisis management group was led in by the prime minister's personal security assistant. They had all been brought in two nondescript government cars with heavily tinted windows. The prime minister was already seated at the head of the plain-looking oval table and waved them to seats on either side of him.

"Ashok, what is the take of your group on the CRAI report on China?" he asked Ashok Sobti, who was sitting to his immediate right.

"It states the obvious that politics prevents our country from recognizing. There is a window of a few years that exists for China to act proactively and aggressively to undermine India in the perceived absence of adequate nuclear weapon and missile capability and, if I may also add, political will."

"How long do you think we have before something major develops?"

Sridhar, who was sitting opposite the prime minister, replied for all of them, "Mr. Prime Minister, the window will open wider the moment the next major terror strike takes place and the government is distracted by Pakistan-originated events. It could be a matter of a few days or a few weeks and almost certainly less than a year to coincide with any major pullout of Western troops from Afghanistan. In the meantime, their preparations are certainly going on. The stepped-up outlays on twenty-seven airfields in Tibet as also the intensity of training exercises of the PLA are sure-shot indications! Upgraded airfields are certainly not to cater for a few thousand Western tourists on a budget holiday."

"So what are our short- and medium-term options?" the prime minister queried.

Speed Ranganathan took up the discussion. "Purely at a conceptual-level squeeze, there are two pressure points that are China's great vulnerabilities and higher priorities than dealing with India—preserving its energy pipeline, including petro-based, coal, natural gas, and uranium, and restive minorities on the periphery, especially from Iran! How you can apply game-changing pressure to these vulnerabilities is a separate issue."

Sridhar then explained that a considerable amount of groundwork had been done over the years as far as Tibet, Xinjiang, and Baluchistan were concerned. "We know where to go to instigate large-scale incidents through local insurgent groups. Our credibility is, however, low with these groups. It is low because we have not followed through on promises of support in the past, as political direction has been absent, but all that will be forgotten if we pump in enough money into their pockets and get them to deal with people who have an ongoing, long-term relationship."

Vice-Admiral Shankar Menon added, "Irrespective of what they do for the foreseeable future, China's energy jugular lies in our backyard in the Indian Ocean squeezed in between SOH and Malacca. One hundred and sixty ships made this transit last year. To threaten it, we need to do whatever it takes to get the Admiral Gorshkov/INS Vikramaditya inducted quickly. We discussed Professor Mathews offering the Kremlin additional off-the-record payments from funds you put at our disposal. Money will settle all outstanding disputes on delivery with the Russians. It will also facilitate our request for another nuclear Akula-class submarine on lease from them."

"Go ahead, Matt. Let me know if there is a need for me to speak to the Russians," the prime minister directed firmly. "What about our energy options? We are equally vulnerable in terms of supplies, and Pakistan is sitting on our supply routes even if they are shorter. I'm seriously doubtful about our ability to do anything of note in Tibet and Xinjiang, but there is little downside to trying. Baluchistan is, of course, a more feasible area for us to operate in. This will create problems for the Chinese as well; at not only the Gwadar port but also for the pipeline project from Gwadar to Urumqi."

Professor Mathews jumped into the discussion. "We need to actively compete with Chinese energy companies that are walking away with huge exploration and development acreages in what I call the 'I3' countries—Iran, Iraq, and Indonesia. Now is the time to pump in a few billion dollars into each of these countries. Maybe we can persuade some of the larger owners of offshore hot money to invest in joint ventures with your state-owned oil companies. It will also be an elegant solution to get the money back into productive avenues! The other issue is that we must signal the United States that we can be formidable energy partners if they do not constrain our political space beyond making noises!"

"How do we do that?" asked the PM.

"Not many people outside the US government know that the largest accessible oil reserves in the world are, believe it or not, in the United States! When a well is first drilled, the oil explodes out of the ground, thanks to the earth's natural pressure. After a while, the pressure subsides, and oil doesn't flow any longer. And it becomes uneconomical to get the oil out of the ground. Just to give an example, the US government survey that plotted and tested old wells has found that in Louisiana, there are discovered accessed reserves of 458 million barrels; in Kansas, 243 million barrels; and in Montana, there are three billion barrels of discovered accessible oil just waiting for the right technology to come along to depressurize the wells and get them to flow."

"And the technology is now available, so we come in and offer tens of billions to leverage it?"

"That's exactly the way to go!" Mathews observed. "The technology that has matured in select hands is called carbon dioxide injection technology, where a hole is drilled next to an already exploited well and carbon dioxide is pumped into it to make the oil flow again. There are also cost-effective ways of tapping the Bakken geological formation that spans twenty-five thousand square miles in the northern region that holds 4.3 billion barrels equivalent by horizontal drilling."

"The Chinese will make similar offers and offer much more money!" the PM said.

"That is the reason we should get lobbyists to work the inside for keeping the Chinese out on grounds of national security. The United States did so with keeping the Chinese out of owning any of their ports, so there is already a precedent to avail of!" Ashok Sobti said, jumping into the discussion.

"Let's think this through," the PM said. "We also have an offer from the Iranians through back-door channels that could create energy space for us at the expense of the Chinese as well. The risks are, however, on the face of it, huge!"

"Is it for help with their nuclear program, since most avenues have been squeezed shut by the Americans?" asked Lieutenant General Randhir Singh. "The Iranian Revolutionary Guards had made a tentative approach while I was posted in Tehran. This was more than a dozen years ago, but there was no follow up thereafter by them."

Surprised at this revelation, the PM said, "This time, there seems to be a hint of desperation amongst the Iranians. They have already scrapped the offer of the naval facility to China as a commitment of their good intentions if we play ball. They have also indicated a willingness to offer additional energy deals on favorable terms. In exchange, Iran wants us to do computer simulations to test the efficacy of their nuke. Apparently, they are not enamored by the word of their top scientists! What do you think we should do? My NSA is not in favor of cutting a deal at all."

Ashok Sobti summed up the dilemma, "As long as there is plausible deniability, there should be no problem in doing the simulations. We also get an accurate insight into their nuclear program. In one stroke, we get greater energy security and perhaps become less unequal to the Chinese. Let's face it—Iran will get a nuke sooner or later."

Sridhar added, "The world's proliferation story is murky as hell. The United States helped Britain. The Russians helped the Chinese, who in turn helped the North Korean nuclear weapons program and also that of Pakistan. Pakistan built China a uranium-enrichment facility with stolen technology from URENCO. In turn, they received not only fifty kilos of bomb-grade material but also complete designs for nukes and missiles. We should go ahead and just structure the deal to get maximum mileage out of it. The Americans will finally total the cost and evolve a method to live with the problem by calling it by another name."

Speed Ranganathan said that there was a manageable downside if linkages between Iran's weapons program and Indian's assistance remained tenuous. "The world assumes that we will play like good boys with our track record! Further, everyone would like to be part of the India growth story and will look away from any evidence that prevents them from doing so. The Iranians are fiercely protective of their national interests, and it suits them if the West regards them as irrational. They may have just made an announcement about giving a base to the Chinese with the intention of cancelling it later once we took the bait dangled in front of us. Have they offered any other proof of their good intentions with respect to India?"

"Yes!" the prime minister answered. "They are willing to provide bases in Sistan-Baluchistan for launching attacks against ISI-sponsored groups in southwest Baluchistan. They are also willing to share intelligence as well. Okay, I have your views. What else can you suggest as a group that may help either postpone a face-off or better prepare us for it?"

Lieutenant General Randhir Singh said, "Sir, there is a huge credibility gap as far as the will of the political class is concerned. You need to have a military response ready for the next major act of terror against us. It has to be limited but effective and managed by giving appropriate signals to the world community about our intent."

"What signals would you suggest as appropriate, general?"

"Firstly, you should take the Iranian offer at face value and plan at least one strike in Baluchistan against ISI-sponsored groups to test the Iranian intentions. More importantly, order preparations for a nuclear test at Pokharan to be completed, if we actually have a worthwhile fusion design. You should be able to order triggering with forty-eight hours of giving notice. Simultaneously, hit known terrorist training camps near the border, if there is a major terror strike in India with an air and ground offensive, making it clear that it is for a limited purpose. Of course, Pakistan will retaliate, and the Security Council will step in to control the fighting. But the political purpose would be served.

"It would also be a good idea to quickly accord political approval for lots of arms purchases from the United States. The 155mm M777 light howitzers would be an easy start, as there are no other untainted contestants, and because of effective lobbying by BAE Systems, which manufactures the howitzers, the administration is keen to push the deal. You need to rush the weapons into Leh and Arunachal Pradesh, as the Chinese have us over a barrel with infrastructure development and the army is badly outgunned.

"If we have to explode a nuke, the US arms lobby will save us from any meaningful long-term sanctions. A few billion dollars of fighter aircraft purchases and strategic lift aircraft will buy lots of political space."

"And what message will the Chinese perceive if we do as you suggest and do some tests at Pokharan?"

Sridhar intervened, "The fusion test will send a message of intent that we are ready to deal with a two-front problem. If it comes to a face-down, we need to try to get an EMP weapon ready, even if it is a crude, heavy device, to control escalation! We will have to take our knocks, but it may just cause a major upheaval in the politburo. It will give them a wake-up call that India is a walk-over no longer and hopefully bring about a less belligerent approach!"

"Thank you for all your thoughts. It certainly gives me more confidence, and we can review progress after some time. Anything else that can be considered at this stage or something that you are working on that I should know?" the PM asked.

"We also need to target the leaders of our own homegrown, two-dozen-plus insurgencies, including the ones operating from Pakistan, Myanmar, and Bangladesh, so that they do not get things to flare up when you have your hands full," Nasruddin Babbar, who had been listening, intently spoke for the first time.

"What will you do?" asked the PM.

"Better that you don't ask the question, sir!" Nasruddin Babbar replied. "You may need to be able to maintain deniability for certain internal actions relating to insurgent groups. Look at the unnecessary flack that the Israeli PM, Benjamin Netanyahu, faced when he authorized Mossad to kill Hamas Commander Mahmoud al-Mahbouh in Beirut, and the hit squad used diplomatic passports to make matters worse!"

"Okay, consider that the question has not been asked! We need to terminate this discussion for the time being. However, one thought I would like to leave with you. I would prefer 25 percent of the allocation of funds that are made available to you to go into cyber warfare infrastructure and also include processes that are currently going unaddressed.

"We need some access to the deliberations of the politburo. Ideally, we should be able to get near-real-time access to the Chinese Internet, telecom, and power grid structures to permit a peep. Currently, we are not even trying to get there!"

Mathews added, "We need much more funding. The Chinese have been breaking into sensitive global telecom networks, and even the defense services are not immune to this. Take, for example, the army's wide-area network. Even if you cut it off from other networks, it can still be accessed via wireless by the Chinese and others like the United States unless we can put in our own microprocessors. This also needs to be quickly extended to the atomic energy establishment, the space establishment, the Tejas aircraft, battle tanks, and radars.

"Since the basic work on an Indian chip has already been done by the CSIR labs, all that we need is to put in a team of four to five hundred people to make a microprocessor and complimentary hardware."

Sobti added, "To fabricate chips quickly, we need to invest in a private foundry overseas and take over a majority stake. Thereafter, we hire security-cleared Indians to work in the more sensitive areas of interest to us! Raja will need to raise much more money from our tax evaders."

The prime minister ended the conversation by saying, "Do it, but hurry, Raja. Make it profitable for them to invest directly in energy-related projects like oil and gas fields in the United States, Indonesia, Iran, and Iraq and uranium in Kazakhstan! We have a lot of lost time to make up.

"Incidentally, I need to take out some insurance for all of you if I am incapacitated for any reason. Ashok, why don't you prepare a single copy in hand of the gist of our discussions that I will sign and you can put away in a State Bank of India locker. If any of your actions on behalf of the nation are called into question someday, it may save all of you a lot of trouble if there is a record of my approval!

CHAPTER 18
CYBER TARGET

Anand Sharma, a not uncommon name in India, had risen past his level of competence a decade earlier. However, this was no indicator of his not rising even higher in the Indian Administrative Service that provided the civil services supposedly steel scaffolding in India, a rusting scaffolding ready to crash if the media was to be believed. However, the fact remained that the practitioners of the supposedly dark art of civil mal-governance in India were indeed the best and the brightest.

A rigorous examination process endeavored to weed out chaff that were not in the outstanding category at an early age. This fine young remaining clay of human potential was then matured. This was done by subjecting it to the white heat of a malodorous political process to preserve its intellectual capacity but strip it of its ethical yeast.

Politics invariably triumphed idealism. The choice was stark and often easily made. Be principled and retire early on a meager pension or shed your inhibitions and youthful ideals and climb your professional Mount Everest, a mountain that invariably exerted a fascinating gravitational pull.

The secret to upward civil services mobility was simple and well understood. Make your minister look good—or at least ensure that he or she does not ever look bad! This ensured above-average grades in the mandatory annual confidential report, the stepping stone to civil servant promotions and perks and postretirement sinecures as consultants to the government. The rule applied especially to media management and in this case, encouraging the minister to keep his mouth shut. Dealing with myriad issues and cases of corruption in front of cameras was tricky. These cases dogged the civil-supplies ministry whose primary focus was to shovel millions of tons of subsidized food items to 120 million destitute house-holds and obtain their votes as a quid pro quo.

Anand was now assistant secretary in the Commerce Ministry, with five years left before he would have been compulsorily retired. Years of consultancy work would thereafter fall into his lap as a matter of course. This would involve leveraging his insider knowledge and contacts. The bottom line would be to facilitate large contracts with hefty commissions.

Much to the surprise of Anand Sharma's contemporaries, he had been selected for the Indian Administrative Service, the prima donna civil service amongst the country's government employees. This happened despite twice failing to clear the mandatory written exam. What nobody knew was that Anand Sharma's was singularly fortunate because he had such a caring father.

Nitin Sharma, a successful government contractor and Anand's father, had spent a lifetime parlaying bribes of various denominations for contracts. Over a period of time, Nitin Sharma had evolved a concept to facilitate deals that needed an inside track. This was preferably provided by a family member to plow through the corridors of power of the Indian bureaucracy. This would be insurance for the clan to prosper in an uncertain future. A systematic man well aware of the intellectual limitations of his only son, Anand, he had no option, he reasoned, but to load the dice in favor of the boy.

A first step was taken by sending Anand to the most expensive schools that were endemic in India to get into the civil services. These academies were generally run by former insiders. This method was regarded as a near guarantee to prepare young people to facilitate entry into secure jobs in government. In the due course of time, by a process akin to insider trading, these jobs could be parlayed into small or large fortunes.

"Do your best always so we can be proud of you" was Nitin Sharma's parting advice to his son, Anand, as he caught the train on his way to more coaching. "And God will take care of the rest."

When coaching did not work its magic, fate intervened. A timely donation of a world-acclaimed, "cheapest in the world," and bottom-of-the-line Nano car by Nitin coupled with a cheap Samsung window air conditioner did the trick. These consumer durables were contributed to the dowry of a low-level government functionary's daughter marrying a policeman. That the father of the bride worked in the Union Public Services Commission, a statutory body that oversaw selection into the top services of the Indian government, including the armed forces and the police, was less than incidental.

After the wedding, it was payback time. The grateful father of the bride ensured that through a typing error, Anand Sharma figured in the list of successful candidates heralded into the Indian Administrative Service Class of 1977. The other Anand Sharma, who actually passed the exam because of his undoubted intellect and IQ of 140, jumped in front of a train shortly thereafter. Mourned by only an ailing mother, he was lost to his country's service forever.

As a young district commissioner in Bihar, a land ravaged by floods, Anand Sharma proved to be a surprisingly efficient administrator. He undoubtedly saved hundreds of lives of flood victims by his timely initiative of calling in army engineers to help evacuate the marooned and plug gaps in flood control dykes. As was so often the case on an otherwise slow news day, he became an instant celebrity with his khaki-clad, slender frame, clipped mustache, and rugged good looks. Anand looked the epitome of a man of action in the field in a country desperately short of role models.

The media hype and a stunning visual of him reaching out from the prow of a boat and snatching a young girl from the rooftop of a largely submerged hut was all it took. The baby python sharing the rooftop being computer-enhanced to look bigger than the girl helped, too. It was enough to ensure an award for conspicuous bravery not in the face of the enemy, the Shaurya Chakra from the president of India, a few months later.

"Brave Heart Snake Charmer," screamed *The Times* of India's front-page headline.

"Noah's Ark in Bihar," countered the *Hindustan Times* in a glowing tribute to the only civil servant in Bihar who worked eighteen hours a day when hundreds were only interested in ripping off the state.

"Asian Hero," proclaimed the cover of *Newsweek*.

At the same time, he did not forget family obligations. Thus, when a prolonged relief effort to feed, support, and shelter a hundred thousand people and reconstruct homes was undertaken over the next two years, Anand was able to ensure that his father's company got a fair share of contracts. Unfortunately, the same media that had lionized him the previous year, were quick to crucify him for inspired but inaccurate bookkeeping, rampant leakages in aid, and the vermin-ridden wheat and rice provided in refugee camps by the family firm. However, as was its wont, the Indian Administrative Service closed ranks. After a half-baked departmental enquiry, only a mild reprimand was administered to Anand for not keeping proper records.

He was sent off the same day on another assignment, far from the glare of intruding media. Now after more than three decades of less-than-inspired performance, he found himself ensconced in an assignment in Delhi, one with little work. The work he did do, however, was out of choice—being honorary secretary to an old-boy network of his contemporaries in government jobs. The members met once a quarter for booze, gossip, and promoting individual interests. These included getting their eligible sons and daughters prospective matrimonial matches.

Anand had got into a routine of surfing the Internet from the office in the afternoons spent in his large, spacious office. Sometimes he would share snippets of information gleaned from the web to the old-boy network so that he could maintain an aura of indispensability. He was careful in avoiding any contact with enticing pornographic sites for self-preservation. This was a precaution just in case his computer was seized by the Central Bureau of Investigations. This was an occupational hazard, for his minister could be investigated for corruption at any moment, which wasn't an unreasonable possibility. The news value of a senior bureaucrat surfing pornographic sites was infinitely more valuable than the same bureaucrat bilking the country for millions. This situation, of course, could arise only if his minister lost the next election to parliament from Maharashtra. If the right-wing BJP came to power, a witch hunt would always be in the cards.

CHAPTER 19
TROJAN HORSES

THE 80-GIGABIT HARD DRIVE INSTALLED ON Anand's desktop computer was one manufactured by Seagate Technology, LLC. It had passed through the hands of a Chinese subcontractor called Huan Tech Private Limited during the manufacturing process, and it had been part of a batch that had been deliberately infected with a Trojan-horse virus. The virus automatically uploaded any information saved on these computers' hard drives to websites in China.

Anand was blissfully unaware that thousands of kilometers away in Hong Kong, every keystroke on his office computer had been almost instantaneously reflected in a shadowy electronic wonderland. It was a realm in cyberspace that was occupied by thousands of patriotic young Chinese geeks working in small, easily replicated teams. These teams remained segregated from each other but supported through hundreds of millions of Yuan of funding. The nominated teams could take over critical networks in thirty-five countries critical to Chinese interests if and when required. Off-the-shelf tool kits allowed even less-than-savvy users to build viruses and Trojans, which meant that many hundreds of additional men and women were available as instruments of state policy through electronic means. The tools they used were advanced enough to allow the viruses and Trojans to change their signatures every few minutes, which made it virtually impossible to generate repair patches.

Standard installed antivirus software was no good at stopping low-volume attacks aimed at limited targets. Traditional antivirus programs detected widespread attacks based on known patterns. They did not fare well against low-volume Trojans. And even when they did detect such attacks, the larger-volume threats automatically got more attention, because a larger, annoyed customer base was involved then. Even as the number of virus attacks had increased on Indian networks in the last few years, the duration of attacks had decreased, making it all the more difficult to detect and deal with. The lower duration of an attack did not, however, dilute its impact. A zero-day attack, also known as a zero-hour attack, took advantage of computer vulnerabilities that did not currently have solutions. People often took advantage of this window of opportunity before a patch was created.

Anand was not a user given to regular checks and updates of software patches. As a senior government employee in India, he was viscerally disinclined to treat a computer system or anything else provided to him freely as his own responsibility. Network administration, wherever it existed, was of a hit-or-miss variety located in ministries not directly connected to national security, so it reacted normally when systems ran into problems, which sometimes meant that systems would become unavailable for the simplest tasks for two days at a stretch.

Malware was also no longer exclusive to malicious websites, and even legitimate mainstream sites served as parasitic hosts to unsuspecting visitors. Attacks were increasingly obfuscated by making them more complex. The attacker could have a server-side polymorphic threat delivered by operating a web server with malware files dynamically generating variants, making detection using traditional signature-based antivirus methods very difficult.

Anand could not have cared less as he blissfully hooked into the net and quickly scanned the free reads on the *Wall Street Journal.* His minister, who was busy politicking in his home state so that he could hang on to his vote bank, relied on Anand completely to update him on the world's commercial developments. With a little luck and the right electoral result, it was still possible to get promoted to secretary rank. If ever he thought of the fact that he was being less than honest in his work ethic, he brushed such misgivings aside as hands-on research that would place him in a good position as a consultant later.

To keep the digital gates to the Indian government wide open and compromise hundreds of computers in key and not-so-vital ministries, a Conficker program was introduced by the Chinese team. It was of such sophistication, using state-of-the-art practices to protect itself, that it was never completely eradicated. This program used flaws in Windows software legitimately installed in Anand Sharma's computer to co-opt all machines that were on his mailing list into a virtual government offices network that could be commanded from China. The system was permitted to lie dormant in the sense that it continued to monitor traffic but did not disrupt it. Chinese authors kept distributing advanced versions of the Conficker worm and eventually reached a stage where Chinese authorities could use any of the computers of Anand's network to instruct all the others.

The civil service's old-boy network that Anand ran as an honorary secretary included senior functionaries in all ministries of any consequence to a hostile-power defense, external affairs, home, finance, and commerce, that being just some of them. It also included the office of the national security adviser. The intra-government net was also penetrated as e-mails and attachments sent by family and friends helped enlarge the network.

On Hainan Island, the information flow was so intense that a data center had to be set up on a stand-alone basis to handle the traffic from India. This would create severe problems for the handlers in due course, as all the data was in English and had to be translated. New algorithms had to be created to separate the useful from the frivolous, and the small team of Chinese analysts soon became a larger team. And the larger team then expanded further till four hundred men and women, many of them English proficient, were involved in exploiting this single opening.

One of the names on Anand Sharma's mailing list was Aspi Engineer, a highly respected bureaucrat of impeccable integrity with a master's degree in political science from the University of California. Aspi Engineer was already being touted to become cabinet secretary, the de facto number-one civil servant in India, in a few years. He had been personally selected by the prime minister to assist the ailing national security adviser, who was considered indispensable because of the dirt he had collected on opposition MPs. Aspi owed this to long stints with both the Ministry of Defense and the Ministry of Home Affairs, not to mention his unique perspective of ground realities.

In the course of vetting India's ministerial-level communications, which were being archived in a database on Hainan Island, an algorithm that red-flagged "border management" spewed out a short document on Aspi Engineer's personal computer. The malware was fed to Aspi's computer through a communication inviting all Anand Sharma's batch mates to join in for a celebration of Diwali, the Indian festival of lights. Aspi opened the document and read the following:

> Border Management
>
> LAC/LOC Related Draft Recommendation
>
> Our land borders extend for 15,106 kilometers as opposed to 7500 kilometers of maritime borders. Unfortunately, our benign neglect of this crucial component of our national security environment has resulted in a situation where we have ongoing territorial disputes with all our neighbors other than Bhutan and Myanmar.
>
> Our maritime disputes are largely under control under the provisions of UNCLOSS, including the Sir Creek area with Pakistan and our implicit naval-led hegemonic status. However, the discovery of oil in the KG Basin in the Bay of Bengal by Reliance Industries makes it highly likely that no satisfactory final resolution will be achieved for the foreseeable future with Pakistan, Sri Lanka, Bangladesh, and Indonesia. The ceding of the island of Kachhativu to Sri Lanka as a political sop was disastrous. This has convinced our littoral neighbors that we are pushovers and crying wolf over hostile Indian intentions is a viable strategy to carve out favorable settlements with us. Our maritime neighbors participating in "The String of Pearls" strategy of giving bases to China will constrain us further, but we can live with it, as nothing material will change.
>
> Approximately one third of our land borders are disputed. The 740-kilometer-plus "Line of Actual Control" in Jammu and Kashmir and the Siachen Glacier Area is fortified and held by armies of both Pakistan and India, and no sudden changes are probable without a full-fledged war. On the other hand, the

4057-kilometer "Line of Control" with China has nine major disputed sectors. The greatest danger to India lies in China unilaterally moving forward into the area claimed by it as part of Tibet or parts of it that actually interest them. The Chinese have built up the infrastructure in Tibet, including all weather roads and railways, right up to these areas. (See map attached at Appendix.)

We must ensure that whatever the provocation by the Chinese, there is no hostile reaction on our part, as there is no way that Indian forces can match the potential Chinese build up. We are unprepared to do this, and it will take a minimum of ten years to produce near-matching infrastructure on our side, given the prevailing geologic conditions in the Himalayas compared to the Tibetan Plateau.

The chief of the army staff seems blissfully unaware of this mismatch and is prone to making bellicose statements about teaching the Chinese a lesson while visiting troops involved in border management. A suitable ambassadorial posting for him in Guyana or Mozambique to keep him out of harm's way should be considered forthwith. Instead, we should ensure through the prime minister that the defense minister includes suitable, politically aware candidates as replacements at the earliest.

The short document would cost India dearly, as it provided the keystone of the strategy that China would relentlessly pursue in the ensuing years with remarkable success. A second algorithm that red-flagged "Response Options to Terror Attacks" was extracted through the malware and shared with Pakistan in an informal interaction between the two army intelligence chiefs of China and Pakistan.

DRAFT RESPONSE OPTIONS

TERROR ATTACKS

Recently, the Indian media has suggested through a series of articles quoting prominent political parties and retired senior government bureaucrats and armed forces senior officers that a leaf should be taken out from the Israeli strategy of immediate retaliation. This is normally done by air strikes against Palestinian targets the moment there is a terrorist attack directed at Israeli interests. We need to discourage any talk of such strikes, as the subcontinental context is completely different. In the case of Israel, retaliation poses little short-term danger against a vastly inferior enemy, at least militarily. Israel also continues to have the unstinting support of the United States.

An automatic tit-for-tat escalation ladder will wheel into motion and could include the use of nuclear weapons in case of an Indian armed response against any further Pakistan-sponsored, large-scale terrorist attacks. Any precedent that we seek to establish with US unmanned aerial vehicles targeting the Taliban will be singularly lacking in support from the global community, less Israel.

US UAV strikes are in connivance and with the tacit acceptance of the Pak Army in spite of the fact that increasingly the United States is upping the ante on what the Pak Army can tolerate. The army, in fact, does the targeting groundwork in most cases against inconvenient Pak Taliban groups that act like loose cannons and undermine its prestige and power. Indian strikes will definitely be viewed to fall outside this envelope.

The Pak Army's reputational concerns vis-à-vis India will automatically call for upping the ante. Any nominal civilian head of state not toeing the line of the army will almost certainly be replaced in a coup. Unmistakable warning signals will be sent via the United States and China so that superpower diplomatic pressure can dissuade India. No one will be left in any doubt that the use of nuclear weapons will follow. There seems to be a definitive assessment made by the Pak Army that India's nuclear capability and political will is stunted and can be handled. To respond to military options by India, Pakistan has already got the United States firmly in its corner, as any threat to move forces from combating the Taliban in the northwest to a face-off with India on the west will unhinge the US anti-Taliban alliance.

China will inevitably constrain our options further by activating the LAC. The logic of development for India dictates that a one-shot response is made to show national will and if Pakistan does a tit-for-tat response, we just absorb it without escalating further so that each side can claim victory to its own people. A full-fledged response is beyond our capabilities. India is at least fifteen years away from building an adequate capability politically, economically, and militarily to do anything else.

Our armed forces fail to appreciate the nuances of the nuclear tango between us and Pak as also with China and need to be kept in touch with reality. Our options may appear pacifist but are in tune with existing realities. It is likely that the continued role of the United States within Pakistan will continue to actively constrain renegade elements from within the Pak Military from instigating and abetting the Punjab-based terror groups like the Lashkar e Taiba from making large-scale strikes in India. This, in any case, is becoming increasingly problematic for them, given the enhanced security measures that I have personally overseen and put in place. US interests are deeply aligned with Pakistan to sort out the Afghanistan imbroglio, and India should expect no worthwhile recognition of its genuine concerns.

India stands alone. China controls the US purse strings and can get away with bringing incremental pressure against India with a range of plausible excuses for the international community. The US is now compelled to soft pedal what it may have called its principles like upholding human rights in Tibet to avoid giving offense to China. A recent case in point was the US president cancelling a meeting with the Dalai Lama kowtowing to Chinese demands. A partial naval blockade of Karachi is about the only response that India can make without upping the ante to an extent that escalation will not be controllable. Ships flying the Chinese flag will need to be handled with considerable finesse if a blockade is implemented.

CHAPTER 20
THE MAKING OF A JIHADIST

THE WORDS OF THE PLEDGE CONTINUED to reverberate in their consciousness:

To the sister believer whose clothes the criminals have stripped off

To the sister believer whose hair the oppressor have shaved

To the sister believer whose body has been abused by human dogs

To the sister believer—

"When shall we go?"

"We could go tomorrow morning? We can catch a bus and be there in an hour Abu" said Zaki.

Abu Ismail and Zaki Mohammad had been friends from childhood and were so mentally attuned to each other that at times they seemed like twins. Both were of middle height and medium built, and they had been born in the latter half of the same year. Their fathers were friends as well, both serving in the same battalion of the paramilitary force, the Sutlej Rangers, and prone to long absences from home. Without strong male guidance, the boys were essentially permitted to grow up on their own, with their mothers having negligible influence after they entered their teens. Both mothers had enough problems, trying to marry off six girls between them in the next few years, that they couldn't even think about what the boys were doing … or complain about them to their men folk on the rare occasions they were back home.

The two friends were fortunate to go to the government high school in Renala Khurd, Okara District in Punjab, where Zaki's uncle was a teacher. Both were considered outstanding students and sure to do well if they could make it to college in Lahore. Both decided that they wanted to become engineers and work in Dubai to become rich and contribute to the dowries of their sisters.

However, fate willed otherwise. They were both exposed to reading *Jehad Times*, the Urdu weekly especially targeted at students, and also the monthly *Mujala-e-Tulba*. The latest issue of the *Jehad Times* quoted the Qur'an on the cover page: "Those who are slain in the cause of Allah are not counted amongst the dead. They are living in the presence of their Lord and are well provided for" (R249).

Abu read out loud from the latest *Mujala-e-Tulba* editorial. They discussed the aspect of the "duty of every 'Momin'" to protect and defend the interests of Muslims, especially in Kashmir, where Muslim women were being raped daily by the Indian Army.

Engineering would have to take a backseat as they decided and visited the Lahore office of the Lashkar e Taiba front organization, Jamaat ud Dawa. Again, destiny played a random card as they almost bumped into Khalid Walad, son-in-law of the Lashkar-e-Taiba founder, Hafiz Mohammad Saeed, who stopped when he saw two strapping, young, neatly dressed men and potential gun-fodder candidates.

It had been a slow month till then, with only three unemployed laborers showing up for recruitment—evidently with the idea of getting fed and not because of any ideological reason. It was a great plus to get educated boys. In time, if they survived, they could become good leaders in their own right.

"You have come to kill the Hindu *baniyas*? The shopkeepers who suck the blood of our people should all be killed!" he said, making a slitting gesture across his throat while stopping in midstride and glaring at them. "Good. We need young men like you to come forward and become heroes. These things have to be done to kick the Hindus out of Kashmir and protect our sisters. Kill them all and come back and teach others how to do so! I will be watching you. Train hard and do what you are told." Khalid Walad looked fiercely into their eyes for a moment and then he was gone, a long clerical robe trailing behind him.

Thirty minutes later, after their life stories had been satisfactorily gone over and their enthusiasm for liberating Kashmir had been listened to for all practical purposes they had been accepted as potential tools of Jihad. They were praised for wisdom beyond their years and told to return the next day with their belongings in a bag that could be comfortably backpacked or carried in one hand. In any case, recruitment as gun fodder for the Jihad had never been a very selective process.

Any young candidate who showed up for selection with working limbs and a record of some attendance at a *madrassa* to acquire the right religious ideology was never rejected. The next morning at ten o'clock, a group of three men went over their stories with a fine-tooth comb and took down all their personal particulars. Thereafter, Abu Ismail and Zaki Mohammad were escorted by a third person on an hour-long bus journey to Muridke. They were brought to a small house with a dilapidated vegetable patch for a garden and then were handed over to Maulana Mufti Fadullah.

"Khalid has personally selected and sent them," said their escort to Maulana Mufti Fadullah, who straightaway motioned to them to sit with the other three young men in the room.

Before he continued his discourse on Hadi's Quran, the Maulana said, "You need to understand in every fiber of your body, mind, and soul what Jihad signifies, what your willingness to participate in Jihad involves, and why this will develop the desire in you to be always mentally stronger than your enemies. Without that mental strength, you cannot dominate your enemies, who in mere numbers will always be a hundred times your strength. Without that understanding, you are nothing … there is no difference between you and the policeman on the street. Any fool can be taught how to pull a trigger!"

They slept on the ground in four small rooms with blue walls. The rooms were motivational in nature in the sense that all the walls were covered with paintings of *Jannat* or paradise. The ingredients were lush green trees and fields interspersed with mountain streams flowing with milk and honey. This lush landscape had houses with red roofs and blue walls. The pleasures of paradise for martyrs were projected so that they were made available through *hoors* or celestial angels abiding there.

The next twenty-one days were a blur as the "Daura Sufa" elementary capsule alternating religious discourses, prayer, and physical training was run for thirty young men of about the same age group as they. This was followed by another twenty-one-day capsule called the "Daura Aam" for twenty-two of the original thirty which introduced them to a range of weapons and explosives, including AK-47 rifles, mortars, Uzis, and sidearm pistols and revolvers.

For the thirteen survivors of "Daura Aam," the final twenty-one-day capsule for confidential operations "Daura Khas" also included swimming lessons and being exposed to daily shows of atrocities on Muslims by the "Kaffir" Hindu Police, border security forces, and the army. Abu Ismail and Zaki Mohammad declined to go home and were sent to Muzzafarpur to live in a finishing camp and practice firing and handling weapons, including dummy surface-to-air missiles and explosives.

They were fascinated by the lecture by the technically savvy Saifullah, who had been loaned by al Qaeda to the Lashkar as a trainer. This happened at the insistence of Brigadier Syed Ali, who had first-hand experience of his military skills. "Saifullah," Arabic for "the sword of Allah", had fought in Afghanistan against the Soviet Union before he was eighteen years old from 1988 to 1991. After the Soviets withdrew from Afghanistan in February 1989, Saifullah matched his skills against the Soviet-backed Afghan forces during the civil war waged by Islamist militants against the Democratic Republic of Afghanistan.

Islamist veterans of that war in Afghanistan were held in reverence by the Muslim community tended to be afforded a romanticized mystique, and they are considered to be victorious Mujahideen or "holy warriors" who defeated the Soviets and their communist (and atheistic) Afghan allies. He had also destroyed a Russian helicopter gunship with a Stinger missile launcher picked up from a fallen comrade. Saifullah was unique in the sense that after he suffered a thigh wound from a ricocheting bullet during an ambush on an Afghan convoy, he went home to Peshawar and completed a bachelor's degree in telecommunications.

Saifullah was a brilliant student and had been sponsored by Osama bin Laden himself to complete a master's in computer science and an

MBA from MIT in Boston as a future investment to the cause of Jihad before he eventually returned home. He was currently loaned to the Lashkar e Taiba to promote greater coordination with al Qaeda. The Lashkar had used him to scale up their recruitment, because word of the arrival of a genuine hero spread like wildfire, and also upgrade the Lashkar e Taiba technology awareness for use against the Indians. This automatically also played up the capability of al Qaeda in the minds of the listeners.

Aside from his remarkable military skills, Saifullah was a natural teacher and used simple words to vividly paint pictures to his class of eager listeners "You must continue to read, read, and read more! Without keeping up with technology, you will be like the blind. You cannot be competent warriors, and this training will be wasted. To give you but one example, the new generation of intelligent CCTVs that are fortunately extremely expensive and cannot be widely deployed by the Indians can spot violent gestures or suspicious movements.

"Active awareness systems integrated into these TVs can detect any kind of unusual activity, including someone raising his hand suddenly, running along a street, or taking an unusual route around a car park. Or recognize sounds such as screaming or glass breaking and can integrate face recognition software to pick you out of a crowd. This technology is also being tried out in conjunction with the unmanned aircraft the Americans are flying out of the Bandari air base southwest of Quetta. Baitullah Mehsud started covering his face to avoid being photographed far too late. That is how he was probably picked up as a target by the American missiles. Behave naturally, merge with the crowd, avoid being photographed as far as possible, and you can still fool the system!"

In the garb of a militant, Hafiz Mohammad Sayeed himself, who was accompanied by Brigadier Syed Ali, visited the camp and spoke to them a few days before their training was terminated. "You must clearly understand what the Lashkar-e-Taiba is doing to ensure freedom from rape from the Indian Army for our women folk in Kashmir. Why did we then attack Mumbai?" Hafiz asked rhetorically, looking at a clearly puzzled Zaki sitting cross-legged in the first row of trainees.

"It is because we are a few entirely dedicated to the service of Allah, and the nonbelievers are many. The Indian Army is the third largest in the world, much of it deployed in Jammu and Kashmir for the past sixty-five years. It is designed to fight expensive wars against Pakistan, with tanks and artillery guns and aircraft. When Pakistan has not been able to attack the Indian Army successfully, can we do so?"

"How do you eat a cold Naan in winter? Can you eat it in one bite?" Again, as he looked around, it was Abu squatting behind Zaki who involuntarily answered, "We can eat the cold Naan slowly in small bites until it is finished. But can we do that to the Indian Army? It will take so many years more. We cannot wait forever! Since we cannot get good results from attacking even small portions of the Indian Army, we attacked Mumbai"

The Lashkar-e-Taiba chief nodded vigorously in agreement. "We terrified all the rich people in Mumbai who spend money extracted largely from the work of Muslim laborers in expensive hotels, who give money secretly to the Congress Party, who demand protection from us in turn and would be happy to let Kashmir go in exchange for safety of their lives. Now every time they go past the Taj Hotel in Mumbai with their whores, who move about with their arms and bellies exposed, they fear for their lives, as they cannot help but remember the days of retribution when Mumbai belonged to a handful of us!"

He continued with a theatrical flourish of his hands, "They will spend five thousand crore rupees in trying to make Mumbai safe. They will hire more police, attain better weapons, try to gather more intelligence about us, bring in more army Special Forces, the best trained ones that they possess, and in the end, all their efforts will be in vain. Their efforts will fail because in the end, they do not have the conviction of their cause like you and the hundreds of young men like you waiting to be trained and sent into India have!"

In a few passing sentences, the Lashkar chief had nailed the paradox of the Indian Army. Organized in corps and divisions for classical surgical strikes by swiftly moving armored formations backed by air superiority fighter jets, it was tied up in hundreds of mind-numbing, resource-draining skirmishes—this inside their own borders in asymmetric wars against both state and non-state actors.

"The Indian Army cannot touch us, for you will be sent to strike where they are not. The choice of where to strike is mine on your behalf. How do they find us beforehand? Impossible! We look like them, talk like them, eat what they eat, dress like them, have informers and helpers amongst them, and in their so-called democracy, the police unlike the ISI here do not have the money and training to gather information in each *mohallah* about the comings and goings of their people. Therefore, do not be afraid when you are sent into India. Our cause is just. You are superbly trained and capable of carrying it out, and it is Allah's will that you will succeed."

Brigadier Syed Ali smiled grimly as the Lashkar chief continued his rant. This lot was motivated enough for the mission he had in mind for them. He turned toward Saifullah, who was standing besides him.

"You've done a wonderful job training this lot, Saif! Now let's see what I can make of them."

CHAPTER 21
THE COST OF TERROR

BRIGADIER SYED ALI WAS A KEEN student of world-wide developments in the military and had carried out a study for the ISI on the effects of terrorism on a modern economy. He reckoned that since September 11, 2001, conflicts had acquired a new dimension. Battlefronts have become more fluid. No longer was it possible to marshal armies at borders only to solve problems with neighboring countries or, if distant, to bomb them from the air like the US Air Force dealt with Libya. Battlefronts were far more immediate and could be running next to a milk booth or newspaper vendor as large metros commenced a working day. Civilian assets had become more vulnerable than military targets as states like his own country Pakistan partnered with the formidable talent and resources of some non-state players like the Mujahidin and Lashkar e Taiba to inflict multimillion-dollar damages on an economy like India. Capturing territory was becoming an arcane concept.

Syed Ali had read the Milken Institute study that estimated the short- and long-term costs of September 11, 2001 to the United States. Outside of the loss of human life, the immediate hit was about fifty-three billion dollars. In the weeks that followed, another forty-seven billion dollars disappeared thanks to lost economic output in the US economy. Plus, another $1.7 trillion disappeared from the US stock market.

Then the costs had *really* started to add up. Airlines and aerospace, tourism and travel, hotels and motels, restaurants, the US Postal Service, and the insurance industry all suffered. Just in the first month, at least 125,000 people lost their jobs. Another 1.6 million jobs evaporated over the next year. And businesses retooling for the new "terror economy" had to spend an extra $151 billion.

In cases of terror that was stretched out over weeks by media coverage like in the United States, the law of unintended consequences and the resulting distortions caused by it took over soon enough. Governments in the West wasted billions they otherwise couldn't have, because every new security bill got passed. Nations fought battles they otherwise wouldn't have, because every conflict suddenly looked connected to the war on terror. Individuals and businesses were not spending money in ways they otherwise would have, because they were afraid to take the risk. Air travel fell. Tourism fell. Trade suffered, and foreign investment dried up. In 2002, twenty-nine ports on the US West Coast shut down for two weeks. Two hundred ships carrying over three hundred thousand shipment containers just sat in the water.

Railcars and warehouses all over the country waited, too, along with freezers and grain elevators and companies that had to shut down their production lines. More jobs disappeared. And the added insurance costs against security shutdowns tacked on another thirty billion dollars to the cost of doing business in America. Yet new estimates put the uncovered costs so far at close to two trillion dollars! All taxpayers paid roughly five hundred dollars extra every year to cover the cost of a bloated Homeland Security Agency.

Syed Ali's report to the ISI had summed up the case for the West. "You can never predict how much a war on terror will cost. Fighting terrorism is like fighting a hurricane you can see forming on the radar when it's headed your way. But you don't know what to expect when it lands. Each enhanced cockpit door on a plane costs upward of thirty thousand dollars. Screening every bag carried by airline passengers cost taxpayers an extra five billion dollars each year, and the training of tens of thousands of connected agencies and personnel ups the tally further."

"It all starts to add up, along with the undetermined future costs of Iraq, Afghanistan, and maybe Iran over the next decade. It could set the West back trillions that it does not possess! Nobody knows for sure.

But the true hidden cost is the risk premium this creates. This is how instability destroys faith in the currency of the afflicted country. The lesson we need to take is that sustained terror attacks on India along with a massive effort to flood the country with counterfeit currency will bring India to its knees within a decade."

In the case of India, a nation that had faced more terror attacks than any other major country, no one had ever doubted that the Indians ability to count, especially money. One had to be reasonable in all expenditures even against terror was the unstated Indian view. The question of only throwing money at the problem did not arise unless there was an immediate election due and votes needed to be garnered.

Ash Conway's research showed that there was a near-unanimous view across the board that Indian governments had been notoriously wasteful whenever it came to pandering to their political constituencies. However, for the current party in power if government expenditure did not create a vote bank or generate adequate kickbacks for the current regime, the incurred expense was considered hardly worth the trouble. Security of citizens, national security, and police reforms were treated verbally as holy cows, and cosmetic expenditures like cosmetic surgeries were loudly advertised but judiciously undertaken. It showed immediate results but delivered little long-term benefit. The aftermath of the terrorist attacks on November 26, 2008, in Mumbai, which paralyzed the city for a week, merited similar treatment over a slightly longer period as the outcry from ordinary people carried on for some months.

Ashok Sobti had summed up the typical Indian response pattern to the prime minister. "After serious terrorist attacks we indulge in saber rattling against Pakistan-inspired terrorism by mobilizing some army units, issuing some advisories to hotels to enhance security, increasing some additional regional deployment of the national security guard and promising additions to coastal security. Add to this we issue a stream of promises via the media that this time the government means business. This is in the hope of lulling the average Indian into believing that the government is serious about looking after the nation's security. Soon enough, the crisis blows over, although the sheer scale of the last attack provided enough grist for government bashing over the next many months."

Instinctively, the Indian establishment knew that fighting terror was not affordable with a big-bang-big-buck approach and played the game indirectly. The default option of doing nothing was employed to curtail any overreaction; diplomatic options needed to be played out even while you are keeping your powder dry, and the country had to be prepared to drag it out over the long haul. This could even take decades till the terrorists and insurgents lost patience and their will to fight. It was all part of the daily grind. Definitely nothing to lose your lunch break over! If you looked like a bunch of wimps in the process, so be it.

Ash Conway's simulation results summed up how home-grown terror was perceived as being tackled. "Within the country where transnational elements are not involved, the out-of-the-box lowest common denominator Indian approach is simple: Negotiate for years. Give amnesty and stipends to troublemakers and killers so that they can live like normal civilians. And if charismatic enough to sway the locals, make the insurgent leaders chief ministers of the states where they had fomented rebellion. This could be made possible through rigging elections in their favor with the might of the state and waiting for five years till the electorate kicked them out in the next round of elections for nonperformance."

Transnational elements affecting Indian security came broadly from either Pakistan or China, although insurgents could be holed up in Myanmar, Bhutan, Nepal, Srilanka, and Bangladesh as well. Pakistan was already reaping the whirlwind, because after they abetted and created the Taliban and terror groups like the Lashkar e Taiba and Jaish Mohammed. Thereafter Pakistan lost control of the major terror groups who turned on their masters. China was not suffering at all by aiding and abetting a dozen insurgencies in northeast India-at least thus far.

CHAPTER 22
LINE OF CONTROL

THE ANTI-INSURGENCY OBSTACLE SYSTEM WAS PUT up by the Indian Army along 743 kilometers of the so-called "Line of Control," with Pakistan in Jammu and Kashmir, where no international border had ever existed. It cost fifty million dollars to install and ten million dollars a year to maintain because of heavy snow that damaged major portions of the fence annually. The nine-foot-high, three-layered system was based on the Israeli model in the Gaza Strip and incorporated with infiltration detection sensors to trigger an alarm at the nearest Indian Army post. There were two barbed-wire obstacles and a concertina wire coil placed in between. There was also a thin electric wire carrying a high enough voltage to severely shock and incapacitate anyone touching it inadvertently.

Where ravines, watercourses, and heavy vegetation made it difficult to fence, mines had been laid. Army patrols operating between the fence and the line of control, men equipped with thermal-imaging and night observation devices, tried to dominate the area and raise the ante for Pakistan-based militants being pushed across to create terror-related incidents. The infiltrating militants were well trained in fence-crossing and equipped with special gloves, boots, Chinese cutters, and ladders. The army also manned posts on the fence but perforce large gaps existed. This was because of manpower constraints, severe mountainous and wooded terrain, and the sheer impracticability of putting disproportionate resources in play against limited threats in a no-war-no-peace scenario. This untidy arrangement, one soaked in blood and dismembered limbs, had continued to be in play in some form or another since 1947. Britain had carved two nations, Pakistan and India, on sectarian lines out of the Indian subcontinent for its own balance-of-power purposes.

Ghulam Nabi was exceedingly well paid for each trip, for he was irreplaceable. This was true at least in this particular stretch of the hills for fifty kilometers or so on either side of the point where they were crossing. Throughout his youth and till 1990, Ghulam Nabi had grazed cattle in these parts, where boundaries had never been recognized, and his ancestors had followed the goats and cows to fresh pastures wherever they existed. Thereafter militancy was instigated in the Kashmir Valley by the Pakistan Army, when it had directed the attention of the victorious Mujahidin to Kashmir after it had driven out the Russians from Afghanistan.

The villages along the LOC, where he had several cousins and immediate family, would keep him informed about the movement of patrols whenever he wanted to cross over. Every three or four months, he would discover a new route between posts. He would then establish the routine of Indian patrols, and then lead a group of militants through the gap, normally before the Indian patrols were launched.

His advice on tactical routing had never once been discarded, with the exception of this last trip. It did not bother him too much. As long as Allah gave him strength to walk, he would continue to leverage his knowledge of the harsh terrain, and unique field experience and survival skills honed by trial and error. He would continue to work at his chosen trade as a pathfinder.

Those guides still active and fit were treasured by the Pakistan Army and handled with kid gloves. Of course, there had been a few cases where the guides had sold out to the other side. These tended to have extremely short careers. As soon as suspicion was aroused after a crossing had been foiled, often with severe casualties, the guide was the obvious suspect. Justice at the end of a bullet followed swiftly after a brutal but short interrogation. The deterrent effect against such misadventures lasted for many months.

Ghulam Nabi had protested about the danger a large group of infiltrators would pose against safe passage. However, for the first time in many months, the major from the Inter-Services Intelligence with the stiletto like eyes and voice like the icy waters of the Jhelum River overruled his advice. The major's one-time boss, Brigadier Syed Ali, who had personally enrolled him in the Hizbul Tehrir Islamist group two years ago, had asked him to ensure this passage.

The major told Ghulam "You will get fifty thousand rupees more for this trip. Wait for the first heavy snowfall and cross over into the forests beyond the wire. The distance is barely ten kilometers beyond the wire, and you will be up in the forested Pir Panjal Mountains before anyone can find you. You will be safely there before it becomes daylight."

"If Allah wills we will reach by then!" Ghulam responded.

"Amin here, who will go with you, will give instructions on how to hide the loads once you reach safety in the Dandaloo Nar Forest cave of a Himalayan black bear that we killed. The locals are too scared to go anywhere near there. I know that you feel there are too many men for one column, but I have no choice. They need to be across sometime in the coming week."

"What about the weather forecast?" Ghulam asked.

The major said "Our weather forecasts indicate heavy snow in the next few days. The Indians do not have any all-weather helicopters available nearby to even try to locate you. It will take them at least two hours after daybreak to move these up if visibility improves."

"We will to be ready to go after midnight tomorrow. When will the satellite pass take place?"

The major answered "The Indian satellite that we are tracking would have made its pass by then, and enough snow would have fallen to bury the motion sensors and perhaps some of the wire. No one knows more about what gaps exist and which exact route to follow in the whole valley. Allah has given you the skills to keep everyone safe. Go now!"

Young Sepoy Om Prakash, Number One Platoon, Alpha Company, with four Jammu and Kashmir rifles, was completing eighteen months at his post at an altitude of 9,800 feet above sea level, with just two months away on leave back at his ancestral home east of Jammu, where his father and his elder brother had tilled three acres of land. His officiating company commander, Captain Sahil Butalia, never tired of repeating his admonition whenever he visited the platoon's lonely post on the ridge overlooking the narrow, empty valley in no-man's-land. Although he was an armor officer attached to an infantry unit, the captain was no slouch at commanding loyalty by an unerring ability to gauge uncertainty and fear in his subordinates.

"The militants are waiting and watching all the time. They know that standing in one place when it is pitch dark and nothing moves taxes the patience of the finest soldier in the world which is you! Hundreds of millions of people in India are sleeping soundly because of you. Make sure that you never betray their trust! The girl who marries you will be lucky beyond words."

And with a pat on the back that sent a shiver of pleasure up the young soldier's spine, Sahil Butalia would be gone—perhaps to tell the young sentry at the neighboring post exactly the same thing in perhaps exactly the same words.

Om Prakash blinked his tired eyes and circled his eyeballs first left ten times and then right ten times and stamped his feet softly on the ground against the bitter cold. Snow was beginning to fall quite heavily now, and even though he constantly wiped the night vision goggles, he could see very little in the thick haze.

That morning, the captain had visited the post again and said, "In a few hours, it will start snowing. Don't take a chance. The Pakistanis will definitely try to send infiltrators across. I will spend the night at your post. If you see or hear anything abnormal, awaken me up at once!"

While Om Prakash struggled with the elements and his desire to sleep, Ghulam Nabi Gujjar, thin and frail of indeterminate age, skilled in finding gaps between the Indian Army posts and along barely discernible cattle tracks of a bygone era, led a seventy-five-man column in a single file line away from Om Prakash's prying eyes barely three hundred meters away from him.

"Halt! Who goes there?" Om Prakash challenged the darkness, not sure whether it was his imagination or he had heard a metallic sound. After about fifteen seconds of peering into the darkness, he was convinced that it had been a figment of his overactive imagination. He, however, woke up his platoon commander, Naib Subedar Ishwar Singh, who in turn woke up the captain.

"Om Prakash heard a metallic sound a little to the southwest of us near the depression."

"Fire six rounds of illuminating now!" Sahil Butalia ordered now fully awake.

Ghulam Nabi's column froze, for he had already instructed them to fight their natural instinct to drop to the ground. After what seemed an interminable wait, Ghulam Nabi got his column moving again. There was a renewed sense of urgency propelled by fear at being picked up after almost being through. It was bitterly cold and not moving and the wind only made it worse

It took a full fifteen minutes for the column to pass a single point. Surprisingly, fifteen men of the column carried heavy camouflaged packs and no weapons. This had been Ghulam Nabi's livelihood for the past seventeen years. The groups he led so surely had always been far smaller and easier to control. By the time the first illuminating round burst high, most of the infiltrating column was already through. The fourth illuminating round drifting low in the westerly wind picked out the last bit of the long column.

As he stood next to the medium-machine-gun crew, Captain Sahil Butalia ordered, "Line of men moving left of the fallen tree-fire!"

The ten-second burst virtually cut down the last four men of Ghulam Nabi's column, but the rest managed to pass into the gap. Only bad luck could stop them now from reaching the rendezvous (RV) with their local contact, who could then guide them to safety.

It was still somewhat dark at 6:00 a.m. by the time Captain Sahil Butalia and his patrol of ten finally discovered the four bodies grotesquely sprawled out in the heavy snow, which almost covered their bodies. The lead scout prodded the bodies with his rifle and confirmed that all were dead. As the men spread out to sweep the immediate vicinity for more infiltrators, one of the bodies sprung to life, rolled over, fired at the captain, and caught him with a round high on his chest. Sahil Butalia, holding a Sten machine carbine in both hands, spun with the impact, dropped on his knees, and emptied half his magazine into the Mujahidin who had come temporarily to life.

Colonel Jai Singh heard the terse firsthand report a few minutes later. "Sir, bad news I'm afraid. We dropped four infiltrators a little while ago—fully armed with AK-47s, two hundred rounds, and a couple of grenades each. I'm standing over the dead bodies. There is heavy snow obliterating all signs of passage, but an unknown number seem to have gotten through our defenses. I got careless and took a bullet through my bullet proof vest for my stupidity, but nothing serious, I think."

"Well done, Sahil. Get the doc to have a look. You'll probably feel the pain later. I'll warn the depth defenses of the brigade, but we'll be lucky to catch them in this snow."

CHAPTER 23
SLOW BOIL

THE VICE CHAIRMAN OF THE CENTRAL military commission, General Xu Caihou, looked at the two men who sat across from him. Both generals owed their appointments as commanders of the Lanzhou Military Region and Chengdu Military Region to the vice chairman's direct intervention.

"We have excellent information of what we have always suspected. The Indian Army and Air Force have been given unambiguous instructions that they will not respond proactively against the PLA opposite Tibet irrespective of the provocation. The chairman has instructed me to put this instruction to as severe a test as possible in a localized action without using more than a brigade worth of the army reserves. However, for deception purposes, we can move some rapid-reaction forces without making any serious effort to hide the movement wherever we consider useful—perhaps opposite Sikkim to threaten to cut off all the Indian northeastern states! That should get them worried."

"Our troops are already crossing into what the Indians perceive as their territory two or three times a week. We have also carried out a few helicopter sorties, flying over areas claimed by them. Obviously, you are looking for far more provocation," General Li Qianyuan, who was responsible for the western area abutting Jammu and Kashmir, observed.

General Lia was the first to speak. "Is there a timetable for this proposed action?" His command included all of Tibet, less the western region, which effectively meant the area opposite the Indian states of Uttaranchal, Sikkim, and Arunachal Pradesh. There was also an interesting possibility of using Nepal's Communist parties to create leverages across the unmanned Nepal-Indian border."

"We need seemingly credible reasons for any action that we are going to take. You will need time to innovate incidents that will sound plausible to the world. The western countries don't need to believe us—as long as they have an excuse to swallow what we feed them. Take a month or so to plan what you want to do," the CMC vice chairman said, offering space for his subordinates to perform.

"The Kashmir terror groups are planning something major. Our intercept units have picked up some Internet and cell-phone chatter emanating from someone called Ilyas Azad, who heads the so-called 313 Brigade within Harkut-ul-Jihad-al-Islami that has close al Qaeda and Taliban links. Interestingly, he was trained in the Pakistan Army Special Services Group. With the specialized training that he has, there are good odds that he will do something that forces the Indians to react against Pakistan beyond just making a noise in campaign speeches. That will give us an opportunity to time our actions," Li observed.

Xu added, "I agree. We will also start exerting pressure through the Indian insurgent groups in Assam, Bihar, Orissa, Chattisgarh, Jharkhand, West Bengal, Arunachal, and of course those present in Nepal, Bangladesh, and Myanmar immediately. It should be an interesting winter ahead!"

"What I would like to do," said Li, "is to capture the Daulet Beg Oldi Airfield in the Aksai Plain during a spell of bad weather to test them out. It is at almost five thousand meters and overlooks the Karakoram Highway. If we are going to pump oil through the new pipeline from Gwadar in Baluchistan to Urumqi, we cannot tolerate being held hostage by the Indian presence."

Lia added, "I agree, but it would be even better to capture the Chushul Airfield south of Pangong Lake—and maybe Fukche Airfield in eastern Ladakh as well."

Xu smiled and said, "Let's not get carried away just yet. But certainly, these options will be put to the chairman to get political clearance. For the time being, I like the option of Daulet Beg Oldi. The world will not notice, and the Indians can pretend that it's nothing much and disputed territory. We will need to stage an incident without any unpleasant surprises to deal with later. We should assume that satellites will pick up enough imagery to nail anything that does not tally with whatever version we ultimately decide to put out if there is any carelessness. The timing of the operation needs to ensure that satellite passes overhead are kept in mind."

"If the terrorists do manage a big operation and the Indians are forced to react, it will get interesting. Pakistan, too, will have to show resolution," Lia added, "and with a little prodding by our support, can be made to undertake an operation against India's Northern Command. Even a divisional-sized one will create a serious command dilemma about using the small reserves that Northern Command already has in place. That will give the Indians no choice but to ignore our operation against Daulet Beg Oldi, plus whatever else the CMC may approve."

"What we can possibly plan on for a subsequent phase that could be launched whenever the Politburo decides is the invasion of Bhutan. Already, we have a built up case for extending our claims into Bhutan by our periodic patrols into the Doklam Plateau. We could simply allege firing by the Indians at Tri Junction in Sikkim. We can claim it leaves us no choice but to walk into our claimed area of Doklam to turn the Indian flank at Tri Junction. We could also prod the Maoist government to be formed in Nepal to ask us for help to resettle the hundred thousand 'Bhupalese' people of Nepalese origin who were kicked out of Bhutan. Many of them will volunteer to go in as guerillas and create chaos in Bhutan for us to restore order."

CHAPTER 24
TARGET!

COOL, CALCULATING, UTTERLY RATIONAL IN HIS chilling professional approach, Brigadier Syed Ali remained up-to-date with developments around the world in the niche history of his chosen craft, terrorism. He would, of course, look at it with a different perspective as an Islamist Pakistan national and not just a Pakistan citizen. Reconnaissance by day and research by night so that no detail of relevance missed his eye for want of effort was all part of his self-developed discipline. The goal had to dictate the target and not the other way around. He functioned like a lone wolf—always alert, with stealth, registering minute shifts in the atmosphere and confident in his craft while he short-listed his options.

Syed Ali was more than aware that so-called Western decadence and imperialism providing an infinite list of attractive targets for terror attacks no longer held as true as it had three decades ago. It was the nature of success that brought in the law of diminishing returns. In the decade of the 1970s, the target of choice that guaranteed instant and rapt attention of the world's wannabe terrorist revolved around aircraft. The hijacked-aircraft and the bombed-aircraft themes held sway over many terrorist groups' imaginations as arrival statements on the world stage, particularly when it came to international flights or hijacked local flights flown to international destinations. Sure enough, aircraft security and airport security adjusted to raise the ante with strong-arm measures, including tighter baggage rules, explosive detectors, sniffer dogs, restrictive access, terror profiling, and many other steps at a huge inconvenience to the travelling public. Never mind the billions of dollars it cost.

Terror groups' attention and innovation had quickly shifted to attacking embassies, because media coverage was almost equally rewarding in the 1980s. Once again, vigorous countermeasures that followed from the most affected countries called for further diversification of the target list. Deputy CIA Director Admiral Bobby Inman, his mindset more devious than most talent available in terrorist hands, quickly recommended robust, commonsense-building architecture and security features for US embassies. Inman, thus, set the gold standard for fortified, America-style embassies that would possibly require a small army to take out. The poorer countries, however, would remain vulnerable in this area, for they found it impossible to spend the huge sums of money that better security was priced at. Syed Ali mentally struck embassies off his list.

The terror evolutionary cycle from 2004 had brought in a more universal target; premier hotels where Western businessmen were staying, striking deals, entertaining, and being entertained at any time of the day. These were places where the local elite, intelligence operatives, and diplomats rubbed shoulders. Hundreds of desirable individual and collective targets attended conferences and banquets at five-star hotels. By their very commercial nature, these establishments existed to rake in large amounts of dollars in every imaginable fashion but at a potential cost to some.

Heavy-handed security destroyed the ambience of these places, and effective countermeasures to enhance protection remained wanting because of cultural, commercial, and political reasons. Each hotel needed to maintain a façade of peace and tranquility and class that encouraged hordes of customers who would eat, drink, shop, play, engineer sexual encounters, and display oodles of bare flesh to create a paradox with the streets immediately outside. Any display of the spirit of hedonism was hated by the terrorist and became a desirable target to be shattered to pieces with explosives and gunfire and arson, leaving blood-splattered streets and rubble and grieving families and a benumbing sense of helplessness and frustration in civil society.

Brigadier Syed Ali was a great believer that a trained militant should preferably be as average-looking as he or she could seem in a given setting. He was all in favor of a surveillance operator wearing off-the-rack, decent quality clothes, being neither fat nor thin with a medium built and features that did not attract attention and easily regressed in the memory of watchful guards and anyone passing by. Effective surveillance needed enough cash—for coffee in a restaurant or to shop in stores or for two or three people to meet in a large reception area for half an hour in a manner that attracted little attention.

The same level of security that existed in a typical Western embassy, such as full screenings of all visitors and their belongings, was virtually impossible to promulgate in a hotel. Dismantled weapons and improvised explosive devices (IEDs) were not difficult for guests to sneak into hotels when they were concealed in luggage. Complacency and boredom setting in amongst the watchers when nothing remotely resembling a terrorist attack had taken place for years was great justification for not upgrading security and perhaps downgrading it several notches, especially during an economic downturn.

Like hemlines on women's skirts moving higher during a recession, terror countermeasures pointed toward exercising economy of effort for the greatest rewards for regrouping or small terror groups that do not have the resources of larger organizations like the Taliban. Instead of building larger bombs to inflict sustained damage on iconic buildings and upstage barricades with vehicle-borne improvised explosive devices (VBIED), the neater solution pointed in the opposite direction and minimized scale.

Small-scale attacks by multiple suicide bombers sneaking in small, cheap IEDs to fight detection created enormous flexibility for the masterminds behind these attacks. Whereas VBID tended to be in discriminatory as a general rule, the individual bomber was a lethal smart weapon that could switch targets at will or switch off temporarily as it awaited better opportunities.

A woman carrying explosives in a handbag or concealing some under her clothes to look pregnant or in her bra to look voluptuous was a much more fluid presence than a man, and the woman could also maneuver through gaps in security, successfully seeking her prey. It appeared counterintuitive at times, but the record of VBID versus small IED showed that more foreigners or more desirable targets were knocked off per small IED than in the case of a big-bang VBID. The greater the number of innocent bystanders killed and wounded from the local population, the more likely the local population would turn against the terrorist. This was one more reason to move away from the big-bang approach.

Syed Ali instinctively favored always including hotels alongside other targets. The challenge of balancing guest comfort and customer service at large hotels was an insolvable problem, especially in India. The 26/11 Mumbai experience not withstanding terrorist attacks were regarded by profit-conscious hotel managers as a problem that someone else would confront, not them. At an individual level, it was disregarded completely, making institutional measures into a cosmetic, "best practices" routine. There was, however, an incremental increase and more visible use of magnetometers and X-ray machines and deployment of protective intelligence and counter-surveillance human assets to keep up with what the business opposition was projecting to woo customers.

It was still uncommon in India to co-opt the hundreds of cooks, housekeepers, valets, bellboys, gardeners, maintenance men, construction workers, and the hundreds of visits made by trades-people with deliveries of food, flowers, and shopping replenishments into an effective neural intelligence system that could help to identify would-be perpetrators of violence. This kind of network was easy to evolve immediately after a strike but soon fell into disuse in an environment where lightening was not expected to strike twice in the same place.

So the cat-and-mouse game of terror versus anti-terror continued. The leading innovators in tactics, strategy, and sheer daring in execution amongst terrorists continued to be firmly a step or two ahead of those who sought to stop them. As militants adopted new tactics, security measures were then implemented to counter these tactics. The security changes then caused the militants to change in response, and the cycle began again. Syed Ali had a unique perspective in this evolution from designing the safeguards commonly used by the Pakistan Military and commercial establishments like hotels and banks in the major cities to promoting innovation to wreck the same safeguards in Afghanistan and India.

The first step of his journey was complete. The big target had to be Delhi for a worldwide impact. The other metros of India were much lower on the scale of importance. Mumbai had already been done a few years previously and had actually resulted in only minimal changes in the security establishment, except for the upgrading of the cosmetic variety of security in hotels and in coastal water's intercept capability by deploying additional small craft. After a few months of posturing and threats by the Indians of going to war against Pakistan, it was business as usual, including meetings between the prime ministers of both countries.

There were, however, some important lessons that needed to be kept in mind from that episode: Strike the rich and the influential. Otherwise, the event would be swept under the carpet all too quickly. Bombing the *bazaars* or shopping places and gathering areas of the poor made for fleeting impacts, creating isolated headlines at best. Don't leave evidence behind that can incriminate the real perpetrators. Cell phones in particular were a no-no, as they were too easy to trace later. The Jihadists involved needed to know very little and preferably nothing of the high-level plot so that they could not give it away under interrogation if taken alive. Keep it simple! Put in the knife where the nation's pride and self-image is at stake and the media would ensure its popularity.

Now that you have chosen Delhi, fill in the gaps, Syed Ali thought. *What can you do to bring Delhi to a halt and make India appear helpless and impotent and incompetent in the eyes of the world? Hijack an aircraft? It appeared difficult with so much security around the airport without a full-scale attack that would have no guarantee of success.*

Attack a hotel perhaps? It would need to be timed with some large international conference at the very least.

Kill a minister? It will probably be easier to organize a hit with a suicide bomber.

Bomb a shopping market? Easy enough, but will not bring the city to a halt. Bomb half a dozen markets? Better than a single market event and not too difficult but still not a country-stopping event.

He ran through a random list in his mind—Humayun's Tomb, VIP colony at Lodhi Road, the Indraprastha power station, cinema theatres. Multiple strikes definitely would create impact, but targets needed to be carefully chosen. He knew the answer would come. He needed to sleep on it. *Read all the local papers every day and listen to the news,* he thought. *Weaknesses are ruthlessly pointed out by the media. Only need to pick up the signals.*

Timing—let's see when any or all of it should be done, he then thought. *Seemed simple enough—when it rains. Delhi will come to a halt on its own. Reactions from police and armed forces will get tied up in traffic. It will have all the makings of a potential black swan event if boosters are put in place. July, August, September during the monsoon months preferably, except the first half of August when security was at it's tightest during the Independence Day celebrations that took place annually on August 15th. Also, not in early July, as the rains may be late or later half of September; the monsoon may withdraw early.*

So that was settled—except that everything would need to be in readiness and standing by for a much longer period. Weather reports would narrow it down.

What about the exact timing of the attack? Preferably at night or before dusk, so it is easier to organize a getaway if required. This will also cause more chaos with important functionaries who have to deal with it back home or on the way there. Not too late at night in any case, as initial impact will be missed by a sleeping city. Much more effective before people go to sleep after a long day working. Also before newspapers commence printing!

Resources required for the strike with the normal complement of small arms, grenades and night vision goggles? Too early to say, but for multiple strikes, multiple teams are required. Say half a dozen targets with two-man teams makes twelve. Maybe a couple of drivers added if locals cannot be used for some things makes fourteen. Some safe houses to keep them separate, at least for now.

He continued, *IEDs will definitely be useful, and of course, someone top-of-the-line to make explosives from precursor chemicals after reaching Delhi preferably. All told, eighteen to twenty trained people maximum and at least eight to ten. It may be better to use a combination of potential Jihadists either from the Jaish-e-Mohammad from the Bahawalpur camp or the Lashkar-e-Taiba lot from Lahore to confuse the investigators later. The Hizb ul Mujahidin could be used to get the armament and other logistic requirements across the LOC in exchange for payment in kind to build up their own arsenal. HUM could easily truck the stuff in small consignments to Delhi through their own transportation workers.*

It would be prudent to arrange lots of spare cell phones and SIM cards to cater to contingencies that were certain to arise. It was trite but true. He had long known that the only certainty was uncertainty in this business. *Don't forget diversionary strikes. Tap embedded resources for gathering information. Getaway routes through Nepal may be best. Where else? Sleep on it. The answers will come.*

He was headed home in a taxi as he mentally recalled the place in Gurgaon where he had made his base for over a decade. It was an outstanding location within two hundred meters of a small police station, and for that reason, it would never be suspect. The house had a seasonal watercourse running fifty meters behind it, with some pools of stagnant water. There was no habitation, not even beyond the watercourse for almost three hundred meters, because the area had an uneven, stony feature unsuitable for construction. There was fallow land immediately behind the house that could be developed into a garden and would explain the periodic use of a vehicle or tractor to bring in fertilizer and gardening necessities.

Brigadier Syed Ali had also arranged long-term leases for three small apartments in low-rise buildings with minimal security in outlying areas of Noida and Faridabad, paid for in cash with minimal documentation signed with fictitious names. He had insisted on telephone and Internet connections being available in all three places. One-on-one communication was established between himself and the three users of his potential hideouts by utilizing the excellent Dropbox service accounts. Dropbox gave 2GB of storage, and it was accessible from computers, from the Web, and even from mobile phones. He could now open separate Dropbox folders on his own laptop, linking one each with the three hideouts, and share information, because the folders were synced with each other.

He was as much at home now in Gurgaon as any place in his own country that could be called by that name with reference to time spent there. And as had happened to him so frequently in his life as soon as he permitted his mind to dwell on the mass of data and logic, the sheer obviousness of what should have been his primary target hit him as if with a hammer.

Syed Ali had always believed that to make a successful operational plan, the commander needed to be present at the spot where he wished to bring his resources to bear. Because part of the choice lay in your sixth sense in the synthesis of many things that the brain did not logically seize upon—the air you breathe, even the foul, polluted air of Delhi, the sounds you hear, including the barking of dogs and cacophony of traffic, the ineffable something in the gait of the man on the street, and the play of streetlights on fleeting objects—understanding fully without the trained eye on the ground was impossible. Never would he have spotted the obvious from an air photograph or Google Earth or any number of reports or even eyewitness accounts.

CHAPTER 25
AND THE RAIN CAME DOWN

IT WAS FALLING IN PLACE BIT by bit. Disciplined thinking always paid off if you stuck with it for long enough, and Brigadier Syed Ali was nothing if not disciplined. You had to have certain qualities to survive in this business of dealing death. At one end of the spectrum, it was almost a purely intellectual calling where you put aside all preconceived ideas to create a conceptual framework for what you were setting out to achieve. Normally, the man who conceived the big idea was not the one who executed it. Someone else did—someone who was younger, physically fitter with great hand-eye coordination and a passion for action and risk, someone not eroded around the edges by the passage of time. In his case, he was attempting to do both, not only conceive and nurture a simple way to bring down a country of a billion people but to personally oversee much of the groundwork for the process.

The meeting with Mullah Omar after Osama bin Laden's killing had been brief. General Hameed Gul, his old mentor, had once again been a facilitator and had set it up. This occurred the week after he had been forced to put in his request for premature retirement from the army by the new head of the Inter-Services Intelligence, an organization he had served with every ounce of his being for a quarter century. There was nothing personal in it, he understood, but no matter how he rationalized it, there was a lingering regret. That was just how things were. Billions of dollars worth of American aid did not come easily. Sometimes you had to give the Americans what they wanted. In this case, the CIA wanted his head because of his past relationships with Al Qaeda and the Taliban.

However, he had foreseen that something like this could happen and had salted away the financial resources and IOUs for favors done in the past. He had no intention of going quietly into retirement. He had nurtured the Jihad in many ways. Now, in a small measure, he would lead it. Independence for Kashmir that rightly belonged to Pakistan had been the initial driving passion. Now it was a cold, driving resentment against being hung out to dry.

He had known both Mullah Omar and Osama bin Laden from a time when they were all young men blazing with passion and idealism to boot the infidel Soviets out of Afghanistan, when he was the provider of guns and opportunities. Truth be told, he had trained them both in many ways. The relationship dynamic had matured without any rancor over the past two decades. Both of them had run organizations that till recently had terrified the world, and he, Syed Ali, had become a mere bystander, a demeaning step down that he would definitely change as soon as possible.

"You have a year to put this together. The Americans would have largely gone by then. Are you sure that you have sufficient time? If you remember, it took us more than a year of effort before we were able to get Ahmed Shah Masood in 2001," bin Laden asked.

"The Lion of Panjshir was a different sort of target, always on the lookout for an attempt on his life. His knowledge of technology was negligible. He never expected explosives to be in a camera taking his photograph. He was also exceedingly well-guarded, even when he was in bed with one of his women.

"It will be much easier to hit India where it will hurt, as we have a very wide choice of soft targets. I will be able to put alternate plans together in the next three or four months, including spending two months in India to fine-tune them. Thereafter, it is a question of outsourcing the strike to the Punjab-based groups with whom you have good relationships like the Lashkar e Taiba, training the assault teams and putting the logistics resources in place. Say another six months. I am sure that all will be in readiness well before a year is out."

"You will need money and help?" Mullah Omar asked.

To retain operational independence, he said, "I don't need any money for the time being. Later, it will be required when we have to buy equipment and make preparations to put people in place. I have enough for now, and many of my arrangements have been in place for years, since I was with the Joint Intelligence Bureau running operations against India. As for help, it is much better that I work alone right now. It will take a few more weeks, but it will be too much of a security risk to involve other operatives at this early stage. In any case, we have sufficient time available."

A month later as he mused about things gonc by and what lay ahead of him, the downpour hit the taxi he had hired. Soon, the vehicle's speed dropped further from the forty kilometers per hour they were managing in light traffic to half that speed. The next traffic light was not working, and there was no trace of any traffic policeman, as vehicles of all descriptions—two-wheeler scooters and motorcycles, three-wheeled scooter rickshaws, light trucks, heavy trucks, cars of all sizes and shapes from the ubiquitous Maruti cars, diplomat-owned Mercedes to dark, tinted Pajero SUVs, not to mention the bicycles and three-wheeled manual rickshaws—fought for every inch of forward movement.

There was already more than a foot and a half of water accumulated at the crossing from blocked drains. It took twenty minutes to cross the intersection, but by the time they had crossed over, Syed Ali was smiling grimly to himself. One more part of the puzzle was seemingly in place.

Delhi had a lot of pretensions as a world-class city. However, if size was a criterion, it was certainly world class in its spread and demographics, with its fourteen million citizens squabbling over space and clean air and water. Compared to any other city in India, Delhi had more road transport at six million motor vehicles of all sizes and shapes, increasing by 2000 on a daily basis, than Mumbai, Kolkata and Chennai together. Its twenty thousand kilometers of roads were variable in quality and width, but very few, especially in the more densely populated areas, were free of potholes.

There were more than 750 traffic lights with underground cabling that was prone to flooding after an hour of rain, he had learnt from the previous night's Internet search. On any one day, a third of the traffic lights were dysfunctional. Because of a proliferation of competing authorities controlling infrastructure, drainage was a gray area that no one owned. Two hours of rain was adequate to bring the city to a crawl. An accident or two in between and construction work could create the necessary synergy to gridlock traffic for hours. Syed Ali let his imagination soar.

Patiently, he sat at the rear of the cab, sharing a packet of biscuits he was carrying with the cabdriver. The rain eventually stopped, and he instructed the driver to go right. "I want to see Lodhi Garden and Humayun's Tomb." Sightseeing always came in handy while making conversation with strangers, and he had always had a keen sense of history.

For the next six days, he carried out a careful survey of the city at different times of the day before he was satisfied. He also made it a point to have a cup of coffee at some major five-star hotels—Intercontinental, Le Meridian, the Imperial, the Taj, and the Sheraton.

He also walked for hours every day. As an infantry subaltern, that was what he had been taught. "Time spent on reconnaissance is never wasted. Do it on foot yourself." Most intelligence operatives would have frowned on the idea of doing something on foot that could more effectively be done sitting in a vehicle where you could use a camera unobtrusively and make an occasional note as well instead of relying on memory.

The calm, composed look on the face of Brigadier Syed Ali as he walked along the inner circle of Delhi's Connaught Place was misleading. He shuffled with a slight limp that was caused by the thick insole in one shoe in order to disguise his normal, brisk, military walk. Thick sunglasses and graying hair along with a plain white shirt and slate-gray trousers created a nondescript look that attracted no second glances. His slow progress belied the turmoil in his mind and was designed to let his experienced eye take in potential targets. His self-imposed mission was to engineer a paradigm shift in the nature of terrorist attacks that the Indians had chosen to guard against.

Syed Ali had already spent a month in India, moving around from place to place to take in the changes from his last visit a few years earlier. The brand new metro system in Delhi was not only world class or better, but the same could be said for its protective measures as well. CCTVs, alert guards, good management—the metro seemed to have it all. He crossed it out of his mind for the time being. It would need major resources to tackle.

The traffic system was, however, a mess that could be exploited. Movement was largely dependent on traffic lights and blinking lights. One inspector generally controlled this mess from a small room high up at his small perch on the twenty-first floor in the Vikas Minar Income Tax office building overlooking the Yamuna River. A pollution haze ensured that he did not see much on most days and relied on the twenty-two traffic nets, including one totally dedicated to VIP movement. There were just forty traffic inspectors and half a dozen vehicles to troubleshoot. In many cases, heavy traffic ensured that by the time they arrived at any bottleneck, the problem had become a crisis. The million-dollar blimp with pan cameras used the last couple of years for crisis management had never been properly leveraged. It could, however, not be ignored.

The advantages of his long ISI experience as a protégé of successive ISI chiefs were manifold in an operation of this sort. With the sort of informal oversight that he had exercised over the Mujahidin opium trade, he had about five million dollars stashed in accounts in Dubai, Singapore, and Mauritius. He also had smaller, rupee-denominated accounts in India, along with two safe houses near Delhi as self-insurance assets.

Insurance, of course, was not part of the tradecraft that he had learned as a young officer mentoring the Mujahidin. Essentially, at the executioner level, you just walked, walked, and walked and looked and listened to everyone and everything and sniffed the environment. This included the most fetid of places reeking of human waste and polluted surroundings if that was where the trail led. This storehouse of sights, smells, and sounds tucked away in your head was chewed up continuously in the mysterious warrens of the mind and spirit in a way that computers could not replicate—at least not so far.

A slow realization over time, shaded by accumulated experience, would come to pass by this process while he walked. An analysis of what he sought would emerge without apparent effort, and in turn, this would conjure options. In time, he would chose and fine tune one of them to execute.

Over some years, a complete Indian identity for Brigadier Syed

Ali as an Indian Sanjiv Malhotra from Moradabad in Uttar Pradesh had been built up. The actual owner of that name, a widower with no children, had disappeared trekking in Nepal. Being buried had never been a favored means of disposing of a body by Hindus in India who were supposed to be cremated, but that turned out to be Sanjiv Malhotra's destiny at a somewhat early age of forty-five years. Of course, needless to say, his passport was never found, nor was his driving license. Officially, he was still alive. It was always better to work with genuine documents than to fake them completely. A change of passport was easily managed on the basis of a change in permanent residence.

Opening a bank account at the State Bank of India, the biggest government-owned bank singularly lax in following mandated "know your customer" norms, took only a day. Thereafter, opening two more bank accounts to split funds became relatively simple.

Buying a small house with a drive-in basement in Gurgaon bordering Delhi followed. It was a fast-developing township with over a hundred companies from the Fortune 500 list, creating tens of thousands of jobs, many of them in information technology, enabled services for North American and EU clients.

Gurgaon had people pouring into it from all over India and the world, thus guaranteeing anonymity from any established, prying neighbors in newer developments. Enterprising brokers in connivance with government revenue authorities ensured that purchase and lease property transactions went smoothly. The norm in India was to transact such deals with large amounts of cash and perhaps 30–40 percent by a bank draft. Syed Ali arranged for the cash to be sent into India through Nepal. Once there, a linkage with the then royal family ensured that it was transported smoothly across the border into India. Thereafter, for a 50 percent discounted value, the fake currency was transformed into genuine Indian currency notes.

Owning a house created instant credibility and provided identification to install a telephone and an Internet connection. A chartered accountant who was suggested by a contact in Delhi had facilitated the creation of a permanent account number for taxation purposes, and his profession was registered as a consultant.

The fact that a large number of clients of this particular consultant were Indians working abroad was perhaps a little unusual to say the least. They had invariably returned home with large amounts of money after they had lost their jobs. That they deposited large sums into their bank accounts and thereafter paid 80 percent of the deposit amounts to Sanjiv Malhotra in monthly installments for consultancy over many months was equally strange but nobody's concern.

Sanjiv Malhotra was also known to travel frequently to the United Arab Emirates on business for long stretches. In every sense, he was an unmarried, model citizen who paid his taxes and minded his own business. The one thing that really set him apart from the average Indian was the fact that he never ever jumped a red light. Getting arrested for a dumb traffic offense would have been poor tradecraft. He went for long walks around the locality sometimes late at night and had an excellent idea of houses that were unoccupied and the barking and car-chasing habits of stray neighborhood dogs.

An arrangement with the State Bank of India's bill-paying service for paying all invoices with respect to electricity, water, and telephone services ensured that no inconvenient issues would arise during long absences. Unoccupied houses by themselves attracted no notice, because many of them had been bought purely as investments during boom times and remained vacant while new owners were sought. However, they needed to be protected, for which he soon found a caretaker with a wife and two small children and a day job as a mechanic who was happy to find rent-free accommodation in the garage.

His personal habits were Spartan to the extreme, and the thought of using these monetary resources for his personal needs was out of the question. However, because he was no longer part of the ISI now and records for these transactions had never been created, he had decided that he was free to use them to facilitate whatever cause he now espoused.

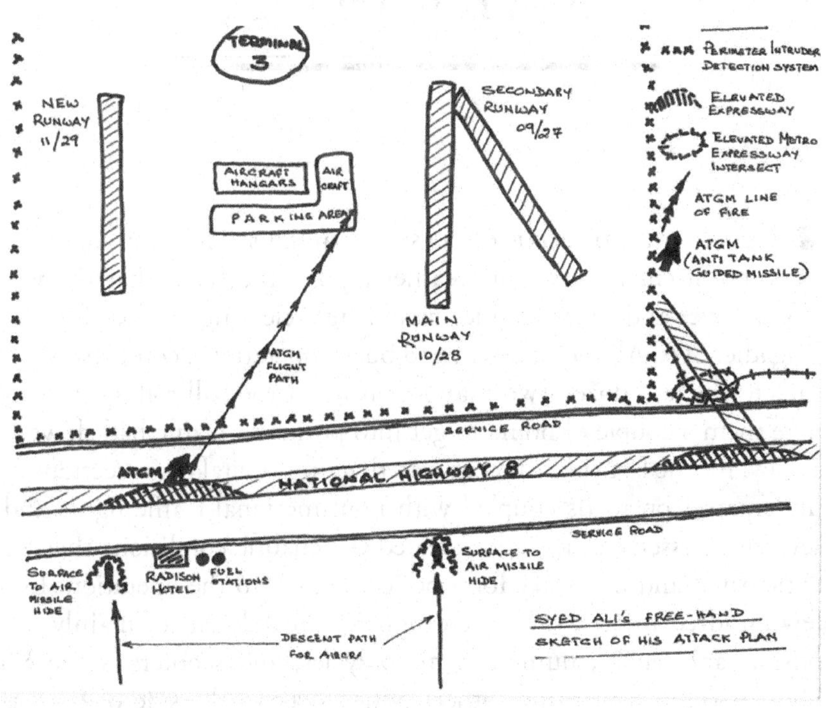

Brig. Syed Ali's hand-drawn sketch of the attack plan

CHAPTER 26
RAPIER THRUST

It had rained more or less continuously for four days with intermittent breaks, but weather reports indicated that the worst was over and that the skies would start clearing by the afternoon. Brigadier Syed Ali took the call and put in operation a complex series of calls to the half dozen two-man teams to set the ball rolling. It would take them a couple of hours to get into position. Traffic had slowed to a crawl for the last three days as waterlogging at vital cross-sections and underpasses on roads coupled with nonfunctional traffic lights and a severely stressed traffic police created the chaotic conditions that were anticipated and necessary for a perfect launch to the operation. Every few hundred meters, there were signs of breakdowns of mainly older buses, cars, trucks, numerous motorcycles, and scooters, some with blinkers on as a warning, others pulled over to the side of both the expressway as well as the service lane.

Indira Gandhi International Airport (IGIA), spread out over an almost-square-shaped area of twenty square kilometers, had graduated from being a seedy, stinking, jam-packed hellhole with overflowing toilets to a gleaming state-of-the-art facility. It was now connected to the city by an eight-lane expressway and the Delhi Mass Rapid Transit system. The new, two-tiered Terminal 3 building that had dealt with thirty-four million passengers the previous year, with arrivals using the bottom half and those departing the top half, provided a world-class experience. Its 160 check-in counters, seventy-eight aerobridges, thirty parking bays for aircraft, seventy-two immigration counters, and fifteen X-ray screening areas, in addition to the ambience created by well-stocked, duty-free shopping and wonderful restaurants, all exuded a general air of efficiency. It was the second largest terminal building in the world after Beijing.

Brigadier Syed Ali took it all in, including the fact that he could have been picked out by any of the four thousand CCTV cameras watching for the smallest untoward move over the more than sixty-five acres of tiles and granite that confronted him. Additionally, window glazing occupied the equivalent of another forty acres of vertical space.

An Israeli intrusion-detection system both physical and covertly included taut wire, buried cable, CCTV cameras, and radars. In addition patrolling by the Central Industrial Security Force precluded anything but a full-fledged attack from breaching the periphery. Security inside the building was watertight as other major complexes in Delhi like the Ministry of Defense, the Parliament Building, and the relatively new metro system were. Elsewhere, such as railway stations, bus terminals, hotels, and shopping areas, it was variable from good to lax.

The answer had been in front of him for days before he had been able to piece it together. Quick-reaction teams of policemen in single vehicles parked at supposedly vital locations were currently engaged in only keeping themselves dry. He looked forward to getting the early reports of his handiwork as soon as he reached his destination. It had taken him three hours to cover a distance of fifteen kilometers to the airport after he had set the wheels of his operation into motion. There was no way that anyone could react quickly in this mess.

"This terminal is so incredibly spacious and well-designed that I don't mind waiting two hours for my connecting flight," said the friendly American woman, a short, sprightly, eighty-something who noticed Syed looking at the ceiling. "The security here is so much better and less obtrusive than anywhere I've been, including back home in Vegas, and everything in this terminal is so classy."

"I could not agree more," Syed replied, smiling down at the diminutive figure. "We Indians seem to have got something right after so many years! Did you know that the counters are Italian, the granite is from Saudi Arabia, the glass that allows in so much light from China, and on the technology front, the state-of-the-art aerobridges from Japan, and the baggage handling and fire safety from Germany?"

As delayed boarding due to a technical snag in the aircraft for his flight to Singapore was announced, he was more and more convinced that his choice of target had been spot on. It was a pity that he had to get away earlier and not see the results of his meticulous plan unfold in front of his own eyes. The Taliban hierarchy had been insistent that they could not take the chance of him being picked up by Indian intelligence, irrespective of the precautions he had exercised. His aim was not just to kill Indians but do so in a specific way.

The loss of life and the potential economic impact of billions of dollars lost aside, the inability of the government to prevent attacks on its own citizens would set back its plans to hold on to Kashmir and negatively influence Indian interests across the world. In all likelihood, the ruling party would lose the next elections, and a weak coalition government would be easier to arm-twist over Kashmir. He couldn't wait to see how the Chinese would grab hold of the opportunity he was about to create. Surely, the PLA would become even more aggressive and constrain the Indian ability to deal with Pakistan even further. He had been really fortunate with the weather in spite of having planned for it. The traffic jams all over Delhi were as good as he could have wished for.

The added bonus was the chance of picking off the prime minister of India and some of his cabinet members with a little bit of luck. The breach of security by a Twitter "tweet" that morning by the junior foreign minister would cost him dearly one way or another. He had accompanied the prime minister and the home minister to Nepal on a crucial two-day visit dealing with a host of crucial security-related issues, including counterfeit currency smuggling into India, insurgent hideouts, and a rapidly increasing Chinese presence in infrastructure projects.

"Wonderful trip to Kathmandu with broad agreement on many issues of mutual interest; I will give an update on some of the things I found of compelling interest after returning to Delhi at 6:00 p.m." The brief "tweet" could not have been more loaded with information.

Barely three kilometers away as the crow flies on the service lane of NH-8, Abu Ismail and Zaki Mohammad, dressed as farmers from nearby areas in off-white pajamas with drawstrings, loose-fitting, long shirts without collars, and loosely tied turbans, were running through a mutually compiled checklist. They were standing next to a battered tractor with the bonnet open, one towing a water tank-mounted trolley with mud-splattered numbered plates. The tractor had all the appearance of having hopelessly broken down. A tractor trolley for conveying water to construction sites was a far from unusual sight, even with the bonnet open. They had already rehearsed this more than half a dozen times.

After they left the key behind in the ignition, the two men moved away from the tractor trolley, carrying loads wrapped in light plastic on their shoulders ostensibly against the weather. They moved down the edge of the service track, avoiding the bumper-to-bumper traffic jam, toward Mahipalpur at a moderate pace, Zaki leading. They also carried large black umbrellas as much for partial concealment as for protection against the weather. Unseen by the men, an elderly farmer accompanied by a much younger woman who appeared to be his daughter observed the scene from the far side of the road.

Twenty minutes after Abu Ismail and Zaki Mohammad were out of sight, the elderly farmer and the young woman unhurriedly walked across the road through the crawling traffic, shut the bonnet, climbed onto the tractor, and very slowly pulled into the traffic on NH-8. A hundred meters down the road, two young men, apparently hitchhikers carrying slim loads covered in waterproof plastic, climbed onto the tractor as well. The tractor labored over the climb onto the flyover overlooking Mahipalpur Village immediately to its right and the airport stretching from the peripheral wall 150 meters to the left and west.

On the crest of the flyover, the tractor appeared to stall and come to standstill. The attractive young woman with breasts the size of large melons that appeared to have a mind of their own, for they swung tantalizingly in the faces of the motorists on the flyover proceeding toward Delhi, was signaling to swing wide of the tractor that again had its bonnet open, signaling trouble.

The two hitchhikers had moved to the front of the tractor and were fiddling with their packages against the comfortably high railing of the flyover. Eight hundred meters away, a number of aircraft were clearly discernible, parked on the tarmac as an aircraft that came in low a few hundred meters ahead of them crossed the highway alignment and sat down swiftly onto the rain-glistened runway, its King Fisher markings clearly legible.

Unknown to Abu Ismail and Zaki Mohammad, a similar scene to what they were enacting was being played out on the far side of Mahipalpur, with two similarly dressed men of medium height parking a battered gray Tata Sumo SUV in a small opening just off the service road some twenty meters short of the first small house of the village. Thereafter, Ishant Khan and Azhar Mahmud opened the bonnet and stuck their heads in to indicate a mechanical problem barely three hundred meters from a police post. Bushes that had grown to more than five feet at places screened them from the post.

The rear seat of the SUV was flat down, and a couple of long packages occupied the booth space and extended to almost touch the front driver's seat. Soon after, both men moved away carrying two long packages wrapped in waterproof plastic and tied with thin nylon clotheslines.

Fifteen minutes later, a vehicle mechanic with traces of oil on his hands and shirt as well as an apprentice boy not more than sixteen years old carrying a small toolbox peered into the bonnet, tightened the battery terminal with a spanner, wiped his hands on a dirty cloth, and started the SUV. Apparently satisfied, Ahmed and his assistant, Fazal, gradually eased the SUV back on to the service track and drove off toward the petrol bunk next to the Radisson Hotel.

IGIA had switched to using a mixed mode of operations on its two operational runways, the main one being utilized by domestic and VIP flights for the most part and the new runway for international flights. Sixty flights were scheduled for the next twenty-four-hour period. Mixed mode meant that flight distances between approaching aircraft on the two different runways was reduced to three nautical miles. As a rough rule of thumb, an aircraft would be touching down on any one runway every two minutes, coming in from the east and flying low across the service lane and eight-lane National Highway Number 8, which ran immediately along the periphery of the airport.

The flight paths for the two runways across NH-8 were about a kilometer apart just before touchdown, adjacent to a flyover on NH-8 and the urban village of Mahipalpur located east of both NH-8 and its service lane. The flyover also overlooked the Radisson Hotel immediately to its east, hugging the service lane on NH-8. Within seventy meters from the entrance to the Radisson that was jam-packed with taxis trying to drop passengers off, there were two fuel stations. These were adjacent to each other with about twenty assorted vehicles in each jostling for space in the restricted area of their premises.

The vehicles in the confinement of the fuel stations also included a replenishment fuel tanker in the fuel bunk closer to the Radisson perimeter wall. The tanker appeared to have an almost-flat tire and was slowly trying to position itself next to the air pressure gauge, which also had a team of two young boys working on repairing tires. Immediately behind the fuel tanker, a dirty white Tata Sumo SUV drew up, blocking any potential attempt by the tanker to reverse.

With a toolbox in one hand and a bag slung over a shoulder, Ahmed, who was accompanied by Fazal, got out of the vehicle after he engaged first gear and locked it up. Ahmed crouched directly behind the tanker, apparently examining something while Fazal walked up to the front of the tanker and engaged the driver in conversation by asking for directions to the next *dhaba* or eating place frequented by the truck trade.

A minute later, the boy and the mechanic, now only carrying a bag and not the toolbox, both walked away separately toward the service road abutting the service station. In a few seconds, they were out of sight behind the boundary wall of the neighboring Radisson Hotel. It was then exactly 5:59 p.m.

The aircraft landing path also passed over the position occupied by Ishant Khan and Azhar Mahmud for international flights on their landing approach to the runway and by Abu Ismail and Zaki Mohammad in the case of domestic flights doing the same. Barely two hundred meters from the boundary wall running along the width of the airport, the two teams could gaze up at the belly of aircrafts touching down at IGIA less than a minute before they actually touched down.

A hundred nautical miles from IGIA, Wing Commander Ashok Kumar, the captain of the prime minister's aircraft, was in a relaxed state of mind as he asked his copilot, Squadron Leader Ramesh Dutt, to take over the controls before they landed. The last couple of days had been tense, especially during the time they had been on the ground at Kathmandu. In spite of the special protection measures taken by the

Nepalese Army to safeguard the prime minister's aircraft and the close watch kept by the commandos of the special protection group, the ultimate responsibility for the aircraft and the prime minister's safety rested in his hands.

He would be glad to see the end of this trip and was already planning the outline of his debriefing at the elite communication squadron office at the Palam Air Base, the Indian Air Force enclave abutting IGIA. The weather had cleared enough for the prime minister's party to be picked up by the Augusta Westland AW101 helicopter operated by his friend and contemporary, Wing Commander Jagat Singh, within five minutes of landing.

The Boeing 737-700 business jet had been delivered in so-called "green condition" at Seattle and custom-fitted by PATS Aircraft Completion Center at Delaware with interiors that included a state room where there was now a conference in progress between the PM and the home minister, meeting room, communications center, and seating for forty-eight passengers, though only half that number, which included a large media contingent, currently occupied the plane.

The aircraft had a state-of-the-art self-protection suite equipped with flares to counter heat-seeking missiles and chaff to counter radar-guided missiles, on-board Internet, advanced navigation aids, and satellite connectivity with encryption. For all practical purposes, it was a flying office from where the PM could do just about anything to run the country, including ordering of a retaliatory nuclear attack. Once on the ground, the aircraft would be guarded around the clock by members of the Garud Commando Force of the Indian Air Force.

CHAPTER 27
RED CHERRY

"So far so good," Abu Ismail remarked as Zaki Mohammad and he jumped over the low boundary wall of the deserted and dilapidated building that they had reconnoitered the previous day. The boundary wall was barely four feet high, but along with the monsoon-fed undergrowth, it provided excellent cover from the service road traffic as they removed the waterproof covering on their loads to reveal two green missile launch tubes, each with a grip stock and a cylindrical thermal battery. The missile rounds had been preloaded in the tubes of the light weight surface-to-air launcher. They were both wearing surgical gloves and carrying Sig Sauer pistols fitted onto belts under their shirts.

"We still have an hour to wait," Zaki said, hunkering down on his haunches to keep his profile below the boundary wall. He had the miniature ELINT (electronic intelligence seeker) with a small antenna perched somewhat precariously on his turban to pick up aircraft radar well before they could see the aircraft.

"I wonder why we have to wait for this particular Boeing 737?" his partner and lifelong friend asked once again. He would position himself at least fifty meters away as instructed by Havildar Sher Khan, formerly of the Pakistan Army's elite special services group. Khan had been crippled by his kneecap being shattered by a bullet, protecting former Pakistan dictator and President General Pervez Musharraf. Through the pain, he had still squeezed of a shot between the eyes of the disgruntled soldier who had single-handedly tried to assassinate Musharraf, an attempt that was hushed up and went unreported in Pakistan.

"Get as close in as possible to the landing area and under the fly path and wear surgical gloves so that your fingerprints are not left on the launcher," Sher Khan had instructed. "If you are close enough, it is impossible to miss a target more than a hundred feet long, especially if it is a commercial aircraft. Even the most advanced protection system in the world needs a few seconds to activate. If you shoot up toward the belly from directly under the aircraft, in two to three seconds, the aircraft will get hit. After that, you need to ditch the launcher immediately. Select a place beforehand where you can cover it and leave it. Preferably, dig a shallow hole in the ground beforehand for this purpose and camouflage it with dirt or rubbish and if possible some vegetation so it is not discovered without a full-fledged search effort."

"We will come to know if we ever get out of this alive," Zaki replied with a nervous laugh. "For all we know, it may be their prime minister! This is definitely a VIP flight. Otherwise, why would we have been ordered this morning not to fire at any plane till 5:58 p.m. and fire at the first one thereafter? Sher Khan had told us that there would be a definite gap of at least two minutes between a normal landing and a VIP plane." Just then, he heard the tiny beep sound growing in intensity, indicating that aircraft radar was in the zone they were expecting. "Are you ready, Abu? This is it. We have just about a minute!"

The Rand Corporation had dismissively observed in a report on the security of Los Angeles Airport that a man-portable, surface-to-air missile was a lesser threat to aviation than a truck or luggage bomb was. The threat was supposedly no more than that of a sniper with a 0.5-caliber sniper weapon, because after all, airliners were designed to fly with the loss of an engine, even if a missile did strike.

Brigadier Syed Ali had also read the report and drawn a different conclusion based on his hands-on experience training Jihadists to fight the Russian Air Force in Afghanistan. The older hand held SAMs were dirt cheap, easily available across the world. They were robust, reliable, relatively idiot-proof to operate, and it was nearly impossible to predict where they could spring up from. Of course, there was a major disadvantage in using these weapons, because plentiful countermeasures were theoretically available to the target. Al Qaeda and the Taliban had virtually stopped planning operations with these weapons for a decade and were focused on suicide bombers and improvised explosive devices innovatively delivered.

He found the idea of using suicide bombers personally repugnant, though he admitted their flexibility and impact imaginatively. He had sent many of his men to die in high-risk operations, but in all cases, they had had detailed contingency plans and resources dedicated to giving them every chance of making it back to safety. He would never have sent a suicide bomber like Al Qaeda in the Arabian Peninsula had in the botched assassination of Saudi Prince Mohammed bin Nayef, a kilo of explosive hidden in a man's rectum! PETN hidden in underwear to be detonated by acid from a syringe was a wasted innovation for bringing down an aircraft on Christmas, a wasted innovation that could have achieved so much more if properly handled by someone like him.

Cyanide pills worn around the neck were another matter. He had always approved of this fallback for cornered operatives faced with imminent capture and thereafter shot full of sodium pentothal or narco, analyzed to extract every iota of information they possessed. Properly motivated men and women would bite into the pills without hesitation.

But what he would do is get his teams into India with each one carrying eight hundred grams of C4 explosive in bearable discomfort in their anal cavities. Four of them had a detonator wrapped in shockproof packing stuffed inside as well—this without any fear of being picked up even by advance body-scanning systems like the newer back-scatter and millimeter-wave gadgets that were reportedly being tested in Mumbai and Delhi airports prior to a projected purchase.

As a matter of abundant precaution, he had chosen to get his teams inside days apart through Nepal, Bangladesh, and Sri Lanka, where screening was far from rigorous. The equipment, of course, had been sent through the porous "Line of Control" opposite the Srinagar Valley. This was thanks to his loyal junior officers in the ISI who had arranged the complex transfer. One consignment had been lost, but that loss had been prudently catered for by him.

It was just too bad that the efficient Stinger missiles were not readily available any more and those that could possibly be refurbished with new batteries and argon gas refills had an inconvenient identification friend-and-foe system that precluded triggering against American- and European-manufactured aircraft. Deliveries of the SA-18 through the Russian-owned company Rosvooruzhenie with end-user certificates generated through the Russian mafia were just too unpredictable to plan on. However, there were tens of thousands of the upgraded knockoff versions of the SA-7 or SA-7b Soviet SAMs abundantly available through the Taliban network, including the HN-5 or Hongying 5 Chinese-made version.

The HN-5 was also known as "Red Cherry" and he had sourced a dozen from Iran just to prove his capabilities to the Taliban. He still had the contacts in the Republican Guards who could be relied upon to get perfectly serviceable, almost new pieces for four thousand dollars each, with a bulk discount of 10 percent. Each Red Cherry with a maximum range of 4.2 kilometers and a ceiling of 2,300 meters had the tail-chase ability to lock onto the engine heat of low-flying aircraft while they clocked mach 1.75. This was good enough, he figured, for his purpose in spite of the drawback of the tiny three-kilo warhead; he would just hedge his bet by using two warheads.

Because he expected a normal approach, Squadron Leader Ramesh Dutt called the Air Traffic Control using his call sign, VVA.

VVA to Delhi: Delhi, VVA arrival in eight minutes. Door now opening in fifteen; request straight-in approach for runway 09.

Delhi to VVA: VVA, you are cleared for the approach to runway 09. Turn right heading 135 to intercept in bound radial. Descending to 26,000 feet call established.

VVA to Delhi: Delhi, VVA cleared for 09. Turning right, heading 135, descending now to 26,000 feet will call established.

Just then, the American Airlines Boeing 777-300ER flying direct to New Delhi from Chicago's O'Hare Airport with 240 passengers, most of them fast asleep, butted in briefly.

A292 to Delhi: Delhi, approach American 292, heavy forty miles out at level 120. Request straight in approach for runway 10, traffic permitting.

Delhi to A292: American 292, copied, turn right heading 140 vectors for ILS runway 10. Descend to level 55. You are number two for landing.

A292 to Delhi: American 292 turning right heading 140 descending now to level 55.

VVA to Delhi: Delhi, VVA established in bound radial. We have the runway in sight.

Delhi to VVA: VVA, over to Tower for runway clearance.

VVA to Tower: Tower, VVA on finals 09 field in sight.

TOWER to VVA: VVA cleared to land runway 09 winds calm.

VVA to Tower: Cleared to land, VVA.

After he activated the power supply to the missile electronics, Abu waited for the electronic supply and gyros to stabilize while his partner, Zaki, did the same with his own launcher. As Squadron Leader Ramesh Dutt, flying barely three hundred feet above their heads, concentrated on getting the landing just right, preferably without the passengers even realizing that they had touched down, both Abu and Zaki put their sights on his tail section and began tracking the 737-700BBJ smoothly they locked the missile on to the plane.

With the planes' near-level flight now, a strong signal of the angular track rate being within launch parameters, a red light in the sight mechanism came on accompanied by a buzzing sound, and Zaki and Abu a fraction of a second later, applying a little depression to cater for the descent rate of the aircraft, each pulled his trigger on the grip stock.

Even before the two missiles had left their tubes, the boosters burned out in the tubes, and the missile was on its way at thirty-two meters per second, rotating at twenty revolutions per minute. Simultaneously, the two forward steering fins as well as the four rear-stub tail fins unfolded. Five and a half meters away and a fraction of a second later, the rocket-sustainer motor activated the boosted speed to 430 meters per second within the first 120 meters, also disabling the final safety mechanism.

Both missiles leaving vapor trails along their near-parallel paths, the lead-sulfide infrared seekers detected all IR radiation below specified wavelengths, tracking in a 1.9 degree limited field of view. The seekers' heads tracked the 737-700BBJ's engine exhausts with an amplitude-modulated spinning reticle, which attempted to keep the seekers' heads constantly pointed toward the target plane. The guidance system of both missiles tracked the movement of the seeker relative to the missile body and used convergence logic to guide the missile toward the target 737-700 aircraft.

In contrast to radar-guided missiles, IR-guided missiles are very difficult to detect as they approach the target. They do not emit detectable radar, and in this case, they were fired from a rear visual aspect directly toward the engines. Situational awareness of altitude and the potential threat was absent, for no intelligence inputs for what was the equivalent of a peaceful sortie were available to the crew. The array of electro-optical sensors in the customized, self-protection suite had a full 360-degree view of the surrounding airspace as the special infrared camera picked up the two missile tracks and locked on to them. The system's electronic brain ran a series of tests to confirm that the two objects being tracked were actually missiles rather than merely something on the ground that appeared to be a threat.

The system was designed to disregard background clutter, such as a sun glint, but no one had generated an algorithm to cater for an eight-kilometer-long traffic jam and thousands of IR spots. By the time the invisible beam of eye-safe, infrared energy was generated by the small laser in order to introduce false targets into the two missiles' guidance system and turn them away from the prime minister's plane, it was a millisecond too late for evasive measures.

What did happen was the following: Simultaneously, the decoy flares were automatically dispensed and activated once the live IR missiles were detected. The flares burned at thousands of degrees, which was much hotter than the exhaust of the jet engine, and the IR missiles would supposedly seek out the hotter flame then, believing it to be an aircraft in afterburner or the beginning of the engine's exhaust source. The missiles' seeker head of both was, however, too close to the plane to be diverted from its track. As both of the men watched the aircraft recede and start sinking below their visual lines of sight beyond the perimeter wall of the airport barely three hundred meters from their location, two bright flashes lit the horizon in the fading light, and an explosion sounded.

It was perhaps the fact that both missiles were launched from fifty meters apart that may have been responsible for the fact that each missile homed in on the exhaust of a different engine on the port and starboard wings before they exploded, resulting in a near-simultaneous loss of power.

VVA to Tower: Mayday, Mayday, Mayday. VVA hit by ground fire. Turning right, launching flare.

> Delhi to TOWER: VVA cleared right. Any assistance required?
>
> Tower to American 292: Go round, direct to SSB VOR. Climb to level 55. Change now to Delhi approach.
>
> American 292 to Tower: American 292 copied, climbing to 55, proceeding to SSB, changing to Delhi approach.

SSB was Sikanderabad, approximately forty nautical miles east of Delhi Airport, where aircrafts approaching to land on runways 11, 10, or 09 had to hold in case of missed approaches. It was also close to the Hindon Air Force Base.

The hydraulic system or the backup system seemed to hold for a few seconds as the pilots struggled to hold the 737-700 level without power before, as if of its own volition, the dying aircraft veered of the runway and crashed into the ground floor of terminal three at 160 knots an hour. Dozens of waiting and transiting passengers near the glass façade overlooking the runway, including Brigadier Syed Ali, watched in horror as a berserk plane slammed square into the terminal. The wings and the mutilated engines came off, slamming into hundreds of terrified commuters as the plane left an imprint just marginally bigger than its size on the façade of the 1.5-billion-dollar terminal.

There were approximately eight thousand people in the terminal that evening when the fuel tanks exploded. There was fire and smoke everywhere within seconds as the blast effect left everyone in the terminal numbed with shock. What had been a disciplined and slightly bored lot of eight thousand or so occupants became a howling, panicked mob, each one looking for escape from the snarling, twisted metal monster that had invaded their minds and bodies. When the final count was done, 489 people would be dead, and 1,146 seriously injured. The prime minister of India and two of his cabinet colleagues, along with twenty-nine others who had accompanied them to Nepal, would figure in the statistics of the dead.

With the distant sound of sirens ringing in their ears, Zaki and Abu put the missile tubes into the shallow hole they had dug near the derelict building and used a broken branch to brush away the traces of digging. They then threw some building debris on top of the spot. From ten meters away, it was difficult to see that the ground had been disturbed in any meaningful fashion. Singly, they walked away from that spot and toward another spot, where they had left the tractor trolley half a kilometer away. Someone would have moved the tractor trolley away by the time they reached the spot where they had initially parked it.

Zaki and Abu had a long walk of a couple of hours ahead of them before they could take a chance and get into a bus that would take them far away from the national capitol region and onward to Nepal subsequently. It had begun to drizzle a bit again, and it gave them an excuse to open their umbrellas and hide part of their faces.

If they had looked back, they may have been able to make out the rear outline of their tractor trolley and a feminine figure carrying a bag slung over one shoulder, frantically waving traffic around it.

CHAPTER 28
SYNERGISTIC STRIKES

"FORGET THE SAUDI ARABIAN AND CHINA Airlines planes!" Alamgir cautioned as Saif coolly positioned himself like he was back in the classroom.

"The Delta first—then we'll see!"

Saif was thrilled to have been chosen to be the first to handle this great piece of equipment in Pakistan—the 9 K 115-2 Métis-MS Russian antitank missile system. NATO forces called it AT-13, Saxhorn-2. Designed by the KBP Instrument Design Bureau with a length of 980 mm and diameter of 130 mm, it weighed only 13.8 kg and could be easily carried for long distances by anyone in reasonable physical condition.

Saif and his partner, Alamgir, were in superb condition after months of grueling training, including a final march of forty kilometers, before their handler was satisfied. The high-explosive, antitank warhead could penetrate 850 mm of explosive-reactive armor. The Russians had field-tested it more than satisfactorily against the Israeli Merkava tank by the simple expedient of funneling it to Hezbollah through the Iranians during the 2006 Lebanon conflict. The semiautomatic guidance system with commands transmitted over a wire link worked like a dream, and there were no problems about minimum range, because the missile was active eighty meters out from launch. A range of 1,500 meters was more than adequate for this mission.

Saif Ali Khan and Alamgir knew that they would definitely be able to take out one of the huge targets that the immovable passenger jets provided out in the open on the tarmac. Firing the first missile would not take more than twenty seconds from the time he rested the launcher on the side of the bridge. The problem could occur on the second launch if some foolhardy driver going around the tractor tried to interfere. This was unlikely, but Alamgir would take care of that with just the throwing knife to keep it quiet. Using submachine carbines would perhaps invoke an unnecessary response if nearby police patrols were vigilant.

The third launch would be interesting, as there was a limit beyond which Zubaida's ample charms would be hard-pressed to distract, and the four of them would have to fight their way out! Saif Ali Khan squeezed off the first antitank guided missile, holding the sight steady on the fuselage of an Air India plane, and he felt his excitement build at the flash of the strike.

Before he could center on the adjacent Delta Airlines aircraft, there was a huge explosion as the C4-crammed IED placed on the long member of the tanker at the petrol bunk next to the Radisson was remotely triggered by Ahmed, and the twelve thousand liters of petrol in the tanker caught fire and exploded in a fireball engulfing the petrol bunk and the service road jam-packed with slow-moving vehicles, a fireball that spread to the Radisson Hotel and a neighboring petrol bunk.

In thirty minutes, the fire would spread to buildings of the village, narrow lanes blocked with all manner of construction material, stockpiled commodities, and piles of rubbish. Ultimately, seventy fire tenders would be involved for the next three days in putting out the fires raging all across the village, fanned by gusting winds.

A series of detonations followed in quick succession. Mangled bodies and cars were flung into the air, and the adjacent petrol bunk also caught fire. The boundary wall of the Radisson crumpled like paper with the blast, and a spate of secondary fires broke out. The blast tore through the windows on the side of the Radisson, and the hundreds of fragments of masonry seriously injured three bankers holding a meeting in a third-floor room.

Two women and a man engaged in a romp in a corner room on the top floor were hit by dozens of small fragments in non-vital areas all over their bodies and eventually crawled out nude onto the fire escape under the full glare of searchlights and TV cameras. The confusion in the Radisson was compounded further by Ahmed and Fazal, who hurled three grenades over the partially destroyed boundary wall of the hotel while they were walking away from the scene.

The explosion hurled two flaming motorcycles and pieces of flesh high in the air, all of which landed on the flyover onto two passing cars. This brought the crawling traffic toward Gurgaon to a complete halt as a woman driving a brand new SUV near one of the cars hit by the flaming motorcycle panicked. Accelerating wildly as she tried to get away, she hit the car directly in front of her and frantically swung right and rammed into the side of a small bus.

On the far side of the flyover, where Saif was coolly swinging his ATGM launcher toward the next target, the shock of the explosion also unnerved traffic proceeding toward Delhi. With a continuing cacophony of horns being pressed, no one was interested in Saif picking off the next two aircraft fuselages, selecting a Northwest Airlines Dream liner and an Air France Airbus. At the same time, Alamgir dropped two grenades on to a police patrol vehicle on the service lane below them. The resulting explosions created more confusion but only resulted in minor injuries to passersby and the three police men in the vehicle.

Meanwhile, at 5:30 p.m., while the SAM teams were moving into position, a series of Syed Ali's other time-planned actions unfolded in slow motion. The process was decontrolled in the sense that none of the participants carried cell phones or were even aware that they were part of an elaborately and innovatively choreographed effort.

Barely a kilometer from one of the SAM teams, there was a busy intersection at the point where a road's junction from National Highway 8 veered off left toward the domestic terminal of IGIA. National Highway 8 continued toward Delhi at this point over a flyover. A cloverleaf design also ensured that road traffic from Delhi could be guided toward the airport with an elevated metro line on concrete piers running transversely across it some fifty meters from the junction. The intersection also catered to streams of traffic proceeding to and from the airport.

The metro link was crucial to moving passengers to and from the airport from Connaught Place, where a direct check-in facility existed that also moved in baggage that was thereafter loaded directly onto various flights. During rainy weather, the metro link was crucial to enable passengers to arrive at the airport comfortably without risking delays in road-bound traffic.

It was near the junction that a tractor trolley carrying an assorted load of bricks and sand, two small concave containers covered with a plastic sheet, and four men equipped with spades and shovels turned off the concrete road. They headed across an open stretch of ground interspersed with monsoon-produced shrubs for the first pier of the overhead rail connection.

The pier supported one end of a twenty-meter concrete span passing directly over the cloverleaf of the flyover carrying traffic to the airport. Two trucks with bricks loaded on them were standing fifty to sixty meters away, apparently unattended. The tractor trolley came to rest so that it largely blocked a view of the bottom of the pier from passing traffic.

Three men dressed as labor unloaded the contents of the trolley near the pier and appeared to fill a rain-created depression near the pillar. Wearing his week-old stubble, similarly dressed in a faded white shirt and slate-colored trousers, the fourth man squatted on his haunches and smoked a mutilated cigarette that he fished out of his shirt pocket. He looked disinterestedly toward the traffic intersection where a police mobile-patrol vehicle was parked facing away from him. After about twenty minutes, the three men apparently finished with the task of unloading the contents of the trolley next to the pier and walked away in the direction of the national highway.

Salim, the cigarette-smoker, stayed put for another five minutes and waited till the three were out of sight before he walked across to examine the work done. Thereafter, as he carried a small bag slung on one shoulder, he walked leisurely toward the intersection two hundred meters away and mingled with a crowd of people waiting impatiently for a bus. Traffic was barely moving, and the constant honking by impatient drivers created a deafening impact.

Brigadier Syed Ali research had made him aware that concrete is a tremendous building material, strong when reinforced and kept in place especially when compressed through pre-stressing techniques. Reinforced concrete pillars supporting the metro line above the flyover had been extensively tested for quality to withstand thirty years of wear and tear. However, concrete is a form of ceramic, with weak lateral strength. Subject to high-velocity explosive shock, it shatters like glass. Once broken, the sheer weight of the broken member tends to pull the adjacent structure down with it.

Concrete supports can be brought down by a ridiculously small amount of explosives. The key to this easily deployable device is detonating the opposing charges at exactly the same time by means of electric detonators or equal-length detonating primacord. When the shockwaves meet in the center of the pillar and attempt to reflect off each other, massive structural damage is created through internal pulverization of the concrete.

He had done the back-of-the-envelope calculation himself more than six months earlier. He had multiplied the diameter of the pillar he estimated at not more than 1.5 meters by the constant five that he recalled from the engineering field manual for Pakistan army engineer regiments. He had added a 25 percent cushion to the result of 7.5 pounds of explosive required, which dictated a total requirement of ten pounds. He figured a maximum of five pounds placed in two suitable concave containers on opposite sides of the pillar to conform to the pillar's shape would bring about the desired result. The collapsing metro span would fall on the airport expressway and kill two birds with one stone, bringing both road and rail traffic to a grinding halt.

Brigadier Syed Ali had left the exact configuration in the hands of Akhtar Ahmed, the fifty-year-old explosives and electronics genius who entered India through Mumbai on a Turkish passport, one of many that he kept for a rainy day. Syed Ali trusted Akhtar because of his professionalism and competence from their days together fighting. At least Akhtar's motivation was clear-cut, and he would make no mistakes. He was doing it for the money, half of which was sitting in his Dubai bank. Fifty thousand dollars for a week's work at what Akhtar construed was a calling was not bad going, he reckoned!

Akhtar Ahmed was a true pro who made his own C4 explosive in small batches for ease of handling that would easily detonate at eight thousand meters per second. He had given a list of accessories that needed to be bought and kept before his arrival so that no time was wasted. It included glass jars, a simple filtering apparatus, sawdust, aluminum foil, heat-resistant containers, protective gloves and eye protectors, tubing, wire, alcohol, rat poison, small nails and bolts, ammonium nitrate fertilizer bags, acetic anhydride and para formaldehyde, petrol, and motor oil.

He also specifically asked for a high-speed, low-noise exhaust fan to be fitted in his workspace to get rid of poisonous vapors arising out of his brewing efforts. However, he insisted on going with Syed Ali to Tilaknagar, the largely unregulated chemical market in Delhi's famous Chandni Chowk, to procure the PIB (polyisobutalene) binder plasticizer he needed. This was commonly used as a calking compound. Another common plasticizer he selected was ethyl hexyl sebecate.

He first made the RDX using a simple seventy-year-old process invented by the Germans that required hardly any equipment. After he placed a measured amount of acetic anhydride in a very large jar, he added about four times the amount of ammonium nitrate and heated the mix in a pan with cooking oil to 80 degrees Celsius. Thereafter, he added small portions of para formaldehyde, which produced poisonous fumes that were both hazardous and flammable. With cooling and filtering, he got fine white powder from the crystals that then formed.

Syed Ali then took powdered PIB and dissolved it in five times the amount of unleaded petrol. He next added a larger quantity of ethyl hexyl sebecate and motor oil to the mix. RDX and petrol were added, and a uniform mixture was formed, rolled out, and allowed to set. This mix was kneaded and set till the petrol smell vanished. The final C4-equivalent product was light gray in color and had the consistency of stiff putty. Akhtar insisted on using a modified, long-range, cordless telephone that he had modified to be a detonator. There was no public provider involved, and it was impossible to jam. Cell phones were getting outdated, and in his inimitable way, Akhtar Ahmed was a fashionable geek.

Salim looked at his watch and let the next metro train pass. *Interesting*, he thought to himself. *Instead of the standard four-coach composition, it had six; perhaps to cope with the increased rush owing to the difficulty of road movement. Three minutes to six—the next one would be perfectly timed.* All that he had to do now was press the intercom switch. *Come on. Come on*, he silently urged on the first coach of the metro train as it approached the explosive-laden pillar. *About twenty meters short*, he reckoned. *This is it.* Somewhere at the back of his mind, he registered the sound of an explosion from the direction of the airport as he pressed the intercom switch.

For a moment, nothing much seemed to happen as the explosives detonated. Then, as if in slow motion, the leading coach briefly appeared airborne at eighty kilometers an hour before it crashed into the ground and the tractor trolley near the pillar. There was an ear-piercing screeching of metal as five more coaches followed slowly behind it. Later, it would be confirmed that 1,690 passengers were involved in the crash. Three hundred and ten died, and 729 were injured to varying extents. The carnage on the expressway was unparalleled. The overhead metro span along with the better part of two metro coaches fell directly onto it and crushed two buses and eighteen cars, killing another fifty-three people and injuring 121 in addition.

No dust was kicked up by the crash, because it had rained. Salim felt the rush of adrenaline as he witnessed this display and he squeezed into the packed bus headed toward Delhi.

In the meanwhile, Ishant Khan and Azhar Mahmud were both looking away from the airport, waiting for their default aircraft target—default by virtue of the fact that it would be the first one to fly over their position after 6:02 p.m. In spite of their training, both looked back toward the airport when they heard the loud explosion when Air India 1 crashed into Terminal 3. Distracted and suddenly fearful, they heard the warning buzz for approaching aircraft in their earphones and turned back to pick up the approaching American Airlines flight 292. To their surprise, they saw the approaching American Airlines aircraft beginning to climb instead of flying almost level over their heads as they were trained to expect.

Ishant Khan recovered quickly and swung his sights in one smooth motion as the plane passed overhead at more than two thousand feet and climbing. A half pressure on the grip-stock trigger activated the seeker's electronics and locked the missile on to the ascending plane. As soon as the red light in the sight came on and he heard the buzz in his headset, he applied a little elevation to cater for the climbing plane and pulled the grip-stock trigger fully and had the satisfaction of seeing his missile unerringly lock on to the target.

Seventy meters to his right, Azhar Mahmud panicked and did not wait for the red light in his sight before he pulled the trigger. At once, his missile leapt away well to the left of the plane and was lost to sight, self-destructing fourteen seconds later.

Captain Greg Mathews, who was piloting the American Airlines 292 with three decades of flying experience retained his cool, and listening to the stricken Air India 1, was half expecting something ugly to happen when he felt his first engine give way and then fought to regain control of the suddenly uneven swing of his aircraft.

A292 to Delhi: American 292, Mayday. Probable missile hit on number-one engine. Turning now to port to take evasive action; have control so far but losing hydraulics. Need to land quickly; will not be able to divert to Jaipur or Agra.

DELHI to Tower: American 292, copied.

At the same time on the Mahipalpur, flyover traffic was flowing in a steady stream around the stricken tractor. No one appeared to be paying attention to Saif Ali Khan aligning his ATGM, partially shielded by the front of the tractor and an umbrella opened out by Alamgir.

Drivers in metropolitan India tended to mind their own business and not get worked up over minor irritants like vehicles broken down in the middle of the road, flagrant breaching of traffic rules by driving on the wrong side, jumping traffic lights, peeing on the road by motorists whenever they felt the need to stop and relieve themselves, pedestrians trying to commit suicide by running across high-speed traffic. Needless to say, a missile launcher at the side of the road was outside their experience. It made no sense but did not seem anything to take personal interest in. Moreover, the sound of the prime minister's crashing plane and subsequent explosion was distracting enough.

Less than a hundred meters away, Ahmed and Fazal walked past the entrance gate of the Radisson Hotel, where a bored security guard with a metal detector was scanning the undersides of cars and taxis that were carrying customers into the hotel. A large group of about twenty foreign tourists were standing outside the main foyer, apparently waiting for transport. Ahmed signaled imperceptibly toward them with his chin, and Fazal immediately took the sling bag and moved a few steps away from the entrance toward the peripheral wall of the Radisson, a wall that was not illuminated.

Fazal dug into the open bag and quickly lobbed three grenades toward the group. The first grenade landed right on top of the group of foreign tourists, ripping into the guts of a group of five. The next two dropped farther away but created more carnage amongst a mixed group of hotel employees carrying luggage, a group of four Indians entering the hotel, and two taxi drivers in the process of helping out their passengers. Ahmed watched the impact of the strikes for a few seconds and walked away along the darker side of the road. Some distance ahead, he could see the boy, Fazal, still carrying the sling bag, headed in the same direction, slowing his stride so that he could catch up with him.

CHAPTER 29
CRASH LANDING

There had been no time for diplomatic niceties. On his way back to Delhi, Ambassador Gerald Johnson, long-term contributor to the Democratic Party, had reacting instinctively, especially after a meeting in the state department. He called up the president directly. Fortunately, following worldwide regulatory trends in other parts of the world, cell phone calls from US carriers had been permitted in India only recently after many years.

"Jack, this is Gerald Johnson. I'm aboard American Airlines 292 circling Delhi after a missile strike on my plane. Delhi is a mess. There are fires and explosions all over the airport. The pilot is struggling to control the aircraft. We need help to land somewhere close!"

"Leave it to me, Gerald. I'll take care of it!" the president said and brought to bear the power and prestige of the most powerful man on earth.

Chairman of Joint Chiefs of Staff and General Joseph Stone had never been called by the president directly and was surprised to get a call at 3:30 a.m. He, however, answered, "Good morning, Mr. President." He spoke in a neutral voice, as if he had been awake all along, listened for all of two minutes, and uttered three words. "Yes, Mr. President!"

This would have been simple, he thought to himself, *if it had been Pakistan*. Fortunately, he had met Air Chief Marshal Harpal Singh, the Indian Air Force chief, a few times when the latter had been the Indian Air attaché in Washington years ago. He placed the call to him, wondering if Harpal would deliver and how long he would survive in the "control the stupid military tightly" atmosphere in New Delhi if he did.

It still took thirty minutes for the Indian Air Force to scramble the MiG-29 fighter jet.

> Delhi to American 292: American 292, you are cleared to divert to Hindon Air Force Base. Follow MiG-29, call sign Tiger 1, coming on your left.
>
> Tiger 1 to Delhi: Delhi, approaching American 292. American 292 from Tiger 1 Follow me. Emergency services have been alerted at Hindon. Commencing descent to four thousand feet
>
> American 292 to Tiger 1: Thank you, Tiger 1. American 292, we have you in sight and following. Descending to four thousand feet, need to carry out one orbit over Hindon to drop our landing gear manually.
>
> Hindon Tower to American 292: This is Hindon Tower. You are cleared to four thousand feet. Follow Tiger 1. There is no other traffic. Cleared to orbit at your discretion.
>
> American 292 to Hindon Tower: Hindon, American 292 losing hydraulics. Stand by for possible crash landing.
>
> Hindon Tower to American 292- American 292 emergency services have been alerted.

When the missile exploded, the copilot hoped for a moment that an engine had suffered an uncontained failure in a state of denial. This happened in spite of Air India One reporting a missile strike a few minutes earlier, but all readings were normal. Then the hydraulic pressures started dropping, and the copilot saw the wing was trailing smoke. The captain could see that the wing was on fire.

Damage, presumably from the missile blast, was concentrated to the left trailing edge along the outboard flap, a place between the engine and the outboard aileron. The outer half of the outboard flap was missing, and the outboard flap track was dangling from the bottom of the wing. About ten feet of the rear spar was missing, and fire-damaged ribs were visible inside the outboard fuel tank. All hydraulic pressure was lost about a minute after the hit, the source said. The low-speed aileron outboard of the damage was supplied by all three hydraulic systems, and there were five spoilers in front of the outboard flap, spoilers fed by the three systems.

Primary flight controls became inoperative, resulting in a total loss of hydraulic pressure, because there was no manual reversion. The stabilizer trim froze, because it was powered only by a pair of hydraulic motors. The crew deployed the ram air turbine with hydraulic pump, but the leaks rendered it ineffective. The crew had problems controlling the aircraft; however, the captain started using engine thrust for control, and he was surprised to find it worked rather well.

The aircraft circled twice while the crew manually extended the landing gear. Greg, the pilot, after he circled the Hindon runway twice while the crew struggled to get the landing gear down, finally lined the aircraft up for a flat, straight-in approach from twenty nautical miles out, following the MiG-29 that climbed sharply instead of touching down to leave the runway clear. His approach and landing speeds were both 180 knots. Having the trim set right when they were hit saved them. The aircraft had flaps retracted, but the brakes worked because they were powered by an isolated hydraulic accumulator.

The crew aimed for the runway, but they were thrown off course and were not properly lined up during touchdown. As it touched down on the runway with the right wheel, the aircraft banked a few degrees to the right, with a slightly nose-up attitude. The aircraft ran off the left side of the runway and went through barbed wires, fences, and dirt before it came to a stop near the fire station. Full reverse was applied, causing a large dust cloud, but even at reduced speed, one wing was almost torn off as the aircraft toppled over on one side.

Gerald Johnson just happened to be sitting on the side that slammed into the ground. His call arguably saved the lives of 220 passengers. However, twenty died, and he was one of them, suffering a severe brain hemorrhage from contact with the side of the aircraft.

Hindon's emergency procedures were superb. The firefighters were screeching to a halt next to the battered, smoking aircraft in under a minute followed by the first of the ambulances. Two Mi-17 helicopter crews had already been scrambled and clearance was being obtained to land them straight into the army's research and referral hospital in Delhi. If only the political leadership in Delhi had had a fraction of the same commitment, hundreds of lives may have been saved.

CHAPTER 30
GROPING IN THE DARK

TWO PRIME MINISTERS DEAD IN THE space of a year was bad news for continuity in governance anywhere. In India, it was especially disastrous, because a murky political process rife with regional overtones and petty politicking had stalled twice. It had managed to throw up, by some sort of miracle or accident, two outstanding, decent, and ethical human beings, both trained professionals before they had switched to politics. Everyone knew that this was not going to happen again. The power brokers would try their best to ensure that lightning did not strike them again after they took the lessons of previous failures to heart.

In a few minutes, gaping holes in area security had bought a large part of the city to a grinding halt. Except for an alert air traffic controller in IGIA, no one else appeared to have a clue about what had struck the city. The fire services at the airport were stretched. Traffic jams all over the city were getting worse by the minute. Along NH-8, all traffic had come to a complete halt. No one knew who was in charge. The police commissioner was barely a month old in his job. No clear-cut lines of authority existed in Delhi because of traditional conflicts between the chief minister of Delhi, an elected politician, and a myriad of central government ministries run by bureaucrats who did not take orders from anyone but their own bosses.

To make matters much worse, a few hours later at 1:00 a.m. the following day, a thirty-gigabyte denial of service attack was initiated from unknown quarters directed at the government and military structure, the power network, railways, air traffic control, the telephony, and media system, and it continued for several days. It was estimated that it involved at least 10 percent of the three million machines available as robot-networks. These were shared or sold as portions of networks to each other and participated unwittingly in this attack. Fortunately, the limited Internet penetration in India meant that, apart from the metros, some semblance of normality in the rest of the country was achieved by late evening. The attacks on the infrastructure, media, and governance systems finally tapered off after a week, up to which time only disjointed accounts of what had transpired in India appeared worldwide.

Cell phones were off the air from major service providers like Airtel, Vodaphone, and Reliance, telecom used by 80 percent of the population in the metros. By and large, landlines were functional, but most people had become totally dependent on cell phones. In most cases, people had little access to landline emergency numbers. Air traffic was a mess, but at IGIA, a basic decision was taken by the airport authority to not permit any takeoffs and to use the clear runway to permit sixty landings and divert all other traffic. It was a brave decision, because no one was sure that more missiles would not be fired.

All the bosses and decision-makers in Delhi had gone home or were stuck on the roads like everyone else—whether it was the fire department, police, telecom providers, power and telephony providers, the bureaucrats in the home, civil aviation and defense, external affairs ministry, and many others required to function as a team in times of disaster or national emergencies. They were just not available anymore.

There was no one to take the responsibility to get hold of the situation and give directions to the line ministries as the prime minister and home minister, two vital cogs to churn the wheels of government, were no more. As fires raged in Mahipalpur and its Radisson Hotel throughout the night, fire brigades struggled valiantly to reach the spots closest to them. Many drivers had abandoned their vehicles and just walked off into the night, hoping to get a lift to somewhere safe. Many had run out of fuel after hours of static running. Ambulance services were all directed toward the airport for the most part.

At 7:00 p.m., the three chiefs of the armed forces had a chat and decided to step in to restore calm while the political drama of replacing the prime minister was played out. It was decided that the general officer commanding the Delhi area would immediately be ordered to restore the situation and local air force and naval resources could be co-opted into this effort. Because he was the least committed, the naval chief was asked to seek an appointment with the president, nominally the supreme commander of the armed forces, to explain what the armed forces were doing and also to assure her that no coup was in the offering.

Ultimately, the old-fashioned radio network of the army units located nearby and the police saved the day. Fortunately, the general officer commanding the Delhi area and the police commissioner had served together in their younger years and kept in occasional touch. More importantly, they trusted each other and could take calls, knowing that support from the other could be assumed.

All inward access into the disaster area except for ambulances was stopped. By early morning, with vehicles generally crawling out of the cordoned area and very little coming in, some semblance of order was restored, though a thick pall of smoke from the raging fires severely hampered these efforts. The biggest problem was dealing with the three thousand injured.

Hospitals in Gurgaon, Noida, Ghaziabad, and Faridabad jumped into the fray and took in almost twelve hundred people, though it took many hours for ambulances to get through and the last casualty was not wheeled into Artemis Hospital in Gurgaon until the following afternoon. In the chaos, families were separated, injured wives and minor children being picked up and taken to one hospital, their spouses landing up elsewhere. This created much heartburn, but the army soon had its way, saying that saving lives was more important than keeping families together. It would ensure families were brought together later. Importantly, no one died because of not getting treated.

The congress party acted true to its DNA, which dictated "look for a precedent." The nearest one that fitted the bill was more than two decades earlier when Indira Gandhi, the prime minister at that time, was assassinated. Her son, Rajiv Gandhi, an airline pilot, was pulled out of the hat and established as prime minister. Under the guise of a national calamity, due process was given the go by the wheelers and dealers in the congress party. The congress party organizations were totally ignored, and the young dynast, Durga Vadera, less than forty-five years old, was touted as the only one who could save the country from collapse. The country's president was pulled out of bed at four in the morning, and the freshly touted savior was sworn in as the next prime minister of India.

As a two-term member of parliament from Uttar Pradesh, Durga had been reelected by a 78 percent majority for nurturing her rural constituency and doubling rice productivity through corporate involvement. She had answered the opposition charges of rigging the election in her first stint as MP by promptly resigning from parliament, a resignation that was never formally accepted. The election commission inquiry had exonerated her from any wrongdoing to sway the electorate. This purported resignation became the core argument of the coterie for selecting a leader in a time of crisis.

"We want a PM who can display courage and who is not afraid of losing her job." At no time did anyone openly come out with the true criterion for selection—the brand value of her grandmother's name!

CHAPTER 31
THE DAY AFTER

It was close to midnight before the first official reaction from the government of India through the new PM, a somber-looking Durga Vadera in a white sari without embellishment, her head covered in the traditional fashion. She was then beamed to the country in Hindi. It was translated in real time by media channels across the globe.

"My fellow brothers and sisters of this great country, I speak to you at a time of great danger to India and as your new prime minister. It is with the deepest distress that I have to inform you that about six hours ago, an attack by terrorists probably supported by a neighboring country resulted in the shooting down of the plane of our beloved prime minister. He was returning from a successful visit to our neighbor, Nepal. The prime minister and thirty people on board, including the home minister, the minister of state for external affairs, members of the media, and the Indian Air Force crew have all unfortunately been killed. The plane crashed into Terminal 3 at IGIA, and it is feared that there are hundreds of other casualties. Simultaneous attacks were also launched by the terrorists on the metro system near the airport, on aircraft within the airport perimeter, and also the Radisson Hotel, where a number of foreign tourists are feared to have been killed and injured.

"Every effort is being made to provide medical aid to the injured, and all hospitals in the national capital region have joined hands in this endeavor. We are also making our best efforts to contact the near and dear ones of those dead and injured.

"I wish to assure you that we will leave no stone unturned to bring the perpetrators of these acts of terror to justice. We will chase them to the ends of the earth and find them wherever they are hiding, no matter in which country. May God's blessings continue to be with our country and us."

The first of the block to react globally under intense pressure from the US secretary of state was the prime minister of Pakistan, Shamsher Jung Choudhary.

"Madame Prime Minister, I wish to extend our heartfelt condolences to the government and the people of India for the tragic, large-scale loss of life in the heinous terrorist attack on Delhi. I also wish to assure the government of India that in the unlikely event that Pakistan territory has been used in any way in this attack, my government will render all possible assistance in carrying out investigations to bring the perpetrators to justice. Both our countries are victims of terrorism, and it should be our endeavor to work together to put an end to this phenomenon and bring the terrorists responsible to justice."

Outside of the loss of human life officially put down at 1,949 dead and 4,778 injured months later by a commission of inquiry, the immediate economic hit was about eighteen billion in Indian rupees, excluding the cost of four new aircraft completely destroyed. In the weeks that followed, another twelve billion dollars disappeared thanks to lost economic output in the economy. Plus, there was another $560 billion that disappeared from the recovering Indian stock market stock capitalization.

Then the other associated costs began to kick in. Airlines and tourists began to shun India. Valuations of hotels and motels, restaurants, brothels, and the shipping and insurance industry all suffered a 60–70 percent drop. Just in the month of September, at least two hundred thousand people lost their jobs. Another two million jobs disappeared over the next year. The damage to Terminal 3, which controlled the flow of passengers in IGIA, was estimated at close to five hundred million dollars. Worse, it was found technically unfeasible to telescope the construction time to anything less than two years.

This time, the government couldn't look away from it. The main opposition, BJP, after years out in the wilderness of Indian politics, now with a new dynamic leader, was first off the blocks. It castigated the congress for years of national security neglect, taking out rallies and processions in every small town in the country, and squarely blamed Pakistan for the strike. Membership in the party, which was a nominal ten rupees a head, mushroomed at the rate of almost five thousand a day for the first three months. Congress allies found it expedient to keep as far away as possible and blame the Grand Old Party for all the security failures. They pointed out that none of the portfolios that really mattered, such as defense, external affairs, and home, were held by any of the allies. The BJP agreed with the congress allies, widening the rift further, and asked for the government to resign.

Durga Vadera had reluctantly agreed to meet the former atomic energy chief, Dr. Anil Kak, at the urging of Cabinet Secretary Shan Surya, who advised the union cabinet.

"Your predecessor frequently sought his views and was to meet Dr. Kak today in my presence. If he wants to see you now at close to midnight, you can rest assured that it is connected with an issue of high national importance. He wanted me to be present as well."

"Okay, but tell him that he has a maximum of twenty minutes."

Dr. Anil Kak said, "Madame Prime Minister, thank you for humoring me at this critical juncture. I won't take long, but I thought it would help you in the long days ahead, when you have to deal with Pakistan and China, if you are aware of certain recent developments. The meeting today with your predecessor was to apprise him with the details of the recent Iranian offer that came outside diplomatic channels."

"And how did you get involved in this, Dr. Kak?" Durga asked.

"The commander of the Iranian Revolutionary Guard Corps wants to ensure there is no diplomatic rebuff from us, and he may have been less than confident dealing with the Indian ambassador in Tehran. In short, the Iranians have little faith in their nuclear scientists' claim to have built a working nuclear weapon. They want computer simulation tests carried out by us to confirm they have a workable system in place. In turn, Iran will give us all the oil and gas concessions that we seek. I got involved because they figured I could get the message to the right quarters and because the emissary they chose, Sohrab Mehrotra, to get in touch with me is the son of an old friend of mine."

Shan Surya asked, "The young multimillionaire Sohrab Mehrotra, who runs the 'Victory Oil Enterprises' group of companies in Iran?"

"Yes, he is apparently rich enough, although I can't vouch for his personal worth. They figure Sohrab has so much self-interest at stake in Iran, along with the right connections in India, including me, that there is a good chance he will deliver. As proof of its keenness to do business with India, Iran has already made a unilateral statement regarding backing out of giving China a base near the Straits of Hormuz. Sohrab had told me in advance that the statement would be made once he had assured the IRGC that the message he was carrying would be delivered to the PM. You need not worry about his loyalties. He comes from a long line of nationalists."

Durga Vadera asked the obvious question, "And what guarantee do I have that the Iranians will not renege on its commitments to us? After all, they've apparently done so with the Chinese, backing out of giving base facilities.

"That is exactly why I asked for this appointment, Madame Prime Minister. To recommend a way to keep the screws turned on Iran irrespective of Iran's intentions." In a few crisp sentences, the former Indian Atomic Energy Commission chief explained his idea.

CHAPTER 32
THE GLOVES ARE OFF

"SO WHAT DO WE DO? WE can't just make a noise like we did last time for a few weeks and then get back to business as usual. Everything has been tried in the past talks, cajoling, and threats to no avail!" the young Prime Minister Durga Vadera addressed her first question to the heads of the nation's military.

The military chiefs were amongst the special invitees to the meeting of the cabinet committee on security, India's highest decision-making body. This was a remarkable backtrack from not too long ago when Murthy, the national security adviser, a former police officer with great political connections to the ruling dynasty, had prevailed with his view that the military and its blinkered vision be largely kept out of meaningful national strategy development. Murthy's offer to resign owning moral responsibility following the terror attacks had been immediately accepted one hour after the swearing in of the prime minister.

Air Chief Marshal Harpal Singh observed, "Nothing immediately that is not of a cosmetic nature … insofar as military action is concerned. The ISI could not have timed this better, knowing that the movement of armored columns off the roads during the monsoon is extremely difficult, as tanks get stuck in the wet ground and lose traction. However, we should seriously start work to push the insurgencies in Balochistan, Tibet, and Xinjiang, if we are not already doing so! The Chinese are bound to leverage our difficulties by stirring up the LAC."

General Kapur, the army chief, interjected, "We could risk a strike in the Barmer sector of Rajasthan, where it is bone dry, but the point is of hitting the terror groups in their backyard in Pakistan's Punjab, more specifically Lahore and Bahawalpur. The international community will have no problems with that type of action. We could alternately launch some air strikes, of course, against suspect locations of terrorist camps, but none of them are stupid enough to stay put there. They would have moved on."

Singh continued, "As far as the three armed services are concerned, our faith in the nature of existing intelligence about terror training camps is not high, and we could be hitting a void and end up only killing civilians. If you exercise a political option to show national will immediately, I will need at least three days of notice to execute punitive air strikes in strength and also cater for the Pak response.

"We will otherwise need to wait up to early October at the very least for favorable ground conditions and then make a limited ground and air strike in Punjab. We have a range of contingency plans for your approval to exercise such an option. Anything more will definitely trigger a full-scale conflict."

"And what do I tell the people of India in the meantime, Air Chief Marshal? The opposition BJP will easily make mincemeat of our ability in parliament next week when it convenes again. It will call for my head as a weak incompetent leader that has once again let India be attacked."

Obviously not expecting any worthwhile answer, for she knew there was none except to tough it out politically, she turned to the army chief and said, "Tell me, general. How do you prevent the Chinese from taking advantage of this situation? I'm sure they must be delighted with the mess we find ourselves in."

"There is absolutely no doubt in my mind that China had an inkling of what was going to happen. It is too much of a coincidence that the Internet-triggered attack on our infrastructure and governance structure through botnets was orchestrated from Hainan Island. The Lingshui Signals Intelligence Facility and the Third Technical Department of the PLA organized it, even if we can't legally prove it. It would have taken a week with almost unlimited resources to set it up so effectively.

"We are making a huge mistake, taking the onus on ourselves to manage border-related tensions. The Chinese are hell-bent on pushing and provoking us every which way! Government orders to avoid Chinese patrols at all costs in disputed areas are having a devastating effect on morale of my troops. Our censors are reporting rising discontent in correspondence from officers and men to their families and friends," General Shiv Kapur, the Indian Army chief, told the freshly constituted cabinet committee on security.

"Ever since our former nuclear scientists rubbished the results of the series of nuclear tests code named 'Shakti' as damp squibs, the Chinese have turned on the heat on us," Singh added. "It also brings into question the very foundation of our commitment to non-first use of nuclear weapons. If we don't have the capability to retaliate massively, it will be easy to test our resolve … or rather the lack of it. It's a great pity that this vital nuclear capability or lack of it has been hidden from the armed forces all these years."

The prime minister appeared to be thinking aloud. "We clearly do not have the luxury of testing another nuke. All our nuclear power plants will be starved of fuel within a year. The Nuclear Suppliers Group led by the Americans will simply cut off fuel supplies the moment we test!"

Admiral Tony Pereira, the newly appointed naval chief, spoke forcefully. He had been a naval attaché to Beijing a decade back and had since advocated a tougher line with China, without having the rank to be taken seriously. Tony had been appointed naval chief in spite of official misgivings about his proactive views on the employment of the defense forces. This had happened only on account of the fact that the other contender for the navy's top job was caught up as a fall guy for the defense ministry. He had been blamed for the cost escalation mess for the Gorshkov aircraft carrier. The aircraft carrier was being purchased after an expensive upgrade from the Russians.

"Surprise them, Madame Prime Minister, by doing something different," the admiral said. "Explode a fusion device at Pokharan to start with. We can live with our nuclear power plants running sub-optimally, if it comes to a pinch, I reckon. In any case, we have been doing so for years and know the ropes of how to manage well enough. We need to get out of the defensive pattern of Boy Scout behavior we have created for the last fifty years!"

"Worth examining if we can do it quickly. There is enough reason to do so! The world will just have to lump it. China and Pakistan, too, will have to rethink all that they have taken for granted regarding our deterrence posture," General Kapur supported the admiral.

The admiral continued, "As far as the navy is concerned, the Chinese overall superiority does not worry me too much. The Chinese Navy has too many constraints operating large forces in the Indian Ocean in general and the Bay of Bengal and Arabian Sea in particular. Besides, I expect the aircraft carrier Gorshkov, which we have renamed INS Vikramaditya, to be available to us in another few months to tilt the balance decisively in our favor—that is, if the latest pricing row with Russia can be quickly settled."

"China also has useful assets in Sri Lanka and Myanmar to compound our maritime problems," the defense minister interjected.

Admiral Pereira replied, "China's second pipeline from the Island of Ramree oil and gas terminal on Myanmar's west coast to Kunming in Yunnan will be particularly vulnerable to our eastern fleet if push comes to shove. Similarly, Hambantota Port built by them in Sri Lanka, Trincomalee, which they use for berthing, and Gwadar on the Pakistan Makran coast are useful assets no doubt but only in peacetime. INS Vikramaditya escorted by a nuclear submarine is a game changer for sea control. I personally do not think that the Chinese can do anything beyond local ground-based actions on the LAC, where they have the advantage of superior communications."

"Any fresh intelligence inputs that may be useful to make a decision?" the prime minister posed the last question to Swapan Dasgupta, the intelligence bureau head.

"I'm naturally a bit cynical about coincidences, but after years of watching insurgent groups operating out of Bangladesh and Myanmar, there seems to be a lot of meetings going on between them and the Maoists in the Red Corridor."

"This business of all the insurgent groups working together for a common aim has been going on for decades, hasn't it? Nothing major has come of it so far!"

"True, but these meetings were sporadic in nature, with some groups being involved and some out of it, with this dynamic constantly shifting. All the leaders have king-sized egos that prevent them from working together more than notionally."

"So what has changed in your opinion?" Durga Vadera asked.

"The Maoists are the ones doing the front-running this time by sending emissaries. Previously, till two years ago, they were totally disinterested in the northeastern groups, even the major ones like ULFA and the NSCN. I think this change of heart can only be explained by someone giving them cash incentives for doing so," Swapan observed.

"It can only be the Chinese if what you say is correct. Money is probably channeled through the Maoists in Nepal, whom they control to a large extent," Ravi Kumar, the research-and-analysis-wing boss observed. "The ISI is the only other candidate who could do this, but it's not its style to delegate in this fashion. It cannot be a priority with the ISI in any case that has its hands full within Pakistan, what with the Punjabi terrorists and Al Qaeda, besides the Taliban keeping it fully engaged."

Newly promoted Home Minister Ch Tompok Singh, who had been listening intently, voiced their collective fear, "If the Chinese are indeed doing this, we can expect things to heat up soon. If I was in their place, I would try to instigate simultaneous actions by as many insurgent groups as possible. This would be in our depth areas in eastern India behind front lines where troops are deployed on the LAC. Trouble through extortions and killings can be easily stirred by making large result-based payoffs to insurgent groups. This may effectively draw away army formations to help an overwhelmed police and thin out troop density. The Chinese would do so preferably only when a ready-made crisis with Pakistan already exists so that we have a tough time deciding what to do on two fronts."

The finance minister, who was also a member of the cabinet committee for security and who had summoned the service chiefs and the RAW director, added "The payoffs to insurgents seem to have been underway for the last few quarters. At least a hundred million dollars has come in as additional counterfeit currency as per revenue intelligence and it all seems to have gone into Maoist hands."

"Thank you, gentlemen," Durga Vadera said. "While I accept that no major offensive can be launched till after the rains, surely we can light up Baluchistan and Xinjiang in the interim period. I want the petroleum pipeline and road projects from Gwadar Port on the Baloch coast to Xinjiang through Pakistan-occupied Kashmir to be delayed."

"We will need the Iranians on board to do anything meaningful in Baluchistan," Ravi Kumar qualified.

"The Iranians will be on board!" Durga Vadera said emphatically. "I will take care of it."

Two hours later, Sohrab Mehrotra and Dr. Anil Kak was ushered in to see the PM in a small office at her residence. The cool, calm, composed woman working late into the night showed no signs of having already gone through a sixteen-hour workday.

"The IRGC may have chosen you to deliver their message, Mr. Mehrotra, but India needs you more than you can imagine! I want you to stress on the Iranians that India will do whatever it takes to do the computer simulations that they need. The logistics involved are complex because of the requirements for secrecy, but that can only cause a few weeks delay. However, in the meantime, Iran needs to work with us to sort out common problems in Baluchistan."

CHAPTER 33
RENT A GUN

AFTER ITS PEOPLE SHUNNED AFGHANISTAN DURING the Taliban regime, India had made a nonmilitary gamble that was welcomed in Afghanistan. It had become a major donor, seeding $1.5 billion worth of power plants, transmission lines, satellite transmitters, wells, toilets, hospitals, high-protein biscuits for school kids, a new parliament building, and most importantly, roads. Freebee visits for Afghanistan's bureaucrats to India along with cosmetic surgery for their women went down extremely well in winning powerful friends. Pakistan, however, nipped this development by repeated messages to the United States that Indian involvement in its strategic backyard was unwelcome. It would constrain Pakistan's ability to fight the Taliban. The United States invariably obliged by keeping India out of multinational initiatives.

Pakistan had seen its influence, which was at a peak during the Taliban regime, wane after the regime was kicked out by the US invasion of Afghanistan post 9/11. Because Indian projects encompassed sizeable areas opposite the Pakistan borders, including Baluchistan, these projects also ensured easy access to Indian embassy staff to Pakistan-sensitive areas. It also ensured the backing of sizeable local populations for Indian-friendly projects.

The Indian decision to support the Baloch insurgents was conveyed to the military attaché in Kabul and the RAW station chief. The ambassador was left out of the loop on many operational issues. This ensured that he could always confidently claim total deniability of Indian involvement. The detailed execution was not interfered with in any meaningful way. It was, however, not expected to achieve any dramatic results beyond causing some additional tit-for-tat inconvenience to the Pakistan Army.

The colorful, charismatic, multilingual Brigadier Reza Ali Khan, military attaché in the embassy of India in Afghanistan, had other ideas. He had spent twenty years of a varied career as an infantry officer in insurgency-related operations. He now happily spent much of his time in Kandahar within easy reach of Balochistan, concocting a vicious brew for his enemy. He had also established good contacts with the Baloch population in Afghanistan in Nemroz, Helmand, and Farah who would provide the direct linkages to the Baloch Ittehad (Unity) in the future and funnel the money needed to fund the various factions. Because he had been at the receiving end of ISI-inspired insurgency in Kashmir for years, he relished this opportunity of giving it back. He would be proactive and open the western front against Pakistan, even without clear-cut orders to do so.

Surinder Malik, the research-and-analysis-wing boss, who had honed his considerable skills in Sri Lanka and Myanmar, was in total agreement with Reza Ali Khan. The operation took off within the first six weeks of the decision to launch, as many months of contingency planning had already been done. There was, however, a shortage of funds that needed to be addressed, because there was no formal policy in place to execute the mission. A meeting with Sridhar, who had been his boss earlier for a prolonged period, resolved that problem off the record. During a quick trip to Delhi, five million dollars was made available to Malik in Dubai through Sridhar to feed the appetite of friendly Baloch sirdars with no questions asked.

The Indian view of Iran as a potential asset against China, especially after the recent overtures by the IRGC through Sohrab Mehrotra, made the Indians walk a tightrope. This was to ensure that the Baloch chiefs they funded did not create problems for the Iranians—at least in the short term. Money in driblets to all the Baloch chiefs who waged war against Pakistan was readily given. The payouts escalated rapidly with the number of confirmed kills or heavy guns and tanks or helicopters destroyed. Bridges and infrastructure taken down brought additional bonuses. A portion of the payouts were arranged on request by various Baloch chiefs in banks in Dubai and Geneva. The service was inclusive of opening accounts. After all, the chiefs were human and would need to retire someday. A time could well come when the leaders wanted to move to a climate that actively discouraged taking potshots at your neighbor or vice versa.

Brigadier Reza Ali Khan and Surinder Malik were delighted to receive explicit instructions to prepare to play a decisive role against China in the future by targeting Gwadar. Their task would focus on the sabotage of the transportation infrastructure to ensure that the energy pipeline to Xinjiang along the Karakoram Highway was delayed. The Baloch Chiefs, unhappy with the Chinese control over Pakistan and the granting of mining leases that were not benefitting Balochistan, were happy to oblige. It got them lots of media attention with negligible risk.

"The Iranians have recommended a couple of targets for us to consider. Needless to say, it serves their interests for us to target Jundallah!" Brigadier Reza Ali Khan, the Indian Military attaché in Kabul told Surinder Malik, the Indian research and analysis wing station head in Afghanistan.

"We can take it that their suggestion is on the level and based on good intelligence," Surinder Malik replied. "The Iranians are extremely annoyed with the ISI promoting trouble amongst the Iranian Baloch inside Sistan-Balochistan through Jundallah.

"Jundallah is just a modified face of Sipah-e-Sahaba and the Taliban. The group would not be able to attack the Iranian Police, the Iranian Border Guard, and the Iranian Revolutionary Guard without help from the state apparatus of Pakistan or the collusion of the occupying powers in Afghanistan. This is one of the reasons that Jundallah fighters have escaped so easily into Pakistan from the Iranian border without problems with Pakistani security forces and border guards. It must also be mentioned that there are several American bases in Pakistani Baluchistan in close proximity to Iran that Jundallah could be using for support in its cross-border raids of Iran."

"It will also give them intense satisfaction if we act on this information and screw up a CIA-sponsored operation against Iran in the bargain!" Reza observed.

"Where can we launch the operation from? It has to be from within Iranian territory!"

"If the training camp run by the ISI and Jundallah combine is west of Kafar, the best place to launch is from within the Bahukalat protected area in Iran. If Iran agrees to the strike, we can take it that the information is genuine," Reza summed up.

The camouflaged, prefabricated huts of the Jundallah training camp were connected to a tarmac road barely four hundred meters away. They could not be seen from the road because of an intervening dune. At any time, two armed sentries were on guard duty. Each hut accommodated ten men comfortably. One of the huts was shared by only four noncommissioned officers, who were the trainers of the group, attached from the Pakistan Army.

The thirty men, none of whom were Balochis, were at the end of their training period. They had just returned from a forced march of four kilometers with loads of twenty-five kilograms each, excluding their personal weapons. Only one man had failed to complete the forced march. With a twisted ankle, he had fallen out after the first ten kilometers and had been left to his own devices to find his way back. As soon as his companions disappeared over the horizon, he activated the tiny GPRS phone hidden in the original soap packaging. His brother had already received half the promised amount of two hundred thousand Pakistan rupees. One hour later, he was picked up by a battered, light, commercial vehicle half-loaded with construction material, and after he travelled another half an hour, he got busy making a sketch of the training camp in the sand and explaining the layout and routine to a dozen Mari tribesmen looking over his shoulder.

Shakeel Ahmed Mari, the heavily muscled, six-foot-tall leader of the team asked a question, "Are you sure about the location of the camp that you have indicated to us on the map, Jabber?"

"Of course I am! I've lived there for two months."

"Good!" Shakeel said and nodded. At this signal, two of the Mari tribesmen grabbed Jabber by his arms and turned him around so the back of his head was facing Shakeel even as he struggled like a trussed chicken. Shakeel whipped out a silenced pistol and put a round into the back of his head. After they dumped Jabber into a shallow grave that had already been dug fifty meters away, the six men set off for the camp.

Without exception, the trainees had gone to sleep fitfully, barely mindful of the dust storm raging outside that reduced visibility to just a few meters. The two sentries, who had also walked the whole day, were dead tired in their slit trenches on opposite sides of the small encampment, their faces almost fully covered in an attempt to keep out the sand. Sand that filled their eyes, noses, and ears and worked its grit into their mouths kept them barely awake by the sheer lack of options. The efficacy of their thermal-imaging sights was reduced to near zero under the circumstances, and the wailing of the wind killed any other sound they could have discerned. They were, however, not worried by not being able to see out in the darkness. No threat from the Iranians was expected. The fieldcraft of the two men who crawled behind each of the sentries was impeccable. The muffled noise of the silenced weapons was barely audible.

Thereafter, five men carrying heavy, ten-kilogram satchel charges placed one each next to the flimsy plywood door of each hut and drifted away to the safety of the lee of the dune. The remote detonation kits worked precisely as planned. The ten men, Shakeel at the center, formed an assault line to prevent firing at each other by accident and walked into the debris created by the blasts, looking for survivors. Sporadic shots rang out from the line as they meticulously searched for bodies. Ten minutes later, the team was satisfied that there were no survivors.

At 3:00 a.m., the news filtered out that the assault team had achieved its mission and was on its way back. On the western fringe of the Bahukalat protected area, Colonel Basher Sistani of the Iranian Revolutionary Guards rubbed his hands vigorously to combat the cold and poured a lukewarm tumbler of tea and offered it to Brigadier Reza Ali Khan. "May this be the beginning of a long and successful partnership between us?"

"Insha'Allah!"

CHAPTER 34
DRAGON FIRE

THE CHINESE SPECIAL FORCES TEAM OF three in the military snow garb of their Indian counterparts waited patiently for over four hours at the Shyok River bend in the frozen reaches of northeastern Kashmir in the area known as Aksai Chin. Late in the afternoon, the leader looked briefly down at his watch. With his GPS now firmly buckled at his waist, he had no problem finding the exact spot desired, not even in the mountains.

"Over there. Next to the big rock," Captain Dingbang said in a low voice full of authority. "Confirm when ready!"

"I have him," confirmed Yong, the thick, burly Han NCO, as the first faint sound of the helicopter engines became audible.

"Get ready … fire!"

The slow, low-flying PLAAF Mi-17 helicopter with the twin engines, whose Uyghur crew had been specifically briefed on the routing he was to follow, did not have a chance as the missile's infrared-homing head struck the engine. From barely a hundred and fifty meters above the level of the ground, the ungainly helicopter plummeted straight into the ground on its side a fraction of a second before the explosion as the fuel tanks ignited. The smoldering wreckage was barely a few hundred meters away by then.

With two other men, Captain Dingbang, whose name coincidentally signified "protector of the country," walked slowly toward the gnarled, twisted pieces of metal, ensuring no telltale sign was left on the ground.

The smell of charred flesh hung in the air. He signaled to the other two to wait fifty meters short and walked around the desolate scene with no trace of emotion, stepping carefully around the wreckage and shooting photographs with the high-pixel digital camera he had been given.

One of the charred bodies on the ground twitched. The captain soon pointed it out to Yong, who moved up swiftly and put a small hand towel that he pulled out of his pocket on to the face of the barely breathing soldier and held the dying man's nostrils tightly together between his callused thumb and forefinger till the twitching stopped.

"He's dead for sure. Shall I check out the other bodies?"

"No need. I have had a good look. The cold will kill them in any case if anyone is alive. Okay, let's move. We have a long walk ahead!"

Corporal Hu, the youngest of the three, kept his face carefully composed. It wouldn't do him any good if Yong even suspected what was going through his mind. He wondered what was imperative about shooting down the PLAAF helicopter, even if all the crew members had been Uyghur. However, he trusted Captain Dingbang, who always led from the front. Still, a nagging doubt seemed to keep cropping up no matter how hard he tried to keep it at bay. His mother, who was a practicing Buddhist, would never have approved, he reckoned.

In translation, "Aksai Chin" meant "White Brook Pass," perhaps beckoning to the tranquility of the area till it was disrupted suddenly by the Sino-Indian War of 1962. The desolate, high-altitude, cold-desert area lay in northeastern Kashmir in the Ladakh area, adjacent to both the restive and seditious Chinese provinces of Tibet and Xinjiang, formerly east Turkistan. At one stage, both these provinces considered themselves independent countries with no claims on Aksai Chin, which was historically a portion of the Kingdom of Ladakh until it was annexed by the princely state of Kashmir in the nineteenth century. The primary cause of the war was the Chinese building National Highway 219, an all-weather road that provided the best connectivity between Xinjiang and Tibet, cutting through Aksai Chin, an area considered part of India.

China had controlled thirty-eight thousand square kilometers of territory in Aksai Chin since 1962. A further 5,180 square kilometers of land had been ceded to it by Pakistan in 1963. There was, however, a gap in between these two areas in which the aircraft landing ground of

Daulet Beg Oldi, latitude 35 degrees north, longitude 77 degrees east, repaired and reactivated by the Indian Army was located. DBO was at a height of 16,200 feet, barely eight kilometers from the LAC.

On September 1st, two weeks after the terror strike on the Delhi airport, China claimed that Indian troops had fired and brought down a Chinese PLAAF Mi-17 helicopter with a handheld SAM east of the Shyok River in the Aksai Chin area. Photographs were distributed to the world media in Beijing, showing the remains of a Mi-17 helicopter lying close to the banks of what appeared to be a desolate stretch of river bank with four dead bodies in combat gear. The names of the two crew and six soldiers killed in the crash were all Uyghur from Xinjiang. Ethnic differences in Xinjiang were expected to be buried with the announcement of Uyghur casualties as anger focused on India.

The bland Chinese TV announcement was received with considerable surprise by the world, for it seemed completely uncharacteristic of the Indians, who had been backpedaling for decades to avoid annoying China. "India has violated the Peace and Tranquility Arrangement between India and China, shooting down an unarmed helicopter of the PLAAF without warning, resulting in the untimely death of six soldiers of the PLA, all belonging to Xinjiang. Defense Minister Shao Wei has personally extended his condolences to the bereaved families and has promised that the perpetrators of this cowardly act will not go unpunished."

Just before the photographs were released at first light, six Z-9G helicopters equipped with infrared sensors, navigation radars, and auxiliary power units for high-altitude operations attacked Daulet Beg Oldi (DBO), suppressing its rudimentary defenses and killing or wounding almost all the twenty-eight members of the small guard detachment that was housed in a small, barrack-shaped, temporary hutment. This happened as they were being lined up for a morning briefing regarding the day's schedule. The small satellite link for maintaining communications with the outside world was also shattered by canon fire in the first few seconds.

The coup de main did not cater for Sepoys Fateh Jung Bahadur and Nar Bahadur of the first battalion of the Eighth Gurkha Rifles Regiment. Both soldiers were on guard duty in a bunker with an adjacent trench near the middle of the 2.2-kilometer-long landing ground. The guard duty was routine. They had become accustomed to it over the past month, and nothing was expected to happen. The assault plan was for a dozen successively echeloned Mi-17s to land a hundred meters apart on the runway two minutes after the Z-9Gs suppressive fire lifted. This had become necessary, because in the rarified atmosphere at over 16,000 feet, each helicopter could only lift four infantry soldiers in addition to the crew. A second and third wave of helicopters was to follow five minutes apart to build up a company of troops.

Although taken completely by surprise, the two Indian soldiers bided their time till the seventh and eighth helicopters touched down barely seventy meters from them and fired at point-blank range, their rocket launcher instantly crippling both helicopters. However, within seconds, they found themselves under fire from the right as the Chinese squads that had already landed homed on to them.

In the meanwhile, on the opposite side of the runway and echeloned three hundred meters away, the other guard trench, engaged now with the company commander having joined them under fire, fired at another two Mi-17s and destroyed one of them. By the time that all the ten men of the guard section had been killed or wounded severely, four Mi-17 and one Z-9G helicopter had been destroyed on the tarmac, making it unusable for fixed-wing aircraft. Forty-four Chinese soldiers had been killed or wounded by the defenders. Twenty-three Indian wounded were eventually taken as prisoners of war.

Half an hour before daybreak, a foot column of a full infantry battalion that had been launched from the Chinese side of the LAC linked up with the helicopter assault force and proceeded to dig in around the perimeter of the airfield. Soon after midnight, six battle tanks had crossed the shallow Chip Chap River on the Chinese side of the LAC and linked up with the forces that had captured DBO. The unexpected nature of the assault had taken the Indian troops completely by surprise, and scattered resistance ended soon after the company commander of the troops was killed.

There was no Indian reaction beyond two reconnaissance flights that flew over DOB, taking the air photographs that would shake India out of decades of mind-numbing stupor. In the meantime, China declared that defensive action by the PLA had been halted and that twenty-three Indian prisoners of war would be released as soon as a flag meeting with Indian forces could be organized.

The Indian Corps commander at Leh, Lieutenant General Kanwar Devraj Singh, had been given unambiguous instructions by the Northern Army commander only a month earlier. "Devraj, under *no* circumstances are you to instigate an incident in Aksai Chin. Trust me—our time will come. I don't care what happens in the interim and how much in the right our troops are or how far inside the Chinese come. Make sure our patrols stay far away from the Chinese. Reduce your patrols if you must. I know that there will be daily violations of the LAC, but please explain the reason to all your formation commanders and do so personally. Tell them to pass the same message down to the last *jawan*. Our soldiers will understand how important it is to be prepared to fight only one enemy at a time. I don't really have the resources to deal with both Pakistan and China together right now if things get out of hand, and Pakistan has to react if the army wants to stay in power."

When the corps commander reported on the ongoing situation at Daulet Beg Oldi, he recommended that action be taken immediately. "I'm sure the government orders did not cater for a situation like this to be developing. It will take a few days, but we should launch a counterattack and use our tanks as well. If we do not react, the next stage can only be worse!"

"I am equally aware of the repercussions. Bring in artillery fire if something else happens. Use infantry battalion commando platoons to lay some ambushes. Play down incidents in your situation reports if you instigate them. Some limited self-defense we can justify. Step up surveillance opposite the Pakistan deployments. It is bound to try something now that the Chinese have played a trump card for them!"

"Okay, sir, will do what it takes. If you hear any complaints about our supposed actions from the Chinese through the government, just ignore them."

Two hours later, the corps commander was called to take a call on a secure line from the army commander. "Things are worse than we thought, Devraj. Satellite imagery has just confirmed that a complete Chinese rapid-reaction force is building up opposite Sikkim. The Russians have confirmed off the record that it was deployed last month opposite Taiwan. I'm willing to bet my next paycheck that the Chinese have decided to turn the screws on us along with the Pakis."

"Is there anything that you want me to do in view of this development?" Devraj Singh asked.

"We can't keep turning the other cheek forever. If push comes to shove, I will give you some more troops, probably a brigade group, but they will have to be acclimatized before you use them to fight at a fourteen-thousand-feet altitude. Forget throwing the Chinese out of DBO. It's too small an operation to make any difference. Figure out something that hurts them a lot more. We've discussed some of these options in the past. Make a firm recommendation of what you would like to do. It won't be easy, given your limited resources, but that is all I can give you for the time being!"

"I can tell you right now what I would like to do! Cut National Highway 219 in Aksai Chin if they decide to use the RRF in Sikkim. It will help immensely if you can also airlift a regiment of T-72 tanks to Leh from Delhi."

CHAPTER 35
FORT MEADE, MARYLAND

Vice-Admiral J. Walter McNeil, the National Security Agency agency's director and former intelligence head for the joint staff, better known as DIRNSA, was as proactive an electronic spymaster as any in the NSA history. He had three flat-screen TVs on his office wall beaming muted channels nonstop according to an algorithm selected by him. He was known to redirect eavesdropping analysis within seconds of breaking stories purely on instinct honed by decades of experience even without further corroboration of the accuracy of these stories.

McNeil maintained that there was a common problem with a lot of terror group leaders, even with the good ones. They stopped following their own advice and started believing the hype of their own infallibility. This was especially so when the world media chipped in with superlatives while it covered stories on them and made them believe that they were indeed special when it comes to killing, raping, maiming, torturing, bombing, and making perpetual fools of the security apparatus. It made them feel different from what they were as ill-educated street kids who are ill-fed, under clothed, and strangers to charity, or even well-fed, rich brats ignored by their parents in some cases.

Communication security within Al Qaeda was a given. You could get killed ignoring the simple steps required to ensure that words thrown into the ether were not traceable back to you. Ayman Al Zawahri made the mistake that even raw operatives were drilled to avoid. He did not, however, completely ignore tradecraft, for he sent a trusted aide named Ilyas Ahmed thirty kilometers south of Quetta to place the call to Bangkok at 8:00 p.m. The phone at the other end rang for fifteen seconds before he broke the connection. Exactly one minute later, the number called him back and disconnected after four rings. Another thirty seconds later, the number called again and disconnected after three rings. There seemed nothing unusual about the calls. The third time around when the phone rang, Ilyas Ahmed picked up and asked, "Has our guest arrived at the airport?"

"No," was the answer from Bangkok before the connection was disconnected.

If the US ambassador had not gotten killed in Delhi, the short conversation would not have raised any alarm bells at the headquarters of the secret National Security Agency. The NSA, located inside an army base at Fort Meade, Maryland, was the US intelligence community's ears around the world, picking up millions of conversations from coded military conversations at PLA bases in the Tibet Autonomous Region, the Russian Northern Fleet in the Barents Sea, *hawala* or illegal currency traders in Mumbai, and the Taliban and Al Qaeda regional networks.

"Al Qaeda or Lashkar e Taiba for sure," Vice Admiral J. Walter McNeil declared as soon as soon as the Indian prime minister's plane was shot down.

The call from the joint chief of staff half an hour later to him set the cat amongst the pigeons at NSA.

"Walter, Joe Stone here. This is just to confirm that Gerald Johnson, our ambassador to India, is dead. He was a friend of the president, and no one fucks around with doing this to the president's cronies. See what you can do to bail out the Indians on this one. They are in a complete mess. The CIA is already on the ball!"

Deputy Director Patricia "Ferret" Holmes, whose ability to conjure up "what if" scenarios, when the heat was on, was legendary, focused the NSA effort on Baluchistan and South Waziristan with her observation.

"If the admiral is right … and with his track record, I wouldn't like to bet against his gut reaction. Whoever planned this in the Al Qaeda *shura* council will want a firsthand report aside from the media. Focus on the immediate six-hour period after the attacks. Let's analyze calls made to outside Pakistan and see if there is a pattern disruption."

Forty hours later, Ali Zakaria, a veteran with fifteen years of experience who spoke half a dozen languages, including Arabic, Farsi, Pashto, and Hindi, walked up to the deputy director with a sheaf of papers in his hand.

"Ferret, we've narrowed it down to about one hundred and fifty calls, most of which are run-of-the-mill conversations. There is one placed from south of Quetta two hours after the attack to a cell phone in Bangkok that seems unusual. Fortunately, the network providers were using the old A 5/1 GSM 64 bit binary code as a ciphering algorithm to save upgrading expenses. We can crack this quickly. Why would anyone from the boondocks outside Quetta be asking about a guest arriving at Bangkok Airport?"

"Zak, you may just have hit pay dirt! Let's get the admiral to lean on his buddies in the CIA and state department."

Tim Cartwright, the regional security officer at the US embassy in Bangkok, placed the early morning call to his golf partner, Kriengsak Niratpattanasai, head of the Thai Immigration Bureau.

"Kriengsak, you will have to take my word on this one, buddy! It will be a huge personal favor if you can trace the number I have sent you by SMS and put a team of your special enforcement division to keep a tag on the owner. Just ensure he does not skip the country while we cook up something to pin on him."

"Can't without a warrant, but I will get you the particulars of the owner in a couple of hours."

Barely an hour later, Tim Cartwright was called and informed by Kriengsak that the owner of the phone number being traced was a Pakistan citizen named Abdullah Qadir. He was a frequent visitor to textile factories and imported quality lace from Thailand to make bras and lingerie products in Karachi. He was also booked on a Cathay flight to Hong Kong leaving in an hour.

"Kriengsak, I owe you one, old buddy! Can you also get me a photocopy of his passport?"

Four hours later, Kurt Cobb, the CIA station chief in Pakistan, was holding a printout of a high-quality scan of Abdullah Qadir's passport in his hand and passing instructions. It had been routed via the CIA headquarters duty staff at Langley.

"We need the best guy we have in Karachi to check this out. Get Nasrullah Ahmed to run a check on Abdullah Qadir. I want to know everything about him, including any identification marks on his ass! We have an input from Hong Kong from our airport guys. He will be in Karachi by Wednesday, routing via Syria. In particular, I want to know the people he has met with in the last two weeks and where he has travelled within Pakistan if at all. Get his bank statement as well if possible."

Two days later, as the preliminary investigation report was e-mailed using a proprietary encryption method, Kurt Cobb grimaced as he exclaimed to himself, "Son of a bitch! Abdullah Qadir is Brigadier Syed Ali's brother-in-law. If the Indians come to know, it will mean war!" He continued reading the report and making notes for his recommendations to the CIA headquarters in Langley.

"Under no circumstances should we take the risk of even passing on this information about Brigadier Syed Ali to our embassy in New Delhi to prevent inadvertent leaks. It is also likely that that Abdullah Qadir was being used by Brigadier Syed Ali to train the leadership of the Indian Mujahideen (IM) in a safe house in Karachi run by the ISI in managing illegal foreign exchange transactions for operations in India. Yasin Bhatkal, alias Shah Rukh, alias Ahmed, is also a seasoned bomb maker who makes innovative circuits and timers for bombs, and he has been photographed visiting Abdullah Qadir on three occasions."

CHAPTER 36
NATGRID

THE KNIVES WERE OUT WHILE SMOKE from the terror strikes on IGIA still lingered in the air.

"Banana Republic of India" was the headline that covered half the front page of the *International Herald Tribune* above the picture of a hundred or more mangled bodies and a wild-eyed woman holding her dead child in her arms, a picture that captured the world's reaction to the ghastly sequence of events played out in Delhi as India was found wanting every which way in dealing with the aftermath of terror once again.

Ariel Dayan, one of the worlds' foremost authorities on fighting terror, witnessed some of the effects firsthand while he was staying at the Radisson on a consultancy assignment to a multinational private security company. He brutally summed it up for BBC journalist Susan Walker, who was based in Delhi.

"Indian governments have not learnt anything from forty years of terror strikes against the country. This is as professional a hit as I have seen in my life, and I will bet an arm and a leg that this is supported by Pakistan's ISI. Two eyes for an eye is the only response that terrorists and their supporters will ever understand. The Indian voter has failed to understand this simple truth and continues to tolerate weak-kneed governments instead of voting with his feet and throwing them out!"

"Almost five thousand people killed and wounded, including the prime minister of India dead, and billions of dollars worth of property destroyed leave alone the economic aftermath. What do you think the Indians will do?" Susan Walker prodded.

"True to form, they will do nothing much besides expelling hot air by empty political speeches. The monsoon is on, so there is a perfect excuse not to launch ground operations against Pakistan, as tanks will get bogged down off the roads. After a few weeks, it will be business as usual. The prime ministers of both countries will meet at the UN Headquarters by accident. The Indians will ask for the perpetrators to be handed over, and Pakistan will ask to see the evidence and agree to do so. And the United States will promise to intercede on behalf of India. After that, there will be no forward movement until a new disaster takes place!"

Till a year earlier, the new home minister, Ch Tompok Singh from Manipur, had looked after the same portfolio in the tiny insurgency-ridden state of Manipur bordering Myanmar in India's northeast before he was selected to be the minister of state for home affairs in the central government. Manipur had more independent insurgent outfits than any place on earth, and Ch Tompok Singh, as a former Indian Police Service superintendent, had successfully fought them all for fifteen years and been awarded the President's Police Medal for gallantry thrice before he switched to full-time politics. He was convinced that the answer to India's insurgencies lay in a different brand of politics based on wider participation by common people. He had listened patiently to the host of brief presentations at the multiagency center, which was the nodal point for the national intelligence grid.

"I don't care what else you have to do. Drop it! This investigation needs to be done first. We don't seem to have a clue as to what happened except for the two men who fired the antitank missiles from on top of the Mahipalpur flyover and crippled three aircraft on the ground. Presumably, there were at least two teams firing SAMs from different locations, as we know that the launches were well separated. There were at least two more people involved in the petrol-bunk explosions and another three or four in the metroline attack. Everyone can't just disappear without a trace. And this definitely does not include the guy who planned this and the explosives experts. Follow the money. Girish, after your interaction yesterday at the Radisson, can you give everyone here a sense of what they need to focus on at least to start with?"

The national intelligence grid had designated senior officers from the Intelligence Bureau (IB) responsible for internal intelligence, research and analysis wing (RAW) for foreign intelligence, Central Bureau of Investigations (CBI), National Investigating Agency (NIA), Directorate of Revenue Intelligence (DRI), Enforcement Directorate, Central Board of Excise and Customs (CBEC), Central Board of Direct Taxes (CBDT), Financial Intelligence Unit (FIU), and Serious Fraud Investigation Office (SFIO). NATGRID had helped to speed up investigations and to preempt crimes by acting on suspicious activities of people under watch by use of more than twenty stand-alone databases. Private bank and transport companies' data was still a work in progress because of vested interests wanting to keep these out.

Girish, a former policeman with fifteen years of investigating high-profile cases on his record, was extensively networked at a personal level across most of the states in India. He represented the National Investigation Agency, the lead agency in the recently launched investigation on the airport terror attacks on NATGRID. "I will keep this short and follow up on e-mail on the Intranet. The Israeli security consultant, Ariel Dayan, was spot on when he made the remark of it being a professional hit to the BBC. It's a no-brainer that the ISI is involved. It has all the hallmarks of a synchronized military operation, and the logistics of getting in the missile launchers and explosives and coordinating the training effort and reconnaissance is beyond any single terrorist organization!"

Nader, the RAW representative, interrupted, "At the official level with the Pakistan Army top brass having to approve it, I would say, 'No.' This is because the army chief needs to cover his butt and save embarrassing his government in case the CIA discovers a connection. However, there is definitely a strong element of collusion at some lower level with real executive power. Perhaps a colonel or brigadier is involved. I would not be surprised in the least bit if it is from amongst the eight to ten ISI officers who were forcibly eased out last year under American pressure for their old links to the Afghan Taliban."

Girish nodded in agreement. "No issue with what you say. It would be helpful if you can get your people in Islamabad or Kabul to get some photographs of these people."

"I will see what we can do, though it may take some time. There are a lot of existing photographs of some of them from the time that they were celebrating booting the Soviets out of Afghanistan, but appearances change over two decades," Nader confirmed.

"Do what you can. We did a postmortem of the attack with the home secretary in a meeting at the Radisson Hotel, with reps from the local Delhi and from the neighboring states of Haryana police, airport security, a special action team of the national security guard, and the telecom regulatory authority.

"There was a general consensus of opinion on a few issues that could help crack this investigation. Firstly, whosoever planned the attack had to be staying for a prolonged period of some months within twenty to thirty minutes of travelling time to the airport. The majority was of the opinion that security outside Delhi was definitely more lax, and the outskirts of Gurgaon toward Delhi was the best bet to establish a hideout or a base for operations.

"Secondly, the sheer simplicity of the plan, stand-alone yet synergistic nature of the different actions targeting flying aircraft, static aircraft, the metro, the Radisson Hotel, and the petrol bunks, and last but not least, the training requirements and logistics of assembling high-grade explosives and missile systems indicates a military mind with practical combat exposure.

"Thirdly and perhaps most significantly our best chance to pick up the trail is to concentrate on the financial transactions and identity creation required for at least one of them to operate in this particular way. As the home minister has suggested, let's try to follow the money. There will be a record somewhere—a bank account perhaps within fifteen kilometers of the airport, close to where the planner stayed, a driving license or a passport perhaps, a hotel or guesthouse booking or bill paid through a credit card, and in case of an assumed identity, an income tax permanent account number, especially if property has been purchased as a hideout for the long term."

CHAPTER 37
DESTINY'S CALL

Chris Healy, the officiating US ambassador, walked into the PM's office and found that beside Durga Vadera, the minister for home affairs, Ch Tompok Singh was also present.

"Thank you for agreeing to see me so quickly. The Ministry of External Affairs people were doubtful whether you would be available till next week."

Durga Vadera said, "Please accept my heartfelt condolences on Ambassador Gerald Johnson's demise. I assure you that we will get the perpetrators wherever they are. All stops have been pulled out, and it should be a matter of a few days at best. I assume you have also come to share inputs available to you on the incident?"

"Thank you for your condolences, Madame Prime Minister. On behalf of the American people, our prayers and good wishes are with you after having lost a fantastic leader and so many people. We will do our best to help with the investigations. As agreed, we will have someone from the FBI here by tomorrow to coordinate investigative efforts with Ch Tompok Singh's people. In the meanwhile, we have picked up some information that may help if true. Apparently, the person who planned and coordinated the attack could have planned to fly out of Delhi to Bangkok prior to the attack. There is a chance that he did not make it and is still in India or is dead."

"How accurate is this information?" Durga asked.

"It is a reasonable conjecture at this stage, connecting disparate pieces. Rob Stevens, the FBI rep, will keep the home secretary posted if anything further develops. I wish you the best of luck. I'm very confident that with you cracking the whip, we will see good progress soon."

While Chris Healy was getting up from his chair to leave, Durga said "Be careful, Mr. Healy. Helping Pakistan is a dangerous business for ambassadors. Your country also lost one when travelling in a plane with the late dictator, Zia ul Haq, when a crate-load of mangoes apparently exploded!"

Ch Tompok Singh reached his office and asked Home Secretary Somal Davar to come and see him. As he recounted the conversation with the US ambassador, he added, "Speak to the civil aviation secretary to have the director general of civil aviation immediately get hold of the passenger lists. My assistant just checked on the Internet that there were apparently only four flights scheduled to Bangkok from IGIA. We need to get the complete breakdown of passengers who were scheduled to travel and their addresses and contact numbers. Get the NIA to first check out those who cancelled their bookings or who did not board their scheduled flights first. The Americans are hiding something for sure, probably Pak-related connections, but let's take them at their word to start with. Keep me informed of progress!"

"It won't take long," Somal Davar added. "I have had the DGCA link the airlines' daily passenger lists data with his office, and NATGRID has access to it on an as required basis."

Four hours later, Somal Davar called up his minister, Ch Tompok Singh. "You were right. There were only four flights to Bangkok the whole day. The last one was delayed and subsequently cancelled because of the attack after the passengers had checked in. Sixty-one passengers cancelled their bookings, and there were seven no shows—perhaps because of the traffic situation. We have constituted a team to track these down. Hopefully, we should be able to complete the preliminary check by midday tomorrow."

"Use NATGRID to get a copy of all the passports of people booked to Bangkok on August 25th, starting from their ticket details. Do this irrespective of whether they boarded, cancelled, or missed their flights. Check with the airlines for those who have definitely left and put them on a separate list. We are clutching at straws, but if the Americans are right, the perpetrator of the attacks will be one of the remaining faces who did not get on a flight to Bangkok. Get a list of all the hospitals in the national capital region where casualties have been sent, although it is unlikely that the perpetrator will be one of these. Get the complete history of these sixty-eight people and track each one down for any link to terror."

It took a complete week of intense police work. An alert was put out for the sixty-eight passengers who had either cancelled their bookings or had not shown up at the airport for one reason or another. The sixty-one cancelled bookings included fourteen foreigners who were prevented from leaving the country after they all tried to leave India from Mumbai.

The forty-seven Indians who had cancelled seat bookings were from eighteen states around India. Many of them were rudely pulled out of bed in the middle of the night and taken to the nearest major police station for cross-examination. One of them was caught with a hundred thousand dollars in assorted currencies in a briefcase and was subjected to third-degree questioning, which included a red chili stuffed into his anal cavity, before he admitted to drug trafficking. There was, however, no connection established with the terror attacks.

Finally, only three names were left that had not been satisfactorily accounted for. All three had checked in for the last flight to Bangkok, which had been forcibly cancelled. All three were dead. As he made his daily round of the Indian Home Ministry, Rob Stevens of the FBI pocketed the three pictures handed over to him by Somal Davar, who said, "These are the pictures of three passengers who were to fly to Bangkok and did not make it. All three are persons of Indian origin, but the picture on top is of Arun Bhatia, a US citizen who owned a software business in Delhi. Sanjiv Malhotra was a local businessman from Gurgaon, who we are following up, and Intikab Alam was a Thai national making an annual visit to family in Delhi and Hyderabad. We would be grateful if you can share any leads on these people that you may have."

"So what news has the FBI unearthed for us, or are the Americans just pretending to help?" Ch Tompok Singh asked Somal Davar.

"Rob Stevens is hiding something! He was absolutely open,

forthcoming, and enthusiastic initially, and now he seems to have clammed up."

"It probably means that they have solved the riddle of the ambassador's demise, Somal! The only logical reason for this volte face in behavior, and I'm now speaking as an ex-cop, is that there is a Pakistan Army or ISI connection with the attack. The Yanks had apparently already established this before you handed over the pictures of the three who died in the terminal waiting for their flight to Bangkok. There is no way they will derail their agenda against Al Qaeda in Afghanistan by giving us evidence of Pak collusion in the Delhi attack. For them, it is a no-brainer to avoid giving us evidence of Pak complicity that can lead to war in the subcontinent."

"We can try to reverse-follow the trail back to Pakistan, starting with these three with a little luck."

"Organize a video conference with the directors general of police in Andhra Pradesh, Haryana, and UP and the commissioner of police in Delhi along with the NIA. Get the dirt on all three, including the last time and place where they masturbated!"

"Sanjiv Malhotra to my mind is the obvious suspect—Hindu name, no known relatives, trips to Dubai, no dearth of money, passport changed recently, an ideally located house for easy access and exit, no vices, no friends—all too convenient to be true!" Shiv Marwaha, the pipe-smoking NIA chief remarked to his old classmate, Lieutenant General Arun Sahgal, the director general of military intelligence (DGMI).

"What do you want me to do to help, Shiv? Sure, it seems to have the ISI stamp. It would require an extremely experienced and competent operative with years of experience to pull this off without a trace. But these photographs that you have produced match nothing in our records. Our military attachés in Afghanistan and Pakistan are still plugging away. One of them has scanned dozens of old photographs from an old studio in Kabul showing victorious Taliban posing with ISI young officers after defeating the Russians, but faces change remarkably over the decades, especially if a cosmetic surgeon is roped in. We also have copies of group photographs of about three thousand Pakistan Army officers from the Internet and other sources, but nothing seems to match!"

Just then there was a discreet beep on the intercom. The DGMI listened for a minute and said, "Why don't you come in and explain? We have no secrets from the head of NIA."

Almost immediately, a thin, tired-looking, clean-shaven colonel with red-rimmed eyes walked in with a slim folder of photographs in one hand.

"Shiv, this is Colonel Rusi Mody. Rusi is our one-stop expert on the Pakistan Military. Everything worth knowing is archived in his head!"

After he shook hands with the NIA head, the colonel remarked, "We finally ran into some overdue luck, sir! There is a photographer in Rawalpindi who is frequently used by Pak retiring officers who have to submit current photographs for postretirement identity cards. His son was killed in a bomb blast last month, and he needed money to look after his daughter-in-law and twin grandsons. He gave us a CD with about two hundred photographs taken in the last year of retiring officers. One of these is a near-perfect match with the photograph of Sanjiv Malhotra, except there is a mustache and beard."

"Well done, Rusi. I knew you would swing it! Have we been able to put a name to the face as well?"

"Sir, the CD included the names of all the subjects photographed! The photograph is that of Brigadier Syed Ali, who served with the ISI almost throughout his service. The CIA forced his retirement from ISI because of his Taliban links!"

"Thanks, colonel. You've just produced the miracle that we needed. Now if you can give me a copy of the CD before I go to the home minister, we can start the process of getting even with Pakistan for this!"

CHAPTER 38
CONFLICT MANAGEMENT GROUP

Ashok Sobti and his team sat around the oval table waiting for Prime Minister Durga Vadera to finish reading the note left behind by his predecessor explaining the rationale for a short-term, parallel, crisis-fighting structure.

"You first need to decide whether you want to continue with this structure or you wish to scrap it. The circumstances have changed since this unofficial shadow crisis-control team was constituted," Ashok Sobti said crisply.

"You need to continue! I will hereafter refer to you as the 'Conflict Management Group' to make it sound like one of the corporate think tanks proliferating in India. It will ensure a degree of anonymity and freedom of action for exactly this kind of national emergency. We need game-changing acts right now to clear the mounting mess. If you did not exist, I would probably have to create something similar. Can you please give me a quick update of what you have achieved already and where it fits into the national response structure?"

"The basic premise we have been working on was articulated by research into current Chinese motivation vis-à-vis India. This was estimated to try to dismantle or at least severely unbalance India by both external and internal threats within a five- to seven-year period. After that, the Americans' recovery from the current financial crisis would act as a constraint on Chinese geopolitical freedom of action. The

China strategy was visualized to be executed in informal collusion with Pakistan, a situation that seems to have already come into existence.

"There are two pressure points that may create a feeling of vulnerability in the Chinese politburo and a willingness to talk rather than rely on armed conflict. These, assessed by Dr. Speed Ranganathan, are energy-centric and related to the Chinese minorities' unrest largely in Tibet, Xinjiang, and Inner Mongolia. Our group is constantly reviewing our mission goals to ensure that there is no conflict with the attempts of the government to ensure national security objectives. Our work is designed to promote unheralded synergy. Sridhar will now give you a brief about what we have tried to do to pre-empt the situation going out of control if push comes to shove."

Sridhar stood up to summarize the group's efforts in clear staccato sentences. "Our first objective as per your earlier direction was to activate Balochistan. The Iranians have been remarkably cooperative since you spoke to their ambassador, and we have had a major success in wiping out an ISI-sponsored Jundallah camp. In the process, at least forty assorted Sunni terrorists have been killed along with some ISI handlers. Pakistan has put a lid on this information instead of blaming India as it normally does when we are not involved. It's more than likely that the camp in operation had the backing of the CIA to unbalance Iran's Baloch population. As we pursue our 'rent a gun' model, we have already pumped in an equivalent of five million dollars to about a dozen tribal heads through banks in Dubai. We have also promised more to those showing results in terms of infrastructure damage and Pak Army casualties."

"Do we have anything to show for this investment so far?" Durga asked.

"At present, work on the Gwadar-Urumqi pipeline, a major objective, has already slowed down, because non-Baloch labor is being threatened with dire consequences. The Chinese exploitation of the Saindal copper-mining lease in Baluchistan has also been delayed for at least eighteen months by sabotage of equipment. Money is also being given to laborers who agree to go home. In case of an armed conflict with China, we have plans to target Chinese oil tankers. We are also making inroads into Jihad cyber groups that can be used to target Chinese workers involved in oil exploration and oil well development activities."

"How has the Pakistan Army reacted to this?"

Sridhar replied, "We have kept the Pakistan Army from thinning out from the province and sending additional troops to face us."

"What about Xinjiang?" Durga queried.

"We have contacted Uyghur groups in Turkey and the United States, but nothing on the ground is likely to happen for quite some time. The Turkmenistan-Urumqi pipeline disruption is going to be a major objective. Lots of young people have been hired to keep an eye on Jihad websites and chatter to target potential recruits from minority Chinese groups. There are other ongoing efforts that have yet to deliver."

Sobti interceded, "Raja will update you about the funding situation for our group's entrepreneurial model so the context in which we are working can be easily understood. Money can be a great leveler for our targeted approach to crisis control. It also gives you enormous leverage for out-of-the-box solutions."

"Thanks, Ashok. Madame Prime Minister, I was given instructions by your predecessor to tap the data bank on tax evaders and create a pipeline for funding projects vital to national security issues. So far we have $2.5 billion in the kitty, mainly offshore. We have also spent approximately seven million dollars on buying significant shareholdings in technology companies. The cash has also sped up new arms acquisitions, primarily from Russia. A watertight structure of trusts and offshore accounts in over a dozen jurisdictions has also been set up that cannot be attributed to the Indian government.

"There are about a dozen research and development boosters, hiring of scientists, including some Russians and Israelis and intelligence requirements for which we have also provided funding. There is also ongoing funding for the CRAI decision-making matrix for anticipating Chinese actions. We have gone way beyond just the political angle. The economic upheaval in the world has resulted in intense debate amongst leading economists, many of whom have direct access to the standing committee of Chinese politburo. We will get an insight beyond governments statistics that are routinely cooked up by the Chinese bureaucracy at all levels to adhere to laid-down targets. The finance minister is being regularly updated on this aspect.

"In addition, we have ironclad commitments from six of the larger, tax-evading, corporate serial offenders for security-linked thirteen billion dollars in investments outside India in the developing world. This is for funding strategically important energy projects to compete with China in Iran, Iraq, Myanmar, and Kazakhstan. About ten billion dollars over and above this figure is going to go into US energy technology companies. This investment will stand us in good stead when thousands of old wells are progressively activated. In the next few months, we will add strategic investments in metals and rare earths to this portfolio."

"Thanks, Raja. Admiral, could you please sum up the armed forces equipment procurement–related national security developments we have been connected with to date for the benefit of the PM?"

"There have been significant gains achieved in completing the aircraft carrier INS Vikramaditya sea trials as well as the fifth-generation fighter-aircraft prototypes that were specifically pushed by your predecessor. We need to thank Mathews for persuading the Russians to take money and play ball. We have also got off to a good start in significantly tightening our cyber security. However, the equipment that we need to wage cyber war has a long lead time and is not likely to be available for at least eighteen months. We also have a trained nucleus of about three hundred talented, young software engineers. These were employed after detailed background security checks, as they will be involved in cyber sabotage targeting China when we need to. We will spin off this group to RAW in a few months when it is fully operational. It can be used as a nucleus for a much larger organization.

"Mathews has again achieved a miracle in getting some extremely talented Russian scientists working for us to create a useable EMP weapon. The work is going on underground in some abandoned gold mines in Karnataka to ensure adequate security. All in all, things have looked up, and we have achieved a fair momentum working together. We had recommended that government sanction be accorded quickly to purchase American 155 howitzers, and some effective lobbying to this end has already been organized by Speed. Nothing seems to have come of it."

"The new CCS has cleared the proposal," Prime Minister Durga Vadera clarified. "As also the issue of doing the nuke simulation tests that the Iranians are seeking. This is subject to the energy tradeoffs being sufficiently high to offset the risks involved!

"Speed needs to make a few trips to Washington again, perhaps along with Raja, to spread the money and organize more lobbyists. We need lobbyists who can deliver on neutralizing knee-jerk reactions that the United States might take against our interests. If the Israelis even suspect that we have bailed out the Iranians, there will be enormous pressure on the US administration from the Jewish lobby to turn the screws on us."

Lieutenant General Randhir Singh spoke for the first time. "Madame Prime Minister, I think your immediate problem is going to come the moment you are forced to take proactive steps against Pakistan. It will be a rerun of the 1971 conflict in many ways, with the United States firmly aligned with Pakistan—that is, unless we start lobbying the US administration hard right now. Remember they sailed the aircraft carrier Enterprise into the Bay of Bengal to pose a threat in being to India? We need to continuously evolve fresh options to deal with the United States. Your government needs to move quickly to get all the major US armament companies on board. Promise them the moon if necessary in terms of orders. Boeing, Lockheed Martin, Raytheon, and company play the rent-a-senator game in their sleep!"

M. J. Mathews, who had been absentmindedly doodling on a scratch pad, interjected, "Madame Prime Minister, I think it would be appropriate under the circumstances to treat this as a war situation. Petty politicking needs to be put aside. It may be appropriate to consider keeping the leader of the opposition fully in the loop on a daily instead of periodic basis. This is especially so when it comes to deciding on proactive actions against both Pakistan and China at some stage! After all, if he wins the election next month, with the crisis continuing to spin along, he may be tempted to throw the baby out with the bathwater."

"Thank you, gentlemen," Durga Vadera said. "I will give Sant Chatwal a call myself. He is still the most effective amateur lobbyist we have ever had. Make some additional funds available to him. I have already decided that if push comes to shove and we have an armed conflict on our hands, we will need a national government. The leader of the opposition can have back his old defense minister's portfolio as far as I am concerned!

"I will also make a quick working visit to Russia next month to talk about our mutual fears about Chinese intentions. I'm trying to time it while the Iranian president is still there so we can have an unnoticed, accidental meeting!"

CHAPTER 39
DEMOCRACY AT PLAY

"How much do you reckon we can take in?"

"Senator Kane, we should be able to raise a million and change tonight. The Indian community has come out of the recession better than most, I reckon. If there is a shortfall, I promise to make it up myself!" Sant Chatwal declared to his distinguished visitor at his plush seven-thousand-square-foot penthouse as the two waited for the other guests at the fund-raising dinner to arrive."

"Thanks, Sant, I really appreciate the amount of time and effort you've put into my campaign."

"The United States has become totally vulnerable to China strategically and economically, and we are doing our damndest to shoot ourselves in the foot further! We don't seem to know who our friends are, and potential friends think we're weirdoes. America needs strong visionary leadership at this stage from someone like you."

"Talking of friends, I presume you are referring to India?"

"Partially, as far as India, a potential US ally in dealing with the Chinese, is concerned, the feedback that is coming in is not encouraging. A recent Gallup survey shows that 77 percent of urban Indians do not view the United States as a serious partner in fighting terror."

"What about Americans of Indian descent?"

"It is also true of a distinct 68 percent majority of US citizens of Indian origin."

Sant Chatwal read from the piece of paper he was holding in his hand, quoting Senator Jim Webb's remarks, chairing the hearing of the US Senate's Foreign Relations Subcommittee. "The inconsistent foreign policy of the United States toward Asian countries has gifted an opportunity to China to enhance its influence over regional countries. American sanctions and other policy restrictions have not only increased Chinese political and economic influence in Southeast Asia, they ironically serve as a double reward for China, because all the while, American interaction in East Asia has been declining."

He then continued, "A lot of people coming tonight are totally pissed off by the knee-jerk reaction of the president in slamming sanctions against India. We invaded Iraq and then Afghanistan after 9/11 in pursuit of our national interests, annoying most of the world in the bargain. Here, we have a case of India showing remarkable restraint, with China and Pakistan in cahoots breathing down its neck! And to add insult to injury, we are in the process of gifting Pakistan, the foremost nuclear rogue, including North Korea, three nuclear plants with an assured fuel supply!"

"Exploding fusion nukes is hardly exercising restraint. All surveys are showing the American people support the president's views."

"That nuke test is actually preserving the balance of power in America's favor. You can imagine how uppity the Chinese will get if they can bite off elephant-size chunks of India. So far, they have been figuring that the Indians have to lump it, because they have been asleep for fifty years without building up their armed forces and border infrastructure."

Senator Kelvin Kane picked his words carefully as if he was treading through a minefield. "I am of the view that inconsistencies inherent in our policies toward different governments tend to create confusion, cynicism, and allegations of what can be best termed as situational ethics."

Sant Chatwal said, "It pisses me off how we've gifted energy security to China! Within the next few years, Beijing is on track to exclusively transfer to its waiting refineries, both oil and locally trapped natural gas via a 2,380 kilometer pipeline from Burma (Myanmar), while we slap sanctions against the Army Junta. The deal is worth thirty billion dollars. The half a dozen giant deals in Iran are much larger, and there was a time when the Shah of Iran was our favorite monarch, driving

American policy in the gulf. We'll probably screw up in Brazil as well over offshore oil and gas given half a chance."

"How would you do it, given a choice?' asked the senator "It would take years of talk to lower suspicions."

Sant Chatwal said, "So what if the Iranians are developing a nuke? Everyone will have them sooner or later. Let them feel good about being able to deal with an Israeli threat. My personal take is that it's us they are most nervous about. Talk to them preferably through the Indians who have developed extremely robust linkages. Henry Kissinger opened up China for Nixon through Pakistan when it was a pariah, because we needed China to tackle the USSR. Now we need Iran to prevent uncontrolled access to oil by China.

"Our interests have not changed just because the mullahs grabbed power from the Shah in Iran. We need to talk to them. Why would they screw around with Chinese technology for oil exploration and development if they had US technology on offer and a genuine partnership? In the initial stages, it could be front-ended by the Indians through someone like Reliance Industries, from whom the Iranians also get the refined stuff. The Iranian refineries are a mess because of our sanctions."

Kelvin Kane said, "We need to win the election first. Then we can play around with some of the stuff you are suggesting. The United States has definitely taken its eye off the ball as far as China is concerned, and we need to fix it pronto. If we need to sup with the devil, so be it."

"Here are our first guests!" Sant said as a group of a dozen men and women strolled leisurely into the huge hall.

CHAPTER 40
RUN SILENT, STRIKE DEEP

"INNOVATE OR DIE!"

Lieutenant General K. P. Singh, the corps commander, had been brutally frank in his final talk with the officers of the armored brigade that was to deliver the cold start that strategy demanded.

"The next terror strike that takes place in India will force the government to take punitive military steps if they want to be voted back to power. Rest assured, gentlemen, that it's only a matter of time—today, tomorrow, a year down the line? Who knows? If we are launched the leading combat groups will buy a lot of casualties with first light—unless you achieve your objective during the night. Any questions so far?"

"Sir, with two or three days notice, essentially, it will be a cold start. Our tank and infantry combat vehicle (ICV) crews will be incomplete. Some will be on courses, some on leave, some doing the hundred and one things that peacetime routine demands. As things stand, we need at least two weeks to be adequately organized!"

"What's your name, son?"

"Sir, I am Captain Sahil Butalia, leading squadron commander of Combat Group 4 HORSE that in turn is the designated spearhead of the brigade."

"I appreciate your concern, but there is nothing much that I can do to increase the notice period. Keep your eyes and ears open to what is happening in the country and assume the worst. Any major terror strike anywhere and you can assume that it is only a matter of days before you are launched. Remember that your enemy may well be in the same boat in terms of readiness!'"

"I think it's quite stupid of you to want to return to your regiment, Sahil, if you are not fit. Are you sure that you have recovered from your injury? You still seem to be walking with a roll like a sailor," his sister, Nivriti, had observed with a jaundiced eye during a quick meeting over lunch he had had with her in Delhi."

"Of course I'm okay!" he had replied forcefully, seeing the concern in her eyes. He had cajoled the doctor into certifying that he was fit to rejoin his men. Sahil was exactly fourteen months older, but they had been almost like twins, as far as being able to read each other's thoughts was concerned. They hadn't seen much of each other for some years, not since she had drifted into a career in journalism by walking in uninvited into the national daily *Hindustan Times* office "for the experience." Sahil had opted for the army in spite of flashes of brilliance with a paintbrush and a penchant for fooling around with hi-tech gizmos that could have led to a totally different career path.

"Someone has to bail the country out if there is a conflict because of your stupid article last week!" he said, smiling over the top of his Coke. "Seriously, I'm proud of you for having written it. Much better than the man-bites-dog stuff that you normally dish out on weekends! Keep up the good work."

The article in question had been pushed by her editor to the front page on a slow news day: "Limited War Must Be an Option for India!" She had argued that India had encouraged terrorist attacks by continuously downplaying the dangers of a war ever since 21/11. This unambiguous message had only emboldened the Pakistan Army. It was now led by a former ISI chief hardwired into thinking of "death by a thousand cuts" to India. She had stressed that the Indian political leadership was unduly stressed by the idea of provoking a nuclear war; whereas on the other side, a military professional knew that his country would cease to exist if a nuclear war was triggered by him but was not averse to trying to scare the shit out of politicians in India.

Al Qaeda's media arm had picked it up and responded immediately with a lead article: "India Looking for War!" It had gone on to say the usual things: "Jihad is a personal, religiously mandated duty for every able-bodied Muslim. It is for you like our heroic Mujahid brother, Syed Ali, to decide how and when and where you are to discharge this duty. But whatever you do, do not wait for tomorrow and do not wait for others. Shame on our brothers in the uniform of the Pakistan Army to forget this sacred duty! You should all wear a veil and hide your faces."

As it transpired, the heavy monsoon rains dictated that the notice would be a prolonged one and none of the fighting sub units would be seriously under strength. The more cynical young officers were convinced that nothing would happen again as far as punitive action by the armed forces was concerned. The new prime minister would take forever to get her bearings, let alone take important war- and peace-related decisions.

Meanwhile, well-defined processes kicked in. Men were recalled from leave, and those who needed to go were stopped. Gunnery training was intensified on the miniature ranges, where a small caliber weapon was aligned with the main gun of the tank and fired at sharply telescoped ranges to build crew confidence. Weapons were thoroughly cleaned. Ammunition and fuel replenishment convoys were arranged and practiced, and sand model discussions at the subunit level of platoon and company were carried out to make sure that every man understood what was expected of him. When the FOOs (forward observation officers) of affiliated artillery batteries were shifted and the engineer mine-breaching trawl tanks joined them, the atmosphere suddenly changed. No longer was it just a game with them playing soldiers.

Captain Sahil Butalia nodded at the young soldier, who had requested a private interview.

"All well with you, Prakash Singh? I hope your father has returned home after his operation."

"Yes sir, I have no problem and have just come to you with a suggestion. The troop sergeant laughed it off, saying that I was mad, so I asked for this meeting with you."

"Perhaps he did not fully understand what you were trying to get across. And what is this suggestion of yours?"

"If we get some racing camels or even one, it will make reconnaissance in front of the tank column much simpler. My uncle, who lives in his village about two hours from here, has been breeding camels to race at the Pushkar Fair for the last thirty years. They can easily do seventy to eighty kilometers in one night! After that, of course, they will require lots of rest and fodder, but we won't require them thereafter, according to your plan!"

"It seems a good idea, and we will definitely look into its feasibility immediately. However, even if it is doable, we cannot ask your uncle, who is a civilian and probably quite old, to ride his camel into war!"

"No problem, sir. I have been riding his camels since I was four years old, along with my cousin, Karam, who is also in the squadron reconnaissance section. They know us and will die running if we let them. All that I need is a few lessons operating a GPS on camelback and a GPRS cell phone to travel light, or for that matter, a handheld radio set will do if it gives enough range."

"What gave you this idea, Prakash?" Captain Sahil Butalia asked.

"Sir, you were stressing on the reconnaissance section that you needed them to lead the advance in their jeeps and keep it quiet, but jeeps can be heard from a long distance at night. And across the grain of the land in the desert, my camel will be much faster!"

CHAPTER 41
NIGHT OF DETERMINATION

Defense Minister Shivaji Bhonsle, dependent on a sizeable Muslim vote for reelection, was adamant in opposing the timing of the Indian offensive into Pakistan that the chiefs of the Indian Armed Forces had recommended to the cabinet committee on security.

"Indian Muslims will be deeply offended. Ramadan represents the ninth month of the Islamic year in which the Koran was revealed to the prophet Mohammed. The actual revelation, according to Muslim tradition, came between the night of the twenty-sixth and twenty-seventh day called 'the Night of Determination' when the chiefs want to launch the offensive."

"You do Indian Muslims a grave injustice, Shivaji. They are nationalists first!" Durga Vadera put the argument to an end. Her secretary had done the homework. "The prophet Mohammed himself led his forces to victory during Ramadan in 624 AD at the Battle of Badr against the desert tribes. In more recent memory, the Egyptians attacked Israel in 1973, and Al Qaeda attacked the USS Cole during the holy month in 2000. We must try to achieve surprise if possible to wrap this up quickly. This may just do it."

For Muslims, Ramadan is a time of introspection, sacrifice, reconciliation, and repentance. It is a time to exercise self-restraint and practice good deeds. Thus, in spite of the tense atmosphere prevailing with India, the Pakistan Army was still caught off guard with defensive formations far from their operational areas.

Combat team "Alpha" had made excellent time leading the combat group, starting twenty-five kilometers east of the Indo-Pakistan border from its assembly area at 6:00 p.m. A medium-intensity dust storm had already started, one that would severely hinder aerial reconnaissance from both sides. Guidance had been nearly foolproof, and at 9:00 p.m., the spearhead of the tracked column was on the verge of crossing over into Pakistan.

Prakash and his cousin, Karam, equipped both with night-vision binoculars, a Garmin GPS, a GPRS phone, and a handheld radio set with spare batteries, and their racing camels, Rani and Shaitan, had been moved a kilometer short of the border into a farm building occupied by the border security forces. This was done to allow both camels resembling overgrown greyhounds to rest for the race of a lifetime. Bahawalpur was exactly a hundred kilometers away. They would both move virtually in parallel with each other but five kilometers apart, leading the armored thrust by an hour and warning of enemy deployments and minefields.

Fort Abbas had been passed from ten kilometers south. Both camels were moving easily at six to seven kilometers an hour in spite of the storm, and their riders had confirmed absence of minefields and enemy by single clicks on the switches of their handheld radios. At about 2:00 a.m., more than thirty kilometers across the border, Captain Butalia's adrenaline level rose as his headphones crackled to life.

"Two-two Alpha, contact, wait out!"

It was the classic report taught in the school of armored warfare when the leading tanks contacted the enemy. Only in this case, the leading elements were outside the playbook, both being camels. As Captain Sahil Butalia waited impatiently, he wondered what had transpired with Prakash and Karam, his two leading tank troops of three tanks, each deployed hugging the line of low dunes five hundred meters ahead of him.

"Two-two Alpha, I passed a TOW missile-tracked launcher three hundred meters on my left—probably part of the enemy 31 Corps heavy antitank unit. I saw the commander as he cupped his hands to light a cigarette. He has given no sign of having spotted me. I have moved a few hundred meters farther west and have spotted another set of tracks—over."

"Two-two Alpha, circle north five to seven hundred meters and see if you can spot anything else out to you. Twenty-two Bravo, do you have anything to report from your end—over?" Captain Butalia waited impatiently for the response from Karam on the other racing camel, Shaitan.

"Two-two Bravo, negative so far. Suggest I circle north of control point forty-seven as well to see if I can pick up tracks or a launcher—over."

"Two-two Bravo, do it quickly but be careful. Report in thirty minutes maximum—out".

It was time to discuss the options with the commanding officer of combat group 4 HORSE.

"Delta, contact is six kilometers away. Suggest I close in with the enemy while my reconnaissance elements are probing. Fields of fire are not more than 1,500 meters, I reckon, and we should be able to close in another four kilometers easy to save time. With the howling of the wind, we may not be even heard."

"Delta, do so. If two-two Bravo reports no enemy, I will wheel the rest of the combat group behind him and continue toward Bahawalpur. We need to do another thirty kilometers before first light. You sort out the TOW elements and follow, as we can't afford to let them hang around on our tail—over."

"Delta, wilco—out."

Thirty minutes later, the combat group had moved on, leaving Alpha to clear the TOWs. There had been five or six TOW launchers arrayed in front, and the enemy artillery had opened up. The two troops of tanks that had deployed first had moved up, one providing cover fire while the second moved. One tank had been hit by TOW fire; however, the crew had bailed out safely, and the covering fire had brewed two M113 APC-tracked improved TOW vehicles.

The sandstorm was easing off, which was bad news for an attacker. As Captain Sahil Butalia moved into position on the northern flank of the TOW deployment with eight tanks and the two platoons of mechanized infantry, Prakash surfaced again.

"Twenty-two Alpha, they are pulling out. I can see three tracked carriers moving west at high speed. I can also see your dust cloud. Turn one quarter to your right, and you can intercept them—over!"

"Two-two Alpha, okay, doing exactly that. Keep watching and correcting our direction if you can—out."

In an exhilarating chase, they closed in to less than four hundred meters and shot up two more improved TOW carriers. In the ensuing melee, one more tank was destroyed as the commander of an APC that had partially shed a track swiveled around and fired off two TOW missiles at less than five hundred meters before it was blown away by a high-explosive round. The mechanized platoon quickly dismounted and was able to capture two prisoners. Major Rathore, the mechanized company commander, interrogated the prisoners briskly and briefly.

"Open your mouth, motherfucker!" he said, putting the barrel of his Sten machine carbine into the rattled enemy noncommissioned officer's mouth. "Now talk!"

The time was 5:30 a.m. when Captain Sahil Butalia spoke again to his combat group commander. "Delta, POW confirms Pak 30 Corps Reserves are deployed fifteen kilometers west of Bahawalpur. Two tank regiments and a mechanized infantry battalion for sure. I am now moving on a parallel track to your south—over."

"Delta, Roger. I will be launching a Nishant UAV in ten minutes. Move as fast as you can and camouflage and deploy after thirty. Orders for you will follow—over."

"Delta, wilco—out."

The Nishant UAV, powered by a fifty-five-horsepower Wankel rotary engine, was rail-launched from a hydro-pneumatic launcher weighing fourteen tons. The catapult was carried on an all-terrain Tatra-wheeled vehicle that could comfortably keep up with armored columns in deserts. While not quite the most current technology, with a cruising speed of just 125 kilometers per hour and a 3,600-meter ceiling, it served its purpose of target tracking and localization during the day and night. Its laser-target capability was adequate for bringing down accurate fire from the Bofors 155mm artillery guns deployed eight kilometers behind the armored brigade. Sixty kilometers deep into Pakistan, the leading units of the two opposing armored brigades ran into each other with a resounding clash.

Combat group 4 HORSE less Captain Sahil Butalia's combat team and combat group 6 LANCERS of the opposing Pakistan Army, which had both led their respective forces, contacted each other while they were crossing from the crest of dunes 1,500 meters apart into the shallow space in between each other's advance. Firing rapidly after a few seconds, the leading elements were inextricably mixed up with each other as they desperately jockeyed to get back behind the crest into comparative safety.

Close-range tank clashes are decided quickly on a kill or be killed basis. By 10:00 a.m., 6 LANCERS had lost twenty-one tanks and APCs versus the thirteen tanks and ICVs lost by combat group 4 HORSE. The intense dose of training in the past few weeks was giving the Indian armor a significant edge. A hail of tank missile and artillery fire from both sides and constant small maneuvers reduced visibility to almost point-blank range, even though the sandstorm had eased. At 10:30 a.m., the Nishant UAV circling the battle area down-linked data showing another Pakistan combat group ten kilometers to the southwest, moving toward the flank of Horse, locked in battle with Lancers.

Colonel Raju, 4 HORSE's commander, immediately ordered his mechanized infantry to face the emerging threat. "Zulu, deploy a pivot of one company of BMPs on eight to ten kilometers of the dune line to our immediate southwest immediately. Engage the enemy combat group at max distance. Delta, wheel north-west and hit them from the flank and rear as soon as possible."

"Zulu, roger, moving now to the line of dunes. Will be in location in fifteen—out," the ICV company commander responded.

"Delta for Zulu, moving deployed estimate to reach control point sixty-six in ninety—over," Captain Sahil Butalia confirmed.

"Zulu, speed up as much as you can. I can see the enemy dust cloud closing toward you already—out," Colonel Raju urged, willing his BMP infantry combat vehicles with their antitank missiles to protect his flank and rear. In the meantime, the Indian 180 Armored Brigade commander had also intervened in the battle and ordered his reserve combat group 16 CAVALRY, to swing around from farther south and take the enemy from the rear.

"Zulu for Delta, I am in position and am engaging roughly twenty to fourteen tanks that I can spot on and off. I can see the dust of your leading troops. Steer quarter left to hit them in the rear—out."

"Delta for Zulu, thanks but please do not fire any missiles once I am closing in with the enemy out to you. Delta one and two, steer left and right of me for the Khejri tree on the skyline by fire and move. Delta three, come in line from farther north. Delta four, remain in reserve but keep me in sight." The orders rang out fast and furious before the decisive stage of the battle was joined as Alpha rammed into the rear of a force three times its size and destroyed eleven tanks for the loss of just one tank and an ICV.

The Pakistani combat group commander, Colonel Imtiaz Rana, grappled with being caught by missile fire on one side and a determined Sahil Butalia hell-bent on closing in at speed in spite of inferior numbers and ordered a barrage of smoke to facilitate redeployment. As his reserve combat team tried to turn Captain Butalia's Alpha's flank to relieve pressure, combat group 16 CAVALRY, completed its maneuver and enveloped the Pakistani armor from the east, coming at it from the direction of the setting sun.

In the next two hours the destruction of the 30 Corps reserve 10 Armored Brigade was completed. It was the first time in more than four decades that a tank battle of maneuver had been fought by two roughly equal forces of about 150 tanks and other armored carriers, each resulting in the near total destruction of one side. When the final tally was taken, the Indians had lost a total of thirty-four armored vehicles, roughly half of which would be eventually recovered and repaired, and had captured or destroyed 119 Pakistani tanks and armored personnel and missile carriers. The script of the limited Indian offensive had suddenly turned. Never in their wildest conjectures had the Indians thought of anything more than a stalemate in the offensive against equal forces to salvage political brownie points against the opposition parties in parliament.

The Pakistan Army's 14 Armored Brigade, sidestepped from an adjacent sector on tracks, underwent a grueling night-approach march into the battle zone. It was picked up by the freshly launched Nishant UAV, and its leading elements walked straight into the new horseshoe deployment of Captain Sahil Butalia's reinforced combat team and lost seven tanks in five minutes. It, however, managed to stabilize the situation and stem the Indian thrust by the end of the day.

The destruction of the Pakistani reserves during a surprise attack had upped the ante in Pakistan. The prestige of the Pakistan Army hung in the balance, if it did not extract revenge for the defeat. What followed was inevitable.

CHAPTER 42
NIGHT OF THE GENERALS

IN THE MIDDLE OF A REGULAR breakfast newscast, the *Times Now* news anchor suddenly interrupted the discussion. "Please stand by for an important announcement by the prime minister of India!" In a calm, flat voice showing little emotion, the somberly dressed prime minister read from her prepared text.

"My fellow Indians, it is with a sense of considerable regret I stand here to inform you that our peace-loving country is fed up with the past three decades of repeated terror incidents being sponsored from across our borders, mainly in Pakistan. Thousands of lives have been lost, including our last dearly loved prime minister, aside from the thousands more who have been seriously injured. Our best diplomatic efforts have been thwarted in bringing the perpetrators to justice in spite of clinching evidence being presented by us.

"My government has been forced to respond to redress this inequitable situation. We have been forced to direct our armed forces, primarily army and air, to take limited action directed against terrorist sanctuaries in Pakistan. It is from these places from where the latest attacks against India in Delhi, masterminded by a Pakistan Army Inter-Services Intelligence (ISI) brigadier have been formulated and launched. We have sufficient and compelling proof of his identity that we are providing to the world community. This action was started last night and will continue for a limited period until the sanctuaries are destroyed.

Thereafter, our forces will return to our side of the international border as soon as possible.

"The situation along the LAC with China continues to remain tense ever since China forcibly occupied our forward-advance landing ground at Daulet Beg Oldi. There is absolutely no truth in the Chinese assertion that one of their military helicopters was shot down by our forces and they were forced to react in self-defense. The critical situation that our country finds ourselves in at this stage has also necessitated the conduct of four underground nuclear tests, including a small fusion device of a nominal yield of forty-five kilotons. We trust that our constraints will be appreciated by the wider international community. If the situation continues to deteriorate, we may have no option but to revisit our current commitment not to be the first party to use a nuclear device. This is an extreme option for us that I pray will not arise.

"We hope that the government of Pakistan will at long last take the measures that we have been demanding for decades to stamp out terror groups trained and financed in Pakistan. Relations between our countries can then be reverted to normal.

"I am also pained to point out that we continue to harbor certain disruptive elements and groups in India who are working at the behest of foreign agencies in organizing terror strikes within our country to create tension and hatred between communities. I urge all right-thinking citizens who may have access to knowledge regarding these groups to bring it to the notice of the police authorities concerned without fear of being personally implicated for any reason. We have in the recent past introduced a 911, toll-free number that you can use from anywhere in the country and be instantly connected with someone who will take your complaint and initiate action on it near simultaneously. All this will be done by keeping your identity secret as a matter of policy, unless you will otherwise."

What Durga Vadera did not include in her speech was the far-reaching decision that had been implemented in respect of Iran. After weeks of dillydallying in passing executive orders to the atomic energy commission chairman, computer simulations of Iran's nuclear fission device had been carried out in great secrecy. The device was unwieldy but would work with an estimated yield of twenty to twenty-two kilotons.

Simultaneously, a conversation was taking place between US Secretary of State Eleanor Griffith Huxley and Pakistan Prime Minister Shamsher Jung Choudhary. "We are monitoring the situation very closely throughout national technical means, including through the predator UAVs that you permitted to be operated from some of your air bases. There is no sign of the Indians doing anything anywhere else except the limited ground offensive in the Bahawalpur area that the Lashkar e Taiba camps have functioned from. I had warned you more than a month ago that credible action, at least at the cosmetic level, was required to be taken by your government against the organization to give the Indians at least a pipe dream to sell their people. You failed completely to take any steps in that direction, and your loudmouthed home minister has further muddied the waters by irresponsible statements. You shot yourselves in the foot and left the Indians with no choice but to react in some way.

"Now please make sure you don't do something more stupid like firing off a couple of nukes of your own or pulling out troops from the tribal areas or, for that matter, getting together with the Chinese and launching a counteroffensive of your own. If you just sit tight for a few days and let me handle this issue, Pakistan will come out of this smelling of roses."

"What is a limited offensive to you, Eleanor, is a national disaster for me and Pakistan. What is the United States doing for Pakistan right now? Nothing of substance we can put a finger on except feeding us empty words of advice!" Shamsher Jung Choudhary retorted.

"You are being backed more than you deserve. Just watch *CNN* after an hour for President Watson's take of the situation in South Asia. The TV crews are just moving in for the press conference. The Indians will pay for what they have done!"

"Get real, Eleanor! Pity you never had to fight an election, unlike your president. The Indians will do what they have to, irrespective of what you threaten to do. I will try to avert an open-ended conflict as best as I can. Now I have to cut this short and go, as we both have things to do!"

The makeup crew had done their best but could not totally disguise the dark shadows from under President James Watson's eyes before he began his broadcast. "A few hours ago, India conducted a series of four underground tests, including what we believe from preliminary results was a fusion nuke. India has also launched an armored strike into Pakistan from its forward bases in Rajasthan, ostensibly directed at terrorist sanctuaries believed to be in the Bahawalpur area. I would like to mention here that not an iota of proof has been provided by the Indian government about the existence of these sanctuaries so far. The United States strongly urges India to immediately call a cease-fire in this conflict and pull back their troops back to the Indian side of the international border. Under the provisions of our law, I am forthwith ordering a cessation of nuclear energy cooperation with India and pulling back all men, equipment, and enriched fuel provided so far for nuclear power generation back to this country.

"We also urge the government of Pakistan not to act unilaterally and increase the scope of this conflict and give peace a chance. The UN Security Council is likely to meet shortly in New York to take stock of the situation and help resolve the conflict. However, to lend teeth to future prospective UNSC resolutions, I have ordered the US Seventh Fleet to immediately locate a carrier-borne task force in the Indian Ocean. This task force will be further bolstered by elements from our sixth fleet based in Bahrain."

The meeting between General Mahmoud Butt, the new chief of the Pakistan Army, and his prime minister had been brief. The lack of chemistry between the two men had never been more evident. "General, Pakistan's interests do not exist in absolute black-and-white terms unlike what you appear to propagate. There are some interwoven strands of gray that we need to balance, like when we agreed to the United States using our bases, although our people are totally against this policy. There is no question of a counteroffensive being launched by the armed forces into India for the time being. I don't care what support the Chinese seem to have promised you off the record. Let preparations remain on course, of course, while we give peace as promised by Watson a chance. We won't explode any nukes for the time being, if the Americans make good on their promise to screw the Indians civil nuclear program!"

"Very well Mr. Prime Minister! I had warned you weeks ago that if the Indians attack, any hope of our achieving any surprise will lie in the speed and violence of our reaction. We could have retaliated by now and also prevented this disaster in Bahawalpur by staging forward our reserves a week earlier. The window for action is closing fast, and along with it, the destiny of our people to live with self-respect. It would not be advisable through inaction to create a situation where we will be forced to use nuclear strikes as the only remaining option."

As the army chief saluted smartly and left, the Pakistan prime minister heaved a sigh of relief. It had gone far easier than he had any reason to expect. He would change his mind soon. Two hours later, as he was in the middle of a spirited address to the Pakistan Parliament, a high-speed convoy of heavy vehicles was already streaming in to surround the building and make nonsense of the security measures put in place by the police. A young, athletic-looking major general in combat fatigues with gleaming boots and a paratrooper's beret walked briskly into the central hall. He was accompanied by a similarly dressed, noncommissioned officer with a slung Sten machine carbine on his left shoulder, carrying a battery-powered, amplified loudspeaker in the other hand, which he handed over to the officer.

"*May I have your attention please!*" a voice used for instant obedience rang out, bringing a hush to the noisy assembly as if by magic. Major General Shahid Khan paused for effect for a moment and then continued, "I am here at the behest of the chiefs of the Pakistan Armed Forces. In view of the enormous physical threat being posed to the existence of Pakistan by the Indian attack, I have been directed to convey to you that a temporary state of martial law is being imposed on our country with immediate effect. Please remain seated, as in a short while, you will all be given further instructions and arrangements made for you to be conveyed back to your respective homes. Thank you for your willing cooperation!"

CHAPTER 43
COUNTER THRUST

THE LAUNCHING OF A COUNTER OFFENSIVE by Pakistan had to resolve two problems to hope for success. Both these problems related to the radar coverage of the Indo-Pak border by the Indians. The first problem involved taking out a tethered 1,700-kilogram EL/M-2083-phased array radar hovering at four thousand feet, mounted on a 240-foot-long aerostat located west of Amritsar. The static coverage system was developed and manufactured by Israel Aerospace Industries' Elta Systems Group (IAI/Elta). The system was designed to detect approaching aircraft from long ranges, especially those flying at low altitudes and using electronically steered, multi beam techniques to detect terrain-hugging objects up to three hundred kilometers away. The EL/M-2083 aerostat unit was capable of providing three-dimensional, low-altitude coverage equal to at least thirty ground-based radars.

The second problem related to a similar system that was much more flexible but provided short-duration coverage. The Indian Air Force had finally acquired the first of three Russian IL-76 aircraft carrying Israeli Phalcon-phased array radars designated AWACS KW-3551 for radar, electronic surveillance, photo-reconnaissance, and spying inside Pakistani territory and airspace. The AWACS was located at Agra. With this enhanced air surveillance and interception capability, the IAF now had foreknowledge of the aerial and ground activity at PAF air bases and air defense installations. The AWACs could detect the number of aircraft flying in the air, parking, or taxiing on the ground. It knew the location and deployment of Pakistani radars, missiles (i.e., SAMs, surface-to-surface missiles, IRBMs), nuclear installations, military concentrations, armor and artillery deployments, POL depots, powerhouses, and vital infrastructure. The IAF AWACs could even monitor air and rail movements and the traffic on Pakistani highways.

The frequent flying of IAF's Russian-built AWACs to obtain a photo and video view of all activity in the air or on the ground to a depth of three hundred kilometers was a very dangerous development and, in fact, a provocation in the prevailing volatile Pak-India relations. With powerful radars and electronic sensors mounted on the AWACs, the Indian Air Force now had an enhanced detection, interception, and accurate attack and ground-strike capability. Aircraft fitted with surveillance radars, sensing and data-collecting electronics, jamming black boxes, and command and control capability were known as AEW (airborne early warning), and they were designed for radar early warning and detection of aircraft, ships, and submarines. But when augmented by early warning and command and control (i.e., intercept capability), these were called AWACs. Thirty minutes after the imposition of military rule in Pakistan, contingency plans to take out the aerostat and ground the AWACs were set into motion.

The call had come without warning. It was a hand-delivered letter by government-speed post the previous afternoon. When she opened the envelope, there was a blank sheet of paper. To her, the green paper indicated "Thursday." The code was simple—the color of paper would correspond to the day of the week immediately to come. Monday to Sunday would correspond to the colors in a rainbow spectrum—VIBGYOR—violet for Monday, indigo for Tuesday, and so on till red corresponded to Sunday.

Sultana Ahmed strapped herself into the cockpit of the Cessna Skyhawk R. She was a well known figure in the small flying club at Patiala for the past two years. She flew at least twice a week when she was visiting and paid cash each time. All that anyone knew about her was that she was a rich, nonresident Indian (NRI) from Liverpool who visited her ailing mother in Patiala from time to time. She was a favored client for a struggling flying club.

Seventy minutes later, instead of landing at Rajasansi Airport at

Amritsar as her flight plan indicated, she flew straight into the 240-foot-long aerostat, thinking she was achieving martyrdom. What she did achieve was a big hole in the Indian radar network that could only be plugged for some hours at a time by AWACs.

Thirty minutes after Sultana Ahmed had taken off on her last flight, Wing Commander Rakesh Nath at the Air Force Station Agra supervised the delicate business of wheeling out the AWACs KW-3551, which he regarded as his own aircraft from the special hangar. The front of the hangar was much higher than the others to accommodate a scaffold structure for maintenance. As was customary on auspicious occasions, Corporal Aziz Mahmoud offered a succulent collection of large Indian sweets from a famous sweetshop in the city to the officers and crew. His brother's wedding had been finalized for the following month. This was just before they boarded the aircraft. Three hours later, the entire crew of the aircraft was taken violently ill, an incident that turned out to be food poisoning initially, and they were forced to land at Adampur. As ISI Chief Lieutenant General Saif Gilani put it to the joint chief of staff, "India's air defense is as effective as a blindfolded whore in a military barrack, lying on the floor with her legs spread!"

The first wave of F-16 aircraft of the Pakistan Air Force the setting sun at their backs, hit Indian forward air bases in North India at Jammu, Chandigarh, Pathankot, Halwara, Adampur, Ambala, and Amritsar, primarily with runway denial munitions. It was critical to keep the runways down and prevent Indian combat aircraft from taking off and interfering with ground operations of the Pakistan armored thrusts for the first twenty-four hours of combat. After that, it would not matter too much, because forces would have fanned out and easy targets would not be easily available.

Not much damage was done to Indian aircraft, for they were encased in blast pens, but all runways were severely affected in spite of well-organized efforts to carry out repairs to craters with quick-drying concrete. The only exception was an AN-32 transport aircraft with thirty-two soldiers taking off from Chandigarh for Leh that was shot down on takeoff by a PAF F-16, all aboard killed.

As successful flash reports of the airstrike and the closing down of Indian air bases trickled in, a wave of six Huey Cobra attack helicopters flying nap of the earth fifty meters above ground level swooped through the Shakargarh salient jutting into India, crossed the international border, and almost simultaneously crossed the antitank ditch and embankment obstacle system impregnated with fortifications. This had been erected to run virtually parallel to the border, dug three to five kilometers in depth. The obstacle also had a mixed minefield of antitank and antipersonnel mines running ahead of it. Any ground attack by Pakistan would be forced to venture through the minefield and take casualties from exploding mines before their men tackled the antitank ditch and the weapon emplacements guarding crossing areas.

As they wheeled around in a brisk U-turn immediately after penetrating the airspace above the obstacle system, the Huey Cobras attacked the emplacements from the rear, with rockets and canon fire delivered using thermal-imaging sights. They caught Alpha Company of the defending Seven Rajput Battalion of the Indian Army responsible for defense of the area under attack totally by surprise. As luck would have it, many soldiers tasked with collecting dinner for their subunits were caught in the open in the initial fury of the rocket barrage.

Five minutes later, twelve heavy-lift helicopters following in the wake of the Huey Cobras disgorged two companies of the Pakistan Special Services Group (SSG) while they hovered close to the ground within six hundred meters of the rear of the obstacle system. These specially trained and selected troops quickly moved up to the area neutralized by the attack helicopters, and at the point of their bayonets, they proceeded to kill all surviving troops. This did not go uncontested, for the defenders, though taken completely by surprise, fought back valiantly after they emerged from their pillboxes to face the rear. Within an hour, opposition ceased, because the defenders were picked off one by one, but not before the SSG companies had lost thirty-one killed and wounded, although they had accounted for more than twice that number of defenders.

Near simultaneously, a brigade group of Pakistan assault infantry commenced move at a brisk walk from ten kilometers away on the Pakistan side of the border. The brigade was grouped with a subunit of tanks and an assault engineer task force with bridging equipment to span the ditch and mine-breeching equipment to clear a safe passage for follow on troops The brigade group had been staged forward in the hours of darkness and had waited in concealment after they had camouflaged themselves for twenty-four hours for just this role in order to quickly link up with the helicopter-borne SSG companies and widen the foothold on the obstacle system before the inevitable Indian counterattack was launched. This brigade group's advance was severely disrupted by a platoon of Seven Rajput deployed within the Indian minefield between strips of mines, along with a troop of three tanks under Lieutenant Suraj Rathore. The Indian forward deployment position had been superbly camouflaged, lying adjacent to a small clump of trees, and reconnaissance elements had failed to pick it up.

Rathore's orders to his troop of tanks were simple: "We will engage the enemy at point-blank range. No one will fire before me! Now is the chance to earn your pay."

The firefight took place at point-blank range, with Rathore's gunner firing three armor-piercing rounds at five to six hundred meters and scoring two direct hits on the assault-brigade tanks before the enemy could react. His two tanks accounted for another three tanks between them. In the smoke, dust, and confusion, they broke contact and retreated, bringing down a heavy volume of machine-gun fire on the assaulting infantry. It was too good to last, and Rathore was killed by an enemy artillery shell landing on his tank. Another tank was lost to a rocket-launcher team that had sneaked in to within a hundred meters. The infantry platoon was also overrun, but not before it had totally disrupted one of the assaulting columns, killing and wounding forty-two enemy soldiers. The two-hour delay this action caused was to prove critical subsequently.

By 2300 hours, the Pakistan infantry brigade finally linked up with the SSG troops. In the meanwhile, the commanding officer of Seven Rajput had also been able to take action by strengthening the shoulders of the breach in his defenses. He did this by moving some vehicle-mounted mobile teams with machine guns and antitank weapons to plug the breach in depth. He had also requested for additional resources to attack the enemy bridgehead into his defenses while he was stabilizing the situation.

When the first armor elements of the Pakistan attackers were finally inducted into the bridgehead, a full-fledged counterattack with tanks and infantry supported by all available artillery by the Indians had developed. The carnage that ensued on both sides was considerable; however, by 5:00 a.m., the Indian counterattack had been beaten back, and the better part of an armored brigade with almost 140 armored vehicles of all types were in a position to head due west and cut off the main Indian lifeline between Jammu and Kashmir and the rest of India.

Farther north, the Chinese divisional commander, Major General Mao Lai, watched the developing situation and gave the go-ahead for the next phase of his operation.

"Northern command of the Indians is tied up by the Pakistani thrust that is on the verge of cutting off the national highway to Jammu and Kashmir. It does not have the reserves to deal with us!' he told his regimental commanders.

The GOC Northern Command landed back at his headquarters after his aerial reconnaissance and walked into the command bunker of his chief of staff. "Although things seem to be under control and Sixteen Corps is confident of preventing any further ingress toward the national highway south of the Hiranagar area, I think we cannot afford to wait any longer. With this current drought raging, we cannot take any chances with the Madhopur Headworks falling to the Pakistanis and blocking release of water into the irrigation system. A good Punjab and Haryana wheat harvest is vital to prevent food riots later. Release a hundred Krasnopols. There is a FH-77 155 mm Bofors battery ideally located to cover the complete breakout area."

"Why not wait for a few hours? Let them induct another armored brigade, and we can truly hammer them in that confined space and maybe launch an armored brigade and a couple of infantry battalions from southeast of Samba to hit their launch pad," suggested the chief of staff.

"No, it will just escalate to a real war from the present conflict in limited areas! They will be forced to consider nukes to retrieve the situation. Why raise the stakes for the Pakistan Army to a level where the self-respect or *izzat* is on the line?"

As distinct from conventional artillery projectiles that engage area targets, the Krasnopol, designed by the versatile KBP Design Bureau at Tula in Russia, ensures destruction of individual targets from covered fire positions by a single shot without fire adjustments. It was ideal against tanks, as it could pick off targets moving at up to thirty-six kilometers per hour. Tanks were rarely able to achieve even half this speed in a fighting breakout. The laser terminal guidance of the Krasnopol fifty-kilogram canon-launched, fin-stabilized projectile ensured a steep attack trajectory for the 20.5-kiloggram warhead against the least heavily armored portion of all tanks. The most heavily armored portion of any tank was designed against frontal attack.

The Nishant UAV had picked up the camouflaged combat group of sixty-five armored vehicles, including tanks and armored personnel carriers waiting to be launched to seize the Madhopur Headworks in a swift operation, along with another helicopter-borne operation. At 1700 hours, as the weak winter sun was fading and camouflage nets were being taken down by the armored vehicle crews dispersed over about four square kilometers, the opening salvo of eighteen Krasnopols hit thirteen tanks and five armored personal carriers, leaving smoking wrecks in their wake. In the melee that followed, armor vehicles frantically trying to drive out of the zone, the remaining eighty-two rounds took out another forty armored vehicles, many being struck twice over as the terminal guidance systems refused to differentiate between living and dead targets.

The much-maligned Krasnopols at the equivalent of thirty thousand dollars, a round dogged by allegations of kickbacks, bribes, nonperformance, rigged trials, and dud fuses for thirteen years, ever since they had been procured, had delivered at the end of their shelf lives. The northern army commander smiled in relief. If he had known they were going to work so well, he would have released only half the number from his strategic stocks. It was time to turn his attention to the Chinese now.

ISI Chief Lieutenant General Saif Gilani saluted and entered General Mahmoud Butt's office at the Pakistan General Headquarters in Rawalpindi. The fate of Pakistan and, in many ways, its neighborhood had been written within its four walls for many decades.

"You sent for me, sir?"

"US Secretary of State Eleanor Griffith Huxley spoke to me an hour ago. The Americans are insisting that we do not widen the war, or else they will cut off all arms and ammunition flows and the billion a year in aid to our country. They have promised to ensure that the Indians sit quietly as well! She is also paranoid about us pulling out troops from the Afghan border and allowing the Taliban to regroup. I have told her that if she gets the Indians to pull back from Bahawalpur, we will cooperate. To make her even more paranoid, I have also threatened to pull out one brigade every week to be sent to the western front with India starting next week, unless we see signs of political movement."

"Word of our offensive into India getting stalled has been magnified by rumors on the streets. The Pakistan public will not stand for this state of affairs for very long, not unless it is convinced that we are proactive against India. Already, the political parties are holding street meetings, saying the Pakistan Army is ineffective and only interested in power!" Lieutenant General Saif Gilani commented.

"Saif, what other nonmilitary options do we have in place to keep the Indians unbalanced? We need to remain relevant in the region and be able to distance ourselves from any culpability that may arise. The Americans will know we are responsible, but they can live with that—as long as they can tell the Indians that we have little control over non-state actors!"

"We have more than fifty sleeper cells all over India, sir. We had a minor setback in a recent raid on a training camp for Indian-origin Mujahideen. It seems to have been inspired by India through Bugti in Dubai but succeeded due to our own carelessness. We lost four promising 'fidayeen' volunteers for attacks in Kolkata, who were the cream of the present crop. Currently, we have four small camps within an hour's drive from the Makran Coast in Baluchistan and the border with Iran. A hundred disaffected Muslim youngsters from India who were brought in via Nepal and Bangladesh are in various stages of being trained. There are twenty-five in each camp, with four instructors who are experts in firearms and making IEDs with local materials. Since recruitment was done mainly through the mobsters we control like Dawood Ibrahim in Mumbai, Amir Raza Khan in Kolkata, Rasool 'Party' in Ahmadabad, and the Bhatkal brothers in Karnataka, we dedicated a camp to each faction to build up local affiliations and promote teamwork. We can unleash the IM across major cities in at least a dozen places near simultaneously! However, the operational aspects are complex and will take at least six weeks to organize."

"Go ahead. That suits us fine. The Chinese will be delighted, as they seem to be controlling India's northeast insurgent groups to some extent. We should see what quid pro quo can be extracted from them in exchange for squeezing the Indians. Look at making a quick trip to Beijing in between to talk to the PLA. I will give the Americans a month to persuade the Indians to pull back to their side of the border. There is no way that the Indians will cooperate without all sorts of guarantees on terrorism the Americans cannot deliver. The Indians are in a bind and can't risk any further escalation of conflict against us because of actions of homegrown terrorists—at least not with the Chinese breathing down their necks!"

General Mahmoud Butt pulled a drag from his cigarette and then said thoughtfully, "It may be also the right time to remind our people of the grave danger that India poses to us in Baluchistan."

"It is certainly possible to do, sir! I will need less than a week to activate our contingency plans!"

Five days later, a small luxury bus carrying half a dozen Chinese engineers from the Saindak copper and gold project at Chagm to Gwadar was ambushed by four masked men fifty kilometers from Gwadar just before sunset. When they heard the gunshots, an army patrol in the vicinity gave chase to the open SUV carrying the assailants and managed to gun down one of them, a man who fell out of the vehicle after he was shot. The other three managed to get away in the darkness. A letter recovered from the dead body indicated that the man, who was in his early twenties, was from the Kutch district of Gujarat in India. All the newspapers ran a story of the Indian RAW agent trying to provoke trouble in Baluchistan in connivance with local sirdars and all the efforts being made to trace the culprits.

"One of the Indian boys being trained who had finished his training decided that he had had enough and wanted to go home. I have already issued instructions to streamline our screening and selection process further," Lieutenant General Saif Gilani explained.

"The incident should be a timely reminder to our Chinese friends of the dangers posed by India to the development of the Gwadar-Urumqi road, rail, and pipeline project! Please remind them of our advice for the past two years for making optimum use of Gwadar. They must sink the

Indian aircraft carrier to ensure that the oil pipeline to Xinjiang remains secure!" General Mahmud Butt observed.

It was Eleanor Griffith Huxley on the encrypted line again. "General Butt, the president is delighted that you have cooled things down with the Indians."

"Ms. Huxley, this is purely provisional as I told you earlier. You need to get the Indians to start pulling out soon. The Pakistan public will not stand for an Indian victory, even if it is notional!"

"General, we will certainly try, but it's not going to happen in a hurry. Meanwhile, you have enough other-than-war options, including with China, to keep the Indians hopping. All I can promise is that we will disregard any evidence of your involvement in the execution of any of these options."

"I cannot promise anything, Ms. Huxley!"

"Surely, you can, general. I wouldn't like to be in your boots if the news of the fifty million dollars sitting in your numbered account in Geneva gets out. Have a nice day, general!"

CHAPTER 44
SINK THE GORSHKOV

ADMIRAL ZHANG WENGEN DID NOT SUFFER fools gladly even the ones who could overrule him.

"We don't have to bother too much about an Indian carrier fleet. The excuse of a conflict in South Tibet or Arunachal Pradesh, as the Indians call it, is adequate for us to take out a carrier in less than fifteen minutes. One Dong Feng missile, with its complex satellite guidance system, an almost nonexistent radar signature and total maneuverability with a conventional one-kiloton, high-explosive warhead is enough to do the trick! If we can take out a 1.5-meter-diameter target in outer space travelling at twenty-eight thousand kilometers per hour, where is the problem with a target two hundred times that size that is static or moving at one thousandth that speed?"

The vice chairman of the central military commission, General Xu Caihou, terminated the discussion then when he said, "Sink the Gorshkov but non-conventionally! The politburo wants it done to make sure that there is no threat in being from India that can disrupt our shipping carrying crude oil from the Persian Gulf. I don't care how difficult it is. You have two years to plan the operation before the Gorshkov refit and upgrade at Murmansk is completed. We will get enough warning before the carrier sails for India. Just ensure that the sinking is attributed to pirates or Al Qaeda and not the PLA Navy. You can assume that anything else that you ask for will be provided from the PLA and the PLAAF and other strategic national assets—satellite coverage, strategic reconnaissance aircraft, shore watchers, Special Forces, equipment, and technology from anywhere in the world. Just name it, and it's yours!"

In Ukraine at Nikolayev South Shipyard Number 444, back in 1978, a modified Kiev-class aircraft carrier was laid for the Soviet Navy. It was launched in 1982 as the Baku, but software bugs in the command and control system delayed its commissioning for five long years. After the collapse of the Soviet Union in 1991, the city of Baku found itself a part of independent Azerbaijan, which resulted in the renaming of the ship as the "Admiral Gorshkov," vaunted for his single-minded expansion of the Soviet Navy. Three years later, the jinx resurfaced, and the ship was docked for a year of repairs following a boiler room explosion.

In early 2004, the Indians sensed an opportunity for blue-water capability at fire-sale rates. They put in a bid to buy the Gorshkov. Strapped for cash after the recession induced in the United States and the collapse in worldwide commodity prices, especially that of oil, Russia approved the sale readily. Russia also agreed to upgrade the carrier by stripping all the weaponry from the ship's foredeck to make way for a short takeoff but arrested recovery configuration (STOBAR). The short-lived name, "Admiral Gorshkov," would be erased, and the carrier would be renamed INS Vikramaditya after the legendary Hindu King who had started life as a salt trader. Years of bickering followed the purchase, and instead of a fire-sale morsel, the Russians would ultimately rake in more than four billion dollars from the sale. This besides the strategically important payoff in keeping the Sevmash yard fully employed at a time of stringent financial distress for Russia, 70 percent of the aircraft carriers equipment would be new and the balance refurbished.

At forty-five thousand tons of full-load displacement with a length of 273.1 meters, beam of thirty-one meters, and a draught of 8.2 meters, INS Vikramaditya's four-shaft geared steam turbines delivered two hundred thousand shaft horse power. It had a top speed of twenty-nine knots, with a range of over seven thousand nautical miles and sustained operations for over forty-five days. The armament suite was formidable with twelve Sandbox surface-to-surface missiles and twenty-four vertically launched SA-N-9 surface-to-air missiles, besides two 100-mm guns, eight 30-mm canons, and ten 533-mm torpedo tubes. It also carried lethal RBU-6000 antisubmarine rocket launchers.

The crowning glory, of course, were the twelve brand new state-of-the-art MIG-29K aircraft fourth-generation fighters with state-of-the-art flyby wire-flight controls operating off a 14 degree ski jump. These would be retrieved after missions with the help of three arrester wires. The aircraft had advanced RD-33 MK engines and additional fuel tanks whose radar cross-sections were reduced by a factor of 4–5 compared to the MIG-29. Twenty Kamov 28 and Kamov 31 helicopters for antisubmarine warfare and airborne early warning completed the lethal mix of firepower. Russian AN-124 cargo planes had already delivered the MIG-29K aircraft to India.

Rear Admiral Kamath, better known as just "KVK," was impatiently waiting to cast off, vigorously rubbing his hands together in the biting cold. He had been promoted to flag rank three months earlier back in Delhi and told to winter in Murmansk until the INS Vikramaditya was ready to be brought home to Karwar near Goa. This would be after the completion of sea trials and rectification of defects. India's latest stealth platform would provide the escort. Naval headquarters had been adamant on the routing. It would be a long haul home, and as an aviator who had cut his teeth on the Viraat's 12-degree ski jump flying Sea Harrier's, he was uncomfortable with the idea that he had no planes on board. They had already been crated, sent to India, and flown operationally by fully trained pilots from land.

He was expected to crawl home at a sedate speed of twelve knots or 22.2 kilometers an hour to conserve fuel and simultaneously train the crew and escort a destroyer. It would take thirty days to do a journey that, according to him, should not have required more than three weeks. He had gone over the route a hundred times in his mind, looking for hidden dangers, although he had been assured by naval headquarters that there was absolutely no cause for concern for a flattop under escort.

INS Vikramaditya Time and Distance Chart

Place From	To	Dist on Leg (KM)	Dist on Leg (NM)	Time on Leg (hrs)	Cumulative (km)	Cumulative (NM)	Heading
Murmansk	N of Finland	350	189	16	350	189	335
N of Finland	Waypoint South	550	297	25	900	486	250
Waypoint South	Faroe Is	1200	648	54	2100	1134	225
Faroe Is	Off Amsterdam	930	502	42	3030	1636	200
Off Amsterdam	Dover Strait	220	119	10	3250	1755	230
Dover Strait	Lands End	500	270	22	3750	2025	280
Lands End	N of Portugal	770	416	35	4520	2441	240
N of Portugal	Trafalgar (Cadiz)	830	448	37	5350	2889	220
Trafalgar (Cadiz)	Gibraltar Strait	450	243	20	5800	3132	150
Gibraltar Strait	N of Tunis	1450	783	65	7250	3915	110
N of Tunis	Malta	520	281	23	7770	4195	170
Malta	Alexandria	1630	880	73	9400	5076	140
Alexandria	Gulf of Suez	450	243	48	9850	5319	170
Gulf of Suez	Djibouti	2050	1107	92	11900	6425	165
Djibouti	Socotra	1000	540	45	12900	6965	080
Socotra	Karwar	2200	1188	99	15100	8153	070
				707			
Total time is 30 days of sailing at 12 knots ie 22.2 km/hr							
This is passage through the Suez canal and takes 48 hrs approx							
Text in red indicates areas where there is likely choke point							

INS Vikramaditya's voyage From Murmansk to Karwar Time & Distance Chart

The sea trials had gone smoothly and were incident free. The Vikramaditya exceeded most of the planning parameters, albeit marginally. Already, the ship's company was acquiring a noticeable élan that boded well for the future. The only discordant note that had been struck was the suspected presence of an unidentified submarine in the neighborhood during a spell of gale force conditions. *NATO or Chinese,* he surmised to himself and put the thought out of his mind.

In his mind's eye, he went over the first leg of the nominated route once again—Murmansk to North of Finland, Waypoint South, Faroe Island, off Amsterdam, then through the busy Straits of Dover, Lands End, north of Portugal to Trafalgar, where Nelson had crushed the French fleet in 1805, and into the Straits of Gibraltar. The refueling tanker would tentatively meet them at sea south of Crete. He would have preferred to have sailed around the cape instead of exposing himself to the bottlenecks of Gibraltar, the Suez Canal, and the pirate-dominated seas of the coast of Africa.

The one saving grace, where he had been permitted to have his own way, was in the escort by the Kolkata-class destroyer, INS Kochi, with its two multirole helicopters. It was a state-of-the-art, 163-meter-long stealth ship with a 17.4-meter beam and a 6,800-ton displacement that could breeze past thirty knots without really straining its four gas turbines. It carried sixteen Brahmos supersonic cruise missiles and forty-eight Israeli Barak surface-to-air missiles. The "Nagin" active towed-array sonar as well as the "Humsa-NG" hull-mounted radar were both world-class.

CHAPTER 45
KING OF THE OCEAN

After a month of initial planning by the PLA Navy, it was decided that plausible deniability had to be maintained for an outsourced attack on an Indian carrier. Some apparent motivation for the attack needed to be created so that the world community would find the attack plausible. The Muslim Jihadist groups that were inimical to India were all based in Pakistan and had no maritime expertise. The ISI could otherwise be easily co-opted into finding the right talent.

Ultimately, it was freshly promoted Major Dingbang, the Special Forces veteran entrusted with causing a flare-up on the LAC in Aksai Chin, who suggested that LTTE "naval" surviving Sea Tiger elements constituted the best viable alternative to launch an attack. He was now seconded to the "Gorshkov Planning Cell." The Sea Tigers had been simply the best in the world in terms of nonconventional maritime experience. In addition, the survivors had a grudge against India for not supporting the Tamil struggle. In the past, this had led the LTTE to assassinate Rajiv Gandhi, the prime minister of India. An attack by the LTTE remnants could never be attributed to China. To set it up, however, it was essential to keep a tag of the Gorshkov from the time it sailed.

The CMC had agreed that the first Chinese Hai Yang satellite dedicated solely to maritime surveillance would be prioritized for the task. Additional assets would be co-opted as and when needed. To retain flexibility and a standby strike option, a Yuan-class submarine would be launched from Qingdao in the Yellow Sea. The Yuan diesel-electric configuration had anechoic tile coatings, a quiet seven-blade screw, extended battery life, powered propulsion, and an oxygen recycling plant. Plus, it was virtually inaudible to detection even to US sensors. It would also neatly solve the problem of delivering large quantities of explosives and stores to the former Sea Tigers, if such actions were necessary.

At its peak, thc LTTE had a fleet of twenty-seven known deep-seagoing vessels engaged in arms, drugs, and human smuggling rackets. The ships traversed international waters under various *nom de guerre*, often registered in Honduras, Panama, or Liberia. LTTE ships transported both weapons and trainees (back and forth) to a port in Turkey from Karachi. The weapons were provided by Harkatul Ansar, an affiliate of Al Qaeda, for the purpose of fighting in Chechnya.

The LTTE had no qualms over letting its fleet be used for illicit purposes whether by the heroin barons of Afghanistan or for gun running to the Abu Sayyaf and the Moro Islamic Liberation Front of the Southern Philippines or by the Harkat-ul-Mujahideen of Pakistan. It did not hesitate to accept a consignment of arms and ammunition from the ISI of Pakistan in 1993. The LTTE had links to the "Golden Triangle" and the 'Golden Crescent" via Tamil Nadu, and Indian officials had adequate proof that these drugs were smuggled out from India through the South Indian coastal area of Tuticorin.

The historically notorious smuggling port of Sri Lankan's northern peninsula, Velvetithurai "VVT," had been the home of the recently deceased Tiger ruler, Prabhakaran, and many leaders of LTTE "core" groups. Through it were smuggled in not only drugs but also weapons, injured cadres, medicines, expertise, and all necessary provisions to wage war against the Sri Lankan Armed Forces. Although the LTTE denied its role in trafficking narcotics as a source of revenue, there were many areas in which the LTTE had mastered and brought to perfection certain terrorist tactics. Both suicide bombing, targeted political assassinations conducted by the LTTE, and those later practiced by Al Qaeda and by Chechen separatists showed that guerrilla tactics were constantly being (and have for some time been) copied and shared by these movements.

The surviving LTTE still has a well-established network of "legitimate" businesses that provided funds as well as logistics for their activities. There were thousands of Chinese in Sri Lanka, especially around the Chinese-built Hambantota Port. Contacting the LTTE would not be difficult, thus writing a new chapter in maritime tactics. A month of effort, however, clearly showed that the top Sea Tiger surviving elements were no longer in Sri Lanka.

It was eventually the Chinese naval attaché in Pakistan who located Iravan through ISI's Brigadier Syed Ali, who was still in service. Syed Ali's links with the Harkut ul Mujahideen, which had a long association with the LTTE Diaspora, also consisting of many former Sea Tigers, ultimately uncovered Iravan on the French Riviera. The ISI, presuming that the Chinese query would bode ill for Indian maritime assets, pulled out all the stops to do this in a month. In time, the ISI would broaden its horizon and suggest targeting the Gorshkov to the PLA to secure Gwadar from the Indian Navy.

The literal translation of the name Iravan meant "King of Ocean," and the name was given for the LTTE Sea Tigers' most versatile commander and the blue-eyed boy of Colonel Soosai, who raised and commanded the Sea Tigers till his death was apt. Iravan had himself been initially trained as a suicide bomber and a frogman and had been in the first batch of ten inductees into the Sea Tigers at the age of sixteen in 1992. Soosai, the canny Sea Tiger chief, however, considered Iravan far too precious a talent to be wasted on suicide efforts.

Given ample latitude to bloom, Iravan was credited with having significantly contributed to the hijacking of the "Irish Mona" and "Athena" and the Chinese ship "MV Cordiality" outside Sri Lankan waters. He was also credited for personally having sunk two catamarans, which were being used as troop carriers, and one freighter of the Sri Lankan Navy in attacks on the Kankesanturai Navy base. He led a charmed life, and even in the thickest of fighting, he had never sustained more than minor injuries.

In 1998, Iravan had vanished, reportedly killed. With an estimated IQ of 160, Iravan had been placed in the genius category, and without any formal education, he had developed a theory of sea control by the time he was in his mid twenties. He had also seen the writing on the waves for the eventual death of the Tamil struggle after a meeting with the megalomaniac Prabhakaran, the LTTE supremo, and had quietly deserted the Sea Tigers. He then made his way to his maternal granduncle's fishing village on the extreme southeast coast of Tamil Nadu, India, and for all practical purposes, he vanished.

Over the years thereafter, he had acquired a marine engineering degree, jobs with a succession of European shipping companies, and fluency in three additional languages besides Tamil and Sinhala, including English, French and Italian. He had also acquired a French wife named Marie, whose father had a yacht-rental business in Nice and terminal cancer. The only misstep he had made in his life was having been unwittingly photographed by a crew member with a camera cell phone shooting a Chinese sailor. Digital enhancements of the photograph would lead to his being tracked eventually.

When Iravan was finally found more than a decade later and gently blackmailed into attacking the "Gorshkov" or else face extrication to China, he still held out until he was promised a fee of ten million dollars. Half the amount was deposited a week later into his existing account in Mauritius. He also asked for logistic backing, including the opening of a shell company in Mauritius and an operating company in Cyprus. This would provide cover, and he would not have to remain away from his new home for prolonged periods and arouse any suspicion to arrange it.

In exchange, he would be forced to accommodate a Chinese handler in the guise of the owner of the new water sports business to ensure that he did not renege on his agreement. Thomas Chu-yu Soong, a strongly built Taiwanese-American businessman arrived a week later to do the job of controller. He was apart from his alias none other than Major Dingbang, a man already bored with his stint as a staff officer and craving action.

Dingbang had volunteered to be sent, already being stifled by inaction. He had taken appropriate action to ensure that a marine commando was not picked in his place by having attended a three-month course run for marine commando officer inductees. Amongst his myriad of skills, he was now also a proficient diver, and an underwater demolition handyman, and he could handle the soon-to-be-inducted, hundred-kilogram, lightweight sonar based on a stolen US design.

CHAPTER 46
SEA TIGER CUBS

It took Iravan a little effort thereafter to locate his old childhood friend and former Sea Tiger buddy, Guru. This was achieved through his Indian fishermen contacts working the waters between India and northern Sri Lanka and indulging in some smuggling as well to make ends meet. Guru had refused to leave Sri Lanka in spite of Iravan urging him repeatedly in the late 1990s. Guru's organizational skills were well recognized by the Tigers, and ideologically, he was too committed to back out of the struggle. Ideology, however, did not supplant friendship. He would continue to insist to the Sea Tiger and LTTE command that he had had no idea of what had happened to Iravan. The time had now come for Guru to accept his friend's offer.

While the LTTE were still fighting their last doomed battles, more than forty child combatants between fourteen and seventeen years of age, all suffering from various stages of malnutrition, arrived at Ambepussa, northeast of Colombo at the Protection and Rehabilitation Center, which was run by the Sri Lankan government. Six months later, as they pored over books in mathematics, chemistry, computer science, and two languages, Sinhala, the tongue of the majority Sinhala Buddhists that they had been trained to kill, and English, no one would have guessed from their neat, clean looks and clothes that there were two common threads that united them. They were all orphans from Sencholai a "rebel" orphanage in the northeastern Kilinochchi district, and they had all been trained to be suicide bombers. This was to be done by activating explosive jackets they were taught to wear as a compulsory lesson.

Karuna and Varuna, the twins who had not known a family since they were orphaned at six months, and their friend, Thayalan, orphaned the same day by a Sri Lankan airstrike that killed both parents, used their spare time when they were not studying or playing to wonder how they would remake their lives after they left Ambepusa. The idea of a Tamil nation and their duty to achieve it was drilled into their beings in lieu of their mother's milk.

The primary purpose of their lives was to destroy the enemies of the Tamil Nation. Their favorite story was the assassination of Rajiv Gandhi, the Indian prime minister, by Dhanu with a bomb concealed in a basket of flowers. They were told that this one act of bravery resulted in India being forced to withdraw its troops from fighting the LTTE in Sri Lanka, but India continued to be an enemy supporting the Sinhalese majority against the Tamils.

The only adult person the three friends could turn to was Guru, who empathized with their plight and urged them to work hard to make an impact on the world when they were older. A soft-spoken man in his early thirties with a huge scar on his stomach where he had been once shot, Guru had apparently arrived out of nowhere. He voluntarily taught them chemistry and math. He was also the lone Tamil teacher for the group and subtly took the three boys under his wing.

One night, when the orphanage students were returning from an excursion to the sea, the bus had a breakdown on a lonely stretch of the single-lane road. The three of them and Guru had gotten off from the rear of the bus to pee on the side of the road while the driver struggled to start the vehicle.

As if on cue, a Sinhalese mob materialized from the front and attacked the tired youngsters in the bus, killing twenty-six of their contemporaries with machetes and spears and setting the bus on fire. When they heard the screams of the mob, the three ran off into a forest nearby as fast as they could, now verbally prodded by Guru urging them to run faster. For all practical purposes, the mob had killed all the passengers in the bus to extract revenge on the Tamils for decades of terror, and there were no more children left to settle. Karuna, Varuna, and Thyalan had ceased to exist.

Eleven days later, they landed, well after midnight, in a trawler on the Tamil Nadu coast at the fishing village that Iravan's family had sprung from. Two weeks later, all four of them had acquired unique, twelve-digit identity numbers with biometric backing under a national experiment for allocating unique identity numbers and acquired manual labor jobs, making roads under the national rural employment guarantee scheme. Six months later, all four of them were issued Indian passports. Guru had become Ekbaal. Karuna had become Chandresh. Varuna had become Firoz, and Thyalan had become Tejas.

The three youngsters and Guru were then funneled enough money through the *hawala* route to buy a small garment-export business to earn a comfortable living without attracting attention. Under Guru's watchful eye, a rigorous fitness regime that included extensive weight training, swimming, and running was started to ensure that they would be ready to deal with extraordinary physical and mental stresses. The export business would also provide the perfect reason to travel to any place in the world.

In the mean while, Iravan had been a busy man, mentally conjuring the nuts and bolts of what would be his most significant mission. He had not been totally unhappy when his presence in France was ferreted out by the Chinese, although he had hidden it well. For him, it was an acknowledgment of his world-class ability and skills in asymmetric maritime warfare. What he had missed for more than a decade was the scent of battle and the closeness of comrades fighting next to each other. All of his former comrades, with the sole exception of Guru, were now dead. The Sea Tigers had survived for years driving loads of battlefield innovation with a paucity of material resources. Even now, he had decided to make do with a strike force of just four people. These would not be available for training until their new identities were in place.

Guru could be trusted with anything, and he was a great planner; however, her did not have the core ruthlessness to be truly outstanding. Loyalty to a comrade in arms was a core belief with him. He could also rely on his instinct to choose from the most ideologically committed young men and the Tamil separatist cause brainwashed into treating India as the great betrayer of this vision. Success could only come from a combination of tactical and technological synergy coupled with flawless execution. Iravan had no doubt that the Chinese would give him the explosives he needed that would otherwise take up too much effort to organize. He just needed to ensure that he retained adequate control over the execution of his final plan.

Maiden Voyage of INS Vikramaditya

CHAPTER 47
THE PILLARS OF HERCULES

IRAVAN EXPLAINED TO HIS YOUNG TEAM with diagrams drawn in the sand. "An aircraft carrier like the INS Vikramaditya is designed to quickly deploy and recover aircraft. It is a seagoing air base. Unescorted carriers are vulnerable to attacks by other ships, aircraft, submarines, or missiles per conventional naval doctrine. We will find our own way to attack the carrier."

No one had, however, taught Iravan any conventional doctrine. The Chinese would track and provide adequate warning to locate the carrier and also make available the assets he demanded. It had taken Iravan barely a few days to decide that if he had to organize an attack against the Vikramaditya, it had to be in his new backyard. The Mediterranean Sea between the Straits of Gibraltar and the Suez Canal was the obvious choice. Earlier in the voyage, a strike base in the Atlantic near Tangiers on the African coast would be problematic. Tighter maritime security by the littoral countries, including Russia, England, France, Spain, and Portugal was a negative factor between Murmansk and the west of Gibraltar. The plus side lay in the new crew of the Vikramaditya, still meshing together in the early stages of the voyage and most prone to reactive errors and thus a potentially successful mission for him. After Djibouti in the Indian Ocean, the Indian Western Naval Fleet would be predominant, and the chances of success would become dismal.

The idea of choosing to attack where conflicting territorial jurisdictions existed between European countries and African ones was appealing. This would hinder both meaningful reaction and investigation. NATO's attempts to police the strait and the Mediterranean had fizzled out some years ago, for no significant threat had manifested itself. NATO did have a theoretical structure to combat threats to shipping headed by an Italian admiral out of Naples. Any incident closer to the African coastline would get snarled in bureaucracy.

Tentatively, he picked out the individual locations in the 2,300-mile stretch of Mediterranean Sea encompassing almost a million square miles that he favored: firstly, in the sea immediately east of the United Kingdom ruled Gibraltar and between Spain and Morocco; secondly, between the Balearic Islands and the Algerian coast; thirdly, going farther east, promising attack sites could be picked between Sardinia and Tunisia; fourthly, between Sicily and Tunisia; fifthly, between Malta and Libya; and sixthly and lastly, between Crete, Egypt, and Libya.

Instinct made him prioritize the eastern edge of the Straits of Gibraltar with the two promontories, arguably one of the Pillars of Hercules, the other being the Rock of Gibraltar. Here, he could choose battle in a constricted shipping lane. Alternately, he could attack the carrier in the sea between Sicily and Tunisia. The Italian island of Pantellaria, almost midway between the two, would provide an ideal base for preparations for the operation, especially realistic rehearsals.

He had already decided on his attack mode: equipment loaded with C4 explosive for suicide attacks. That was an intellectual exercise he had continued doing since he had deserted the Sea Tigers, and he would turn to the country with the greatest seafaring tradition of the modern era, the United Kingdom, for his wish list. It was a change to be able to splurge on cutting-edge technology instead of making do with odds and ends.

The first bit of equipment he favored that the Mauritius-based company would acquire for its Mediterranean water sports company registered in Cyprus was a 2.5-million-dollar XSAR military interceptor boat. It could do 155 kilometers per hour or eighty knots, carry a dozen passengers if needed, and run circles around any escorting destroyer or frigate that accompanied the Vikramaditya. Importantly, it could carry enough fuel for a thousand kilometers. A stripped-down version without armaments would attract more envy than curiosity. Six hundred kilograms of C4 could be easily stuffed into the hull compartments.

The second cheaper boat, the scuba craft manufactured by Creative Worldwide, cost barely two hundred thousand dollars. The four-hundred-kilogram machine generated 160 horsepower and could do eight kilometers per hour or almost forty knots before it dove to a depth of thirty meters. The boat's power was harnessed by the advanced twin-tunnel hull that provided low-speed stability and high-speed dynamic lift for a jet-powered, air-cushioned ride. Once under the surface, the boat was powered by electric thrusters and lithium batteries and employed intuitive controls to replicate flying underwater. The boat had adequate internal stowage for four hundred kilograms of C4 explosive. A rigid, inflatable hull ensured readiness to launch using compressed-air bottles in thirty seconds. An overall length of 3.9 meters and a beam of 2.3 meters made deck storage simple.

Major Dingbang, aka Thomas Chu-yu Soong, exuded confidence and a faint air of menace from his large, tightly muscled frame. In a few days, Iravan realized that he was deferring to Thomas on all details of his plan. It was Thomas, with his military and commando training who unerringly pointed out that the best place to attack the Vikramaditya was nearer the western edge of the Strait of Gibraltar in spite of unpredictable sea conditions, rather than the eastern edge. In a passage of fifty-eight kilometers, the strait was at its narrowest at 12.5 kilometers between point Marroqui in Spain and point Cirres in Morocco in the west and widest at the eastern end at twenty-three kilometers between the Rock of Gibraltar under UK control in the north and either Jebel Moussa in Morocco or Mount Hacha in Ceuta, which controlled by Spain on the African mainland to the south.

The other relevant issue was that the speed of the carrier and escort was predictable at less than twenty-three kilometers an hour or eleven knots to avoid collisions with sperm whales, and it would be easier to work out an attack profile than it would have been with an unpredictable speed. Thomas also mooted the idea of adequate backup force and raised the requirement for procuring scuba boats to three and also for a diversion to delay any preemptive armed response by the carrier.

Plenty of distractions were always available for any ship officer on watch crossing into the straits. Ninety thousand vessels a year passed through, and there were always a dozen or so vessels of varying sizes making the transit at any time of the day or night. In addition, there were ferries running transversely across the strait from Spain to Morocco. There was always a good chance for the Vandavals, Levante, and Sirocco winds influencing weather and producing the infamous mists and dust clouds to reduce visibility.

Conceptually, once firm intelligence of the carrier Vikramaditya crossing the straits along with its escort or maybe more than one escort was available, his choices were straightforward. He could position his yacht to sail in the opposite direction and get in between the carrier and the escort(s) and offset to both before he attacked the carrier with the scuba boats. The other option was to pre-position the yacht to sail in the same direction and let it be overtaken by the escort(s) before he initiated action. The time and space issues would need to be worked out and practiced repeatedly, but a fortnight of rehearsals should have worked for him. He had organized similar sessions with the Sea Tigers often enough.

Now what remained to be set up were the choice of a plausible cover story and the choice of a yacht large enough to carry the attack craft but small enough not to attract too much attention. It was here that the multifaceted talents of Thomas, also known as Major Dingbang, came in handy.

"What distracts a sailor the most at sea?" Thomas asked Iravan while they were trying to conceptualize a plan to tackle the carrier and its escort.

"Always a woman … or the thought of one!" said Iravan with a broad smile.

"The first thing we should do then is to provide the Indians on watch with a glimpse of more than one woman, preferably with almost nothing on!"

"And how do we arrange that?" asked Iravan.

"Simple! You hire them from France, Spain, or Italy with your contacts. It's a safe bet that with a brand new carrier, the Strait of Gibraltar will be crossed in broad daylight. Choose some lingerie models with big boobs and a professional photographer to arrange a shoot for 'Mediterranean Aqua Adventures Private Limited' after the carrier leaves Murmansk. Promise them a bonus for the short notice. We can pick up the models from Algeciras and organize a floating shoot under the nose of the carrier on the deck of a fancy sailboat."

"And hit them with the scuba boats and the interceptor boat when they are distracted."

"Something like that!" agreed Thomas.

"There is just one gray area," Iravan said. "While I'm certain that you will be able to give us sufficient warning of the carrier's approach to the strait, we still need to position ourselves close enough to its sailing route. If we can't do that without arousing suspicion, we risk being blown out of the water!"

"So what is the answer?" asked Thomas.

"I reckon the ships will have to cross into the strait three to four kilometers from the southern edge. We'll just have to place our powered sailboat somewhere near the western entrance to the strait about five kilometers from point Cirres on the southern shore. We can do this once we are reasonably sure about the carrier's timing of crossing into the strait. From the photographs you provide, we should have no problem in recognizing the Vikramaditya and its escort."

Thomas shook his head, indicating disagreement. "May be possible, but we need a foolproof way of doing so. We can drop the boats beforehand a few kilometers short and move alongside the carrier at a respectable distance. The boats can then position themselves closer to the coast so that the carrier and escort have to cross between our two locations. Thereafter, give the ship's company an eyeful of luscious flesh for half an hour or so and make our move."

Iravan said somberly, "I suggest that you part company with us before we pick up the models. I cannot guarantee anyone coming out of this alive."

Thomas smiled and said, "No way, my friend. I have to keep an eye on our investment in you. I'm sure you will find a way to keep us alive like you did in all your actions with the Sea Tigers! I trust your survival instincts. Besides, I am the only one with the technical knowledge to ensure that we locate and attack the right target irrespective of weather and light conditions. I have ordered some very expensive pieces of equipment that will be with us in a few days, which should ensure success!"

CHAPTER 48
DAUGHTER OF THE WIND

The island of Pantellaria, the literal translation meaning "Daughter of the Wind," lies in the Strait of Sicily, a hundred kilometers from Sicily and even closer at seventy kilometers to the Tunisian coast. The island had been chosen by Iravan as a base for the rehearsals that would make or break the operation. The priority now was to rehearse the attack drills until they were performed flawlessly. Ideally, this would happen without a single word being spoken after the initial "go" order was given. Cell phone calls were traceable in retrospect, and the use of Tamil by Iravan and the strike team would only delay trained investigators.

The two pieces of passive sonar equipment based on stolen US patent 4641290, dated February 3, 1997, were encased in a waterproof, suitcase-style enclosure. Instead of a towed array, there was a small float of ten inches with three powerful nanotechnology-based hydrophones set off at 120 degrees to each other. A miniature floating antennae with a fifty-meter lead was also included. This was a far cry from the massive towed array used by current Chinese submarines, but it would identify the carrier with absolute certainty twenty kilometers away.

The high-speed interceptor boat in which Iravan and he would ride would make it possible to shift locations every thirty seconds to theoretically perform a somewhat perfect triangulation of the carrier and escort location within five minutes. This could be done with an error of less than one hundred meters. The sonar data was displayed on a laptop via a wireless Ethernet connection. The data could also be mirrored in one of the scuba boats as long as the antenna was sticking out of the water.

For passive sonar to be useful in identifying the Indian INS Vikramaditya and its escort, INS Kochi, the targets' radiated noise characteristics are critical. Otherwise the sonar would pick targets without being able to identify them at a distance.

The radiated spectrum from INS Vikramaditya like for any other ship consisted of an unresolved continuum of noise with spectral lines in it that could be used as a unique classification distinct from any other ship. The acoustic intelligence software also pirated from a US defense contractor would pick out the carrier from a babble of maritime noise much like a mother identifying her child's voice through the babble created on a school playground.

The INS Kochi's radiated spectrum had been available for some time, for a Chinese trawler looking for more than fish in the Bay of Bengal had picked up the ship's noise signatures a year earlier during Kochi's proving trials in spite of Kochi's built-in stealth characteristics. The same data had also been acquired to add to the PLA Navy "war book" a month earlier during the proving trials of the carrier near Murmansk.

Thomas's role in the operation for interpretation of the passive sonar data was crucial, and the rehearsals were as important for him to refine his interpretation skills as they were for Iravan's suicide squad to get their act right. Iravan's undoubted past successes had generally been based on attacking anchored targets by entering enemy harbors by stealth at night. Here, the targets were moving and distinctly dangerous, even if total surprise could be achieved.

Iravan, however, was undoubtedly the playmaker, exuding the natural authority of a dozen successful operations without ever raising his voice. Guru and the boys, Karuna, Varuna, and Thyalan, hung on to his every word. He made it clear to Thomas that he needed to keep quiet and let him play the leadership role. In any case, there was a working language issue that only he, Iravan, could address. Thomas was impressed with not only the absolute command that Iravan exerted but the quick diagrammatic debriefs drawn with a pointed stick on the secluded beach that Iravan conducted for all of them after each rehearsal.

Initially, they would take one of the scuba boats with four hundred kilograms of weights stowed in the watertight compartments towed behind the interceptor to conserve fuel and position themselves near a shipping lane. Iravan would choose a random ship radiating at least 165 decibels of sound to guarantee a large enough vessel length. He would then say, "Attack," and time Thomas as he did his calculations for an intercept. He would then order any two of Guru's team to steer for the intercept position and go fifteen meters underwater and listen to the sonar sound of the approaching ship "target." The attack team then tried to get into an attack position as quickly as possible without alerting the ship, and it would stay underwater until the ship had clearly passed.

By the fifth day, Thomas could confidently place the attacking scuba boat within two hundred and fifty meters of the approaching track. The scuba crews were naturals at the game, and after the third day, they were able to regularly mock-attack the bottom of all passing ships. The attack vectors were based on the loudness of the sonar approaching and receding sounds. Because it was important to clamp onto the target bottom of the carrier in the actual attack, this was practiced on the speedboat bottom. A far larger target extending 290 meters would pose fewer problems.

The second week of practice drills included all three scuba boats, Guru and Thyalan in the center and the twin brothers on either side conforming to their movements. The scuba whistles they carried to attract each other's attention in an emergency had a limited thirty-meter range, which meant that they needed to remain within that range. Guru, the former math teacher, had also calculated that in the event of the carrier's track being more than four hundred meters from where they were located, any target moving at a speed of more than ten knots would probably avoid being intercepted. The carrier had to be slowed down or veered toward them some way as soon as it crossed into the strait. Iravan said he would ensure that and to leave the problem to him.

"How will you slow the carrier down or make it veer toward the scuba boats, Iravan, if it is required?" Thomas asked him as they took a needed break in the small cottage they had rented for the season.

"You and I will loiter on a parallel track until the escort crosses our position laterally. We will then move across the bow of the carrier without warning at not too great a speed!"

Thomas grinned and said, "And you think that the captain will automatically order the carrier to slow down?"

"Of course he won't, but he will turn to starboard by a few degrees, which should do the trick! Who in his right mind will risk an accident with a brand new carrier? We can zip away at thrice his speed in case he goofs. It was part of my getaway plan in any case. One of Jorge Thierry's smuggling pals will pick us up in his trawler in a couple of hours. We will then disappear after we sink the interceptor—unless, of course, one of the helicopters fires a missile at us!"

CHAPTER 49
THE GHOST IN THE ROOM

ALTHOUGH HE WAS USED TO VISITING the corner office in the senate building of the Kremlin, General of the Army Aleksandra Mirinov, head of Russia's Counterintelligence Service (SKR), looked ill at ease in a civilian suit that barely enclosed his bulk.

"We kept track of the electrical engineer, Viktor Konev, working on the Gorshkov upgrade for more than two years. The *mafiya* got him employed in the Sevmash shipyard on behest of their Chinese connections. Konev had little choice when he could not repay a gambling debt. He has been passing on weekly information on the Gorshkov construction progress along with certain drawings and blueprints. There are at least a dozen known spies working for the Chinese across Russia that we have tabs on. I think the time has come to pick them up before they do any significant damage!"

Vladimir Putin leaned back in his chair, his hands behind his head, deep in thought. "Not yet. Let them be for the time being. Just ensure that there is no serious compromise of technology. We need to take a long-term view of this development."

Admiral Vladimir Klichugin, the navy chief, added, "We picked up a submarine using a magnetic anomaly detector (MAD) from a helicopter during the first sea trial of the carrier after Mirinov issued the warning about Chinese infiltration into the Sevmash shipyard. Interestingly, the frigate that launched the helicopter recovered some diesel traces where the MAD marker was dropped. The lab reports took a lot of time, but the diesel is from one of the refineries supplying diesel to the Hainan submarine base. It was definitely a PLA Navy sub. If I was heading the PLA Navy and wanting to secure oil flows in the Indian Ocean, I would definitely be working on ideas to knock off the Gorshkov! The best time would probably be early on with a new crew while it is raw and untrained on the voyage to India. Our satellite picked up the Gorshkov west of Gibraltar this morning. If the PLA wants to do something, it should be in the coming week, or it will become increasingly difficult!"

Mikhail Sapunov, the head of the Federal Security Service (FSB) and longtime confidante of Putin, added, "Our analysis directorate feels that with the decline of America and Europe, the balance of power in Asia has tilted strongly in China's favor. Russia's interests are getting increasingly marginalized. It is the rise of China, our immediate neighbor, and not the United States located thousands of kilometers away that should worry us! Whatever we try to do, China will be the ghost in the room keeping watch. India is our natural, undeclared ally for the future. India is getting hemmed in by the broadening of the Sino-Pak defense cooperation. There is also the possibility of a political accommodation between the United States and China that should worry us."

Anatoly Serdyukov, the defense minister, added, "I think we should offer the Indians another Nerpa-class nuclear submarine, which they are informally asking for, to help them gain an edge in the Indian Ocean region. This will also scale up their ability to stare down Pakistan, along with the new improved T90 tanks that are almost ready to be shipped. The Indians will be happy to provide additional funding for the T50 PAK FGFA program as well, if we promise to speed up the program. We have also facilitated the hiring of some of our retired scientists by Professor Mathews for the Indians. Apparently, they are interested in developing an EMP option against the Chinese."

Putin suddenly stood up and walked around his large office, weighing what the three powerful men in the room were getting at. "Mikhail, warn the Indians straight away that there may be a threat to the carrier. Get the analysis directorate to work out possible ways in which the threat may manifest itself in conjunction with Vladimir's people. I can see problems multiplying with China regarding the cornering of gas supplies from Central Asia and Turkmenistan in particular. We need to do everything possible to ensure that China's energy requirements are constrained. It's the easiest way to constrain their growth. Mikhail, incidentally, is there any substance behind what Ambassador Andropov is surmising? He feels that the new Indian PM has secretly tapped into the enormous wealth of its citizens who have evaded taxes to gain strategic freedom of action and acquire assets that India has not been able to afford so far!"

"We are working at it, but she seems to be pushing a lot of security- and energy-related projects, including ones with us, with huge sums of money that are going unreported!"

"Good, why don't we then get some of the money for the new gas pipelines and energy-related projects through Indian participation instead of looking for Chinese funds and creating long-term problems for ourselves?"

CHAPTER 50
THE STING

THE TWENTY-FOUR-METER TEAK SCHOONER SAILBOAT THEY had rented for the decoy operation, whose crew of three they had paid in advance for six months, was a work of art. It had the classic sailing lines of ships from a different era, with all the modern and safety gear to go anywhere in the world in comfort. The diesel engine could, if needed, churn out a top speed of thirteen knots when the wind failed. It could easily accommodate the interceptor boat and scuba boats on its spacious deck. Captain Jorge Thierry at the age of sixty-five, after four decades of end-running law enforcement agencies without ever being charged with breaking the law, could be both selectively blind and deaf. The amount of money being paid to him and his two nephews, who constituted the crew, was added insurance to maintain that status.

Thierry arrived at Pantellaria as indicated by the schedule given to him to pick up the half a dozen scuba enthusiasts and their equipment, which included three scuba boats and a high-speed interceptor boat. The night before, the Chinese submarine had made its rendezvous with Thomas in the interceptor boat south of Pantellaria Island. It delivered the C4 explosives in portable packs, which they would load into the waterproof compartments on all the boats at night. He showed no curiosity when he was told to go and pick up the camera crew and four models at Malaga on the southeast coast of Spain while the interceptor boat and scuba boats stayed offshore for some deep-sea diving.

Thomas had ensured that he had picked up the Indian ships twenty thousand meters west of the Gibraltar Strait after the satellite's last early warning pass. He had then performed the target-motion analysis taught to him and determined the range at eighteen thousand meters, the speed at eleven knots, and the course at 097 degrees. He had passed on the information to Guru, Karuna, Varuna, and Thyalan, who were known to him as Ekbaal, Chandresh, Firoz, and Tejas, names affirmed by their Indian passports, and they, in turn, had entered the information into their state-of-the-art inertial navigation systems.

Conceptually, it seemed simple. The powered sailboat, including a bevy of well-endowed lingerie and swimsuit models, had sailed toward the narrow western end of the strait and positioned itself where the Indian warships could not help but notice the expanse of skin on display. Simultaneously, the three attack scuba boats would position themselves at 90 degrees to his calculated approach corridor. The boats would deploy approximately thirty meters apart in the track worked out by Thomas and conform to Guru's movements in the center boat. They would target the bottom of the carrier. Hopefully, one of them would be successful. In the event of failure, Iravan and he would ram the carrier with the high-speed interceptor boat and cripple it. If the scuba boat attack succeeded, Iravan and he would get away.

The destroyer, INS Kochi, had a trick up its sleeve. It crossed into the strait with a helicopter ranging low ahead to search out impending dangers. The crew reported no untoward activity on the purported course. There was an empty VLCC oil tanker cruising three nautical miles ahead. There was some kind of modeling activity happening on a sailboat just north of the approach, but it was safely out of the way of the destroyer.

Four shapely young women wearing almost nothing were prancing around on the deck. One pointed her bottom toward the helicopter crew legs spread well out and straight, arms reaching energetically for the deck behind her heels. The pilot circled the sailboat twice and recommended to his ship that it alter its course marginally to take in the sight. The photographer on the mainsail acrobatically taking pictures went unseen but added to the atmosphere of professional models at work.

As the destroyer surged into the straight, Captain Jorge Thierry changed tack and started turning his sailboat around on a parallel track. He also closed imperceptibly closer to the Vikramaditya to ensure that all hands on the carrier deck got a close look at the bevy of women models strutting for the camera. Half a square meter of wispy, see-through lingerie would have sufficed to account for all the fabric worn by the voluptuous, oil-sheen skin of the four models on view. Hopefully, the crew of the carrier would go on looking at the nubile young flesh until it was too late.

Iravan was smiling broadly, back on stage after more than a decade. Major Dingbang, also known as Thomas, also felt the tingling sensation of approaching battle as he redid his calculations, positioning the interceptor boat broadside and parallel to the course for the INS Kochi. The three assault scuba boats under Guru's command tucked inside the flare of the interceptor maintained a neck-only status for a few moments till they submerged completely. They were quickly lost to view, except for the bobbing motion of the thin antenna linked to the interceptor's sonar receding from Iravan. Guru's intercept course would place him directly under the escort destroyer's course in a few minutes. He would then make adjustments so that his attack position was optimized by the time the carrier crossed his position perhaps five minutes later.

The interceptor boat's radio on channel sixteen cackled to life. "Boat on my starboard bow, do you hear me?"

"Loud and clear, battleship," Iravan responded.

"Shift to channel seventy-two. I am approaching you. Please keep clear of my starboard bow!"

"Keeping well clear, battleship I value my skin!" Iravan responded, making a marginal adjustment away from the INS Kochi.

As the INS Kochi went past, Iravan started to edge the interceptor closer to the following INS Vikramaditya's projected path.

It seemed as if the entire crew of the carrier had turned out on deck to witness the photo shoot on the graceful, old sailboat. There was a loud roar of approval as the girls seemed to relish the attention they were getting and adopted provocative poses that would have been regarded as obscene in a porn film. Rear Admiral KVK Kamath permitted the boisterous display of approval with a slight smile on his face. *No harm in letting his men ogle*, he thought to himself. That was all anyone was going to get. It had been a long haul for the past few months, and it would give them an excuse to jerk off in the head. The grizzled captain of the sailboat waved to them and steered a bit closer to the carrier as it looked down upon him from what appeared to be a tantalizingly close distance and overhauled him. The distraction was going to be costly.

The aircraft carrier's navigation officer yelled into his mike. "Stupid bastard, stay out of my way altering course to starboard!"

The INS Vikramaditya turned 10 degrees to starboard, and with the turn catching was righting itself by five degrees when it came almost directly onto the waiting scuba boats ten meters below the surface of the Mediterranean. In the process of correcting the turn, the speed of the aircraft carrier dropped to eight knots, giving Karuna, Guru, Thyalan, and Varuna the few vital seconds they needed to achieve what they regarded as immortality. The Vikramaditya had four shafts, each of which ended with a propeller. The attack profile of the three scuba boats targeted the two starboard shafts, Karuna and Varuna both aligning closely, Guru and Thyalan in the center. The longest shaft with the propeller at the end protruded about thirty meters from the engine room. It was the one adjacent to which Thyalan aimed the magnetic clamp. It connected with a metallic clump barely perceptible in the scuba boat a fraction of a second before the four hundred kilograms of C4 explosive detonated and Karuna and Varuna made contact. The force of the explosion killed the four attackers almost instantaneously and made the carrier lurch dangerously to starboard. For a moment, it seemed as if the INS Vikramaditya would keel over, but the slowing carrier gradually righted as Rear Admiral KVK Kamath fought to establish control and the firefighting equipment kicked in.

"Sabotage!" the thought was uppermost in KVKs mind as the fleeting thought of not becoming a vice admiral was brushed aside. "Sink the boat," he ordered. "The fucker set us up!"

"Congratulations, Iravan. You are still the best. You've done it!" Major Dingbang aka Thomas shouted so that he could be heard over the roar of the engine as Iravan sped them away eastward at sixty knots with the light of battle still in his eye. All the while, he was keeping a watchful eye over his shoulder for a pursuit helicopter.

"I will miss Guru, Karuna, Varuna, and Thyalan. They were the best team I ever had," Iravan commented. "I will miss them."

"Not for very long," said Dingbang, producing a small pistol from the back of his waistband and shooting the startled Iravan in the chest. He felt a momentary remorse in killing someone who had been a comrade for so many months; however, orders were orders, and one could not afford to be sentimental in this business. Distracted by his thoughts, he held the straight course that Iravan had set and was completely unaware when the Sea Eagle air-to-surface missile fired by the INS Kochi's multirole helicopter hit the interceptor in the rear, and the explosion flung him high into the air and into the sea. His life belt kept him afloat but unconscious as the two marine commandos in the helicopter were lowered into the sea to retrieve him. They also retrieved Iravan, who was critically wounded but alive. Surgeon Commander Bipin Pillai, who cleaned up the mess in Iravan's chest and abdomen, would ensure that he lived.

Two weeks later, a much subdued Admiral Tony Pereira finished his briefing to the cabinet committee on security. His offer to resign, taking moral responsibility for failing to anticipate the attack, was rejected by the CCS. "It will take a minimum of two years to make the Vikramaditya seaworthy again, although the Russians have promised full cooperation. Two of the main engine shafts will have to be machined afresh in Russia. The two prisoners are completely under wraps for the time being, but there seems to be no doubt at all that China is provoking a conflict. It appears the Chinese now have a relatively free run in the Indian Ocean area. We, too, need to resort to other-than-war techniques to drive the lesson home to them that two can play the same game. Unfortunately, because of our convoluted inter ministry communication links, the warning from the Russians took more than two days to be delivered to the navy, since a weekend and sloppy staff procedures interfered with the dissemination!"

After the CCS meeting broke up, the PM sent for Ashok Sobti and Sridhar. There was fire in her eyes as Durga Vadera spoke to them, "Are you ready to give the Chinese a taste of their own medicine?"

"Yes, we are just waiting for your go ahead.' Sridhar answered.

"Let's do it quickly!" Durga ordered.

Narayan Patel answered the phone on the second ring. "Sorry, wrong number!" the voice from the other end answered. The process was repeated twice again with the same response each time "Sorry, wrong number!" The fourth time the phone rang the same voice asked "Will you come to the party tonight?"

Narayan Patel answered "Yes of course, I'm just waiting for my wife to get dressed." The die had been cast.

CHAPTER 51
RED CORRIDOR

Ashok Sobti had kicked off the discussion in a small auditorium in the Santhanam Foundation. "While terrorism is mounted by 'outsiders' on the local community and local support is bought and coerced, the insurgencies in India are an acute manifestation of economic and political deprivation. The reason of widespread lack of good governance is not going to go away in a hurry. At a strategic level we need to deal with our insurgent movements especially in eastern India while tackling China and Pakistan as well.

While terrorists seek to undermine the government in much of India, insurgents continue to strike at the government itself. Their endgame is to make it too expensive for state governments to continue business as usual and concede demands for autonomy within the heartland of India and in those areas closer to neighboring country borders like with Pakistan, China and Myanmar for secession from India. Nasruddin, there is no one better suited than you to bring everyone up to date with the current situation."

Nasruddin Babbar said "Out of India's six hundred districts, almost a third in the states of Bihar, Orissa, West Bengal, Jharkhand, Chhattisgarh, Madhya Pradesh, Maharashtra, and Andhra Pradesh have portions where the writ of the Indian state is questionable. It has been supplanted by left-wing extremists loosely associated with the Communist Party of India (Marxist).

There are eight districts—Aurangabad and Gaya in Bihar, Bijapur and Dantewada in Chhattisgarh, Chatter and Palma in Jharkhand, and Malkangiri and Raigarh in Orissa, where the state does not exist at all in terms of governance except on maps. The ultras hold complete sway, extract protection in cash and kind, dispense roughshod justice through the muzzle of a rifle, destroy transport and communications and behave in a more reprehensible manner than the authority they wished to replace. Of late, in a bizarre marketing twist for ideology, the promotion of the Marxist line is sought by arranging small loans for businesses and even weddings.

There is a second category, too—Khammam in Andhra Pradesh, Balaghat in Madya Pradesh, and Gadchhiroli and Gondia in Maharashtra, where control lies generally with the state during the day and entirely with the Marxists by night. The locals at least have no doubt that daylight hours of government sway do not count."

"What exactly is the Red Corridor?"Speed Ranganathan asked.

Sridhar butted in "The 161 trouble-torn districts out of the 630 in the country form the euphemistic 'Red Corridor.' This extends almost a thousand miles from Nepal in the north of India to our famous temple town of Tirupati to the south in Andhra Pradesh. With the fragmentation of Nepal politics continuing, the Maoist cadres, who toppled the king of Nepal, continue to gain influence in the country's politics. Their political bent has become covertly more and more pro-China and anti-India. The Maoist combatant cadres are integrated with the Nepal Army, and now part of it is ideologically in tune with the Maoist cadres operating in India. Nepal is, therefore, becoming an increasingly favored haven for rest, recuperation, training, and planning of Indian Maoists."

Ashok Sobti added "We are all aware that in the last forty years the Indian parliament has paid no attention to these problem districts. The fact these areas are only rarely mentioned in the national media may have something to do with it? The occasional story by urban-centric-oriented reporters and interviews with Maoist leaders in remote jungles by cub reporters are exceptions to this norm."

Nasruddin Babbar continued "India has an internal security system that had been hijacked by apathy and a deep-rooted nexus of the executive and the criminal politician class. This cozy setup was challenged in a few short months in West Bengal when the trouble moved to Lalgarh, a word that can be loosely translated as "Red Fort," in the district of West Midnapore, less than a hundred miles from Kolkata. This was an uncomfortably close distance for both the political class and the media to ignore when Naxals took over the location and fought a pitched battle with state and central police forces that took two months to muster.

For three decades, the Communist Party state government in West Bengal has succeeded in keeping the state free from Naxal (Maoist) influence. A brutal police offensive coupled with initiation of land reforms whose numerous beneficiaries shunned the rebel path and an engineered split in the insurgent ranks in the 1970s forced the guerilla activities into the neighboring State of Bihar."

"How did the present trouble come about?" Speed asked.

Sridhar commented "The impact of incomplete land reform programs was felt and rural incomes dropped sharply. Across West Bengal, the state government virtually abdicated its authority, allowing its local strongmen and their goons to treat their areas as virtual kingdoms. In the tribal belts, the impact has been the worst, allowing the Maoists to return with a vengeance. This has been through a Trojan-horse front termed innocently enough as 'the People's Committee against Police Atrocities' that is winning the propaganda war."

Lieutenant General Randhir Singh who had been listening quietly spoke for the first time. "The short-term strategic answer to our problems is the judicious application of force. We cannot wait for governance to kick in. Nasruddin needs to be given the resources to target the top insurgent leaders that he has asked for in the past right now to take them out of the equation. It will create the strategic space to better deal with China and Pakistan."

Nasruddin Babbar said "I entirely agree with the general! Greed is the key. If we throw enough money at key personnel in the insurgent groups they will sell their mothers as well. West Bengal is where I intend to focus to start with."

Arif Mohammad, the man only known to them as "Bhai" or "Brother," put it bluntly to the PCAPA leaders, opening the bulky suitcase that he was carrying. "Count it—three million rupees here; a million rupees for each of you to look after your families. You may all well be famous at the end of it as well! Convert the mass protests by the tribals into violent agitations. If you can control these three districts for a year, I will be back with more."

As he got up to go, he added in a matter-of-fact voice, "There is no such thing as charity in this world. Don't even think of running away! I promise you that your daughters and wives will pay the price wherever they may be. Think of what they will look like once a hundred of our Maoists are through stuffing every orifice in their bodies with their cocks!"

Building opinion against the state's attempt to use disproportionate force and violence was artfully orchestrated by Chhatradhar Mahato, the Maoist mouthpiece. Women Maoists masquerading as villagers told journalists how police had strip-searched them and then defecated and urinated on stored drinking water they had to bring from their only water source five miles away.

Swaying public opinion is easy, especially because past lumpen behavior from the custodians of law and order does not engender trust in the affected population. Calcutta celebrities, including filmmaker Aparna Sen, poet Joy Goswami, and theater personalities like Shaonli Mitra, contributed their might in hamstringing the state response and discouraging the police effort. This was done through being media savvy anti-establishment and being instantly available to give sound bites to deadline-stressed journalists. The national commission for women muddied the waters even further in similar fashion and ensured that the districts of Bankura and Purulia also become contested Maoist bastions within the space of five years. Fear pervaded Kolkata after three decades of relative peace.

There was also acute discord between the central and state police forces. Lots of funds and additional central forces were being pumped into West Bengal in a belated attempt to tackle the insurgency. A lack of institutional mechanisms to ensure that at each level of deployment there was effective control, however, contributed to dysfunctional governance at the grassroots levels while the police and para-military forces combated the militants.

All the while, the state government dithered in its response. The core issue of development and empowerment of the tribal population continued to receive only lip service, and nothing much changed in their lives in terms of food, health, education, and infrastructure.

The opposition parties scented blood as sample polls showed that the population of the state had had enough and were looking for an election to throw out the government.

What remained was the engineering of a media-friendly incident before the elections to destroy the remaining credibility of the state government. The killing and kidnapping of some low-level police officers for ransom provided the spark. Twenty-four policemen, including constables, inspectors, and home guards, were present at the Sankrali police station when the Maoists struck at 1:30 p.m. with everyone present eating lunch. Not a single shot was fired in retaliation. Not a single policeman was armed. The practice was to keep weapons locked in trunks for safe keeping.

The officer in charge of the police station was abducted from his nearby home, where he also had gone for lunch unarmed. The police station had six WWI vintage .303 rifles, three revolvers, one pistol, and 180 rounds of ammunition all locked up in the storeroom. Policemen felt that the weapons recently issued to them were no match for the sophisticated semiautomatics of the Maoists, so keeping them locked up was safer. A few days later, the high-profile Rajdhani Express train was stopped by tribals with bows and arrows, and the drivers were taken hostage. A powerful message had been delivered to the people of West Bengal—the Communist Party of India state government was helpless and ineffectual in the face of the Maoists, whose day had come.

All that was required now was lubrication of the insurgency with dollops of money and low-key publicity shunning individuals like Arif to shape future events. The first major success came when the unseen war against the state introduced a game changer by targeting a complete company of the Seventieth Central Reserve Police Force unit at Arif's urging. The ambush was sprung in the Mukrana Forest of Dantewada District after the paramilitary force was returning after an unsuccessful sweep for insurgents.

The anonymous phone call that led to the operation was made from a telephone booth at the Raipur Railway Station by Arif, who posed as a militant looking for a reward of a hundred thousand rupees. Superintendent of Police Dantewada was told about the location of a Maoist camp of thirty in the center of the forest. Arif promised to guide the force from a village called Tadmetla. A tribal was positioned as a fake guide to tire out the company on foot through the thickest part of the forest by taking it on a wild-goose chase and then disappearing before the trap was sprung. Thereafter, three hundred Maoist cadres ensured the massive headlines splashed across the complete front page in the *Indian Express* the next day: "Maoists Butcher 125 CRPF Men!"

CHAPTER 52
THE PAWN

It had taken the best part of three months to set up the second meeting. Arif walked around the deserted school building in Chakadoba in West Bengal's West Midnapore District, smoking his third cigarette. He waited patiently for the Maoist insurgents to show up. He knew they would be watching him from the edge of the jungle beyond the playground. He had put a lot of effort into fixing this rendezvous.

They came for him just before dusk. After he handed over the rucksack that he had been carrying on his back, he was silently escorted by two men to a clearing in a jungle after a brisk one-hour walk. Maheshwar Rao, formerly one of the rising stars of the People's War Group before it merged with the CPM and once school and college friend, sat on the ground with his legs crossed under him. Unsmiling, he gestured to Arif Mohammad to sit down opposite him.

Arif Mohammad was born in Chakadoba but had spent twenty years in Nizamabad, Karimnagar, and Kudapa districts in Orissa, where his father had worked in the forest department for the government. A brilliant student who went on to get an engineering degree, he was proficient in half a dozen languages that included Bengali, Oriya, Hindi, Arabic, English, and Chinese—a unique mix. Bengali and Oriya were his default languages by virtue of his surroundings while he was growing up with other children. Arabic was taught to him by his father in a haphazard fashion to read the Koran when he was between ten and twelve years of age. English came to be familiar only in college in Bhubaneshwar so that he could read compulsory engineering textbooks. To round up this somewhat eclectic mix, he picked up a functional smattering of Chinese working for an iron trader who utilized the ports of Vishakhapatnam in Orissa and Haldia in West Bengal to export ore in mainly Chinese-owned ships.

By the time he was forty-five years old, married, and the father of three girls, he was appointed the manager of the export office in Haldia because of his Bengali-speaking background. This also suited him, because he was close enough to keep an eye on his ailing parents, who had gone back to the small family farm in West Midnapore and depended on him to supplement their meager pension. He was also facing a midlife crisis.

He was bored to distraction by his perfect wife, who gave in to his every whim and was now pregnant for the fourth time. He was losing his hair, worrying about the fact that three daughters had to be married with a fat dowry in the coming few years. He was also fed up with having been a perfect husband and doting father, an act that in recent months was sending his blood pressure through the roof. And to precipitate matters further, he was worried that sooner or later he would have to arrange a heart bypass operation for his father. He needed lots of money to meet his responsibilities, much more than he could have ever hoped to have earned.

Because he felt hemmed in by forces he had no control over, Arif reluctantly accepted an invitation from Subodh Mukherjee to celebrate the wedding of his son. Subodh, a customs official he had known for many years, was a gregarious character of his own age, one not averse to mixing business and pleasure. Arif's job demanded that he paid Subodh off in cash on a consignment basis to facilitate speedy shipments of ore.

"What you need, my friend is Chinese *chooth* to dip your cock into for a few hours to bring you back to life," Subodh commented as he and half a dozen men from the bridegroom's side walked down Bipin Bihari Street toward Mahatama Gandhi Road in the bustling neighborhood of Bow Bazaar.

They finally turned down a crooked lane into the city's oldest Chinatown and climbed two floors into a dimly lit, shabbily furnished room. After a few minutes, they were shepherded by a matronly woman into a much larger room with a group of men holding glasses of liquor, arrayed in a semicircle around a dimly lit stage.

A naked, fair-skinned woman with large breasts and long hair was lying face down on a mattress, her knees drawn up and her bottom sticking out. She was moaning softly while her fingers played with her pubic area.

The men watching her almost missed the approach from a side curtain of a massively proportioned, very dark-skinned, equally naked woman with an oiled body rush up to her, a long leather whip in one hand and what appeared to be a tubular object in the other. She cracked the whip hard against the other woman's bottom, leaving an angry red welt and forcing her to turn around on to her back and draw up her knees. In a flash, the dark-skinned woman had mounted the other woman and thrown away the whip. The tubular object was revealed to be a large dildo that she guided into her own nether regions, and though the smaller woman whimpers, the dark-skinned one also rammed the dildo into the cunt of the fair-skinned woman.

As the men watched the riveted action, some of them beginning to unzip themselves, Subodh murmured something into the ear of the same matronly woman who had escorted them into the room. She stood next to him as he pointed to the bulging erection of a visibly excited Arif.

A few seconds later, Arif found himself shepherded into a tiny, neatly arranged room almost entirely taken up by a double bed. A bedside lamp on a side table outlined the silhouette of Lily Chang, who was of indeterminate age, had seemingly flawless skin, and flaunted the build of a sixteen-year-old, with jet black hair and a soft tingling laugh. In spite of a momentary reservation, he was captivated and transported into another world as she gestured for him to sit down and then knelt at his feet to remove his shoes.

"Don't move. Let me do it for you," she said in flawless Hindi, unbuttoning his shirt and pulling down his trousers and cupping him in both her slender hands. Without further ado, she lifted her skirt to reveal the smooth shaven area between her legs and guided him in one smooth movement after he fumbled a bit with his aim. It was all over in a minute as he squirted his seed into her and emerged from his inadequacy with shame. She murmured softly and held him in the crook of her arm for a long while, and as he relaxed, she squirmed out from under him and took his limp member in her mouth, coaxing it into a full-fledged erection, and gently lowered herself onto it.

And that is how it all began—smitten by cupid's indiscriminate flaming arrow, driven to distraction over the ensuing months to visit Lily. He was spending vast sums of money that he could not afford until he finally took thirty thousand rupees out of the company account, hoping to replace it later, and got sacked as the accountant called up the owner.

At the height of his despair, Lily introduced him to Wu-Tai Chin, who conveniently turned out to be a Chinese iron trader looking for a representative in India. Fat, balding, sympathetic, he had an uncanny knack for anticipating what Arif was thinking. Within six months, Wu-Tai, now half-friend, half-father, proposed a simple method to make Arif financially sound enough to arrange a bypass operation in Kolkata's Apollo Hospital for both his parents, marry off his daughters, and facilitate the continuance of his ardent passion for the incomparable Lily. What Arif would never know was that aside from being his mentor, Wu-Tai was also the play master for China's Ministry of State Security in Kolkata.

All the while, Maheshwar Rao and he met periodically every six months or so for a quick meal and a chat. While he did not approve of what his friend was apparently doing with the People's War Group, he kept his feelings to himself.

Maheshwar Rao had now been head of the Communist Party Maoist guerilla operations in West Bengal, Jharkhand, and Orissa for three years. He was also a member of the left party's politburo, the underground outfit's highest decision-making body.

His predecessor and a dozen cadres had been killed in a successful police ambush while they were robbing a bank following a tipoff by Maya, a disgruntled woman colleague whose sexual advances he had ignored. Maheshwar Rao, the sole surviving member of the raiding Maoist group, had escaped the police trap and had personally interrogated Maya. Unfortunately, she had taken a long time to die after one of her eyes had been slowly taken out with a bayonet. His rapid elevation to the politburo had soon followed that event.

In fifty years, the Maoists were India's biggest threat as far as internal security was concerned. Their writ ran where the terrain was favorable, where masses of people could be persuaded or compelled to cooperate, and where the lack of even rudimentary roads hindered security forces from operating efficiently. In spite of this control, they remained a shadowy group, preferring to live in jungles from where they periodically emerged to carry out guerilla attacks and shunning all forms of publicity.

Because people had lost all faith in governance provided by the state and were too disorganized to combat the terror unleashed by the Maoists, the insurgents became the de facto government, dispensing quick, heavy-handed justice and collecting donations in cash or in food.

"Have you brought the money?"

"We have it here," said one of Arif's escorts, putting down the heavy rucksack loaded with bundles of thousand-rupee notes.

"Good, wait with the others until I send for you."

"I have brought the money as I promised," said Arif. "Have you been able to get an agreement from the others who are living in peace camps after cease-fire agreements?" The others included groups as disparate as Dilip Nunisa's Dima Halam Daoga (DHD) and Bir Singh Munda's Birsa Commando Force, which had signed cease-fires with the government more than six to eight years ago but were plainly dissatisfied with their treatment in the ensuing years. Recent adherents of cease-fire agreements included a faction comprising two companies of the twenty-eighth battalion of the once dreaded Arabinda Rajkhowa's United Liberation Front of Assam (ULFA), United People's Democratic Solidarity (UPDS), National Democratic Front of Bodoland (NDFB), and Adivasi Cobra Militant Force (ACMF). All these could be easily contacted by emissaries, especially if they could deliver money.

"All are agreeable. I have also contacted our friends in Myanmar and Bangladesh, but ULFA and PLA want more money. NSCN want a hundred Kalashnikovs by the end of the year," said Maheshwar Rao.

"It is entirely up to you to bring them in line. I will arrange for the weapons but that will take two months to smuggle in to you. There is no way I can obtain so many locally. My offer is very fair. Twenty million rupees for you alone after you deliver for this year. After that, annual payments depending on what you can deliver. Make a template for the type of terror incidents that you can engineer, and we can work out a scale of payment for each. How you want to share it with the others is entirely up to you to decide. I would seriously suggest that everyone should take some money offshore. I can help with the mechanics of opening accounts if necessary.

"If Al Qaeda can coordinate and direct Muslim Sunni groups all over the world, I see no reason why the Maoists cannot be the mentor and director for all groups fighting Indian-sponsored oppression. Al Qaeda has the vision do so, even if it does not have the strength and resources necessary.

"You, on the other hand, have the numbers and the staying power to defeat the Indian state. Most importantly, you already have the major resource required—that is, dedicated man power. You have lots of potential recruits waiting to be tapped in the tribal areas in particular. Anything you lack, I will be able to help you obtain."

"And what is the guarantee that I can give my politburo that you will deliver the money? I can hardly take the responsibility on the basis that we played together as children, a fact that all my people are incidentally well aware of!"

"My life should be guarantee enough! I will stay with you as a hostage until February. If you can remove a woman's eyes, you can also cut off my testicles!" Arif Mohammed replied, looking Maheshwar Rao straight in the eye. "Our destinies are now intermingled for better or for worse. This is just the start. Once you deliver, we can move on to more important issues that concern the Maoists."

CHAPTER 53
EASY MONEY

Raja Santhanam had brought up the subject of the vast amounts of illegal money flooding into India to support terror and insurgent groups as a strategic concern.

"We have a problem. People need to have confidence in the country's money, and that lasts as long as their government strives to preserve it with sensible policies. The core of the idea behind money is trust and promise, belief and faith, as evident in the peculiar cultural need to mark it with the head of national leaders like Gandhi and heroes."

When trust breaks down, people experience something like a crisis of faith. This is what is being experienced by the people of India now as more and more gold is being bought. Somewhat surprisingly, however, people from Nepal, Bangladesh, and Pakistan in the neighborhood continue to have more confidence in Indian currency than in that of their own countries."

Speed Ranganathan commented "There is an iron law in economics. Quality and quantity vary inversely, which is another way of saying that when you add more of something, each unit is worth less than the unit that preceded it (assuming everything else remains unchanged). Certainly, this is true of money. The more money in a financial system, the less each unit of it is worth. Money is many things: the touchy-feely stuff consisting of coins rattling in pockets and notes turning slightly soggy on a humid day, the stuff piled up in bank vaults, increasingly too, the electronic stuff moving at the speed of light along the vectors of financial networks. In India it is ultimately gold that is trusted as money and that is why there is such a huge demand for it."

Sridhar added "The Reserve Bank of India, the Union Home Ministry and all of India's national security agencies are on the same page on only one issue. They have absolutely no clue of how to stem the flood of freshly minted but fake Indian currency (FMIC) into India. This is estimated at about sixty billion dollars worth in circulation. This is the Indian version of what the Americans have made famous as "quantitative easing," printing trillions of dollars to ease the pain of economic collapse. In this case, the intention of our enemies is clearly to bring about the economic collapse of India through rendering the rupee useless."

A collective finger in the dyke against counterfeit currency had yielded a miserable equivalent of twenty million dollars in a year of unremitting but wasteful effort. It cost five times as much as the recovered currency, aside from the time wasted in dozens of coordination meetings at all levels. Mohandas Karamchand Gandhi had his exact likeness emblazoned on each fake note. The man revered by the Indian on the street as the ultimate Indian hero was paradoxically being used to defraud the Indian people after he had been assassinated more than six decades ago.

Sridhar added holding up a five hundred rupee note "The better forgeries are clearly works of considerable art and technological skills combined. When held up to the light, the portrait of Gandhi and multidirectional lines along with the electrotype mark show distinctly as you can see here in this note. Held under ultraviolet light, dual-colored optical fibers are clearly discernible. The security thread on rupee notes of a hundred, five hundred, and a thousand denominations has a machine-readable, windowed security thread with a color shift from blue to green when viewed from different angles. These notes glow yellow in reverse, and again, under ultraviolet light, the text glows on the obverse side."

In the ultimate homage to the handicapped, the portrait of Gandhi, the Reserve Bank of India seal, the guarantee and promise clause, the Ashoka lion emblem, and the governor's signature were in indented or improved intaglio print to ostensibly assist the blind in identifying currency notes. In India where the handicapped were treated with some disdain and even ramps for wheelchairs at airports were a rarity, not to mention at the more commonly used train stations, this was actually done more as a security measure rather than an act of genuine concern for the blind.

In the tight security environment of the Malir Cantonment in Karachi, Munir Ahmed, former engraver of the Reserve Bank of India—that is, till he was found drunk on the job and dismissed in 1990—permitted his guards to escort him to the neat, two-room set a kilometer away. He would rest for the next twelve hours before he would return to work again under escort the next day. Had he been a Pakistan citizen, he would have been an honored one for the rash of troubles that he was causing by his knowledge of the stability of India's financial system. He would, however, finish his life unsung and unwanted by his country of birth.

Unknown to Munir Ahmed while he slept, arrangements for transporting his art in the form of millions of rupees of Indian currency were being set in motion at Nepal's border with India in the Terai Region at Birganj, through which 80 percent of Nepal's trade with the outside world passed. Brought into Kathmandu by international airline flights in suitcases lined with foil to evade detection by day's end, thirty million rupees in fake currency would have travelled from Nepal to India, concealed in sacks on bicycles, three-wheeled rickshaws, horse-drawn Tongas, and even the backs of pedestrians. This was, of course, not the sole entry point for fake currency entering India, but it was certainly one with the least amount of logistics pain. It also reduced the overall risk of detection and confiscation at the border.

Bir Bahadur Rana organized his daily dispatch of ten bicycle riders, each at roughly ten minutes intervals from twenty kilometers short of Birganj, each carrying a hundred thousand fake Indian rupees. Today, he would be one of the riders as well. Once a week, he made a trip himself to ensure that he remained updated on changing conditions at the border crossings and familiar with the guards at the borders who had to be given their cut, part of which would be passed on to politicians on both sides of the border.

He was not greedy like most of the other courier organizers and almost instinctively hedged his risk. In the unlikely event that one of his cyclists was picked up across the Shankaracharya Gate crossing the bridge into India, he could make up the loss in a few days through his commission of 0.5 percent. Normally, this game was staged by the customs on both sides once every four to five weeks to prove that they were on the job and not taking bribes. It was a tested system that kept almost everyone involved happy.

As Bir Bahadur cycled into the walled compound of Bhujbal Singh, a chartered accountant living in Raxaul who was reputedly one of the better known fake currency dealers in the area was carefully watched by Arif Mohammad. Arif had come to pick up twenty million rupees of superior quality notes that had been arranged by his Chinese handler and which he would eventually hand over to the Naxals.

The money would be transported back to West Bengal in waterproof tarpaulin hidden in a consignment of Basmati rice favored by gourmets the world over. While he was curious about the organization behind this delivery, he kept this curiosity firmly under check and looked suitably bored with the process. He had been given a hundred-rupee note to be given as a receipt to Bhujbal Singh. Presumably, the number on the note would have been passed on to Bhujbal in advance.

This was one of the most porous borders in the world; so much so that it was not even marked at many places. Livestock went across to graze, and people move around freely to work, shop, and smuggle. Criminal gangs ferried narcotics, fuel, timber, shoddy electronic goods, and currency printed in Pakistan, Bangladesh, and Thailand. It was brought into Kathmandu by paid couriers, transported overland to Birganj on the Nepal side of the border, and then taken across by smugglers into the hands of the distributors on the Indian side at Raxaul.

Pakistan's Inter-Services Intelligence has streamlined this operation over two decades, organizing the printing in the sanctuary of their own cantonments and then using Dawood Ibrahim's D Company to do the dirty work of transporting it into Dubai and other gulf destinations to remove any direct Pakistan link before it was funneled back into India. Connivance with high-ranking Nepali officials and Indian border police was rampant. Upgrading of technology to keep pace with currency innovations by the Reserve Bank of India was an ongoing story.

There was one major problem with using counterfeit currency

for operational purposes. It was difficult to handle for even medium-volume transactions. If you wanted to perhaps buy a van, for instance, to transport arms, ammunition, explosives, or personnel, you would need to pay for a new one with a bank draft.

Paying for a secondhand vehicle in running condition would require two to four hundred thousand rupees. A currency note of over a hundred rupees was subject to examination by the seller. Even if he did not know the difference between a forged bank note and a genuine one, it was still a risk. There was, of course, a choice and another risk of changing fake currency for genuine notes through someone in the trade.

Anyone could sneak into India easily enough, especially through Nepal, but to instigate violence on a large scale in an urban area, it needed an existing underground organization to help with the logistics. Alternately, it required a fake bank account, stolen or fake credit cards, and some basic identity document like a phone bill to be able to operate at an appropriate scale. For most necessities, including weapons and explosives, cash had always been king. You just needed enough of it. For Chinese-funded operations, any interception of the odd currency consignment would never be traced back to them. In the template of convenience used by Indians, these hauls would be automatically attributable to Pakistan and the ISI.

CHAPTER 54
BUTTERFLY'S FLUTTER

Lily Chang served them steaming hot tea in mugs, left some peanuts and almonds on a table for them to munch on while they talked, and vanished to shop for vegetables.

"In our connected world, the flutter of a butterfly's wings in one part of the world can indeed trigger a hurricane elsewhere. Make Rao an offer he can't refuse! If you align it with what the Maoists are doing in any case, Rao will jump at it. What do you make of my choice of districts? Will the center react if there is sufficient trouble in them? Let's go through the list state-wise," Wu-Tai Chin said and then paused to hear Arif Mohammed's reaction.

Arif Mohammed was impressed by the obvious homework that had been done by his controller, Wu-Tai Chin, but hid it well. The targets were all high-poverty, low-literacy districts with acute water problems controlled by the Maoists, also known as Naxals or Naxalites, where the government of India was collectively throwing money at the problem. The equivalent of $1.4 billion a year was going down the tubes without apparent results. *Much like what the Chinese were doing in Tibet and Xinjiang*, Arif reckoned. *That's where they must have got the idea!*

"It's quite unlikely that the Maoists will be able to do all that you have outlined in so many districts in different states," Arif observed.

"We will see. What about Sonebhadra in Uttar Pradesh and Bihar's districts of Jamui, Jehanabad, Gaya, Arwal, Aurangabad, and Rohtas?"

"Great choice in UP, as the Maoist foothold will get a chance to expand and spill over into and from four neighboring states, with whose police forces coordination is nonexistent. Bihar's districts selected by you are firmly in control of the Maoists, and the state government will be forced to ask for help."

"And the four districts in Andhra, Srikakulam, Vizianagaram, Visakhapatnam, and Khammam?"

"They are all districts that Rao has a personal interest in and would love to tighten his hold further and where the central government will be forced to react since the congress is running the state so far. The maximum reaction can be expected there, I reckon."

"What about Bastar, Dantewada, Kanker, Rajnandgaon, Surguja, Narayanpur, and Bijapur in Chattisgarh?"

"In Chattisgarh, again, you seem to have picked where the Maoists are firmly entrenched, but the center is not really interested, because they are not controlling the state."

"What about the districts in the remaining states? You have the list here?" Wu-Tai asked.

Arif quickly read through the list. "Again, why have so many districts in Jharkhand-Bokara, Chatra, Garhwa, Gumla, Hazaribagh, Latehar, Lohardaga, East Singhbhum, Palamau, and West Singhbhum? The center will be forced to ignore most of them by the state governments who are keen on a settlement of the problem by peace talks. Balaghat in Madhya Pradesh is understandable, but the state government has adequate resources to tackle the rot. Gadhchiroli and Gondia in Maharashtra will get instant attention, as the industrial heartland of India will become easily accessible thereafter, and the ruling party is holding power tenuously in the state."

Wu-Tai Chin smiled and then continued, "The logic of my selection will take time to manifest itself, but humor me and stick to my list. Offer Rao ten million rupees a district. He should unilaterally declare a cease-fire for two months or slightly more and offer peace talks with the government to lull it into complacency. It will also enable him to make all the preparations required for the following period. After the cease-fire period ends, there should be one violent incident in every selected district every week for at least a ninety-day period. Tell them that there will be sizeable bonuses for large incidents like attacks on Jharkhand's thermal and hydroelectric plants that stop generation of power."

"I cannot understand why you have kept West Bengal districts out of your list after our recent successes there."

"I have done so because the states' western districts are already on fire. Why waste resources on a done deal! Police stations are under lock and key, and policemen don't dare to venture out after dark, even if one of their own is killed. The strikes on the police by the Maoists that we experimented with have been more successful than I anticipated. It's time to move on to do bigger things."

Arif disagreed. "In West Bengal, the key lies in Kolkata. We should focus resources entirely on areas surrounding the capital, where the Maoists already have a strong urban base. You need to focus on North and South Parganas districts and Howrah!"

In the adjoining room, Lily Chang switched off the small recording device, pocketed the tiny tape, and then left ostensibly to buy vegetables. A girl had to look out for herself, and there was nothing like an insurance policy in bad times. For thirty minutes, she stood on the side of a road near a major traffic light that had just turned red. Suddenly, a battered-looking taxi jumped the red light amongst squealing of brakes and loud abuses that completely jammed the road for a few moments, and then it slowed down near her, the sliding door of the passenger cabin open.

"Quickly, sister!" said the grinning, turbaned Sikh cabdriver looking into the rearview mirror. "No one can follow us now."

Superintendent of Police Rizvan Babbar, working with the criminal investigation department, offered her a steaming hot cup of tea while he played back the recording that Lily had brought.

"Nice work, Lily! Well done. I've also confirmed with Fortis Hospital that your mother's triple bypass operation is set up for Wednesday. She will be there for a week, and you can stay with her. Don't worry about the bills. I've taken care of that."

After she left, he picked up the secure phone and punched in a Delhi number. It was picked up on the second ring, so he knew it was safe to talk and there was no one else in the room with his father.

"Hello, Rizvan, any news on the Maoists?"

"You were totally right, Father. The Chinese are paying big money to the Maoists to direct their operations and bring the northeast groups on board. I'm sending you the details by secure e-mail!"

CHAPTER 55
FEAR IS THE KEY

WU TAI-CHIN'S LOGIC OF SELECTING DISTRICTS to be hit by Maoist violence for the next three months was simple. All the thirty or more districts were connected to each other, and the Maoists already had a good foothold in each. Instigating violence simultaneously would impose severe restraints on not only the state government law and order machinery in Bihar, Jharkhand, Chattisgarh, Orissa, and Maharashtra but also overload the central governments already overflowing plate of woes. Internal security overload alongside attacks by Pakistan and China would paralyze the decision-making process. It would be completely outside the experience of the government and would inevitably cause severe compromises with preserving India's security in the immediate future. Ignoring violence anywhere was not a solution for more than a couple of weeks, for it would become more difficult to stamp out later.

When the events came about, the intensity of the violence spilling across state boundaries took India by surprise. The truce declared by the Maoists had held up for more than two months without a single incident of violence that could be attributed to them. The sophistication of the attacks stretched the police resources of the involved states like a rubber band within a fortnight. The pattern was similar everywhere—the economy was being targeted. They were uprooting of railway tracks and fleeting attacks on small isolated stations, setting trucks ablaze, opening fire at state transport buses, attacking construction workers at energy infrastructure locations, a systematic attack on mobile phone towers for disruptive shutdowns.

The effect on coal production in India was almost immediate. With coal stocks being depleted, load shedding was the immediate response of the thermal generation plants. Large-scale attacks on police forces were completely avoided for the first month. Just as suddenly in the fifth week, seven landmines were exploded under police jeeps within a period of three days in Jharkhand. As the police hesitated to get on the roads, especially at night, a full-scale attack was launched by a hundred Maoist cadres on the DVC-Chandrapura five-hundred-megawatt thermal power plant in Jharkhand, and twenty-seven engineers and workers were brutally killed, their heads lopped off. Power production and industrial production in the region slumped by 25 percent overnight after the attacks.

In a measure of its desperation, two army divisions that were being newly raised in Assam and Arunachal Pradesh were told to divert a brigade group each to Jharkhand and Bihar respectively. In addition, three units of the army's Rashtriya Rifles were diverted from counterinsurgency duties in Kashmir to stem the rot. Wu-tai-Chin's gambit was succeeding much beyond what he had envisaged.

However, Wu Tai-Chin was also orchestrating events in the northeast. Again, the impact would greatly affect the economic arena.

In a race to establish first-user water rights and preempt Chinese designs on the Yarlung Tsangpo water, the Arunachal Pradesh government had decided to activate hydroelectric projects on the Subansiri, Siang, and Lohit River basins. The Subansari hydroelectric project was the largest of them, a run of the river project on the border of Assam and Arunachal Pradesh located at North Lakhimpur. It was also the project that had made distinct progress under the National Hydropower Corporation.

The National Democratic Front of Bodoland (NDFB) was tasked to stop all work on the project for ten million rupees. They achieved it by the simple expedient of kidnapping the superintendent engineer and two of his assistants at gunpoint during a thunderstorm and holding them for ransom. Fourteen laborers were also killed in the same operation, resulting in a labor strike that paralyzed the project for the next three months. An attack on a local police station killed all the twenty policemen who were caught asleep after a harrowing week of investigative and protection work. Two police constables were also abducted and held for ransom. Work was only resumed when an infantry battalion from the army was located at the project site, denuding force from the border with China. A series of road blockades instigated through locals at Dhemaji and Lakhimpur, however, stopped all movement of material to the site.

The violence was extended through all the northeast insurgent groups and dozens of environmental-related NGOs (nongovernment organizations) to target twelve projects of the National Hydropower Corporation, effectively putting fifty thousand megawatts of potential power projects into limbo. Another newly raised infantry brigade that had still to receive its full complement of equipment had to be diverted to quell disturbances in Assam.

Simultaneous attacks in other parts of India by the Indian Mujahideen resulted in a nation under siege. Each day, the target seemed to be a different city or town. There appeared to be a total change in the strategy followed in the attacks that made it obvious that they were being orchestrated by the ISI. The senseless, low-risk bombings of the past decade, random bombs going off in crowded shopping areas to project India as an unsafe destination, were replaced by a far more sophisticated approach.

The major cities that were better policed were avoided. Disruption of railway services in times of conflict was far more effective than merely garnering headlines. In a two-week period in early winter, bomb blasts with IEDs and magnified shrapnel effects hit a string of railway stations. Targets included ticket counters, transport stands, tea and food stalls, and main platform entrances at peak hours. No security measures to deter strikes existed in any of these places, because they were all designed to tackle threats within station premises and not at the approaches to these.

Starting in the east near the Siliguri Corridor in West Bengal at stations like Islampur, Siliguri, New Jalpaiguri, moving west to Katihar, Purnia, and Kishanganj in Bihar and then into Uttar Pradesh to include Azamgarh, Ghazipur, Ballia Robertsganj, Moradabad, and Aligarh, a series of bomb blasts ripped through the bodies of hundreds of innocent commuters, hawkers, vendors, and beggars, overloading emergency services just after most doctors had left for home. Farther to the west in Punjab, Muktsar, Faridkot, and Mansa were targeted, not to mention Hiranagar and Samba in Jammu and Kashmir. A large number of Indian Railways staff and labor also became terror victims. More than 1,200 people across north and east India lost their lives, and at least four times as many were wounded.

Train services, including the movement of guns, tanks, ammunition, and fuel to troops deployed to face China and Pakistan, were severely hampered. As precautionary security measures were put into place across northern India, a further wave of IED attacks hit railway stations in Jodhpur, Sikar, and Nagaur in Rajasthan followed by Bhuj, Palanpur, and Mehsana in Gujarat, all happening on the same day in a two-hour period after sunset. Mob frenzy took hold in half a dozen towns, and a number of innocent youths with beards were stoned and kicked to death.

As the nationwide toll mounted, smaller incidents that had received only passing mention instead of headlines were analyzed in a series of lead articles by the *Hindustan Times* correspondent Nivriti Butalia titled "Farewell to India—Siliguri Corridor Being Cut by Sino-Pak Collusion." In a meticulously researched coverage, the story traced the linkage between the coup engineered in Nepal by China to bring the Maoists in total power by installing Machida the successor of Prachanda as the PM and the arming of thousands of Bhupalese (Bhutanese of Nepali-origin camping in Nepal since 1990) to instigate anarchy in Bhutan.

The second article's front page had a blown-up photograph of two hooded youths on a Honda motorcycle, hurling a piglet head into a mosque in New Jalpaiguri. The story went on to describe how these young men had been recruited by the Hizb ul-Tehrir in Bangladesh, which also received money from Saudi Arabian fundamentalists through the ISI. With small payoffs to the border security force personnel, they were smuggled into India to live with distant relatives and await instructions.

The last of the series painted a grim end for the northeast states of India as they were being severed from the rest of the country. The communist government in Nepal under Chinese tutelage would unleash sizeable numbers of the radical younger generation of Bhupalese enrolled into insurgent outfits like the Bhutan Tiger Force, the Communist Party of Bhutan, and the Bhutan Maoist Party into Bhutan to create anarchy and invite a Chinese walk-in to restore order. The friendly Bangladesh government would be replaced by a radicalized one after a series of political assassinations triggered by the ISI.

With the newly created army formations already largely sucked into insurgency-related missions, the stage was set for the PLA's next move. A little help from the ISI set the ball rolling.

CHAPTER 56
AN EYE FOR AN EYE

THEY HAD MET UP AGAIN IN the African restaurant of the Safari Park Hotel in Nairobi at midday. Narayan Patel downed another beer, keeping up with the three Somalis he only knew as Guleed, Hadeef, and Beyle. Traditionally a teetotaler community and strict vegetarians, the Patel community was flexible in their approach when it came to business, but Narayan drew the line at eating meat.

The real estate business Narayan ran had been inherited from his father. Atul Patel had come to Kenya seventy years earlier as a petty trader and moneylender and had worked his way up to controlling small parcels of real estate business in lieu of unpaid debts. Remarkably, he had done so without making any enemies.

Narayan had imbibed the two lessons that his father, Atul, had repeated on an almost daily basis: "Retain contact with the family and friends in Veraval on the Gujarat coast. Look what happened to Indians in Uganda under the dictator Idi Amin when so many were killed or kicked out! Retaining a foothold in India may also save your family's collective ass. Secondly, never lose a customer through lack of effort. Make him a friend over time by investing in the relationship." The annual pilgrimage to the land of his ancestors was a must for two weeks every year. It had become part of his DNA and had taken him very little time to realize how beneficial it was to his business as well. Lots of Indians with unaccounted cash had bought real estate in Africa through him to diversify their risks.

Yash, his second cousin, who worked or at least had worked for the Indian government, had made the offer casually during his last visit. "Would you like to try to make a million dollars in cash for a few weeks of work?"

"Who wouldn't?" he had replied.

"Good. I may be able to set up something for you in the next six months. By the way, do you know any Somali pirates? I hear some of them are buying commercial property in Nairobi."

Yash had obviously done his homework he had quickly realized. "Some Somalis are my clients. Whether they are connected with piracy is something I have no knowledge of."

If important clients wanted him to drink with them to build up a relationship, Narayan would oblige. Fortunately, he had a natural ability to remain reasonably sober irrespective of the amount of beer he drank. His clients, however, did not have the same ability in many cases.

"Patel, how much do we need to buy the building we saw this morning?"

"Two million US—the dollar is not what it used to be, Guleed. I might be able to get you a hundred and fifty thousand off if you have the cash."

"No way can we get that kind of money in a hurry! I guess we'll just have to forget about it, Patel. Thanks for the beer," Hadeef added despondently, chewing at a large mouthful of Nyama Choma, the grilled meat specialty, while he slumped in a corner of the sofa.

"Maybe there is a simple way out. Depends on how badly you want to collect steady rent from a good European multinational company and retire from your business," Narayan Patel said and signaled for another round of drinks.

Beyle, six feet four of corded muscle with a deceptively soft voice, gulped his beer and asked, "How simple?"

"Nothing different from what you normally do, so it should be simple enough. This time, though, I will choose a target to prey upon and take to Haradheere."

"We are still listening," Beyle said under his breath.

"This time, it has to be a Chinese VLCC tanker and any two other Chinese ships in the next three months," Narayan said. "However, there will be no long-drawn negotiations over the ransom money, unless you want to amuse yourself. I will pay you five million dollars plus transfer the building we saw to your names. The choice is yours! In addition, you get to keep the ransom money. My only condition is that the negotiations should be spun out for seventy-five days, at least for the oil tanker."

"We want five million in advance. It's not easy to take over a Chinese tanker, with their PLA Navy always at hand."

"Take one million as a down payment now. The balance payable here in cash when any western TV channel reports the hijack as successful! After that, I will give you two hundred thousand dollars as advance for each of the other two ships and eight hundred thousand dollars on completion of each mission. You have two weeks from the time I give the word for you to board the first ship."

"It's a deal!" Beyle replied, putting out a huge hand for Narayan Patel to shake.

The navigation instruments of the Shenzhen indicated 12 degrees 22 minutes north and 48 degrees 23 minutes east. The high-speed boat with dual engines appeared on the radar, closing in to the three hundred thousand DWT tanker carrying two million barrels of oil at twenty-three knots. It was followed by two other similar boats, each spaced well apart with an eight-man crew, all armed with Kalashnikovs. In addition, in each boat, one man readied a rocket-propelled grenade launcher. Captain Zhao Peng pushed the emergency security button on the ship in order to alert the ship owner, the state-owned China Shipping Company, through satellite phone. He also radioed a request for help from the nearest military vessel. Because he went by the book, he followed the security protocol ordering avoidance maneuvers in spite of the fact that he knew that a fully loaded tanker had no hope in hell of running away from a speedboat at least 50 percent quicker. Zhao simultaneously sounded the ship's alarm, announcing that they were under attack by pirates, and ordered the activation of the water cannon to repel boarders. He then barricaded himself and the steersman, who was on watch at that time, on the command deck.

Four pirates from both port and starboard sides led by a bare-chested Beyle clambered aboard using aluminum ladders, making light work of the seven meters of freeboard of the tanker. They first turned off the water cannon. Coolly, they then assaulted the command deck, reducing the toughened windows to shreds. Within fifteen minutes, Beyle had complete control of the ship.

The closest military vessel in the area, the Pakistan frigate Gazni, was about 120 kilometers away, but it still launched a helicopter. The crew led by Lieutenant Imtiaz Bux was told to fire at will at the pirates. In the meanwhile, twenty pirates had boarded the tanker and assembled the crew on deck around themselves. When he saw the crew and pirates intermingled on the deck, Imtiaz Bux fired two missiles in frustration and sank two of the speedboats manned by a single pirate each. The two boats were sunk, and both the pirates were severely wounded and would die in a few hours. Hadeef, who had also clambered aboard, slapped Captain Zhao Peng twice in a fit of rage at his loss and showed him a spot on the chart to sail to.

After two days, they approached the small town of Eyl in Put Land Province on the Somali coast, and the Shenzhen dropped anchor about five nautical miles from the coast. After they anchored, a Somali negotiator in a tattered T-shirt and plastic sandals who surprisingly spoke Chinese in a hesitant fashion appeared. Zhao was ordered to get in touch with the security officer of the China Shipping Company, and each member of the crew was made to speak to him. The negotiations would be conducted by a specialist company based in London, the center of the global shipping industry where the financial and legal aspects would also be resolved. Because there was an issue of blood money that had to be resolved, it would take almost a hundred days of negotiations before an unheard sum of twenty million dollars would be dropped on board the tanker by a small seaplane and the crew as well as the taker would be freed.

The SMS message to Narayan Patel was brief and left him smiling. "Watch *CNN*!" As the update on the situation from Patel reached Sridhar by a series of cutouts, he briefed the crisis management group. "Retribution is sweet—an eye for an eye after forty years of waiting, even if it is a smaller eye! It's a pity we didn't ask them to sink the Shenzhen."

CHAPTER 57
COLD DESERT—RIPOSTE

Lieutenant General Kanwar Devraj Singh was clear in his mind that it would be a fortnight before the brigade and tank regiment he had been promised would be ready for battle. In the meanwhile, he couldn't sit on his butt. It was asking for further trouble from the PLA.

At the end of the conversation with the army commander on the secure line, a plan had taken shape in his mind. It was simple and straightforward, as all good plans should have been. Sometimes a few trained and dedicated men could do the task when thousands could not. Insert three squads each of five men, using the high-altitude parachute-penetration system (HAPPS) across the LAC using "intruder parachutes." Also alongside, give them the wherewithal to optimize their intrusion. An intruder, parachute-based, controlled-aerial delivery system would carry and deliver the ammunition, explosives, and other stores required by the dedicated team to disrupt and interdict the high-altitude, cold, desert, western highway connecting Xinjiang and Tibet. Repairs to bridges and culverts would be virtually impossible in the subzero extreme winter at 13–14,000 feet above sea level.

Conditions were ideal. A strong westerly was blowing at this time of the year. With the release taking place at an altitude of nearly thirty thousand feet, the paratroopers would ride the wind and glide more than eighty kilometers from where they first jumped off. There would be no radar signatures. To assist interdiction of the highway by the air force later, each squad was carrying a laser designator as well to light up potential targets for laser-guided bombs from aircraft to find their mark within a meter of the desired impact points.

The participants were all volunteer Khampas from eastern Tibet, a part of which had been spun off by the Chinese after they had annexed Tibet into Sichuan. Their parents had fled Tibet, chased by the PLA, in the early 1960's, and crossed into India. They had been handpicked by the inspector general of the SFF. All were qualified free-fall parachutists and had been trained by US Green Berets. All had been instructors at the SFF Parachutist Training School in Sarsawa. A fire to liberate Tibet burned constantly in their hearts and had not dimmed over the past decades.

Presently, all were in the process of tying up the final details and checking the equipment. The countdown would begin at 1700 hours when they would all commence the process of inhaling oxygen to de-nitrogenize their bodies and blood. Jumping out at thirty thousand feet could make the blood boil if this was not done. The oxygen consoles were fitted inside the specially modified C-130. They carried enough oxygen for the pre-breathing process and the requirement of flight just prior to the jump. Thereafter, the para jumpers would switch to the man-portable oxygen equipment in the parachute harness.

Preparations were also on for selection of the second-set insertion a day later. This would be led by handpicked veterans from 9 Para SF under Major Balraj Gurung with Captain Arun as his second-in-command.

In addition, Devraj had also planned to infiltrate some surveillance detachments of the Para SF and Ladakh Scouts for operations in the areas just behind the Chinese forward defenses.

He could not wish away the delay that the process of induction and acclimatization to fight at fourteen thousand feet above sea level imposed. However, if the air-inserted squads achieved even partial success, the Chinese would have their hands full. It would become even more interesting if someone had the gumption to target the Qinghai-Lhasa railway line simultaneously.

Company leader Dawa was the most experienced of the lot. As he gathered his Pinjas, there were tears in his eyes. He hugged them all and invoked the blessing of the Dalai Lama. He then dug inside his pocket and took out a large pebble. It was something he had carried with him for the last fifty years from his home at Lhasa.

He took Tshering, Wangyal, and Lama aside and instructed them to carry out a final check of all the equipment. He himself took the rest for pre-breathing exercises. It was a painful process. The fitting of the mask had to be checked to ensure there was no leakage. All communication thereafter would be by hand signals. Thondup, Wangdus, Thupten, and Philze with Tshering comprised the first squad. They were to operate in the general area of Rudok.

Another squad under Lama was to land in the general area of Churkang and move south of it. The Dawa-led squad was to operate even farther south, closer to Shiquanhe and the Chinese missile site built into the mountainside.

An hour before departure, route navigation had to be painstakingly evolved and checked. They were waiting for the weather and wind report from the metrological section—wind direction and speed at every thousand feet. Based on the inputs received, the waypoints and bearings to guide the parachutists were worked out, checked, and then rechecked.

At 2000 hours, the lone aircraft started its engines and taxied down to the runaway. All the fifteen squad members mumbled silent prayers as the aircraft hurtled down the runaway and was soon airborne. A circuitous flight route had been worked out that went over Kargil and then on to Indira Col before they turned southeastward to follow a track along the "Line of Control." From a height of thirty thousand feet, it would be impossible to see and identify features, especially at night, but then the GPS each squad possess would get them wherever they needed to go. Still north of the Pangong Tso Lake, the warning buzzer beeped. It was show-time. The squads immediately switched their oxygen supply system from the console to their personal cylinders on the parachute. Then in a line, one behind the other, they shuffled forward toward the ramp. The dispatchers indicated the outside temperature to be minus 55 degrees Celsius and wind speed at just over forty-five knots.

As the ramp slid down, a blast of cold air hit them at gale force. Even while the biting cold was expected, the ferocity of the wind still caught them off guard for a few seconds. After a small beep, the first squad dived out. The dispatchers ejected their loads by the controlled-aerial delivery system. The other squads followed at one-minute intervals.

Company leader Dawa was the last man out of the aircraft. As he went out into the slipstream, years of training and discipline kicked in, and he found himself doing a mental count.

"One thousand, two thousand, three thousand, four thousand, five thousand" Dawa allowed himself time to clear the slipstream. If the chute had opened in the slipstream, it would have been torn to strips. During free fall, the altimeter helped, but in this case, the requirement was to drift only to a safe distance. The squad members jumped and pulled their ripcords after they cleared the slipstream.

As the chute deployed, Dawa could make out the outline of the other chutes. When he tugged hard at the left toggle, he took a sharp left turn. He assumed the lead and set on the designated course, riding the strong westerly. Periodic corrections had to be made to cater for the change in wind pattern at varying altitudes. He reached down and adjusted the seat straps for momentary comfort. It was going to be a minimum thirty minutes to touchdown. He glanced back every now and then to check if all, including the loads, were still intact. The ground could still not be seen despite the ambient luminosity of high altitude. The altimeter indicated twenty-seven thousand feet. *Another sixteen thousand feet to descend*, he reckoned. The time was getting on to 2330 hours. They should be touching ground in another ten to eleven minutes. As he looked down, he could now discern the ground of the high-altitude desert. He mentally thanked the Dalai, as it was clear he would be landing east of the western highway as intended. There would be nearly five hours of darkness to establish a hideout, conceal their tracks, and hide their stores after they retrieved them.

The first day, all three squads were to remain concealed and rest. They were told to just observe the ground for enemies, rest up for the arduous next phase, and do nothing else that may have inadvertently given away their positions. There was to be no communication between the squads whatsoever. An encrypted, high-speed Morse burst would be sent to indicate that the eagles had landed and established their nests.

During the next night, they were to receive the Para SF detachment. The interdiction operation fireworks were planned for later.

In the meantime, induction of the tanks was going on by air. By the second day, the first squadron of T-72 tanks had arrived led by Major Sahil Butalia, who had been pulled out from operations against Pakistan, for he had done a stint in Ladakh when terrain and altitude trials of the tanks had been carried out some years ago. His experience would be a big help to crews flying straight into a hostile fighting environment from the plains they had trained in. IL-76 and C-130 transport aircraft had operated nonstop to induct whatever was required.

The airfields at Nyoma and Fuchke had been energized. Heavy-lift Mi-24 helicopters were available to move whatever Devraj wanted to the forward battle zone.

A steady stream of information was coming in. The Chinese had moved up their BD regiment, and their defenses were fully manned. A mechanized regiment had also been inducted, which in turn had created the requirement for adequate armor to counter it.

The Chinese media had gone into overdrive, releasing satellite pictures of the Indian buildup and exaggerated news ascribing warlike designs to the Indians against the spirit of past joint agreements between China and India. Internet blogs encouraged by the PLA dissected Indian warlike moves and praised Chinese restraint in the face of grave provocations.

The second phase of the air induction had gone off with out a hitch. However, the linkup between the Para SF and Dawa's squad could take place only after a delay of twenty-four hours. Hundreds of Tibetan grazers, who had been evicted from the forward villages, were camping nearby where the para had landed but made no attempt to inform the Chinese authorities.

Sergeant Hu of the fifteen military intelligence communication unit was worried. As he worked at his folding desk with an old field telephone, he pondered over the daily report of communications. All was routine. There was a marginal increase of radio traffic, but what puzzled him was the report of three encrypted transmissions occurring between midnight and first light in the past five days. Who? What? Why? He had no answers. But something was amiss.

Tshering and Lama were safe. A lot of convoy movement along the western highway was taking place. The last three nights, Dawa and the Para SF boys had been constantly on the move, four to five hours of walking every night to establish a new hideout to avoid detection. The GPS now indicated they were just about five kilometers southwest of Shiquanhe. Extreme caution had to be exercised.

Contrary to general perception, the bareness to the Tibetan terrain offered great opportunities in camouflage and concealment. Though one could see for miles, the rock- and boulder-strewn landscape, with the constant play of evolving shadows, played havoc with perception. The folds in the ground were very deceptive and could hide large numbers of troops from most observers.

Everything going so smoothly was paradoxically a cause of worry. Devraj was thinking about Murphy's Law and the inevitability of things going wrong. Devraj took a mental stock of his buildup. By interchanging two battalions from his ground-holding brigades, integrating the existing mechanized company with the inducted armored regiment, he had a combat team and adequate infantry ready and poised to make a surprise foray into the Chinese side.

He decided to spend the night at Chumathang. He was tense and needed to relax. All loose ends for a raid on the small hamlet of Dumchelle, which housed a Chinese regimental headquarters and its logistics elements on the Chinese side, had been coordinated. The men were ready. Air activity has increased manifold during the last three days. Sporadic engagement of the forward defenses by artillery had also increased just as patrol clashes had as well. However, it was nothing that was not expected.

At 2000 hours, Balraj and Gurung were lying just three hundred meters north of the suspected missile site to the West of Shiquanhe. The balance of the squad was busy laying IEDs and landmines along the western highway, both to the north and south, as it entered and exited Shiquanhe. Roads leading to Churkang had also been mined. Gravel tracks made it all simpler to execute.

Norbu fed in the coordinates of the missile site and sent out a burst to the attack aircraft under Wing Commander Joy Bhowmick, who was already on the way. They were to fly south, cross the Wakhan Corridor, and follow a route along the Karakoram Range. Contact would be established with the code sign "tango sierra papa."

Simultaneously, another flight of Su-30 MK-III aircraft was also airborne to attack the Hotan Airfield.

After a scrambled beep, Joy Bhowmick knew what had to be done.

A similar beep on Balraj Gurung's headphones ensured that he had pressed the trigger. The missile site was lit up by the laser designator. The laser-guided bombs swooshed down, riding the invisible beam to which it was now slaved. Multiple explosions sounded in the air as the bombs exploded within the hollowed-out cavern.

By 0400 hours, Major Sahil Butalia reported that Dumchelle was invested and that four armored personnel carriers of the PLA mechanized unit had been destroyed.

Movement of Chinese convoys brought ground traffic to a halt. The western highway had been disrupted at a number of places. Five major culverts had been blown up. Approaches and exits to these culverts along with the debris had been mined. By the morning, rioting between the locals and the Han civilians had broken out. The PLA was shooting Tibetans on the slightest suspicion.

Such panic and confusion prevailed that it was easy for Dawa to easily commandeer a truck. There were still three hours of darkness available. After the accomplishment of their mission, all squads headed west to the designated pickup point. Helicopters were expected just before daylight.

As they hugged the ground and the valley contours, the Mi-17 helicopters weaved their way to the designated landing to pick up Dawa and his men.

"What took you so long?" Dawa queried the pilot as he slid his backpack off his shoulders and reached for the steel thermos and the sweet tea that it contained.

In Beijing, the vice chairman of the central military commission, General Xu Caihou, spoke to Hu Jintao, the most powerful man in China, who was also the chairman of the CMC in addition to his other roles as president of China and general secretary of the Communist Party of China.

"It's a minor tactical setback that we should privately welcome," Xu Caihou explained.

"How can you justify a military setback that ruins the reputation of the PLA?" Hu Jintao reacted angrily.

"The escalation in violence creates the ideal window for us to respond to the warlike Indian posture. As soon as the last regiment of the RRF reaches south of Lhasa, we have the perfect provocation to permit the PLA to launch a retaliatory attack in Sikkim and Bhutan."

CHAPTER 58
THE SILIGURI CORRIDOR

THE MOST VULNERABLE PART OF INDIA was definitely the Siliguri Corridor, a narrow strip of India only twenty-one to forty kilometers wide at places that separate Bangladesh from Nepal. Siliguri, a multihued town of 1.6 million people, the largest city in North Bengal, was nestled at the base of the Himalayan Mountains in the plains, and it was the gateway to northeast India's seven states.

Bangladesh continued being home to hundreds of Islamic militants in spite of the new government trying to clamp down. Pakistan's Inter-Services Intelligence used its existing network from 1971 for funneling very large sums of Saudi-origin money to sponsor waves of illegal immigrants into India's most sensitive areas. More than nine hundred mosques and over a thousand madrassas built with mainly Saudi funds also provided safe havens for militant organizations, including SIMI (Students Islamic Movement in India), with strong links to the Hizb ul Mujahid in Pakistan-occupied area of Kashmir. The Siliguri Corridor was a powder keg waiting to explode in India's face. The demographic profile of the area had already been radically altered with cynical Indian politicians seeking to promote a reliable Muslim vote bank by ensuring voter identity cards to the illegal influx.

Drugs, firearms, and explosives inevitably followed, the smugglers promoting the influx of twelve million, as did generally peace-loving Bangladesh citizens into the promised land of their dreams in Assam and West Bengal. Election results in the two states of Assam and West

Bengal were significantly impacted by the votes of people who had not been through a due process of changing nationality but still given votes. A similar situation would not be permissible anywhere else in the world.

A small but significant minority of the immigrants were the new flag bearers of radical, Sunni-style Jihad. In a democracy as diverse as India, it was hazardous for the political class to associate an ethnic or religious group with acts of political violence or terrorism. Careful, fine-combed profiling of groups within communities was taboo except for the majority Hindu community where no bar existed. Intelligence collection with respect to subgroups that had been subverted or ripe for subversion was negligible at the organized level. The Jihadist cult had, therefore, been provided unlimited freedom to flower and direct itself at the soft effete state that had provided the sustenance to bloom in the first place.

The Siliguri Corridor was also a place where the strategic perceptions of China, Pakistan, and important segments of Bangladesh and Nepalese Maoists overlapped. Thus, it was only a matter of time before the belated Indian internal response of flooding the area with military and paramilitary forces would be put to a test.

Siliguri, the fourth largest town in West Bengal with a population of 1.5 million people, was the transit point for air, road, and rail traffic to the neighboring countries of Nepal, Bhutan, and Bangladesh. It hosted well over six hundred thousand visitors and tourists a year, many of them visiting the towns of Gangtok, Rangpo, Kalimpong, Kurseong, Mirik, and Darjeeling in the vicinity. This passage of people further compounded the security problems for the plethora of paramilitary and military force bases in the corridor, including the Indian Army, border security force (BSF), Central Reserve Police Force (CRPF), Shashatra Seema Bal (SSB), and the Assam Rifles as well as the Indian Air Force's Bagdogra Airfield, which was close to the town of Siliguri.

The three-day war game was organized by the Indian army's 33 Corps headquarters in the Siliguri corridor military base at Sukhna under the shadow of the terror strike in Delhi. It was being attended by senior officers from all of the army's eastern command responsible for the defense of all the northeastern states of India as well as a liberal representation from the corresponding eastern air command, for any operations against China would have to be joint army-air efforts. The army chief and defense minister were also expected to attend briefly on the closing day. Small, freshly painted boards leading into the Siliguri cantonment showed arrows pointing in the direction where exercise "Dragon Fire II" was being conducted.

Meanwhile, every three hours or so, a circling Chinese telecommunications satellite was overhead, probing for cell phone numbers and conversations originating from the Siliguri cantonment. A disgruntled employee of the telephone regulatory authority of India (TRAI) had procured and sold the personal GPRS cell phone numbers of three hundred senior military officers ranging from major upward for a hundred thousand rupees. This act also ensured that his son could pay fifty thousand rupees as a bribe for admission into the regional engineering college.

Ran Bahadur Rana, a Nepalese Maoist, had paid the money through his cousin in Siliguri. Ten days later, the list had found its way to Li Jie, the commercial attaché in the Chinese embassy in Kathmandu, and was soon in the hands of the PLA intelligence directorate thereafter. All that was now required was to track origination of calls from three hundred cell phones and wait till the calls originated from roughly the same area. That would happen in any army, air force, or navy when the users were brought together for training purposes.

The Dong-Hai 10 land-attack cruise missile was a masterpiece of reverse engineering and was a lesson to third-world countries how military technology could be developed on the cheap, even if it took the time and considerable coordination of a host of national assets. Two unexploded US Tomahawk cruise missiles as well as numerous sub parts from war zones as far apart as Serbia, Iraq and, Afghanistan had been bought for fifty thousand dollars each from Osama bin Laden's agents. These assemblies and sub assemblies were studied, taken apart, and used to leverage the Hong Niao or "Red Bird" family of Chinese land-attack cruise missile development. The engine was developed on the superior Russian turbofan TRDD-50 engine that had been acquired through the purchase of half a dozen Kh-55 Raduga cruise missiles from Ukraine in the 1990s.

With a range in excess of 1,500 kilometers and a warhead of four hundred kilograms of high explosive, the missile was now loaded onto a platform launcher that carried three missiles. The PLA second artillery corps cruise missile brigade located at Jiangshu, Yunnan Province, in southern China had shifted three launchers well south of Lhasa in early August under the command of Colonel Liu Jiangping. The position was barely three hundred kilometers from Siliguri, but no one was willing to take any chances with the Americans.

A short flying time by moving the missile launchers closer to the intended target would ensure that there was no way that the unencrypted GPS could be jammed from satellites. Terminal homing, including the combined inertial navigation system (INS), GPS, and the terrain-following radar (TERCOM) would ensure that the strike point was within ten meters of the chosen point. The missile would penetrate any low-level air defense system of the Indians with ease because of the stealth-technology elements coupled with the effect the curvature of the earth had on detection.

Dragon Strike II had run smoothly enough. Eastern Command and Eastern Air Command were sanguine that any Chinese thrust would be severely punished. The year 1962 had since passed, a time when professionalism in the armed forces was at a premium and exposure to combat and training of the PLA gave China a distinct edge. As the defense minister rose to address the gathering, there was a brief stir of anticipation amongst the people, the Army Chief Shiv Kapur, half a dozen three-star generals, two air marshals, nine major generals, three air vice marshals, and over a hundred other senior officers present in the new state-of-the-art auditorium, two projection systems reflecting the defense minister's brooding face.

Meanwhile, a few minutes earlier, three kilometers north of their position, Colonel Liu Jiangping had picked up the secure phone in his command post, listened for a minute, and said, "Yes, we are ready and will launch in thirty seconds as ordered!"

"General Shiv Kapur and officers of Eastern Command and Eastern Air Command, I realize that this is an unusual moment. No defense minister has ever addressed a gathering of combat-ready officers at a time when a very fine balance exists between peace and war with both China and Pakistan. I will keep this very short, as I know that within an hour, all of you will be headed in different directions to rejoin your commands. There is no question of accepting China's claim to Arunachal Pradesh. I wish to assure you that unlike at some times in the past, the entire nation stands behind all of you in this time of trial. Equipment and ammunition shortfalls are being made up rapidly, and no stone will be left unturned to support you in the field."

As the defense minister turned to gaze directly into the eyes of the front row of the gathering before he continued, two cruise missiles struck the auditorium roof, went clean through, and simultaneously exploded. Fifty-nine officers died instantly, including Army Chief General Shiv Kapur, and seventy-three were wounded, of which only less than half would ultimately survive after months of rehabilitation. Miraculously, the defense minister survived, only obtaining a very large bruise on his face that would persist for weeks. At one stroke, the entire senior leadership of the eastern theater of operations had been eliminated. This would have much to do with the course of events in the near future. Soldiers deployed for battle had been rendered directionless in a few seconds. Five minutes later, the low-level pass of a Chinese satellite would beam photographs with a resolution of sixty centimeters of the mess created of the auditorium.

As soon as the immediate damage assessment report was received, Colonel Liu Jiangping gave his waiting crews the signal to stand down. No more missiles needed to be launched. Confirmation of success would thereafter pour in from the uncensored Indian media.

CHAPTER 59
THE WAR WITHIN

Ashok Sobti and all members of the crisis management group were struggling to preserve an air of calmness as they took stock. The missile strikes and the death of the army chief and the top military leadership of Eastern Command had created a huge leadership vacuum in the military. The Chinese would be turning up the heat very quickly.

"We need to be ready to give our views when PM Durga Vadera asks," Ashok Sobti opened the discussion.

"I have no doubts that everyone in the NSAB providing guidance to the cabinet committee on security along with us in the crisis management group will be generally on the same page now that the Chinese threat is clearly revealed," said Vice-Admiral Shankar Menon. "We need to respond quickly to show resolve but at the same time keep the conflict from spiraling out of control."

Lieutenant General Randhir Singh added, "The first step we should again recommend is taking out the Qinghai-Tibet railway line. If the Siliguri Corridor is directly threatened, the EMP limited option should be step two."

"I doubt whether the PM will have time for us for quite some time. She will have her hands full. I think this is distinctly going to be a multilevel threat, and we should expect escalating violence within the country, stirred by both China and Pakistan," Sridhar observed. "I think it's time for Nasruddin to activate his plan and target the insurgent leaders. I've activated some of our dormant assets in Bangladesh and Nepal as well to assist. I have also paid more than a million dollars to three generals in Myanmar through our Mauritius account. I have promised double the amount on a head-count basis if they crack down hard on ULFA, UNLF, and PLA insurgent cadres sheltering in Myanmar. The Telecom Regulatory Authority of India (TRAI) board has agreed to give us continuous GPS updates on all the numbers we requested. The national security guard (NSG) has been warned to stand by dedicated resources."

The next day, Wu-Tai Chin walked out of the Chinese consulate at Salt Lake City, where he had gone to collect visas to China for some business associates. The sun had set when he got into his car. His phone rang thrice and then stopped before it rang again. After the third ring, he said "Hello … wrong number." He then drove quickly to the bus stand on the main road, where Arif quickly slid into the front with him.

Wu-Tai Chin got straight to the point. "Arif, you need to organize a meeting with the Maoists this week. Promise them another twenty million rupees to step up attacks across the thirty districts we agreed upon. I've made the same arrangements for you to collect, the money although it would be so much easier if they did not insist on cash."

Arif said, "I'll try to do it quickly, but there is no chance of persuading them to open accounts in tax havens. They don't trust banks. Slow down; there is a police barrier ahead."

There was a long line of cars crawling slowly ahead as the policemen on duty appeared to be meticulously examining car registrations and driver licenses. Vendors of everything from ice cream to cigarettes, from balloons to aphrodisiacs noisily plied their trade to the frustrated drivers. Some cars had been pulled over to the side of the road ahead of the barrier to negotiate the bribe amounts for minor infractions. Without being noticed, a teenage boy with a sharp spike in his hand punched the rear tire and ran off in the opposite direction toward a crowd of people at a bus stop.

"The tire has been punctured!" the teen said to a potbellied man who had thinning hair and wore dark glasses.

"Well done. Here is the other fifty rupees that I promised."

As the boy ran off again, the potbellied man dialed a number on his cell phone.

"Get ready!"

The two men in the nondescript, stolen pickup truck with exchanged registration plates extinguished their cigarettes and waited with the quiet confidence that came from years of working as a team.

"License, insurance, and registration documents please?"

As Wu-Tai Chin handed them over, another policeman tapped the opposite window. "You have a flat tire at the rear right. Better change it there," the second policeman said, helpfully pointing to a curve in the road on the opposite side. Wu-Tai Chin edged his car across the road to the spot indicated by the helpful policeman and got out to inspect the tire. He motioned to Arif to keep sitting in the car to avoid unnecessary exposure. He then took out a jack and spare tire. He was in the process of jacking up the wheel when the pickup truck hit Wu Tai-Chin at seventy kilometers an hour and kept on going straight.

As a startled Arif heard the sound of the impact and got out of the car, he was picked up by two policemen.

"Come with us. You are a witness to this accident!"

The next day, the *Asian Age* had a small corner on the front page with a short write-up: "Wu-Tai Chin, a Chinese businessman in the iron trade, was hit by a speeding truck while he was changing a tire. Investigations were in progress, but there appeared to be no eyewitnesses, according to the police."

Arif Mohammad was petrified. He had never imagined such fear as the kind he now encountered barely three hours after being picked up by the supposed policemen. Arif had been drugged and taken for interrogation to a safe house in West Midnapore, where in four short hours, he had blurted out everything he knew. The two former Special Forces veterans had their Mutt-and-Jeff interrogation technique down pat. The first interrogator played the brute, and the second one played the benefactor. The technique would not have worked on anyone who had been trained to withstand interrogation, but Arif Mohammad had never been subjected to such training. Moreover, enough factual information was known about Arif through Lily to facilitate a quick interrogation.

The first man had slapped Arif around for ten minutes, which had felt like hours to Arif, without asking a single question. He had then had him stripped of his clothes by an equally burly assistant and said, "Screw around with me, and you're dead motherfucker! Now talk."

The first time he had hesitated to think, he was forced to bend over and touch his toes. Thereafter, a green chili, the infamous "Bhoot Jholakia" variety from Assam, the hottest chili in the world at 855,000 Scoville units of pure capsicum, was briefly inserted into his anus until the burning drove him crazy. "Next time, it will be something else!"

In the interrogation that followed, Arif had been led through his first encounter with Wu Tai-Chin and meeting with Maheshwar Rao. Thereafter, he gave information about how the financing was arranged and the instructions passed on to the Maoists for coordinating other insurgent groups.

The soft-spoken interrogator had come into the room just when the fire in his anus was reducing him to a total wreck. "Stop it!" he ordered and put an end to the torture inflicted by Arif's first nemesis, a barrel-chested, dark-skinned man with brooding eyes that appeared to peer into a man's soul. Arif was given his clothes back and briefly permitted to use the bathroom and told to apply a soothing ointment to ease the pain of the burn.

"You have no choice actually, Arif. Your benefactor, Wu Tai-Chin, is no more. If you cooperate with me, your daughters, parents, and your wife will be safe for all times to come. Otherwise, nasty things can happen to young girls and old people on their own. You will have no reason to worry about money. Otherwise, there is no place for you to run where I will not find you."

Maheshwar Rao had responded to Arif's call for an urgent meeting after two days. As Arif waited in the clearing at Chakadoba at midday to be contacted, he was unaware of the GPRS device with the extended battery in the heel of one of the boots. He was made to wear the boots along with a complete set of clothing provided to him for the meeting. Arif and his two escorts had walked for two hours before they had reached the camp. There had been at least a hundred Maoist soldiers in the camp when Arif had dumped his rucksack with two million rupees before Maheshwar Rao.

"You must step up attacks in the thirty districts we agreed upon. There must be at least one a day, if you want the rest of the money. I will bring it exactly after a month, if you follow my instructions. Otherwise, the deal is off."

"I will need to discuss this proposal with our politburo. Fortunately, four members are right here. You will need to spend the night with us before I give you an answer. Some of them might want to talk to you."

It had been the first and only time in the turbulent history of India that the full resources of the armed forces had been used against an insurgent group. There had always been a widespread understanding that in a democracy fighter aircraft, attack helicopters and artillery had no role to play while you were fighting your own people irrespective of the provocation. The idea had always been to leave an opening for insurgents to come back into the mainstream of civic life after they had renounced force. The PM overruled the national security adviser.

"We're not playing games here. China and Pakistan and apparently certain elements in Bangladesh are supporting dozens of insurgent groups. It's time to send a message that kids' playtime is over! The cabinet committee on security has approved the use of whatever force the national security guard wants to use."

Colonel Deepak Choudhary, deputy commander of the regional national security guard center in Kolkata commanded the operation. The UAV had been launched an hour after the GPRS device had shown Arif moving from Chakadoba. The plan entailed having a UAV constantly over the operational area until termination of the attack by the NSG, providing a real-time video link.

The plan of attack on the Maoist camp was simple and based on achieving complete surprise. "We'll establish the stops covering all the eight jungle trails that you can see from the UAV feed by last light tonight. It will take us the best part of the day to move into position. There are apparently almost a hundred armed Maoists that we have physically counted in an area of about eight hundred square meters from the center of this clearing. The leaders seem to be using the four huts at the edge of the clearing as their living accommodation, and Arif Mohammad seems to be in one of them as well."

Major Krishnan interjected, "My squadron has just completed a training cycle. I would like to volunteer to lead the air assault."

"Okay, Krishnan, I know how much you dislike walking! At first light at 0430 hours tomorrow, two advanced light helicopters will be led in the air assault by Krishnan. They will bring suppressive rocket and canon fire to take out the Maoists in the four huts while Krishnan's men rappel down into the clearing and secure it. Ensure that you have enough loud-hailers with you to call upon the Maoists to surrender. This is to ensure that we are not accused of violating human rights in the future as and when the conflict with the Chinese and Pakis ends. I will command the eight teams that will use the stops as a firm base to go in and mop up, along with the tracker dog teams. We will have the ALHs on call for tactical support till the operation is over."

Surprise had been complete. Maheshwar Rao, after a session during which he discussed the proposal brought by Arif, a meeting that had extended till well past midnight, had woken when the first ALH had clattered overhead and the sentry had fired blindly to bring the whole camp to stand to. He scrambled to his feet from the floor, where he had been lying entwined with Dipanwita, his luscious second in command, whose reputation for cold-blooded murder exceeded all her male contemporaries in the insurgent group. The first rocket salvo blew the two off their feet, and by the time the concussed Maheshwar Rao surfaced, the headless Dipanwita lying across his body, the first stick of landed commandos had barged into the huts after they tossed in concussion grenades. By midday, the operation was over. Krishnan and two of his men had been killed in spite of their body armor, and there were eight other casualties. Out of the 103 Marxists present, thirty-two eventually surrendered, half of whom were severely wounded. The rest were all killed.

Nasruddin Babar had other tricks up his sleeve as well. Hitesh Sakia, one of the up-and-coming new breeds of ULFA leaders based in Dacca, was thoroughly disillusioned with a movement gone astray that was only enriching the leaders. Sakia had secretly negotiated to surrender for amnesty to return to India. He had, however, been persuaded to stay on as an informant by Nasruddin for far greater rewards than what a surrendered ULFA officially designated as SULFA could expect. Sakia had usually reported through a series of dead letter boxes. The most important intelligence breakthrough occurred when he reported that a Bangladesh DGFI-sponsored but ULFA-organized meeting of insurgent groups at a ULFA-owned hotel was in the works. Nasruddin Babar was barely able to complete his preparations to leverage this knowledge, mainly because the schedule remained undecided for many weeks.

The meeting was finally held to coordinate simultaneous operations for a large number of Assam-based insurgent groups. These included Muslim United Liberation Tigers of Assam, United Liberation Front of Barak Valley, Islamic Sevak Sangh, United Muslim Liberation Front of Assam, Revolutionary Muslim Commanders, and the National Democratic Front of Bodoland. DGFI sponsorship automatically guaranteed a safe environment for the discussions and kept the Bangladesh police out of the locality altogether. There was as incentive in the form of a cash grant of one million rupees to be paid in cash to each attendee. The money was provided by the vast tentacles of ULFA into all parts of the Bangladesh economy and protection rackets that were run both in Assam and Bangladesh.

Not surprisingly, each of the insurgent groups had sent at least three delegates. The show of strength had everything to do with the fact that not one group trusted any single individual enough to let him accept and deliver a million rupees, which was being put up by ULFA, back to the parent organization.

The Padma River was the spawning ground for the delicious Hilsa fish, which could otherwise be found as far as a thousand kilometers away in the Bay of Bengal. Self-styled master cook Azhar Ali specialized in making "Eilish Mash Torkari" or Hilsa fish curry, the hotel specialty. This was regarded as an essential delicacy for important occasions. He was early to work and had diligently prepared the spice mixture containing cardamom, clove, pepper corn, freshly ground mustard paste, bay leaves, and very little cooking oil. Before he finished, he added the small vial containing a mixture of Escherichia coli (E. coli O157:H7) and a snake-derived virulent form of Salmonella gallinarum provided to him with the advance payment that would buy him three acres of land in his village on the Assam border.

The meals were carried into the small meeting hall from the kitchen in metal trays by two trusted ULFA members. The metal trays had compartments to separate out the main dishes so that the discussions could go on without interference. Separate individual bowls that contained generous helpings of the Hilsa fish curry were distributed along with the food service trays.

Two hours after lunch, the twenty-four participants from seven insurgent groups had finally agreed on a broad agenda of cooperation that essentially preserved the status quo of independent operations in self-designated territories. There was one important clause that Major Imam Siddiqui, the DGFI controller who had put in an appearance after lunch, was able to ram through as an ISI surrogate. It was that there would be a threefold jump in insurgent attacks by all groups in a three-month period after the monsoons. The agreement was hammered out by displaying open suitcases containing the million rupee payoffs and implying that the money could be held back in the absence of agreement. It was also implied that more money would be forthcoming to the groups that carried out the most successful strikes.

In retrospect, if Major Siddiqui had partaken of lunch, things may have worked out differently for India. Within forty-eight hours of the meal, eighteen participants, who were trying to avoid crazed, rampaging mobs on the streets with blood in their eyes, developed influenza-like or gastrointestinal symptoms with abdominal pain, vomiting and expelling bloody diarrhea. Only three ULFA members were able to get expert medical help and survive after months of suffering. The remaining nineteen, who had to safeguard a large sum of money and had to travel through primitive rural communities, all developed severe problems in the bowel and colon and were forced to take shelter where they could find it, paying fortunes in protection payoffs for self-protection.

Only the Muslim United Liberation Tigers of Assam and the National Democratic Front of Bodoland managed to retrieve the million-rupee packages meant for them. Some of their representatives had not eaten the Hilsa, as they had gorged only on the mutton, exchanging the Hilsa bowl with their companions. They had also planned their journeys back more carefully than the others had. The remaining insurgent groups that attended the Dacca meeting lost all their representatives to renal failure in the ensuing three months. The needle of suspicion was directed at Major Imam Siddiqui. It seemed too much of a coincidence that he had arrived only after lunch was out of the way and that he hadn't had to partake. Insurgent unity would be a dead concept for the next decade.

To make matters worse for insurgent groups, a crackdown by the army in Myanmar on insurgent camps forced many of them to return to India and live under the constant threat of attack, undermining their capability to take any decisive action. The sole exception to this was the Pakistan-backed Indian Mujahidin, which kept pressure on the Indian state by the constant bombings of major cities across India, especially Hyderabad, Cuttack, Raipur, Patna, Ghaziabad, Meerut, Lucknow, Ahmedabad, and Coimbatore, successfully fanning communal riots between Hindus and Muslims on a regular basis.

CHAPTER 60
MOTHER OF SATAN

Chrono Satellite Broadcast (CBS) was amongst the most popular TV channels in the country. At one time in 2007, it had been shut down for telecasting provocative news, documents, discussions, and talk shows against the Bangladesh government. The whole country went into shock when it featured a breaking news headline "Bangladesh is far worse than Pakistan!" during the national election campaign and then went on to run a short video clip of a woman being caned.

"Please stop it," she had begged, alternately whimpering or screaming with pain after each blow on her buttocks. "Either kill me or stop it now."

"Hold her legs tightly!" an off-camera voice had interjected as she had squirmed and yelled.

The news anchor commented, "Nazma Bano, twenty-four, endured several cane lashes as her neighbors watched helplessly. The flogging was ordered by a group of religious leaders of her village in Moulavibazar District after she eloped with her boyfriend and married him secretly. The trial and punishment occurred as recently as in September this year. She was sentenced to a hundred lashes. The young woman, haunted by the public humiliation, never really understood why she had been punished. CBS was sent this video clip, which was taken secretly by MMS a few minutes after this event by an unknown person. Our investigating team managed to briefly interview the victim reeling from trauma a few hours ago."

"Is it a crime to fall in love with the person you like and marry him? I did not protest the flogging after the so-called prosecutors threatened to expel my family from the village," said Nazma, nursing both her physical and mental wounds. "I was flogged in front of my neighbors, friends, relations, and other people of the village. Only my mother dared to intervene to save me. And she was thrashed, and her arm was broken. Where is Begum Sahaba, the prime minister? Being a woman, I expect her at least to give me justice and come and see me."

"Is this type of punishment common in other areas in Bangladesh?" asked Rashmi Querishi, who had been sent to interview Nazma.

"Of course it is. This type of trial and punishment is a common practice in our country's remote villages, near the borders in particular, which are controlled by the mullahs. The village leaders pronounce '*Fatwa*' (religious edict) and shame Islam."

The world media pressure was intense. Derogatory references to the Awami league's close connections to the fundamentalist Khelafat e Majlesh Party for a pact and unwillingness to bring the perpetrators of the outrage to justice created intense pressure on the prime minister. A close campaign could swing either way by a calculated gesture of decency or statement.

The prime minister drove for an hour on a dirt track of a road to reach Nazma two days later, and she was followed by at least twenty TV camerapersons. Security was a far cry from what prevailed in Dacca. Here, there was just no time for even perfunctory measures to be put in place.

She was escorted to the small hutment and had to stoop low to entire the darkness of the interior, where, wailing, Nazma moved into the waiting arms of the gray-haired lady older than her grandmother. Instead of the soft flesh and warmth of a nubile young women, the prime minister was surprised by the hard feel of a bulky object pressing against her a microsecond before the explosion.

It was tri-acetone tri-peroxide (TATP), also known as "Mother of Satan" for the damage it inevitably inflicted on the limbs of the amateur bomb makers who use it. TATP, though chemically unstable and given to explode with little provocation, was easily made from available household chemicals. It contained no nitrogen, and thus it was undetectable by commonly used methods. Unlike most explosives, it did not combust on detonation. It decomposed into acetone and ozone, creating a trans-sonic shock wave. The energy in the compound was released when the bonds were broken. The suicide belt also included dozens of ball bearings that wrecked havoc in the closed confines of the hut, blowing Nazma, the prime minister of Bangladesh, and four of her special protection group into smithereens. Nazma and the prime minister's decapitated heads were found ten meters outside the hut, both staring grotesquely at each other.

Since the assassination of Sheikh Mujibur Rehman, the architect of Bangladesh and its first premier, every regime in that country had fostered anti-Indian forces within its territorial ambit. Indeed, Begum Khaleda Zia, a former premier, had gone to the extent of calling the northeast insurgents "freedom fighters." The crucial leverage that Bangladesh had gained in its endeavor to create instability in India was the large number of its own people now residing on Indian soil. The Bangladeshis had a novel way of "legalizing" their immigration in India. The relatives in India reportedly got the names of those across the border, people who were included in the voters' list during enumeration. As their names finally appeared in the list, messages were then sent across to them to finally cross over. It was this population that reportedly created a buffer of noncombatants for the militants, and they utilized them as perfect cover.

Lieutenant General Saif Gilani, head of the ISI, summed up the operation in a few minutes for his boss. "It's a great pity that we had to get rid of Brigadier Syed Ali! His professionalism aside, he was also a master psychologist. Personally, I had grave doubts whether a female prime minister brought up in luxury would react at all. Syed had a dossier on her and her political counterparts the size of a telephone directory. He was sure that she had a soft streak, especially if it came to vying for votes, and would empathize enough with the plight of a woman getting whipped to fly to one of the remotest outposts of Bangladesh. She had a track record of making her presence felt on half a dozen similar occasions, especially where women were brutalized."

"Well done. I was wondering whether all our investments in the

DGFI, the media, and the mullah-led parties were adequate or more needed to be done. It will be interesting to see what the Chinese politburo and PLA do now to take advantage of this opening. Let the riots begin!"

"The Bangladesh DGFI was all in favor of changing the pro-India government. The ISI links with DGFI continue to be strong. After all, we trained them and handed over a going concern for supporting anti-India groups in Assam, Manipur, Nagaland, and Meghalaya. Ideologically, we are on the same page as far as the threat from India is concerned."

A rumor was spread by the DGFI through the Jamaat-e-Islami, the Muslim fundamentalist party, that a Hindu woman had assassinated the PM. Within hours, the whole country was aflame as systematic attacks on the Hindu communities were mounted across Bangladesh. Places where Hindu women were raped by rampaging mobs inside temples included Barisal, Bhola, Pirojpur, Jessore, Khulna, Kushtiah, Bagerghat, Feni, Tangail, Noahkhali, Sirajganj, and Munshiganj in a far worse replay of the 2001 riots. At least seven hundred Hindus were killed in the mob violence.

As the news spread into India and ten thousand Hindus fled into West Bengal and Tripura, the atmosphere was supercharged, and communal riots broke out. Over three thousand Muslim families found themselves on the receiving end of vigilante groups crazed with alcohol and opium, murder, rape, and pillage on their minds. Some of the oldest survivors of the grim days of the partition of India said that it was 1947 all over again but worse.

CHAPTER 61
THE DROUGHT

The specter of drought was once again looming over all of India after a 30 percent shortfall in monsoon precipitation, the exception being some states like Gujarat and Orissa that contributed nothing to India's grain reserves anyway. Central grain stocks were a mere twenty million tons for a 1.2 billion population down from a peak of fifty million tons just a few seasons earlier. Crucial food security for poor rural workers was facilitated by issuing unique identity numbers for each citizen. However, there was little left to distribute in terms of food now. Prices of essential cereals had doubled in the past three months and were predicted to double again by the end of the year.

Worldwide, the story was also grim. The Murray-Darling River system that irrigated Australia's food bowl and created huge surpluses for export had become a stagnant pool. Half of California, North Virginia, Iowa, and most of Texas had been declared federal disaster areas. Grasslands and lakes in Argentina had dried up, and vast areas in northern and central China were reeling under water and fodder shortages. Riots threatened to break out as the Communist Party of China fought to retain control over an increasingly vociferous population stridently blaming it for the water crisis, shortages of potash fertilizers, and an inability to fund second-generation agricultural reforms to benefit farmers.

The Food Corporation of India (FCI), a government-controlled corporation, was meant to fill a role in making food grains available from surplus states to deficient ones within India. Inefficiency and corruption were so deeply entrenched and institutionalized in the FCI that it had a budget of more than ten billion dollars annually and that it had come to symbolize the evil inherent in public services delivery and failed governance. The Canadian government released that a tender for seven million tons of wheat for export had been snatched up by China, because the Indian bid had been filed after the date for closing. *Times Now*, a TV news show, attributed the delay in filing to the FCI bureaucracy being bought off by the Chinese for large cash payments abroad. This resulted in angry and violent demonstrators setting fire to the FCI headquarters in Delhi.

Reports of a thousand farmer suicides and famine deaths from thirty districts across India and pictures of starving orphans trying to eat grass hogged the media space. It was, however, a secretly taken video clip by a ministerial aspirant in Andhra Pradesh that set the cat amongst the pigeons. It showed a group of twenty politicians from the ruling dispensation wolfing down a seven-course meal at a private party in a classy spa. The other half of the clip showed children groveling in garbage heaps for food less than a kilometer away. The parliament that was in session was repeatedly disrupted by opposition calls for the government to resign.

As the government of India struggled to cope, the four horsemen of the apocalypse, supposedly famine, death, war, and conquest, seemed to urge their mounts forward. The BBC reported that China was all set to cut water flow from the Yarlung Tsangpo River going into India and Bangladesh because of its own requirements to fight the drought conditions in the vast agricultural region of northern China astride the Yellow River.

Finance Minister Vikram Chandra's advice to PM Durga Vadera was straightforward. "Let's not panic … yet! We need to look more critically at what is happening in China as well. The CRAI research that we commissioned based on the inputs provided through the cyber research cell is just in. Asha Kumari delivered it a few hours ago and spoke to me, making an interesting case for a potential great depression in China, even with its trillions of dollars of reserves. There is a cross section of top economists, whose e-mails and phone calls we tapped and translated and who are providing inputs to the politburo. According to them, a potential economic crisis is brewing, compounded by the drought and water scarcity.

"Twice before in history, a country has, under similar circumstances to China, run up foreign reserves of the same magnitude. Both cases turned out badly for long investors and brilliantly for anyone dumb enough to have bet against the markets.

"The two cases where countries rang up reserves of a similar magnitude to China are the United States in the 1920s and Japan in the 1980s. In both the cases of the United States and Japan, the high reserves were symptoms of terrible underlying imbalances in those countries. So those reserves were ultimately 'useless' in protecting those countries from a bust.

"The United States and Japan stories are similar. The United States in the 1920s and Japan in the 1980s had sharply undervalued currencies, rapid urbanization, and rapid growth in worker productivity. Both of those great booms were followed by massive busts. Stock markets fell 80 percent from peak to trough. Japan's stock market at a peak was around forty thousand in 1989. Today, over twenty years later, it is around ten thousand, a fourth of the earlier level. The United States crashed in 1929 and didn't recover until World War II.

"China is seeing the same things the United States and Japan saw during their boom years. The booms ended up fueling the creation of too much credit. This led to excess capacity, which then created the 'lost decades' for the United States and Japan. China could easily end up down the same road. There are too many commercial complexes that are built on debt and lying vacant. There is far too much excess manufacturing capacity, and to cap it all off, national debt is fudged at 16 percent of GDP. In actual fact, it is possibly 125 percent of GDP. They are warning of a Dubai-type collapse in the next few years, if financial discipline is not restored quickly, even if unemployment shoots up.

"India's own financial position will become precarious in a few months of combating the drought. The Chinese are apparently better off, but the Communist Party is wary of potential food riots in the countryside. China will also be looking at stopping the fighting quickly, short of giving up any vital national interests! If push comes to shove, I think you can afford to lose a few hundred square kilometers of territory in the Himalayas to make peace. It happened before in 1962 after losing thousands of square kilometers, and the government survived. After all, how many voters live in the Himalayas?"

"Interesting, our biggest advantage seems to be that we can get our citizens to swallow much more crap than the Chinese!" PM Durga Vadera observed. "If the Chinese miracle is faltering, we have the making of a new strategy. Stop the fighting. Start talking and make all the right noises, and give them nothing that they don't already have. However, for this to be successful, we need to hurt them enough initially without getting them to acknowledge any damage and without creating a media free-for-all that will force China to up the ante. I think we should take the final steps to worsen their drought situation by knocking off additional power coming on stream from the Yarlung Tsangpo. If we don't make a noise and crow over it, forcing them to make a disproportionate response, we may just be able to get it to work. If it doesn't work, the BJP will win the next election in any case, and I can always get back to teaching at IIM Ahmedabad!"

CHAPTER 62
THE TRAIN TO LHASA

PM Durga Vadera had insisted that the cabinet committee on security needed to be updated monthly by the service chiefs who felt their concerns were not even being heard by the political class. Air Chief Marshal Harpal Singh was finishing making his case for target priority in Tibet in case of conflict with China.

"As far as the joint chief of staff is concerned, we believe that the number one target for the Indian Air Force should be the interdiction of the Lhasa-Gormud railway line. For China, this line is extremely important militarily, economically, and politically. It vastly increases transport capacity and speed and makes it simple to deploy troops in Tibet as well as exercise control over the population. It makes extraction of significant strategic reserves of uranium, lithium, chromites, copper, borax, iron, and oil possible."

"But that is so for all railway lines! What is special about this one that the joint chiefs have accorded such a high priority? It cannot have much impact on the battle at the LAC, which may not last more than a week or two," queried Finance Minister Vikram Chandra, who was part of the cabinet committee for security.

Air Chief Marshal Harpal Singh explained, "There are some important differences with normal railway lines that may permit alternative routing and can be easily repaired. This one permits no such flexibility. Much of the Lhasa-Golmud line is between four to five thousand meters altitude in extreme weather conditions that reduces human work capacity and causes high-altitude sickness. Damage can take months to repair. The other problem is permafrost, which means frozen soil to a significant depth. During summer—and the sun's radiation is intense in summer in Tibet—the uppermost layer thaws, and the soil collapses as ice turns to water. Special construction techniques are required, including building the railway on bridges whose foundation is deep enough below the thawing layer. This also makes it fundamentally more susceptible to air attacks."

General Shiv Kapur, the army chief, added, "We have multiple choices in targeting, and the PLA cannot protect them all. We can choose targets amongst thirty kilometers of tunnels and 286 bridges as also the Lhasa-Golmud pipeline and optical cable that runs close to the railway. If we succeed, the Chinese cannot move up additional troops and supplies for months. The road capacity will also get further constrained by the necessity of supplying civilian populations. With a large proportion being of Han origin, these people cannot be simply ignored."

PM Durga Vadera intervened, "In other words, there could be a natural tendency to terminate a local conflict fairly quickly if they cannot sustain a buildup? It could also mean a shift of focus elsewhere or perhaps, in a worst case scenario, as an excuse to use one or two low-yield tactical nuclear strikes. We can only consider this option if major national interests are at stake. However, the air force must prepare for such an eventuality in any case. Air Chief Marshal, I want you to see me every fortnight for a few minutes to keep me updated. If there is anything required out of the box, let me know!"

"Sir, if you want me to guarantee that the Lhasa-Golmud railway line is taken out for at least a year, then you must give me the tools to do the job," Air Marshal Ken Doyle, the air officer commander-in-chief of Eastern Air Command, told Air Chief Marshal Harpal Singh.

"What else do you need?"

"Two of the Su T50 PAK FGFA prototypes will do for a start, if you want a guaranteed result!"

"Not possible, as we don't have the trial prototypes yet. However, as you are aware, much of the stealth-defining designs were also built into your Sukhoi 30 MK-Is located at Tezpur," the air chief observed.

"Not in the same class at all as a fifth-generation fighter. I flew the Sukhoi T50/PAK-5A prototype when I was in Russia last month. Even at this stage of development, it has everything we need to do the job. Thrust vectoring enhances the turning ability by redirecting the jet exhaust in a way that will put a ballerina to shame. You can fly into the highest mountains in the world undetected and, if you are suicidal like the Japanese kamikaze lot of the Second World War era, into a road or railway tunnels as well without being detected. The low probability of intercept (LPI) radar is outstanding. The energy of the radar pulse is spread over so many frequencies that no radar warning receiver that the Chinese have will trip. The stealthy radar-jamming technology that seems to have been pinched from Thales Spectra will also hide our own suppression efforts."

"Come on, Ken. I've known you for long enough. What are you getting at?"

"The Sukhoi Design Bureau conceptualizes the components and electronically transmits the information to their manufacturing unit in Siberia, the Komsomolsk-on-Amur Aircraft Production Organization. No time is wasted, and their work ethic is exceptional. Alexander Klementiev, the director, is an organizational genius. Get him two hundred million dollars, and he will produce the prototypes we want within six months!"

Durga Vadera was surprised when Air Chief Marshal Harpal Singh asked for his first appointment to see her just three days after the cabinet committee for security (CCS) met. Singh came straight to the point and explained how the proposed strike in Tibet would be launched when approved by the CCS.

"Madame Prime Minister, we need to short-circuit our procurement process if we are to be able to do this. Our established defense procurement procedures will never work."

"Leave it to me. Everything will be in place by the end of the week. I guarantee that!"

After the air chief had left his office, the prime minister spoke into her intercom, "Send in Dr. Santhanam right away please." In under a minute, Dr. Santhanam walked into his office and was greeted with a terse smile. "Doctor, I have an indirect SOS for you from the air force.

They need two hundred million dollars to be paid to the Sukhoi Design Bureau. Will you do the needful please? You'll get the money back, of course, but even with my intervention, it may take six months at least to work out our own procedures!"

The simulator rehearsals were over at the air force base of Chabua in Upper Assam. Now it was show-time, to deliver or die trying. Squadron leader Vikas Joshi and Flight Lieutenant Kuldip Chand walked across to the prototype T50 PAK FGFAs hidden under camouflage and strapped themselves into their respective cockpits. The flight jackets and antigravity suits that they wore were tailor-made for each one of them. An important feature of their flight jackets was the chest bladder, which automatically balanced pressure and also functioned as a life vest with an emergency transmitter. As each pilot entered the cockpit, they brought with them a small metal box that sufficed as a data transfer unit, the mission data stored on it. During the mission, it would digitally record every sequence and situation for post-mission debriefing. This would be invaluable for launching subsequent Su-30 MK-I follow-up missions if required. As they put on their flying helmets, started the aircraft engines, and rolled onto the camouflaged runway, the world changed. The integrated helmet-mounted display (HMD) started to provide real-time data superimposed right in front of their eyes. No matter where their heads faced, they had access to full control of flight parameters, sensor data, target cueing, and weapon status. The HMD also featured an integrated chemical/biological respirator and night vision camera options.

Their target had been chosen with care. An unambiguous message was sought to be sent to the PLA and the Chinese politburo. Thirty years of infrastructure development on the Tibetan Plateau could not be matched on the Indian side when it came to power projection for Asian supremacy. There were other hard choices that existed to make the aggressor feel the pain, choices made possible entirely by technology.

The Kun Lun great mountain system of Asia extended three thousand kilometers. From the Pamir's of Tajikistan, it ran east along the provincial border between Xinjiang and the Tibet autonomous region to the Sino Tibetan ranges in Qinghai. It stretched along the southern edge of the Tarim basin, the infamous Takla Makhan or sand-buried houses, and the Gobi Desert. The 1,142 kilometers of the Golmud-Lhasa railway line included a 550-kilometer section under permafrost. Here, repair and maintenance under frigid temperature conditions along with strong winds and thunderstorms every third day or so, not to mention the lack of oxygen, made working conditions many times more difficult than it was in the flat plains at low altitudes. Common sense dictated that any attempt to put the railway line out of commission be directed at a place where repair involved a Herculean effort and lots of time. The Kun Lun mountain tunnel 4,648 meters above sea level was 1,686 meters long but was characterized by an elevated rail track that was necessitated by the permafrost. This was the target for the two aircraft. A successful strike to block off even one end would entail at least a year-long effort to clear it. The bonus would be lopping off the fiber optic cable link to Tibet as well.

The train from Golmud was packed with PLA soldiers returning from leave to rejoin their units in Tibet. Packed to capacity with 936 passengers, the train had fourteen cars, two with cushioned berths occupied by PLA officers, eight semi-cushioned berths, and four ordinary cars without any cushioning.

To cope with the lack of oxygen on the Qinghai-Tibet Plateau, the train cars had been equipped with two oxygen supply systems. One was a "dispersion-mode" oxygen supply system, with oxygen spreading in the railway car through the air-con system; the other system, like that of an airplane, offered each passenger individual access to oxygen, and passengers suffering breathing difficulties at high altitudes could use a pipe or mask to take more oxygen. The trains running on the Qinghai-Tibet railway were driven by three computerized engines at one time (made by US-based General Electric or home-based Dongfeng Locomotive Factory), which showed great traction, brake power to guarantee the reliability, and comfort. They could also speed along at a hundred kilometers an hour even in the permafrost part of the line.

Normally, the engines would have breezed through the tunnel in just over ninety seconds. Eighty seconds into the journey, the Brahmos cruise missile fired by squadron leader Joshi from fifteen kilometers away slammed its three-hundred-kilogram high-explosive warhead into the southern exit of the tunnel. It hit a pier supporting the elevated track, sending chunks of concrete and snow into the air, totally obscuring visibility as the train hurtled into the debris and was derailed. A few seconds later, the northern entrance of the tunnel was hit by another cruise missile and largely blocked. Nine hundred soldiers of the PLA lay entombed. It would take the arrival of better weather four months down the line before the bodies would be recovered, many of them showing signs of considerable struggle to fight their way out in the darkness that followed the conversion of the Kun Lun tunnel into a temporary tomb. Otherwise, the intense subzero temperature inside the tunnel ensured that all bodics rcmained perfectly preserved. It was the single largest setback on any one day for the PLA since Mao's Long March, which set China free from Japanese oppression.

"Take out the right two!" squadron leader Joshi ordered his wingman as the encrypted data link from the satellite showed four Jian 10 fighters on an intercept course, 150 kilometers short of the Himalayan crest climbing toward them eighty kilometers away.

"Wilco! Don't think they've spotted us," Flight Lieutenant Kuldip Chand said, locking his radar onto both targets and launching two ASTRA BVR missiles at targets eighty kilometers away while the mission leader did the same for the other two oncoming enemy fighters. The four Chinese pilots got a warning of less than five seconds before they picked up the missile-active radio seeker and the fifteen-kilogram fragmentation directional warheads found their targets.

CHAPTER 63
THE SILENT BOMB

Professor MJ Mathews explained to the Crisis Management Group "The electromagnetic pulse effect was initially observed during the testing of high-airburst nuclear weapons. Simply put, it is the production of an extremely high-intensity but short-duration electromagnetic pulse measured in hundreds of nanoseconds. It propagates away from its source with ever-diminishing intensity, producing a powerful magnetic field within the vicinity of the explosion. The strength of this field is sufficient to produce short-lived transient voltages of thousands of volts, resulting in irreversible damage to a wide range of electrical and electronic equipment, particularly computers, radios, and radar receivers. Computers used in data processing, communication systems, industrial applications, road and rail signaling, and those embedded in military systems, such as signal processors and electronic flight controls, are all vulnerable unless military platforms are suitably hardened."

Raja Santhanam asked, "So would all commercial devices like desktop or laptop computers and cell phones in particular largely built up of high-density metal oxide semiconductor (MOS) that are extremely sensitive to high-voltage transient exposure of even a few volts be a write-off if exposed to EMP?"

Mathews answered, "Definitely so—shielding electrical equipment provides very limited protection, as cables running in and out behave very much like antennae in guiding the high voltage transients into the equipment. Going back in time in the 1962 "Starfish Prime" test, during which a nuclear weapon was detonated four hundred kilometers above Johnston Island in the Pacific, electrical equipment more than 1,400 kilometers away in Hawaii was affected. Streetlights, alarms, circuit breakers, and communications equipment all showed signs of distortions and damage."

"I thought we were discussing a non nuclear EMP weapon?" Ashok Sobti asked.

Mathews explained "You are right, but it is important to understand the difference. A nonnuclear or improvised EMP is a radio-frequency weapon rather than a gamma- or X-ray-frequency one. While it is easier to conceal and does not require a missile, a nonnuclear EMP must be detonated close to the target and does not produce as much damage as the nuclear version, affecting largely localized areas. But such a weapon could be harnessed as an "e-bomb" (electromagnetic bomb), a stand-alone weapon that is easier to hide and maneuver. For countries like India, the preferred way to build an "e-bomb" quickly and one that we are readying is to use high-power microwave vircator devices. You will be pleased to know that with Russian assistance we have a non-nuclear EMP weapon almost ready for use."

The fundamental idea that was well understood by the normally sloppy Indian Defense Research and Development Establishment (DRDO) was that of accelerating a high-current electron beam against a mesh or foil. Many electrons would pass through the anode, forming a bubble or space charge behind the anode. Under proper conditions, this space charge would oscillate at microwave frequency. If the space-charge region was placed into a resonant cavity appropriately tuned, very high peak power was obtainable.

The unwieldy 4.5-meter HPM designed by DRDO contained three main components: a power generator in the form of a flux compression generator (FCG), a microwave-source virtual cathode oscillator, and an antenna that radiated the resultant high-power microwave radiation. The FCG was like a battery that ran on a stick of dynamite. In the FCG, the energy was primarily stored as chemical energy in an explosive, plastic C4. It all started with a twelve-volt lead acid battery—the seed source—at one end of a pipe. The C4 was placed inside the pipe and surrounded by a winding of insulated wire. The battery provided the seed current that generated a DC magnetic field.

A second pipe surrounded the coil. Detonating the explosive pressed the inner pipe against the outer, rapidly squashing the magnetic field and generating a pulse of electromagnetic energy. The major advantage of the FCG was that it cost just a few thousand dollars. The problem the DRDO faced was that the smaller the FCG the less efficient it was. And engineers also had to balance the amount of explosives needed to generate the right amount of power with the unwanted destructive force the explosives caused.

The FCG's energy pulse was fed through an inductor, producing a voltage of about a thousand kilovolts. That much voltage powered the vircator, which made the microwaves. It was actually the simplest HPMs that could be put together. The vircator was basically a vacuum chamber enclosing a mesh-screen anode and a specially designed cathode from which electrons poured.

The major problem area in determining lethality was that of coupling efficiency, which was a measure of how much power was transferred from the field produced by the weapon into the target. This was the problem that the three Russian scientists from Tomsk, Yekaterinburg, and Nizhny Novgorod, under Dr. Alexander Safin, all of whom had worked together for decades, were expected to resolve. They had been persuaded out of retirement by M. J. Mathews with help from an oligarch who employed dozens of former KGB members. This was looked upon approvingly by the FSB, the Russian successor to the KGB, after the breakup of the Soviet Union. The scientists were confident that they could miniaturize the device to under 2.2 meters within a year for a bonus of three million dollars. Collectively between them, they had 108 years of experience working on EMP-related devices.

CHAPTER 64
BUDDHA'S WING

MINIATURIZATION WAS ESSENTIAL TO FACILITATE DELIVERY of the EMP weapon. Deniability after use was an important ingredient that needed to be ensured to prevent escalation of any conflict. There was also a requirement to preempt the necessity of extensive delivery testing. This would have become necessary if the weapon was to be dropped by the air force. A related development for an out-of-the-box solution to a delivery vehicle was making good progress under Raja Santhanam. Alexander Safin and the Russian scientists were also of the view that for defensive operations in the Himalayas, it would be better to pre-position the larger versions of the EMP HPMs near the crests. They could then be fired whenever required without bothering about the effects of weather or visibility.

The American space agency NASA in a joint development with MIT, Georgia Institute of Technology, the National Institute for Aerospace, and M-Dot Aerospace, in which Raja had acquired a sizeable interest through third parties, had finished developing a promising delivery-vehicle technology for a personal flying machine. This was based on extremely light but tougher composite materials capable of propelling soldiers eighty kilometers behind enemy lines. It could also be used for individuals and private businesses like bank couriers to fly over congested roads for short distances. Raja realized that the innovative technology also provided an out-of-the-box solution to the EMP weapon delivery issue.

The miniature helicopter and aircraft was less than four meters high with a four-meter wingspan. It was named the Puffin, after a small water bird famed for being able to land on impossible terrain. One of the acquirers of the technology was the innocuously named Millennium Aero Sports Private Limited (MASPL), which was controlled by a Raja nominee.

By the time the Puffin low-noise, electric VTOL, personal air vehicle reached limited production, an optional modification had been carried out by MASPL to reduce its maximum speed to 160 kilometers per hour from 240 kilometers per hour and reduce its ceiling from nine thousand meters to seven thousand meters. This also resulted in the range being extended to 150 kilometers with a full load to facilitate reaching close enough to the Yarlung Tsangpo Great Bend Gorge hydroelectric project from within India. The machine designed to carry two-hundred-kilogram loads could be remote-controlled by a pilot flying alongside in a separate machine at a safe distance to escape the blast effect of the explosive in the HPM.

Because the weight of none of the pilots with a full load of protective clothing and weaponry was more than ninety-five kilograms, the cruising range was further enhanced. It was possible for a pilot to fly close enough to the EMP weapon carrying Puffin to control its flight and single-shot detonation and still have the turn-around range to reach back within thirty kilometers of the Indian border, where the pilot could even be picked up safely by an advanced light helicopter (ALH). The Puffin was an ugly piece of work, looking extremely awkward, with wings too small to apparently fly. In practice, it worked almost flawlessly and only cost two hundred thousand dollars apiece.

The six volunteers for flight training from the special frontier force were all second-generation Tibetans who were less than twenty-five years old. Each one of them had traditional names, and all had sworn an oath to fight to free the land of their forefathers from China. Karma, meaning "star," was the natural leader of the group. Dorjee, whose name signified "thunderbolt," Lobsang, the "kind-hearted," Sonam, the "fortunate one," Tenzin, the "protector of righteousness," and Dawa, "born on Monday" had all been classmates in Dharamsala, the Dalai Lama's preferred place of residence in the Himalayas, and natural friends.

They had all excelled in commando training at the secretive "Establishment 22" in Chakrata, where the CIA had once trained their predecessors. They had all undergone parachute training at the Indian Army Parachute Regiment facility at Agra and had already spent many months of their young lives patrolling the chilly heights of the Himalayas across the LAC. A more skilled, dedicated, and enthusiastic group of young people willing to risk their lives for a homeland that they had never really seen would have been difficult to find. Stoically, they wore the amulets containing the cyanide pills around their necks. They were all confident, though, that their military skills would preclude the act of biting into the amulets. They were all sent for three months of flight training at different places around India, places like Guwahti, Patna, Bhubaneshwar, Bhopal, Patiala, and Amritsar, to avoid undue attention. They needed the confidence from basic aeronautical skills to handle the Puffin. The strong winds that pervaded the potential target area in southeastern Tibet would demand these skills. However, only one of them would be launched on the first crucial mission. The rest would be on standby in case of failure and for subsequent tasks in Sikkim and Bhutan.

When the Puffin container containing ten completely knocked-down machines finally arrived at Kolkata Port, it remained unopened and was cleared through customs with clockwork precision within fifteen minutes after Ashok Sobti's clout and a few discreet phone calls. It was then dispatched by train to Jorhat and collected by an air force team from the air base. There, it was opened and flown in helicopters to unnamed helicopter pads in the extreme northeast of Arunachal Pradesh.

In the meanwhile in the upper reaches of the Dibang Valley, unseen by the media and curious eyes, the SFF team waited impatiently but not without fear. They were joined there by Flight Lieutenant Ravi Singh, who had spent six months at the MSPL facility in Seattle putting the "Puffin" through its paces. This included two months in remote parts of the Rocky Mountains to understand the altitude effects on the "Puffin." For all practical purposes, Ravi was the test pilot for the machine, having survived a series of near crashes in the first month.

"Listen to what I tell you very carefully," Flight Lieutenant Ravi Singh advised his new students. "With all the effort that all of you have put into your training so far, it would be a pity if you get yourself killed in a flying accident even before reentering the land of your forefathers! This is the most important thing you—any of you—have ever attempted in your lives."

The group had been raised on stories about Pemakö and the significance of the Yarlung Tsangpo to Tibet from childhood. The stories spoke of one of four major rivers that flow off the slopes of Mount Kailas in western Tibet, a peak holy to Buddhists and Hindus and Jains. It drained the north slope of the Himalayas. Thereafter, it abruptly bent south and sheared across the mountain barrier before it plunged down toward India, where it became the Brahmaputra. In its hidden course through the mountains, the river and its tributaries carved the Tsangpo Gorges. Just before the main current swept around "the Great Bend," it was joined by the Po Tsangpo flowing in from the north. From here, the Yarlung Tsangpo crashed through its Lower Gorge (which had also never been run) on its way to the Indian border about 150 kilometers away. In its southern reaches, the Lower Gorge cut through dense, subtropical jungle haunted by tigers.

Cradled in the Lower Gorge was a region called Pemakö. Ancient Buddhist texts declared, "Just taking seven steps toward Pemakö with pure intention ... one will certainly be reborn here. A single drop of water or a blade of grass from this sacred place—whoever tastes it—will be freed from rebirth in the lower realms of existence." Tibetan Buddhists believed that the Great Bend was home to the goddess Dorjee Pagmo, "The Diamond Sow," Buddha's consort. The gorge was her body, the surrounding peaks her breasts, and the river her spine. They swore an oath to each other that they would prevent the Chinese from defiling Pemakö, even at the cost of their lives if necessary.

The complexity of hydroelectric engineering made for demanding construction projects. A water-retaining structure was used to dam up water in the reservoir at the highest potential level possible. Pressure pipes known as "pen stocks" led the water into the spiral casing and then into the turbines. The water was then removed by a "draft tube" suction pipe and diffused into the river or a lower reservoir.

Exploiting water power required the use of a water turbine, which converted potential and kinetic energy into mechanical work. If a generator was fitted onto the turbine shaft, as was the case in the huge

Yarlung Tsangpo Great Bend project, the mechanical work could be converted directly into electric current. A directed stream was designed to hit water turbine blades of the turbine runner curved in an opposite direction. In this way, the blades were turned and received mechanical energy from the water. Mechanical energy of water would be converted into mechanical energy of the shaft, and subsequently, it would be changed to electric energy in electric generators. The electric energy generated would then be transmitted to consumers via an electric grid consisting of distribution equipment, transformer stations, and distribution lines.

All new developments in the area of water turbines became possible only with the use of computational fluid dynamics (CFD) simulations, using incredibly sophisticated software that was far easier than model tests. Because the Francis turbine developed in the United States in the nineteenth century was the most commonly used turbine, CFD tests designed for this turbine in particular permitted easy feasibility studies. The crisis management group's team of hackers had managed to obtain access to the CFD studies without too much difficulty. This was done primarily by hacking into the e-mail accounts of dozens of foreign consultants who were roped into "the mother of all hydroelectric projects." This work would swing the decision of employing EMP to halt the Yarlung Tsangpo forty-thousand-megawatt hydroelectric project and prevent diversion of water to the Gobi Desert and northern areas of China.

The Yarlung Tsangpo hydroelectric project was going to be a game changer, not only from the point of view of resolving north China's water woes but also from those who wanted to bridge the electricity-generation shortfall and connectivity issues. While China was the world's second biggest electricity producer after the United States, grid problems and inadequate generating capacity caused severe shortages. Lack of investment left China with limited transmission capacity between grids. China's uneven distribution of natural resources and their distance from the main demand centers made improvements to the grids imperative. Eighty percent of coal deposits lay in northern China while 67 percent of hydropower was concentrated in the southwest; however, 70 percent of energy consumption took place in the central and coastal areas.

China had abandoned the aim of achieving power balance within each regional grid in favor of a unified national power market in which electricity transfer would be more frequent and take place over much longer distances. Load requirements had been increasing so rapidly in large cities due to industrialization that only 50 percent could be supplied by local electricity generation sources of 220 kV or below, the rest having to be brought in over the regional trunk grids.

Although five of the six main grids were interconnected, Xinjiang and Tibet still remained largely isolated. It was visualized that the development of rural grids would also raise consumption demand from farms, village enterprises, and households and tide over much of the separatist urges in exchange for the good life of a modern consumer. At present, rural consumers deferred purchases of washing machines, clothes dryers, and air conditioners because of limited access to power and exorbitant electricity costs in rural areas compared to the cities. This was due to high-transmission losses that could only be checked by grid upgrading.

The Chinese government required that at least 60 percent of transmission equipment come from Chinese suppliers, so domestic companies predominated in manufacturing capacity. However, both switchgears and cables faced intense competition, for there was excess production capacity because of low-entry barriers and technology requirements. Substandard transmission products for a less-regarded region sneaked in oiled by large bribes. Quality mattered less in Tibet and Xinjiang. In addition, once the manufacturers of the microprocessors in the main power plant on the Great Bend were identified from the hacked e-mails, Alexander Safin organized a series of experiments and guaranteed that when the EMP was triggered, a series of nasty events would take place.

CHAPTER 65
SILENCE OF THE LAMBS

"THE 33 CORPS HEADQUARTERS IN SILIGURI has been attacked by Chinese cruise missiles and dozens of officers were killed, including the army chief. Three days ago, the Chinese have also started their trial runs for the Yarlung main power station, which has been hooked up to substations in Lhasa and also to the national grid at Chengdu. We are on a thirty-minute standby for launch," Flight Lieutenant Ravi Singh went over the mission details for the last time. "We have also been warned to be ready to move to Bhutan or possibly Sikkim at two hours' notice."

Karma had been the natural choice for the mission. Right from the beginning, he had led by example. He had proved repeatedly that he was in a league of his own when it came to guiding the EMP equipment into trial delivery zones. He was repeatedly told by Flight Lieutenant Ravi Singh that no heroics were required. He was required to maintain a steady speed of 150 kilometers per hour for both vehicles, and he needed to explode his load three kilometers away from the dam. This was to be done while positioned over the river three kilometers south of the project site. The debris from the explosion would fall into the ten-knot stream and disappear from sight in under a minute. He needed to be at least three hundred meters from the exploding carrier Puffin to ensure his own safety and preferably already turned homeward when the remote detonation was triggered.

The SFF group had animatedly discussed the logic of targeting through the e-bomb amongst themselves for days. Some things were crystal clear. The forty nanosecond pulse of the e-bomb would produce very high voltages in the extremely fragile gate insulation of the microprocessors controlling the hydropower facility. The computer-controlled circuits, relays, and sensors could all be taken out if you got close enough before you detonated so that little or no power was dissipated in the air. Secondly, the EMP would cause ionization that would force arcing between high-voltage devices, but any destruction would be caused by the power these devices controlled, not so much by the energy added by the EMP itself. Thirdly, for the EMP to work, it had to exceed peak power levels, exceeding the design parameters for civilian equipment and the protection provided by the dissipative arrays, low-impedance grounding system, and the transient voltage surge suppressors.

Karma said good-bye to his friends, who were lined up to see him take off from the high-altitude helipad, and gave a fleeting but awkward hug to each in his weather-protective gear.

He whispered to Dorjee, "Look after the others in Bhutan. I will not be coming back!"

Dorjee nodded his eyes, which were moist with suppressed tears. "I know, but I will still pray that you return to us. Go now and save Pemakö before it is too late."

Ten minutes later, the full moon shining unhindered through the pure mountain air and dawn an hour away, Karma closed his visor, waved to Ravi Singh, and began accelerating vertically to climb through the Himalayan passage of the Dibang River in his EMP-protected Puffin.

Fifty-nine minutes from takeoff in the transient period between first light and the light of the full moon, his GPS waypoint indicated 3.2 kilometers from the Yarlung five hundred thousand high-voltage transformer downstream from the huge dam. Karma was quickly past it as he flew a hundred meters behind and slightly above the EMP-carrying Puffin. This was the moment he was supposed to have turned around and hit the remote detonation button. He held course for another sixty seconds till he could see the huge block of the powerhouse and then detonated the EMP device. The blast of the C4 trigger explosion was like a body blow, but he managed to control the air-cushion vehicle through the turbulence for perhaps thirty seconds; however, it was losing power fast, and it disintegrated as it hit the center of the Yarlung stream. Karma died fifteen seconds after the cold water of the river entered his lungs. A minute later, there was no trace on the water of the two "Puffin" vehicles or the deadly load they had carried. Karma had independently come to the conclusion that he needed to get in closer than what the scientists had worked out for a successful outcome. His own life was inconsequential, for his spiritual belief had told him that there would be a reincarnation of his spirit in human form again.

Cascading failure was common in power grids when one of the elements failed and shifted its load to nearby elements in the system. In turn, those elements were pushed beyond their capacity so that they became overloaded and further shifted their loads onto other elements. Cascading failure then resulted when a single point of failure on a loaded system resulted in a spike across all nodes of the system. This surge current could induce the already overloaded nodes into failure, setting off more overloads and thereby taking down the entire system in a very short time.

Once started, the failure process would cascade through the elements of the system like a ripple on a pond and continue until substantially all of the elements in the system were compromised or the system became functionally disconnected from the source of its load. In Alexander Safin's experience, it was calculated that if one of the five-hundred-thousand-volt transformers on the Yarlung Tsangpo was taken out, the Tibetan grid would collapse altogether.

Inside the main transformer station on the Yarlung Tsangpo, the EMP chewed through the protective hardware that failed, unable to sense the presence of the arcing fault quickly enough. Excessive current eventually caused the windings on the station's power transformer to overheat, severely cooking its innards and raising the flammable mineral oil within to the boiling point. In a vain attempt to prevent the transformer's tank from exploding, pressure release valves vented steamy clouds of superheated oil vapor. The foggy mist of hot oil then ignited the arc, causing it to explode in a ball of flames. In the process, hundreds of gallons of flaming mineral oil were dumped onto the transformer. Local firefighters could only watch from a distance, because there was no way to safely fight this fire. Within an hour, the transformer station and thousands of square meters of auxiliary equipment was a total loss and would take a minimum of four years to reestablish.

The switching surges on the extra high voltage (EHV) electrical power transmission systems initiated conductive plasma channels called streamers, which led to flashovers to other phases or to ground, causing circuit breaker trips and unplanned outages. Streamer formation and growth was the major limiting factor in practical EHV power transmission system designs. This phenomenon constrained the maximum transmission voltage to about 1.2 million volts AC. In this case, the highest operating AC transmission voltage was 1.15 million volts through a seven-hundred-kilometer transmission line that connected hydropower from the generating plant on the Yarlung Tsangpo to the national grid. The break under regular load conditions (approximately two thousand amps) created a much hotter and extremely destructive arc comparable to a fat, blindingly blue-white, hundred-foot-long welding arc four times hotter than the sun that vaporized the contacts on the air-break switches and then worked its way along the feeders, melting and vaporizing them along the way. Large swathes of Tibet were immediately left without power to battle the harsh weather conditions.

The failure of the process-control technology resulted in the water passage into the turbine closing too quickly and water hammer resulting, which put very strong dynamic pressure on the penstocks, distorting them in the process. The process of replacement would be fraught with risk and take two years of accident-ridden work. The damage would only become evident during the trial run of the new transformers.

The extent of damage would not be known for years. At no stage was there any mention in the Indian media about the proactive decisions of the new PM resulting in a game-changing shift in the perceived balance of power in Asia. Twenty-five billion dollars worth of investment was lost for a decade, a fact that China hid for many years from its own people. It was obvious that the Gormud-Lhasa railway line's susceptibility to modern aerial weapons was fully exposed by a small-scale operation.

Further, the colossal shortfall in power now had to be made up for through on-site, diesel-based generation. Fuel now had to be transported by road into Tibet for the civilian population, further eroding the logistic sustainability of building up a dozen divisions for a limited conflict against India. The quick-fix solution for dismantling India no longer existed. It would be back to the slow grind of encouraging insurgencies and betting on the inherent incompetence of India's governance to facilitate an internal collapse. In the meanwhile, the silence of the Indian lambs, without making any claim of operational success, provided balm for the Chinese dragon.

CHAPTER 66
LOST KINGDOM

"We need an excuse to invade Bhutan, one that the world will lump easily without having to react, disapproving our intervention," the president of China and chairman of the CMC, Xi Jinping, observed.

"Helping a neighboring, friendly country to restore law and order after the constitutional head is attacked should be good enough," General Xu Caihou offered.

"Get one of the Maoist groups in eastern Nepal to do the job, but we need to be ready in a month."

"Bhutan has the lowest level of security anywhere in the world. There will be no delay. I guarantee it."

Xi Jinping nodded and then said, "I know the PLA's reservations about the need for this operation and appreciate your willingness to push it. Water has enabled Bhutan to enjoy the highest per capita incomes in South Asia. India is exploiting Bhutan's thirty-thousand-megawatt hydroelectric potential, although it has been slow to wake up."

As he read from a note, he added, "Three 1,500-megawatt projects are on stream at Chukha, Kurichu, and Tala. Three others with 1,760-megawatt total capacity—Punatshangchhu I and II and Mangdechhu—are undergoing trial runs. If we cut off two thousand megawatts that are going to India, it will kill their new industrial production capacity in West Bengal and Assam. It will also kill all potential foreign industrial investment in northeast India. That suits our strategic aim."

General Xu Caihou nodded and continued, "Maybe we should start work on diverting the surplus power into our grid through the Chumbi Valley soon."

A landlocked kingdom of less than forty thousand square kilometers and less than three quarters of a million people, where GNP stands for "Gross National Happiness," Bhutan is located at the eastern end of the Himalayas. It is bordered to the south, east, and west by the Republic of India and to the north by China's Tibet autonomous region (TAR). Bhutan is separated from the nearby state of Nepal to the west by the Indian state of Sikkim. It is separated from Bangladesh to the south by a thin strip of West Bengal. Being adjacent to the disputed Tawang Tract in the Indian state of Arunachal Pradesh, which is also claimed by China, Bhutan served a buffer function. Bhutan had significant strategic leverage with India as a benign northern presence to safeguard the Siliguri Corridor.

A transition from an absolute monarchy to a constitutional monarchy under King Khesar Namgyal Wangchuk without any blood on the streets was an exceptional happening in South Asia. Unlike the native population of Sikkim, who had lost their identity to immigrant Nepalese and were forced to join India, the king of Bhutan had acted promptly to preempt any such possibility. The churning movements for democracy had erupted almost simultaneously in Nepal and Bhutan. There was also the concern in Bhutan over the exploding population imbalance on account of the large number of Bhupalese (Bhutanese of Nepali extraction). Together, these triggered the efflux of Bhupalese from southern parts of Bhutan into Nepal for reasons of personal safety in 1988. The Maoist insurgency grabbing power in Nepal in 2006 hastened the king pushing Bhutan into adopting a multiparty democracy.

Bhutan had remained independent for two thousand years until China decided to change the course of history. Its borders with China were largely not demarcated. Bhutan had a two-hundred-square-kilometer border dispute with China, its only other neighbor with whom it had no trading or diplomatic relations. Wherever the watershed along the Masang Kungchu range was clearly defined, the border had been demarcated, because China had no interest in invading India through seven-thousand-meter-high peaks. It was in the northwest portion, where the spurs dropped toward Chumbi Valley, an area which was of military strategic value to China, that China conveniently created a dispute. The Chinese aim was to enlarge the Chumbi Salient to also include the Dolam Plateau and Dokala in Bhutan so that it could secure a larger launch pad along the Amo Chu River so that their troops could launch into the vulnerable Siliguri Corridor.

Almost a decade earlier on November 13, 2005, Chinese soldiers had crossed into Bhutan from the Chumbi Valley, instigated disputed territories between China and Bhutan, and began building roads and bridges. When Bhutanese Foreign Minister Khandu Wangchuk took up the matter with Chinese authorities after the issue was raised in the Bhutanese parliament, a Chinese foreign ministry spokesman soft-pedaled the issue, claiming that the two sides were continuing to work for a peaceful and cordial resolution of the dispute. The stage was being set for a future walk-in.

Previously, in December 2003, after six years of negotiations with Bodo, Kamtapuri and ULFA militants, and Delhi's friendly persuasion, Bhutan's small six-thousand-man army flushed out Indian insurgent groups from thirty camps in east Bhutan. The India-Bhutan Treaty of Perpetual Peace and Friendship of 1949 was revised thereafter to reflect sovereign equality. This was achieved by dropping the provision on Bhutan being guided by India in its foreign policy. Now the insurgent groups, which were fully funded and equipped by Chinese money and state-of-the-art weapons, were back with a vengeance, and the pitifully small Bhutanese Army was fully committed to combating them.

Not unlike the Palestinian refugees nurtured for nearly two decades in camps on a heady mix of UN handouts, Maoist ideology and Nepali polity in East Nepal, a number of Bhupalese dissident groups like the Bhutan Tiger Force, the Bhutan Maoist Party, and the Communist Party of Bhutan had sprung up. These were clandestinely supported by the Chinese to stretch the Bhutanese resources even further. Bhutan's relations with Nepal had soured over the ethnicity of the refugee issue.

A sizeable Indian military training and administration team

(IMTRAT) located at Ha and Thimpu since 1962 had trained and prepared Bhutanese security forces to meet multifaceted internal and external challenges. It also provided Bhutan its inventory of weapons and firepower, although Bhutan was theoretically free to procure from other sources. All roads inside Bhutan had been built by an Indian border roads task force.

Water enabled Bhutan to enjoy the highest per capita incomes in South Asia. Relations between India and Bhutan were cordial in the cooperative use of Bhutan's thirty-thousand-megawatt hydroelectric potential.

The king of Bhutan's Toyota Land Cruiser was easily recognizable from a distance. In a country of few privately owned vehicles, it was in a class of its own. Til Bahadur and his team of Bhupalese insurgents had stolen almost twenty kilograms of blasting explosives during a thunderstorm from an Indian road construction task force almost a year ago and cached it safely for the right opportunity. They had chosen a damaged culvert on the road between the border town of Phuentsholing and Chimakha to the north, where all vehicles had to slow to a crawl to get across. Their hideout on the mountain slope overlooked the culvert from five hundred meters away.

Til Bahadur's order was a single word—"Now!"—watching the Toyota SUV climb the last bit of the broken approach to the culvert through his small pair of binoculars. The blast lifted the SUV high up into the air and tossed it into the deep gorge below. Hundreds of pro-Nepalese leaflets were found near the assassination site by investigators a few hours later. King Jigme Khesar Namgyal Wangchuk ultimately became a mere pawn, instigating a bloodbath against Nepalese in the southern Dzongkhaps or districts of Bhutan. The Maoist Nepalese government, of course, requested China help with restoring law and order in Bhutan to safeguard people of Nepalese origin.

The orders were clear. *Zhao da* (early war) would take the Indians out of the power equation in Asia for a long time to come. All feasible contingencies had been catered for with redundancy built in. Nothing had been left to chance. Speed and relentless offensive action was the way to go. The Americans, normally so full of hype, described it best:

"Shock and awe." There were just forty-eight hours left. Everything was ready.

General Wen-Chung Liao permitted himself the luxury of dreaming for a minute as his staff officers scurried around and implemented his latest directions. *Yiyou shenglue*—victory through superiority over inferiority was how his meticulous campaign against the Indians would be remembered.

The Jampheri Heights overlooked the Dolam Plateau and were the key to reaching the Jaldhaka River in India. The linchpin of the plan was for the PLA to secure these quickly. Thereafter, the Siliguri Corridor-noose could be tightened at will to choke the Indians. The Indian Army chain of command in the northeast had already been decapitated after it had been taken out by the cruise missile strike on 33 Corps headquarters. In addition, Indian Air Force assets that could effectively interfere were temporarily grounded with ongoing strikes and would be kept in that condition to sustain a favorable air situation for his rapid reaction force.

Assassinations of national leaders in Bangladesh and Bhutan, Gurkha Land agitations in Islampur subdivision of Darjeeling District, Hindu-Muslim communal riots sponsored by Harkat-ul- Mujahidin and Tabligh-e-Jamaat in Jalpaiguri and Cooch Behar Districts, and plans by the ISI and DGFI to cover the complete corridor area between Bhutan and Bangladesh were already overwhelming Indian police and paramilitary forces in the region. To add to this misery, Maoist hit-and-run attacks across the 1,751-kilometer border between India and Nepal but more focused toward the southeast adjacent to the Siliguri Corridor were being facilitated by members of the Nepalese government who had been handsomely bribed. The Indian leadership, if it behaved true to type, was expected to behave like a rabbit caught in the beam of a high-powered light—frozen and unable to react.

CHAPTER 67
CHECKMATE

At 5:00 p.m. Indian Standard Time, just as darkness enveloped northeast India, five Chinese geosynchronous satellites facilitated the precision-guided missile (PGM) strikes on airfields at Bagdogra and Hashimara. The Indians had always presumed that their ability to carry large payloads from their airfields located closer to sea level would compensate for the larger PLAAF numbers. The PLAAF would be hindered by taking off well above three thousand meters from the Tibetan Plateau, where altitude would severely diminish payload capability.

Concurrently in rapidly thickening mist in the floor of the valley, three PLA battalions commenced their infiltration for occupation of what was called the MS Ridge at the southern tip of the Chumbi Valley.

An air-mobile rapid attack force regiment dropped by the PLAAFs 15 Air Corps on the Dolam Plateau was preceded by a battalion-sized, helicopter-borne assault just as the favorable air situation was guaranteed by the PGM strike. The Royal Bhutan Army unit had been bolstered greatly the previous night by the arrival 29 PUNJAB in the vanguard of the newly raised Indian 380 Independent Mountain Brigade that was following up.

The Bhutanese PM, who was totally out of his depth in the emerging threat to his country, had been painted a grim picture of Chinese and militant organization capabilities and intentions by the Indian ambassador. He quietly agreed to whatever the Indians wanted to do. The reinforcements, who were standing by in Cooch Behar District, were moved a few hours later. Unfortunately, they had no time to prepare defenses and were caught out in the open.

The battle for the Jampheri Ridge, which overlooked the Dolam Plateau, raged for seven days, Chinese, Bhutanese, and Indian units inextricably mixed up at times. The arrival of the first of the three infiltrating battalions moving along the Amu Chu River slowly but surely swung the battle in favor of the PLA by the sheer weight of numbers. Both sides suffered more than six hundred casualties in a closed-quarter battle fought more by accident than by design. It was brutal hand-to-hand combat of an intensity unseen anywhere in the world during the past three decades.

The capture of the Jampheri Ridge would pave the way for capture of the Bindu Barrage on the confluence of the Bindu and Jaldhaka Rivers on the Bhutan-Indian border by an airborne assault. The NE could then be severed with ease.

Development of a drivable track along the Amu Chu River for the PLA was a vulnerability that could drastically slow down offensive operations. This had been negated by creating a dedicated engineer-regiment task force with the most modern earth-moving equipment. The equipment was from the great global mining conglomerates of BHP Billiton and Rio Tinto who were lured by tax sops and massive mining concessions in Tibet. Guns, ammunition, and fuel would follow in the wake of the road construction. In the interim period, helicopters and aircraft dropping bombs and rockets on Indian and Bhutanese positions and logistics loads for the PLA attacking troops would solve the problem. In any case, the much vaunted Indian Air Force would have been sufficiently crippled by the missile attacks on their airfields, and its army was eventually tied up in knots with the million mutinies that had erupted.

The first attacks went as planned under full-moon conditions to facilitate the employment of helicopters in treacherous, mountainous terrain and marginal weather conditions that should have caught the defenders napping. However, the Indians and the Bhutanese offered stiff resistance, throwing the time plan of Lieutenant General Wen-

Chung Liao out of the window. In addition, despite the Indian 33 Corps headquarter being destroyed, the 380 Mountain Brigade now double its initial strength with reinforcing troops, was in reasonable control of the tactical battle. There was no vestige of panic setting in anywhere. The junior leadership of the infantry battalions in contact with the PLA fought and died to the last man, seeking no quarter and giving none.

Brigadier Shaitan Singh, the commander of the Indian, brigade was also given four EMP Puffin vehicles and two EMP bombs under the command of Flight Lieutenant Ravi Singh and two SFF pilots, Dorjee and Lobsang. The EMP option was to be used only with prior approval of the Indian Army Eastern Command headquarters. An advanced light helicopter came with the team and was camouflaged and concealed next to a makeshift helipad a few kilometers south of the Bindu Barrage.

The Indian Air Force squadrons were bruised and battered by the pounding but had survived the missile attacks in fair shape because of incessant training and robust backup operating procedures that withstood the mauling. Their airfields at Bagdogra and Hashimara were rapidly resuscitated and made operational.

The infiltrating and assaulting troops had suffered causalities in numbers higher than they had planned. The Chinese operation was barely on track. Lieutenant General Wen-Chung Liao ordered more missile attacks against the airfields, and the Indian infantry positions on Jampheri Ridge were hammered by fighter aircraft and attack helicopters, each flying three missions a day in spite of weather and terrain hazards in the high mountains. All resistance had to be crushed by a massive application of force. "The Indians must be given no respite," he had ordered repeatedly.

By the seventh day, he was on the verge of the breakthrough that he was hoping for. Despite valiant heroics by isolated platoons and companies, the Indian resistance had started to perceptibly weaken. Jampheri Ridge was about to fall, and then the gateway to the Bindu Barrage would open.

Two severely damaged bridges across the cold Torsa River had survived the hit-and-run bombing raids by the Indian Air Force. PLA engineers estimated that at least two days would be needed for repairs, because the spare components had not yet arrived. As they waited for induction, the third regiment had been unable to induct more than a company on the captured ridge.

The CMC took an early strategic decision to interfere in the ensuing battle. The prestige of the PLA was at stake. It ordered a pooling of an additional forty-eight helicopters, including Russian Mi-17 helicopters, some aging Sikorsky S-76s, and twenty-four of the modern and new fly-by-wire Euro copter EC-175. These had been renamed Z-15 for European aviation majors to get around US technology embargos. These were sidestepped from the neighboring military regions to Lhasa in order to support the thrust and pump of additional forces till road-based communications could be made viable again.

Meanwhile, a great surge in militant attacks that had been promised by the Maoists, disgruntled Nepalese Gurkha, and the various Muslim insurgent groups based in Bangladesh accelerated sharply, worsening the internal security environment in eastern and northeastern India.

To rebuild the tempo of operations, Wen-Chung Liao ordered sequential helicopter-borne operations of a battalion each. One would reinforce the Jampheri Ridge. The other would capture the Bindu Barrage in conjunction with an airborne assault by a regiment using a combination of Il-76 aircraft that could carry forty-eight tons each and some Boeing 747F-400 requisitioned from Cathay Pacific to land heavy loads once a landing field was secured.

Lieutenant General Wen-Chung Liao decided to ensure success of the reinforcement effort by using the two dozen state-of-the-art Z-15 helicopters, which were designed to operate with the lowest noise signatures seen in Asian skies. His PLA combat engineers had torn a large enough helipad from the lower Jampheri Ridge portion captured by the regiment, which desperately needed fresh troops to preserve the momentum of the break in attacks.

This time, a change of tactics and technology, a weak moon at 2:30 a.m., would facilitate the landing in wicks of three helicopters touching down simultaneously to disgorge their troops and take off within thirty seconds of touchdown. The chances of Indian interference were negligible, and they were no match technologically.

It was a pity that each powerful Z-15 could carry only ten soldiers instead of its designed load of sixteen because of the rarified air at eleven thousand feet. The more numerous Mi-17 fleet could only manage five at best instead of the eighteen it had been designed for. There was no way the Mi-17 could do the job at night in spite of expensive night-fighting upgrades.

Well below their top-rated cruise speeds, the twenty-four Z-15 helicopters in formation were spread out in eight wicks over a distance twenty-four kilometers, flying at a steady 120 kilometers per hour. Within each wick in arrowhead formation, the separation between helicopters was exactly 135 feet.

True full authority digital engine control (FADEC) had no form of manual override available, placing full authority over the operating parameters of the engine in the hands of the computer and backup computers. If a total FADEC failure occurred, the engine would fail, and pilots would have no means of manually controlling a restart. The cockpit featured four displays as well as a central mission display, every third Z-15 connected by a link to Lieutenant General Wen-Chung Liao's operations room and also to the CMC in Beijing. The flight management system (FMS) determined the aircraft's position and the accuracy of that position even in pitch darkness.

The sensors in the FMS included GPS receivers of the highest accuracy and integrity, not to mention an inertial reference system (IRS) that provided inertial navigation data and flight control data to other systems. Radio aids included equipment that determined position every ten seconds as a further backup.

The quiet, even tone of PM Durga Vadera reflected the steely determination in her eyes at the end of the briefing by the Joint Chiefs of Staff.

"Use the e-bomb. Use all the four remaining ones if we need to. We'll face the consequences when they come! I doubt that it will trigger a nuclear response, but I will work out of the underground national command center till it blows over in case we need to respond further."

Flight Lieutenant Ravi Sharma saluted as he entered the command post of Brigadier Shaitan Singh.

"Our airborne, early-warning aircraft has picked up at least fifty to sixty helicopters heading for the Jampheri Ridge. They appear to be Z-15s from their radar profiles. They should arrive in another forty minutes at their current speed and course."

"I'd better be off, sir. Dorjee will be my backup in case I fail! You can get all your communications switched off after fifty minutes till 0500 hours."

"I know you'll succeed. Best of luck, and see you on your return!"

"Thank you, sir."

"The prime minister herself has been monitoring the battle situation for the last few days and has approved the use of the Puffins against the PLAAF. The army commander has conveyed the news to me himself fifteen minutes ago. You still want to launch the attack yourself?" Brigadier Shaitan Singh asked.

Ravi smiled and exclaimed, "Of course, sir! I would not miss this for the world. Otherwise, what will I tell my daughter when she asks a few years down the line, 'What did you do in the war, Daddy?'"

The night vision goggles he wore were superb, and the intercept bearings on the hardened GPS had already been punched in for this eventuality. The colored, elevated lights on the south face of the ridge put up by the infantry were double visual insurances. As both the Puffins took off, Ravi muttered a silent prayer. As he banked the Puffins south of the ridge, he could see the navigation lights of the leading helicopter of the first wick down below and perhaps two kilometers away.

Flight Lieutenant Ravi Sharma did not hesitate, not even for a second, as he pulled the e-bomb trigger, and the forty-second pulse of the vircator instantaneously triggered extreme voltages coursing through the fragile gate insulations of the twenty-four Z-15s within range.

Two hundred kilometers away, as Lieutenant General Wen-Chung Liao watched the looming approach to the Jampheri Ridge on a giant LED screen in his operations room via the data link, the screen suddenly went blank and was full of static. FADEC and FMS in all twenty-four Z-15s and all the microprocessor-driven systems failed simultaneously as the peak attack voltage far exceeded design parameters.

Down below, almost three regiments of attacking PLA forces and their fire support and control regiments suddenly found themselves without any communications. When Brigadier Shaitan Singh launched a spirited counterattack with an inferior battalion the next night, the PLA troops, unable to call in aviation resources, were barely able to hold on to a third of the captured area without communications and fire support.

The Siliguri Corridor was safe—just about.

CHAPTER 68
THE HAJJ

THE TWO BROTHERS WERE AN INDISTINGUISHABLE part of the teeming millions undertaking the Hajj. Dressed alike in the *ahram*, the pilgrim's dress of unstitched white cloth, a sign of forsaking the material self along with shedding one's natural attire, they had arranged to make the journey of faith together one last time. Chanting *labbaika, Allahuma, labbaika* (For thee, I am ready. Oh, Allah, for thee, I am ready), they had spent the duration of the Muslim pilgrimage to Mecca in November of that year almost shoulder to shoulder, and the closeness that had characterized so many years of their lives began to permeate their beings again as they did God's work.

They performed all the rituals that they had last done together more than two decades earlier. The *tawaf* involved going around the *Kaaba,* the cube shaped building which acts as the Muslim direction of prayer, seven times in a counterclockwise direction. The next ritual involved running seven times between Al-Saifa and Al-Marwah hills in memory of Abraham's wife's search for water for her child, Ismael. The older of the two was hard put to complete the distance with his illness. Thereafter, they had gladly drunk the holy *Aab-e-Zum Zum* water in memory of the spring that quenched Ishmael's thirst. They had gone on to Mina and reached the Arafat Plains. They had participated in the ritual stoning of the devil by casting stones at the three pillars, and the younger one could not help but notice the beads of sweat that showed on the face of his elder brother.

Finally, when they returned to Mecca and shaved their heads before they performed the feast of the sacrifice, the elder brother Naseeb had said, "Akram, before we finally go tomorrow to Medina and offer prayers at the Majid-e-Nabawi, I would just like to remind you of something in our past with your permission."

Surprised by the statement, Akram answered, "My brother, who has been as much of a father that I never knew, you know that you can say whatever you want to me at any time. You don't need my permission!"

"I am going to die before the next year is past its first quarter, my life's work to bring about the end of the house of Saud unfinished. The cancer cells would have won the battle by then. When you first flew an aircraft, you had made me a promise, remember?"

"How can I forget, Naseeb, my brother? You had sacrificed fifteen years of your life after our father's death to educate me and send me to college to study aeronautics and finally make me a pilot. You let me realize my childhood dream of flying by joining the King Fahd Air Force Academy. Whatever you wish will be done. If possible, I will do it while you still live! Just tell me."

When Naseeb explained in ten minutes how he wanted the promise to be made good Akram's face went white.

When he saw the alarm on his bother's face, Naseeb quickly responded, "Forget it, my brother. I must be going mad to ask you this after all these years when you have made a new life. I have absolutely no right to do this! Years ago, when I did not have the money for your training, Sheikh Osama, with whom I had worked beside for so many years, came to know of it. He had already made a fortune by then and simply sent the money to me in a package with one of his sons. Two years later, he asked me to go back to our ancestral land in Yemen. He wanted me, with my background as an *imam*, to guide our people in the meaning of the Koran for the long struggle ahead with the West profiteering from oil belonging rightfully to us Muslims.

"One of those who learned at my knee as he proclaims to all his visitors is Naseer al-Wuhayshi, the present head of Qaeda in Yemen. He escaped from a high-security prison some years ago and sought me out recently. He asked me whether his old teacher's family would be willing to make the ultimate sacrifice of a family member to set an example to the other Jihadists."

"No, my brother, you have every right," he said simply. "For a moment, I forgot my duty." The color was now returning to his face. "I promise that it will be done while you are still alive to see the results. That is the least that I can do. In any case, the house of Saud has denied me what should have been a rightful promotion to a base command!"

Back in Prince Sultan Air Base, Colonel Akram Abdolhassan was a changed man from within. He had a keen sense of history that was promulgated by his basic military training. This had been given an edge by meeting his brother again and the inherent inequalities in Saudi Arabia between the royal family and its self-perpetuation of personal interest characterized by all the prize appointments in the Royal Saudi Air Force being cornered by the royals. There had been numerous attempts to take out the house of Saud over the decades. None of them had succeeded, because they had been inadequately focused, including the Al Qaeda attacks on the refineries in 2006.

He had attended a training session at the base run by US Special Forces a few years ago. Their target matrix went by the acronym CARVER, of which he had made a note. It stood for criticality, accessibility, recuperability, vulnerability, effect on the populace, and recognizability. Assassinate a royal, and a dozen others would vie to replace him. The source of their power was oil, and it was oil that had to be targeted to create severe shortages.

Criticality of supplies to the world was assured by Ghawar, the giant facility that supplied five million barrels a day or more than 6 percent of world production. With the world economy on an upswing and peak oil in many of the world's largest fields having come and gone, even the disruption of large fields like Berri, Zuluf, Marjan, Abu Sa'fah, and Qatif could disrupt the world's economy. There was also a built-in redundancy within the system of hundreds of drilling platforms and lots of pumping stations, not to mention a built-in redundancy in the processing and loading facility that would ensure that recovery was reasonably swift—that is, unless the damage inflicted was sufficiently large. Billions of dollars poured into air defense aircraft, guns, and missile systems and also into ground security had not been wasted, for they provided a high level of protection from severe damage. There was no guarantee of being able to cause a large enough blaze in perhaps

Abqaiq to create a crisis situation, not unless it was done by an insider willing to risk his life.

The closed tribal system that kept Akram from flying the F-15E Desert Eagle fighter aircraft was a windfall in his plan. The A330 MRTT, which was recently delivered to the twentieth squadron (airlift and air refueling) at Riyadh, was a three-point tanker for refueling by means of wing-mounted pods and advanced refueling boom systems. Each Royal Air Force Saudi Airbus A330 MRTT was able to deliver sixty-five tons of fuel in its air-to-air refueling role at a distance of a thousand miles from base, following up to two hours on station. In addition, fully topped up, it carried an additional forty-six tons of fuel to keep it on station like a giant teat that the Tornados and Desert Eagles would feed off to keep flying without landing to refuel. The A330 MRTT aircraft featured greater fuel capacity than most others did and spacious lower holds to transport larger payloads. All of the fuel was carried entirely within existing tanks in the wing and tail. This left the whole cabin free for 272 seats in the A330 MRTT's troop-transport role and its entire cargo hold free to carry military equipment on pallets or in containers.

It was the seventh night of the air force and air defense exercise designed with major assistance from the US Air Force personnel posted in Saudi Arabia. The last phase involved the defense of Saudi Arabia's primary oil export terminals located at the Ras Tanura complex (six million barrels per day capacity and the world's largest offshore oil-loading facility). This included the port at Ras Tanura (2.5 million barrels per day capacity) and the Ras al-Ju'aymah facility (3–3.6 million barrels per day) on the Persian Gulf. More than 75 percent of Saudi oil exports were loaded at the Ras Tanura facility.

Air crews of the of the Saudi Air Force and the Air Defense Hawk SAM batteries unused to prolonged stress and further sapped by the 41 degree C day temperatures were like sleepwalking zombies. Akram's A330 MRTT with a full load of 111 tons of fuel picked up from Riyadh instead of Jeddah, the operating base far to the west, loitered in a circuit which took it as far as 120 kilometers to the west of Ras Tanura without attracting attention.

Suddenly, at 3:30 a.m., much to the relief of all the twenty thousand participants, the prince, because he was concerned about the deterioration in the king's health, suddenly called off the exercise. He was thinking ahead of the requirement for both the RSAF commander as well as the Royal Air Defense Force commander, who might have been immediately required for the state ceremonies in case he became king. It was also better to keep control and preempt any possible coup attempt by having their physical presence next to him.

Orders were being awaited by the tanker crew after the exercise was called off. Akram let his co-pilot fly for the last four hours, and now the aircraft was on autopilot, repeating the circuit. There was no reaction when Akram unstrapped himself and went past the advanced refueling boom operator facing the opposite direction for the next refueling mission and walked to the toilet in the rear with a small zip-locked bag in one hand.

Once inside the toilet, he took out a silencer from his flying suit and fitted it onto his service pistol and tucked it into the small bag before he carried it back to the cockpit. When he entered the cockpit, the co-pilot peering intently at his instrument panel, it took him less than ten seconds to fish out the silenced weapon and shoot his co-pilot in the nape of his neck. He then quickly whipped around and shot the startled boom operator twice in his head. The silencer was more to reduce the muzzle velocity of the round and not put a hole in the aircraft's pressurized cabin than to prevent noise. It had also given him a fraction of a second more to deal with the boom operator, who reacted slowly to a suppressed shot.

Methodically, he strapped himself back in his seat and took the controls off autopilot. He then set a new course of 079 degrees for Tarut Island and commenced a descent to two hundred feet. Unsurprisingly, the ten-minute flight went unnoticed, for with the termination of the exercise, the entire air defense and air force machinery had wound up shop for the night! The air traffic controllers had loads of fighter landings to handle and little time for an errant tanker.

The Ras Tanura Sea Islands were a complex of manmade islands interconnected by walkways located approximately one mile northeast from the north pier. In total, there were four islands, which stretched in a single-file formation over a distance of approximately 1.7 kilometers, pointing approximately northward. Every sea island rested on piles at a water depth of approximately twenty-six meters at low tide. Furthermore, each island consisted of a loading station and two berths, having four to six mooring dolphins and two to four breasting dolphins per berth. The oldest of the four islands had been commissioned in 1967, and it was currently isolated and abandoned in place. The three active islands provide berths for six ships simultaneously. Seven crude oil lines and two bunker lines, all subsea and ranging in size from twenty to forty-eight inches in diameter, were used to deliver crude and fuel oil to the six operational berths.

The fourth manmade structure was an extremely important component of the Ras Tanura oil export complex. Built in the shipyards of Shikoku Island in Japan, this island was transported nine thousand miles over forty days before it was installed. It became a largely self-sufficient addition to Ras Tanura's first three, somewhat similar islands. Twelve hydraulically operated loading arms were lined up, six to a loading berth. These arms, which linked a tanker's manifold valves to the island's loading lines, were twenty-four inches in diameter, the world's largest, and could rise and fall ninety feet to accommodate the difference between empty tankers and fully loaded tankers at different levels of tide.

In the middle of the deck, a 221-foot crane rose in the air with a jib boom that was 167 feet long and strong enough to lift fourteen tons. Control towers and flood lighting and fire-monitoring towers had been erected at the corners. The crane and control towers had been linked to the control house with elevated bridges, and the control house opened onto the deck from an elevator.

In earlier flights, Akram had always regarded the island as akin to a giant water insect. The narrow, 1,750-foot walkway over the water gave the manmade structure a body like a needle, short appendages protruding symmetrically from either side. Six of the appendages were mooring dolphins to which loading tankers were tied. Four appendages were breasting dolphins to absorb the impact of the giant ships and hold them at a safe distance from the loading facilities of the main platform. He now aimed the tanker aircraft at the bottom third of the crane, and just before impact, he opened the controls for the air-to-air refueling hoses to dump aviation fuel at the rate of five thousand liters per minute and create a curtain of trailing petroleum vapor to magnify the blast effect.

An alert, freshly promoted battery commander gave the order to launch barely fifteen seconds before impact and a pair of L-70 40mm air defense guns opened fire simultaneously. A missile strike a hundred meters short of the crane target and numerous hits by the L-70s hastened the crash into an area near one of the dolphins, where the Golden Geese, a VLCC almost fully loaded with close to two million barrels of oil, was being topped up.

Topping up was a very dangerous time when a person was handling oil. As the tanker became full, crew members were absorbed in opening and closing oil to direct the flow into the side cargo tanks and maintaining close communication with the pumping facility to decrease and finally stop the flow of liquid. There was also an element of trailing vapor in the air as crude oil replaced the remaining air in the tank.

When the A-330 tanker and its seventy tons of aviation fuel and trailing vapor crashed, the explosion rattled windowpanes thirty kilometers away and largely destroyed the functional integrity of one third of the fourth island. The pumping facility crew and seventeen other highly trained workers were killed, resulting in crude overflowing the VLCC tanks within minutes.

Fires broke out in two loading tanks and quickly engulfed large parts of the Golden Geese. Captain Pedro Gonzales, a cigar-chewing giant of a man, dazed and bleeding from the blast, fought valiantly to control the fire from spreading. At midday, the port authorities ordered them to evacuate ship, because by then much of it had been gutted and seven crew members had lost their lives. Two of the other islands with operating terminals cleared ships from their terminals in minutes, and efficient, well-rehearsed, preventive measures ensured that the fire did not spread.

Eventually, it would take another three days to ensure that the fire was totally brought under control. As the conjectures in the world media mounted about the origin of the attack, the extent of damage and the resulting long-term impact of a minimum of nine million barrels a day not being shipped for three days and at least three million barrels a day of crude exports being lost to the world markets, crude prices jumped by the second and finally peaked a fortnight later at 199 dollars a barrel.

Tanker and marine insurance rates doubled by the end of the week as the world reeled in shock, and early estimates gave a ballpark figure of two years to get reestablished.

Al Qaeda in the Arabian Peninsula took immediate credit and posted an Internet message to *Al Jazeera*, the Arab news network, that included pictures of the martyr Akram Abdolhassan from the time he was a child to his commissioning into RSAF. *Al Jazeera* immediately broke the news to the world in more than a dozen languages and followed up with a broadcast of an attack on the Turkmenistan-China pipeline by Uyghur rebels as well as an attack on a pipeline in Iraq that took a further two hundred thousand barrels a day temporarily off the market. To add insult to injury, Somali pirates hijacked a Chinese VLCC tanker carrying two million barrels of oil and held the crew and tanker to ransom for $150 million. An attempt by a Chinese frigate to intervene failed. In the following week, two smaller Chinese ships were also hijacked, although no ransom claim was received.

The call by the UN secretary general to China and India for a cease-fire to cool down oil and sea freight and insurance prices was magnanimously agreed to by the Chinese. China called a unilateral cease-fire without prejudice to its claims on India in Arunachal Pradesh and Aksai Chin. The Indians responded to the gesture the same day, calling it an act of statesmanship that it hoped would lead to peaceful resolution of the conflict.

CHAPTER 69
DELUSIONS

THE COMMANDER OF THE ARMY OF the Guardians of the Islamic Revolution of Iran, General Mohammad Ali Jafari, was in a fix. He was doubtful about how his plan would play out and unexpectedly asked for the opinion of his subordinate. Normally, he confined himself to giving executive directions without any preliminary discussion.

"Maybe we should just do this through diplomatic channels?" Jafari posed the question to Suleimani.

Brigadier General Qassem Suleimani, the Qods commander, had gained importance in the eyes of his boss. This was thanks to the success achieved by his selection of Sohrab Mehrotra to work the back channels to the Indian establishment. Sohrab had successfully convinced the Indians to undertake computer simulations to establish the viability of Iran's fission nuke design. Suleimani looked ahead to the day he would rule the roost and occupy the office currently occupied by General Jafari. He would also do all that was necessary to achieve this distinction. If it was Allah's will, as he had little doubt it was, he would succeed.

Suleimani answered, "India's foreign policy establishment is notorious for delay. In any case, the decision had to be taken by the PM and her rubber-stamp cabinet committee on security. It would be better to send Sohrab Mehrotra to do the job. He has billions of dollars in contracts at stake to safeguard. The Indian ambassador has nothing at risk, since he is retiring after two months. We also know from past experience that he can't deliver on even small commitments."

"Okay, talk to Mehrotra, since he seems to trust you. Tell him the Indians have a month to make up their minds. This is not an open-ended offer!" said General Jafari, terminating the meeting.

The same battered Mercedes with the same surly driver had once again fetched Mehrab for the meeting. After more than a year of regular interactions on almost a monthly basis, the two men were at relative ease with each other.

Sohrab said, "You sent for me, general? Is there anything that I can do?"

"Our scientists have evaluated the report brought by you on the computer simulations done in India."

"Is it not satisfactory, general? Is something wrong?"

Suleimani then said, "We have no quarrel with the report contents and its logic. However, the report needs to be taken to its logical conclusion. That is where you come in. Are you aware of what a nuclear initiator is, Mr. Mehrotra?"

"As far as I know, it is some kind of a device needed to assure an adequate supply of neutrons for a fissile explosion to work optimally."

Suleimani smiled and said, "Precisely put, Mr. Mehrotra. You seem to have put all these months of shuttling up and down as an intermediary to good use! The report prepared by your nuclear scientists has analyzed that our fission weapon is workable but has a question mark over the efficacy and reliability of the uranium deuteride initiator."

"It's commonly whispered that you got a workable design from the Pakistani scientist Dr. A. Q. Khan. So why should it not work for you as well? Unless Khan deliberately with held something critical?" Sohrab Mehrotra could not resist flaunting his confidence and temporary indispensability.

Suleimani ignored the remark. "My proposition is simple, Mr. Mehrotra. We want your scientists to tweak the design to make it less temperamental and make it work reliably every time."

"That was not part of the agreement with the Indians."

"I agree with you. This is a fresh offer that we are making. You give us a working initiator, and we will guarantee a three-year delay in supplies to the Gwadar-Urumqi oil pipeline. If Western technology and funds to develop the Yadavaran and North Pars fields can be brought in by India in joint ventures with us, we will create space for you to work there as well."

"Your contractual commitments to the Chinese will not permit any outsiders."

"There is enough ambiguity in the contracts to permit outside participation in the Iranian national interests. Needless to say, Mr. Mehrotra, we will also demand your participation in a financially substantive fashion!"

"There are also contracts in Iraq, Mr. Mehrotra, close to our common border, where Iraq is looking for partners where we could help." Suleimani threw in some additional bait.

"You will use your influence over the Shia-majority Iraqi government, which wants to speed up development of its giant southern fields?"

"Yes, Mr. Mehrotra, that is exactly what Iran will do for India, once India proves to be a reliable enough partner."

The CIA estimate on the Central Asian energy scene made interesting reading:

> *China is continuing to make a serious push to gain access to Central Asian gas. This can be seen from the increased investments in the pipeline that links Turkmenistan, Uzbekistan, and Kazakhstan. Gazprom is being squeezed out of the project, and this has set the stage for Central Asian competition between Beijing and Russia. Gazprom future plans have been assuming that Turkmenistan will sell virtually all of its export production to Russia. However, the new agreement between China and Turkmenistan implies that the new pipeline is a priority commitment for Turkmenistan. The text states, "The gas for export to China will come from fields on the right bank of the Amu-Darya River," but it adds, "If additional volumes of gas are required to build the Turkmenistan-China gas pipeline, the Turkmen side can guarantee gas shipments from other gas fields." The Russians, as a key supplier of gas to Europe, are facing a supply crunch thanks to China's spanner in the way of pipeline and infrastructure investments. The Russians are going to lose at least $100 billion a year from Europe on this account and Putin is hopping mad at China. The money is desperately required for modernization of the Red Army and the mining sector.*

Everything has played out beautifully so far. Eighty percent of our forces are out of Afghanistan. The army is firmly under control of the government in Pakistan once again and seems to be in no hurry to move out. Obviously, the army once again justifies the takeover in the national interest for the moron on the street. Once again, we only need to talk to one guy for cooperation, unlike say in India. In New Delhi, we have to try to press a hundred buttons simultaneously to get the Indians to do anything. So far, General Bhat is playing ball. I reckon we couldn't have written a better script so far, except for the inconvenient rise in oil prices. I guess within six months, prices will start falling again as the world's economies take another tumble."

The US president, in a mellow mood as he puffed gently at his cigar, contemplated the steps he still needed to take.

"The Russian competition with China is, of course, the icing on the cake," CIA Head Francis Leap responded. "We know from sources close to their politburo standing committee that China is developing greater ambitions. It wants to use its foreign currency reserves to have a major say in marketing gas from the Caspian directly to Europe, bypassing Russia completely. It will encourage the Russians to develop Siberian prospects using Indian investments to counter-squeeze China. I wouldn't put it past Putin to sabotage some of the four thousand kilometers of pipelines that the Chinese are laying across Central Asia. It will also help us to play off the Russians and Chinese against each other, depending on the agenda we wish to pursue."

"How are we making out in the back-channel negotiations with the new government in Tehran?" the president asked Eleanor Griffith Huxley, the secretary of state.

"The Iranians have assured us through the Indian tycoon Sohrab Mehrotra that under no circumstances will they give a base to China in SOH. The Indians are also working to get Tehran to talk to us seriously. They also want to keep China on a short leash for energy. India hopes to achieve this by getting large-scale investments and technology from the United States in joint ventures with Indian companies like Reliance Petroleum. The Iranians, not surprisingly, agree with them. Ever since we signed the nuke reduction treaty with them, the Russians are also hedging their bets. Putin seems to be veering around to the view that the long-term threat to Russia is from China and not the United States."

"What's this about the Indians helping Iran with its nuclear program that CNBC has put out?" the president asked.

"We can't prove it—or at least not yet—but one of the NSA former employees who produced that report you liked about the Chinese cutting India to size to spite the United States thinks so. She is working in India currently and got this from her Indian boyfriend, who works closely with the IRGC in Iran," Lieutenant General Jacob Long, the national security adviser, responded.

"Supposing we need to squeeze the Indians hard for cooperation in Afghanistan?" the president asked.

Francis Leap then said, "If it's necessary, Mr. President, we have the resources to carry out a trial by the Western media purely on insinuations. Indian TV channels that have relative freedom from libel laws will pick up the story and turn the heat on to their own government to come clean."

"Eleanor, you were to speak to the Indian PM?"

"I did speak to the Indian prime minister a few hours ago, implying that we have proof about India's help to Tehran in developing a nuke capability. Of course, Durga Vadera, who is a real tough cookie, denied it outright. She doled out the normal crap about how India is the only country in the world that has not contributed toward nuclear weapons proliferation. She also forcefully pointed out that US policies have in fact rewarded proliferators like Pakistan. I, of course, disagreed and conveyed that we are open to being shown that India is not helping Tehran develop nuclear weapons."

"Jake, we need a lever to preserve the balance of power in Afpak in spite of our scaled-down presence."

"We should tell the Indians that in the interest of stability in the region, the United States is considering extending a civilian nuclear deal to Pakistan. We are doing so as Pakistan has been able to address our nonproliferation concerns adequately. When the Indians object to it, we offer a deal if they put boots on the ground in Afghanistan. Say an infantry division to start off. This can be to ostensibly safeguard Indian-created infrastructure assets and safeguard Indian workers. When they do so, we reconsider helping Pakistan's nuke deal!"

The president smiled and said, "Brilliant, Jake! We also tell General Mahmoud Butt that if he helps the Taliban in Pakistan, we'll get the

Indians to increase their presence in Afghanistan. That should also make the Chinese equally unhappy."

"I've cancelled all further appointments for the day. This had better be worth it," Vladimir Putin said. "Alexei, give it to us in a nutshell!"

Alexei Miller, chairman of the Gazprom management committee, was understandably nervous. He figured that if Putin needed a scapegoat, he would automatically be the first choice. In reality, Gazprom was only a proxy for the Kremlin, where all the strategic energy-related decisions were taken. Any chances of following the example of Medvedev, one of his predecessors promoted into the Kremlin, were finished.

"Gazprom is being squeezed out. Our short-term strategy envisaged a major increase in purchases of Central Asian gas. We have no means to offset declining domestic gas production in the short term, and we are purchasing a hundred billion cubic meters of gas from Central Asia. Gazprom was counting on Turkmenistan to provide the bulk of that gas, with purchases slated to go to seventy to eighty billion cubic meters a year. Gazprom future plans have been assuming that Turkmenistan will sell virtually all of its export production to Russia, and we can reap a windfall, selling the gas in Europe, where the prices are exploding."

Deputy Premier Igor Sechin was responsible for the Russian energy sector. He said, "China's Investment Promotion Agency of its commerce ministry is pulling out all the stops in wining, dining, and whoring with the leaders of Turkmenistan, Uzbekistan, and Kazakhstan. This is to gain additional access to Central Asian gas besides investments in the 1,833-kilometer pipeline that links Turkmenistan, Uzbekistan, and Kazakhstan, which guarantees them thirty billion cubic meters of gas for thirty years. China is asking for an additional forty billion cubic meters, which has set the stage for Central Asian competition between Beijing and us. The additional draft agreement between China and Turkmenistan implies that the additional gas is now a priority commitment for Turkmenistan."

"What else are the Chinese up to?" asked Putin, looking toward Mikhail Sapunov, the federal security service chief.

"The Ukrainians are also being encouraged by Chinese investment to again steal gas that Gazprom is routing through Ukraine's old pipelines, thus compounding the shortage in Europe. The Chinese are putting the squeeze on us hard. The European commission has been sounded to sell Caspian Basin gas that China will develop, as it is the only country with the requisite cash reserves, directly into Europe. We stand to lose at least $150 billion a year in potential energy sales."

Anatoly Serdyukov, the defense minister, said, "What the Chinese are doing is logical to them. They perceive Russia as an old woman sapped by the economic turmoil who will supply China cheaply with the arms and commodities required to build its military and economic strength. China is in expansionist mode while they sweet-talk us into cooperating. They are also flooding Siberia with millions of illegal immigrants to change its demography."

They all waited patiently as Putin appeared to gaze out into nothingness, weighing his options. It was time for a calculated message to go to Beijing. "We need to push the Indians a lot more to preserve the balance of power in Asia. What we are doing is not enough. Anatoly, go talk to them some more. See what additional arms they want. Push the joint armament ventures into increased production. Give them whatever they want from our stocks—aircraft, tanks, warships! Take Mikhail with you. The Indian intelligence efforts have always been laughable. Amongst other things, get them to push the Uyghurs into attacking the Horgo's end of the pipeline in Xinjiang. Maybe you can help with cutting the deep end under the Lli and Syr Darya crossings. We also need to do something about the United States, Anatoly."

Anatoly Serdyukov said, "US Military progress in Afghanistan with reduced force levels and an accelerated NATO pullout will be difficult this year. Afghan security officials recently have issued similar warnings, noting that the number of violent assaults is likely to increase with the spring thaws. Some fifteen provinces in the north, east, and west face a serious threat from insurgents, and the situation is declining in provinces bordering Pakistan and Iran."

Mikhail Sapunov added, "Current flashpoints include Marjah and Kandahar, where a fresh offensive has been stalled by the Taliban. Meanwhile, military and civilian development efforts—a key component of the US strategy—are being focused on some eighty districts. Most of them located on or near Afghanistan's Ring Road is only facilitating the move of drugs into Russia."

"Let's help them suffer some more. Anatoly, work out opening logistics corridors for the US forces in Afghanistan so they are not tempted to pull out early. Try to negotiate a quid pro quo by destruction of Afghan poppy fields!"

"I take it, Madame Prime Minister, that you desire an independent evaluation of India's current situation by the crisis management group and our possible options to remedy this situation?"

"Precisely, that is exactly what I want you to give me. I'm flooded with a host of contradictory advice from the national security council that I'm not comfortable with," Durga Vadera agreed.

Ashok Sobti paused, gathering the collective threads of perceptions within the group to create a coherent theme. "There are two positive fall-outs of this crisis, Madame Prime Minister. Ash Kumari has prepared a follow-up report on China. It indicates that there is almost a unanimous groundswell of opinion in China against the leadership. Your bold proactive response in attacking the Qinghai-Lhasa railway line and the communications of the rapid reaction force of the PLA invading Bhutan has forced a rethink of the Sino-Indian strategic equation."

Speed Ranganathan added, "India is no longer regarded as a walkover but as a wily enemy that needs to be strategically pressurized without necessarily provoking a conflict. This may lead to major purges in the standing committee of the politburo. It is widely seen to have goofed by first provoking a conflict-like situation and then backing down. There is a widespread perception in China that the only gainer from the recent conflict has been the United States."

"So we need to encourage this and get everyone in the government to refrain from media-bashing the Chinese. Drumming up jingoistic responses from the Chinese side is stupid. What about the second positive that you see?" Durga Vadera asked.

"Our people are willing to give you a long rope to get us out of this mess intact and get terrorism in some sort of control. They recognize that economic growth will suffer but instinctively realize there is no alternative. They are willing to bite the bullet."

"Seems far-fetched to me from the flak I have personally been getting in the media!" Durga Vadera observed.

"This is confirmed by a private Gallup survey we commissioned all across India as also a new assignment to CRAI through Ash Kumari to assess the mood of people in power in India. It included all political parties with at least five MPs. Seventy percent are not buying the pitch of the opposition that your mishandling of the terror strike in Delhi has led to the conflict with China and Pakistan—also the breakdown of internal security."

"Perhaps you are right, but the mood can change overnight. Ask anyone who has fought an election!" the PM said.

Sobti amplified, "We believe that the survey gives you a window of opportunity of perhaps two years. This is at a time when China may be fumbling with the new standing committee of the politburo establishing its writ."

"What about the negatives? Or are there too many to count? This aside from India being surrounded by enemies and being chewed up from the insides by antinational entities in conjunction with China and Pakistan, let alone Bangladesh and Nepal."

Sridhar interjected, "The major negative is that there is a better than 50 percent chance that if we don't mend our ways, we will lose the complete northeast. The PLA, though sitting in Bhutan and parts of Sikkim, is deemed to have lost huge prestige and is thirsting for revenge. More than a thousand soldiers getting killed in the tunnel and the invasion of the Siliguri Corridor having to be aborted is causing heads to roll, and a major shake-up is underway. There are already reports of a dozen training camps for the northeast insurgent groups and Maoists being set up to up the ante in the coming months."

Durga Vadera looked at Lieutenant General Randhir Singh. "What would you do in my place, general, aside from replacing half a dozen governors with men of backbone to keep non-governance in check?"

"There is no silver bullet, but you have a huge amount of credibility at present that you mean business. This credibility exists both with friends and enemies and can be leveraged. I would take a leaf out of the Israeli strategy against the Arabs and signal by deeds and not words that enough is enough. Now it will be an eye for an eye. Most of the insurgent groups have lost their leaders and should be amenable to a carrot-and-stick approach."

"We will take a tougher approach as you suggest general, what else?" the PM asked.

Lieutenant General Randhir continued "We need to launch a

relentless campaign to root them out whether in Bangladesh, Myanmar, or Nepal by assassinations, trans-border raids, and air strikes. Quickly open up the region to 100 percent foreign direct investment in agriculture and food processing and infrastructure to tackle unemployment and fast-track new all-weather roads. A large foreign investment presence will also preempt open conflict. We should look at unilateral trade concessions to Bangladesh to give the new PM a chance to establish firm control over the government. We also need to keep reminding Bangladesh that China is robbing them of water upstream."

"I agree with your recommendations against the insurgents. For the long term stuff we need to study the implications more fully. What about the Chinese sheltering, training, and arming insurgents, general?"

"The Chinese understand *realpolitik* well enough, Madame Prime Minister. Support their militant minorities fully in Tibet and Xinjiang while officially denying it. Once small incidents mount, they will get the message," Lieutenant General Randhir Singh replied.

Vice-Admiral Shankar Menon added, "One of Raja's companies in Israel has developed a high-altitude, solar-powered aircraft. It is capable of staying aloft at high altitudes for six months at a time to conduct around-the-clock surveillance and reconnaissance. It contains a sensor suite, power-generating and storage apparatus, and radar-imaging apparatus. We should deploy a prototype immediately over the Siliguri Corridor so we are not caught napping the next time around."

"Work on it quickly Raja. The Chinese won't wait for us!" The PM looked at Raja who nodded assent.

Sobti said, "You also need to take a call on doubling the defense budget to 5 percent of GDP, keeping the prevailing situation in mind. Even the opposition can't object. With increased defense spending, economic growth will slow, but it's important to signal the world that we will do what it takes to ensure our security."

Vice-Admiral Shankar Menon then said, "It's the sort of signal that North Korea has taught the world to respect! Moreover, the large armament companies will ensure that the United States does nothing to harm our essential national interests, if fifteen to twenty billion dollars are at stake!"

" I take your point. Why don't we also look at sending an infantry division or even more into Afghanistan and support it by sea through

Iran along with say an armored brigade as the new army chief has suggested?" Durga Vadera asked. "After all, the international community has been questioning our commitment and has frozen us from the Afpak debate. With Iran backing us, there will be little threat to our logistics pipeline. It will ensure that the Taliban is kept on ice for the time being and has no hope of getting back into power. The Russians are all in favor of such a step, and the Chinese will be decidedly unhappy, especially with their copper project about to come on stream, to have Indian troops in the vicinity. In the meantime, we will complete our border infrastructure development to send a clear signal to China that it's better to settle our differences by talking."

"The one positive we have is the continued willingness of Iran to play ball and deliver on energy issues and stonewall China where our interests are involved. Dr. Kak was spot on with his idea of only partially confirming their nuclear weapon capability. We have Iran on the hook!

The ISI head, Lieutenant General Saif Gilani, saluted smartly as he entered the president's office in Islamabad. Life was so much simpler without trying to keep tabs on a civilian government in Pakistan.

"Eleanor Huxley told me this morning that the Indians might be asked to send troops into Afghanistan to look after infrastructure assets. This is ostensibly to enable the Afghanistan National Army to free resources to manage the internal security situation," General Mahmoud Bhatt said. "Obviously, the United States does not trust us to manage the Taliban and the vacuum they've left behind! The question is does it also create an opportunity for us to get firm control of the Taliban groups within Pakistan once again."

Lieutenant General Saif Gilani, the ISI chief, smiled and said, "The United States will be doing us a favor. If the United States and NATO have failed, what chance does the Indian Army have in Afghanistan? India does not have a tenth of the air power projection capability of the Americans. It will also enable me to get the Tehreek-e-Taliban Pakistan to target a real enemy along with Mullah Omar's forces. We can also redirect the Lashkar e Taiba and Kashmir militant groups once again, as they have been restive."

General Mahmoud Bhatt took another puff from his cigarette

before he continued, "You need to ensure that the Islamist groups are kept on a short leash in Assam and the Siliguri Corridor. The Chinese presence in Bhutan is enough to bleed the Indians for years. We don't want a situation where India has to stop pouring resources into a black hole and let their northeast states spin off as independent entities."

"I will personally ensure that, sir. We will ensure that your strategy is followed. Bleed the Indians in the northeast, bleed them in Afghanistan, and bleed them in Jammu and Kashmir!"

President Xi Jinping, also the new chairman of the CMC, was decidedly unhappy after he read the report analyzing the unsatisfactory conflict with India. The feeling was unanimous as the freshly constituted standing committee of the political bureau assembled for its first meeting.

Li Kegianj, the vice president and author of the report, appeared to speak for all the politburo members. "We have made fools of ourselves. Sun Tzu had warned us of what was likely to happen centuries ago!"

The slide projected on the wall where they sat read, "If you know the enemy and know yourself, you need not fear the result of a hundred battles. If you know yourself but not the enemy, for every victory gained, you will also suffer a defeat. If you know neither the enemy nor yourself, you will succumb in every battle."

Li Kegianj continued, "We talked ourselves into believing that the Indians were a doormat for us! In our hurry to undercut the United States, we picked on a supposed ally. We had a winning strategy in place against the Indians straight from Sun Tzu that we dumped. We should get back to it immediately!"

"And what strategy are you referring to?" inquired Zhou Yongkang, a man who was not a "princeling" beholden to anyone except his own hard work for his seat in the politburo.

The slide came on again and read, "The skillful leader subdues the enemy troops without fighting. He captures their cities without laying siege to them. He overthrows their kingdom without lengthy operations in the field."

Li continued, "We had a successful working strategy in place to dismember India that we lost sight of in our eagerness to cut down

American influence. The complete northeast of India, including eight of their states, would have fallen like a diseased arm in ten years. It still can, and we should immediately focus on that. The Indians had been leaning backward to accommodate our every whim for half a century but will no longer do so.

"In our hubris, we forgot our own backyard and left strategic assets, including the Qinghai-Lhasa railway line and the Yarlung Tsangpo Great Bend dam, vulnerable. India had a vast inferiority complex ever since their army was thrashed by the PLA in 1962. All that psychological edge has now vanished."

Xi interrupted, "And what we have done is shoot ourselves in the foot by not realizing how vulnerable PLA logistics continue to be! Two prototype aircraft and two dozen Tibetans have not only created setbacks in Aksai Chin but also virtually crippled an RRF with dozens of aircraft and helicopters in Bhutan and effectively blunted our ability to threaten India in the short term. Where we could build up ten PLA divisions in a few weeks opposite any part of northern and eastern India, we are lucky to support what BD regiments already deployed.

"We had taken over the leadership of Asia and were well established to do the same to tap the vast resources of Africa. The world has acknowledged that Tibet is ours and not an independent entity forcibly occupied by us. We have agreements with the Central Asian republics to tap their energy resources and ease out the Russia's. Han are immigrating into Siberia, and it is only a matter of time that our influence will be felt across Russia. The recent months have seen a strengthening of US power in Asia primarily because of our policy miscalculations with regard to India. We need to set this right!"

He Guoqiang, who headed the central commission for discipline inspection, cleared his throat and then started, "I propose that we should have Zhou Yongkang looking after attaining our strategic interests in India and South Asia full-time. The problem seems to have arisen out of losing focus on what we thought was unimportant. Fortunately for all of us, India refused to take advantage of its temporary successes through the media and saved us face. We should ensure that the Indians do not get a second chance!"

He Guoqiang smiled as the others nodded assent. If Zhou Yongkang succeeded, it would take at least a decade to pass a value judgment. The committee would remember it was He Guoqiang's suggestion that had led to this state. If Zhou failed, He Guoqiang would be the automatic front-runner for becoming the next general secretary, president, and CMC chairman.

EPILOGUE-DOGS OF WAR

THE EIGHT MEN IN THE NEW Shura council were in a somber mood. The frail wraith of a man with only his burning zeal to keep him alive had had the last laugh. He had sent for all of them with a message that it was time for him to go and that they needed to elect someone in his place. None of those present had the same depth of conviction that all things were possible. You just needed to extend yourself, do your best, and leave the end result to Allah, who knew best.

The voice that had emanated from the near skeleton was surprisingly strong as he geared himself for one final effort and answered their murmured greeting. The scarred, freshly oiled, and loaded Kalashnikov lay lengthwise in front of him, creating a physical barrier between him and the men who sat on the ground opposite him. Normally, the rifle always lay to his left side.

"*As sala'amu alaikum*" Peace be upon you, the eight men greeted him with near reverence, almost in one voice, marveling at the strength of will keeping the disease wracked body going.

"*Walaikum as salaam*" And unto you also, peace, the leader replied. I must thank all of you for having appreciated the requirement for absolute secrecy. It permitted me to not share details with you in organizing the attack on Ras Tanura. It was Allah's wish that it succeeded the way it did. In a way, this is a bigger success than the attack on America on September 11, 2001. This will affect the whole world and finally bring America to its knees. Inshallah, our plan for obtaining nuclear material will deliver results soon as well. The Americans spent more than a hundred million dollars to safeguard Pakistan's weapons, but we have the key.

"The way forward is now automatically unfolding. You should focus on overthrowing the puppet Afghan government and reestablishing the rule of our Taliban brothers. That at least is my suggestion after you have helped in reestablishing our presence in Iraq. No leader has emerged in Iraq that can truly command the loyalty of all its religious sects and ethnicities. The rejection of many hundreds of Sunni candidates from fighting the last American-rigged election has opened the way to go back. The world will now be unfortunately increasingly dominated by those unbelievers from China. As America and Europe fade, we must prepare ourselves to deal with those persecuting our Uyghur brothers in Xinjiang."

He held up a frail hand with what appeared to be a number of small sticks sticking out on one side as the murmur in the small room became louder, all of them trying to talk at the same time.

"I will not be around when you do all this. These sticks in my hand are all of equal length except one. You will each take one, and I will then tell you what is to be done next to take our movement forward."

Perplexed by the odd instruction from their revered leader, they leaned across and did what they were told. He then pushed his rifle a few inches toward them.

"The doctor has said that to live a bit longer, I will have to be put on opium injections to kill the pain. That is not the way of the warrior! He who has the shortest stick should come forward."

Slowly, reluctantly when it became obvious that he had actually pulled a stick a good three inches shorter than his contemporaries, Abdul, the man with the freshly hennaed beard, came forward slowly. He was also known as "Abdul the Bomber" for the highly successful bomb attacks he had organized in Iraq and Afghanistan against American troops. He reluctantly picked up the Kalashnikov pushed feebly towards him, cocked it, and in one swift movement, put a bullet through the head of their leader who was looking him straight in the eyes for any sign of wavering.

"This has been worse than killing my own father! I have obeyed our now-dead leader without question all these years. With this act, I have also made my bid to replace him as your Amir! Is there anyone amongst you who will contest my claim?" Abdul said a few seconds later.

The bomber looked around into the eyes of the eight men arrayed in a semicircle around him. He could see flickers of shock, disbelief, and confusion, but no challenge was forthcoming. No one had the wits and gumption to contest his claim. *It will come later*, he then thought. *Perhaps the claim would come from Salim, the Sudanese, who fancied himself cleverer than the rest of the Shura Council. Let it come*, he told himself. He would deal with it then!

However, now was the time to leave his stamp on operational planning issues "I would like the Shura to first consider my proposal. The Americans have still not learned humility from Iraq and Afghanistan and Ras Tanura, as they go back home with their heads down and their dignity like that of a man who has soiled himself. The infidels continue to insult Islam by desecrating or threatening to desecrate the Koran. Their president, in his weakness, says that the laws of his country do not permit action to be taken. We must again hit them in their homes like in 2001."

"Let it be soon!" Mohammad Younis, the youngest of the Shura, made his preference clear. "It would be fitting to strike America again on September 11th next year? Let America be punished for not only permitting but encouraging the burning of the Koran."

The Xinhua news agency is the official press agency of the Peoples Republic of China. Xinhua's International Affairs Department issues a twice weekly publication named *Guoji Neican* or 'Internal Reference on International Affairs' which is devoted to important articles written by reporters all over the world. The article by Nivriti Butalia on Durga Vadera for *The Hindustan Times* 'Know your MP' series had been pulled out of the archive and read by a staffer in the Eighth Bureau of China's Ministry of State Security (MSS). He was in the process of updating a profile of the Indian PM for the Minister of State Security.

The staffer's report highlighted the quote from Durga Vadera before she became PM "I have no doubt in my mind that China is by far our major threat. China has been emboldened by past and continuing success against a comatose Indian polity to continue to raise the ante. We are a country without any allies, practicing hide-bound, flat-footed diplomacy and without the backbone to match force with force and guile with guile!"

The quote was now on the slide being projected on the small screen in the office of Zhou Yongkang freshly appointed by the politburo to look after China's strategic interests in India and South Asia. The Minister of State Security allowed the quote to remain displayed and commented "Mark Tully, who formerly worked for the BBC for decades and is an extremely shrewd observer of the political scene in India, told our Ambassador in New Delhi that India has had only two prime ministers with the balls to deal with China!"

"Who are these?" Zhou Yongkang questioned.

The Minister of State Security Zhang Guangyu laughed sardonically and said "Firstly, Indira Gandhi who dismembered Pakistan and created Bangladesh showing two fingers in the process to Richard Nixon's Seventh Fleet that had sailed into the Bay of Bengal. Now Durga Vadera has, to give her due, upset our time frame to correct the balance of power with the US by giving the PLA a bitter lesson in Tibet."

Zhou Yongkang commented thoughtfully "It's a leadership issue that we failed to recognize and we are suffering for our stupid mistake. We seemed to have gone by our experience of the last quarter of a century when the Indians displayed a total lack of spine dealing with us. Don't you have a contingency plan to remedy this?"

"Of course we have a contingency plan that the Second Bureau can implement. The second-line Indian leadership consists of geriatrics. Almost all the senior cabinet ministers are party hacks with limited talent and almost all have physical liabilities including cardiac, diabetic and prostate problems. Cabinet meetings are held with pee breaks after every 30-40 minutes. There is no one with the will and stature that Durga Vadera now commands."

"How will you take Durga Vadera out of the equation? What is her weakness?" Zhou inquired.

Zhang explained "She is hard as nails! Her three adopted children are her only weakness that we have established. Once you give the order she will be neutralized through them. Much of the year except for vacations the children are more than 300 kilometers away from her attending boarding school in the mountain town of Mussoorie. In bad weather the place becomes inaccessible even by helicopter. The security provided to the children is quite low on her specific direction. She has ordered this so that they can grow and socialize with their peers in a more natural environment. We have contacts with an Indian underworld don in Dubai to do the job. We also have a backup in place through the Lashkar e Taiba in Pakistan who have dormant cells in India through the Indian Mujahidin for such tasks. A Han shoemaker in Mussoorie with Indian citizenship placed by the MSS will coordinate the strike if these options fail."

"Can we avoid killing the children?" Zhou asked.

"Once she resigns as prime minister we will release the children."

"And if she does not?" Zhou posed the question.

"In that case we'll have no choice but to eliminate them—painfully one at a time in case she wants to change her mind in between. In any case her decision making abilities will be sufficiently crippled for our purposes. Do not worry about any disclosure; the Peoples Republic of China will never be connected to this mission. I will personally ensure that."

Zhou Yongkang smiled for the first time during the meeting. "Go ahead Zhang! You also need to ensure that the Indians have their hands full with other problems that arise simultaneously to divert the leadership's attention."

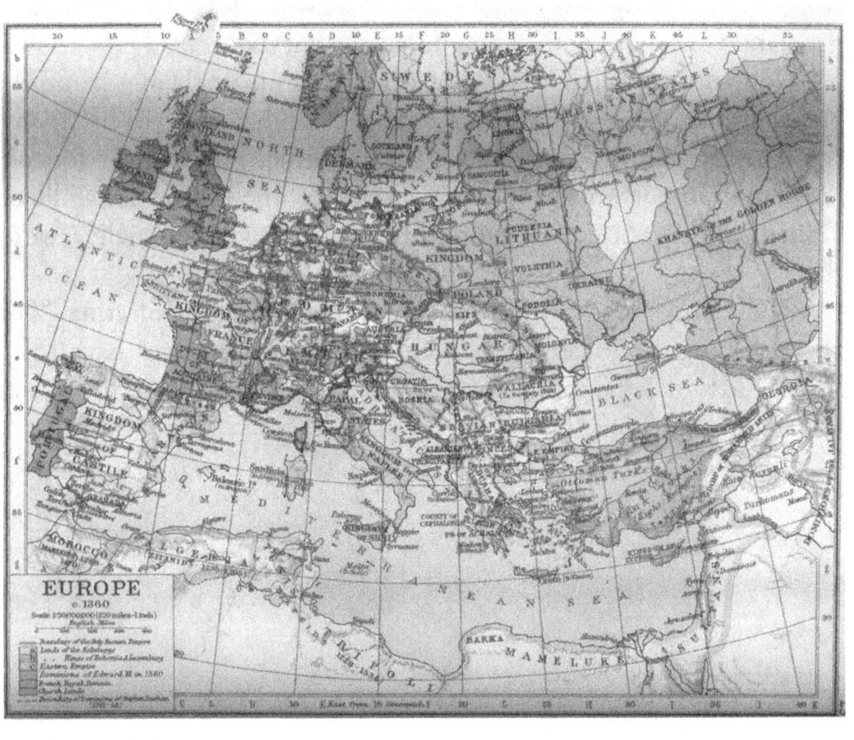
EUROPE
c. 1360
SWEDEN
NORTH SEA
ATLANTIC OCEAN
KINGDOM OF FRANCE
KINGDOM OF POLAND
LITHUANIA
VOLHYNIA
PODOLIA
HUNGARY
WALLACHIA
BLACK SEA
GEORGIA
KINGDOM OF CASTILE
MOROCCO
MEDITERRANEAN SEA
BARKA
MAMELUKE

About the Author

Bob Butalia was born in 1947 in Punjab, India, the son of a Cavalry officer. His early schooling was at St. George's, Mussoorie. In 1963 he followed the family tradition and entered the National Defence Academy as a cadet. In 1967 he received his commission as a 2nd Lieutenant in Hodson's Horse, the Regiment his father had commanded.

Bob is a graduate of the Defence Services Staff College, Wellington. He saw active service during the 1971 Indo-Pak War and took part in the Battle of Bassantar, the largest tank battle of the campaign.

He is married and has two children. Their son Sahil is a Captain in Hodson's Horse, and daughter Nivriti is a budding journalist.

Bob and his wife Rekha live in Gurgaon, India.